PRAIRIE FIRE

In 1887, in the ranchlands of the Oklahoma territory, the beautiful Kathleen Calhoun is ready to start a life of her own. A chance meeting brings the handsome Raven Sky into her life. Sky is gentle and educated, but he is also a Creek Indian . . . Kathleen's attraction to Raven Sky is undeniable, but her dreams are haunted by the Indian savages who brutally murdered her parents. Torn, Kathleen flees Oklahoma and the arms of her beloved. Deep within, she knows she must return to the firm embrace of Raven Sky to feed the flames of her desire . . .

Books by Patricia Werner
Published by The House of Ulverscroft:

THE WILL

PATRICIA WERNER

◆

PRAIRIE FIRE

Complete and Unabridged

ULVERSCROFT
Leicester

First published in the United States of America
in 1988

First Large Print Edition
published 2006

The moral right of the author has been asserted

This is a work of fiction in its entirety.
Any resemblance to actual people, places or events
is purely coincidental.

British Library CIP Data

Werner, Patricia
  Prairie fire.—Large print ed.—
  Ulverscroft large print series: romance
  1. Frontier and pioneer life—Oklahoma—Fiction
  2. Creek Indians—Oklahoma—Fiction 3. Oklahoma
  —Fiction 4. Love stories 5. Large type books
  I. Title
  823.9′14 [F]

  ISBN 1–84617–331–0

Published by
F. A. Thorpe (Publishing)
Anstey, Leicestershire

Set by Words & Graphics Ltd.
Anstey, Leicestershire
Printed and bound in Great Britain by
T. J. International Ltd., Padstow, Cornwall

This book is printed on acid-free paper

1

March 1887

Kate pulled her buckboard up next to several other wagons and buggies waiting at the small wooden depot on the north side of the tracks. A crowd had gathered in Tulsa to meet the train from Vinita. Cattlemen strode the platform in high-heeled boots. Bronze-faced Indian mothers held children. In the stockyards west of the depot, cattle lowed.

In the distance, the train whistled. Kate gathered up her calico skirts and climbed down, placing one calfskin-booted foot on the steps to the crowded platform, to watch the train pull in.

'Afternoon, Miss Kate,' said a familiar voice.

She looked up at Doc Johnson, one of the many white settlers who had come to Tulsey Town, as the Indians called it, when the railroad was laid.

'Hello, Doc,' she said.

'Quite a crowd here,' said Doc. 'Five Tribes delegation back from Washington.'

'Oh? I didn't know. I came to meet my brother.'

'He on the train, too?'

She nodded. The train jolted to a stop as they spoke, and yells went up from the crowd. Kathleen stretched her neck to see her brother disembark. As steam billowed up from the engine, her gaze caught several figures in dark suits and stiff collars who descended from the train.

The last man in the party emerged and looked silently over the crowd. A puff of steam lifted, and Kate stared at the tall Indian in a custom-fitted suit, a white stand-up collar stark against his coppery skin. She noticed the sharp definition of his strong cheekbones, high, flat forehead, and sharply jutting chin.

Sweeping the crowd, his eyes met hers briefly, and she quickly looked away. She searched again for her brother, trying to avert her eyes from the Indian. Doc Johnson had noticed the tall Indian descending from the train, too.

'That's Raven Sky,' he said, 'the Creek chief's second son, skilled in diplomacy, educated in the East.' Then Doc lowered his voice, directing his next words to her alone. 'The Indians need more like him, if you ask me.'

Kate nodded as she watched Raven Sky make his way through the crowd. He approached a regal old man surrounded by Indian women in cotton and gingham dresses. The children stood shyly behind their mothers' skirts. Kathleen lifted an eyebrow, wondering idly which one of the women was Raven Sky's wife.

The regal older man watched Raven Sky greet his people. Then two Indian boys brought his leather-covered trunk and tossed it in the back of a waiting wagon. As the party departed, Kate remembered she had not yet located her brother.

'There's Wendall,' said Doc Johnson. Wendall's familiar form appeared on the platform as he reached up and helped a woman down. He was dressed in a dark coat over a green vest, starched collar, and black tie. His high-heeled boots were the only remnants of his usual western gear.

'Wendall,' Kathleen cried, waving.

'Hello, Sis,' Wendall called as he strode toward them. He crushed her in a hug.

Kathleen smiled proudly at her brother, glad he was back from his banking trip to St. Louis. Looking up at him made her stand a little taller. His broad shoulders, blue-gray eyes, and dark brown hair contributed to his ruggedly handsome appearance. Wendall was a well-respected man in these parts, and Kathleen was proud to be his sister.

She suddenly noticed a woman coming toward them through the thinning crowd. She wore a brown linen traveling suit with a pink ruffled blouse and a fancy flowered hat. A beaded handbag dangled from her arm. She looked familiar, but it took Kate some time to realize she was looking into the face of one of her old school friends from St. Louis.

'Sis, you remember Molly Ladurie,' Wendall said, taking off his hat.

The other woman stepped forward and smiled at Kate, clasped both of Kate's hands, and kissed her cheeks. The sweet scent of perfume floated delicately from Molly's throat. Large brown eyes looked out from her rosy, rounded face framed by brown ringlets that hung gracefully from under her hat.

'I remember Kate,' Molly said.

As she looked at the pretty face, Kathleen felt her eyes widen with surprise. Finally, her face lit with a smile of greeting.

'Molly Ladurie, how long has it been?'

The other woman gave a soft, musical laugh, and Kathleen was suddenly self-conscious about the way she looked. Wisps of the light brown hair twisted into a knot at the back of her head had come loose during the ride to town. Her calico dress was plain.

'It's been a long time, Kate, as I recall. Two years?'

'At least.'

'You escorting my sister?' Wendall said, shaking hands with the Doc.

'No, no,' said Doc Johnson, clearing his throat and raising a hand in mock protest. 'Just here, same as the rest of the town, to find out what happened in Washington. Bumped into Kate here and stayed a few clumsy feet away from her, that's all.'

At the mention of Washington, Wendall's eyes clouded. He glanced in the direction of a group of black-suited Indian and white men who were engaged in a heated discussion at the other end of the platform.

'You travel with the delegation?' asked Doc Johnson.

Wendall brought his eyes back to the Doc. 'We were in the same car. The Indians are worried by the rumors that the government is trying to break up tribal governments and allot their lands to individual members of the tribes.'

Doc Johnson grunted, 'Only a matter of time.' He cleared his throat, looked around the depot, and gestured toward the stock-yards and the one- and two-story buildings nearby. 'Statehood will eventually come to protect the rights of the men who've made improvements in these parts.'

Wendall nodded curtly to Doc.

5

'Perhaps,' he said. Then he took his sister's arm and asked, 'Did you bring the wagon?'

She nodded, sensing the irritation in his voice. He must have learned something on the train that caused him concern. She knew that the whites in Indian Territory talked continuously about getting more land away from the Indians. The town already owned as many parcels of land as the Indians would sell.

Kate bobbed her head toward the end of the platform. 'The wagon's over there.'

'I'll see to the luggage, then.' Going back along the platform, Wendall called to a lanky boy shuffling about in the dirt below them. 'Tom Ridley, how 'bout giving me a hand with these trunks?'

'Sure, Mr. Calhoun.' The boy scrambled to the platform and picked up one end of a deer-hide trunk with iron handles. Near it stood a smaller trunk made of wood and leather and an assortment of carpetbags and smaller traveling cases.

As Kathleen considered the luggage, she began to realize that there could be only two reasons for Molly to bring so much luggage from St. Louis. Either she had come for a very long visit or she had come to stay.

'This way, Molly,' said Kathleen.

Molly held her bonnet as she followed Kate to the wagon.

'Thank you, son,' Wendall said, tossing Tom Ridley a few coins when he and the boy had loaded the buckboard.

'Sure thing, Mr. Calhoun.' The boy gave a salute as Wendall picked up the reins and guided the team away from the station.

Kate turned to the woman beside her. An unsettling feeling had claimed her stomach, and she had to work hard at appearing convivial. 'It's good to see you, Molly. What brings you this far west?'

Wendall spoke for Molly. 'We've got some news, Sis, but let's get to the ranch first.'

Wendall turned back to concentrate on the road, guiding the team well to the right of a deep gully caused by recent flooding.

Kate looked past Molly to study her brother's profile. His strange manner caused nervous feelings to flutter through her, and the muscles in her jaw tightened. She held on to her seat with one hand. Finally he glanced over at her.

Wendall smiled. Kathleen had a no-nonsense countenance, to his way of thinking — a straight-forward sort of face. He approved of that. You always knew where you stood with Kathleen. Something tugged at his heart as he glanced at his little sister, her blue eyes lighting up her tanned, angular face. She was a fighter. But then she had had to be, just as he had.

'How are things at the ranch, Sis?'

'Hank found a calf with a broken leg,' she said. 'I watched him set the bone. I think I could do it myself now.' Pushing a lock of hair off her forehead, she glanced at Molly, who sat between them surveying the flat landscape.

They had four miles to cover between town and Wendall's ranch — his only because his late wife was a half-blood Cherokee, and Wendall's marriage to a tribe member had given him rights to the land held in common by members of the Cherokee Nation.

To the west, low undulating hills and woodlands thick with blackjack and post oak followed the riverbed. To the east, cattle dotted the range for miles.

For twenty years, cattle drives had crossed the prairie on their way to Kansas and the railroads that carried meat to the hungry East. Lush grasses that once fed herds of buffalo now supported thousands of cattle. Cattlemen like Wendall Calhoun negotiated with the Five Civilized Tribes for grazing rights, and the Indians made a fortune from their white tenant ranchers.

Now branding pens, drift fences, headquarters, and ranch houses attested to the fact that the white settlers had come to stay. The grazing land was fenced now, and neighboring Indian and mixed-blood farmers complained when Wendall's longhorns got into their crops. But he bought thousands of bushels of corn and tons of hay from them each year, so they tolerated his presence.

Finally, the Calhoun ranch came into view. Ranch house, outbuildings, corncribs, storehouses, and corrals spread over several acres. Running north on Bird Creek from the Creek Nation border and east from the Osage line almost to the Verdigris River, it was the largest cattle ranch in the Cherokee Nation.

As they pulled up to the ranch house, Kate gathered her skirt in her hands to climb down. Two figures approached from the barn, and Wendall stepped down to greet Hank and Tex, his half-blood ranch foremen. Both were dressed as he usually was, in chaps, denim pants, and cotton shirts.

Like most of the cowboys who worked for Wendall, Hank Prather and Tex Rupert were sons of white trail drivers who had lingered in the area after the days of the great cattle drives.

'Supper'll be ready in an hour,' Kate said. 'You must be hungry.' She noticed how Wendall waited to assist Molly to the ground, and a slight feeling of annoyance swept over her. If the woman couldn't learn to get out of a buckboard wagon by herself, she wouldn't last long here.

'Rhubarb pie?' Wendall asked as he took off his hat and came around the wagon.

She nodded. 'And roast pig.' Kate struggled to remember her manners. 'You must be tired, Molly,' she said. 'There's a guest room.' She glanced uncertainly at her brother. 'I'll show you.'

'Thank you, Kate,' Molly said. 'I'm about done in.' And she followed Kathleen up the steps to the house.

Kate showed Molly upstairs. 'I'll have Mattie bring some water so you can wash.' Then, with a look of apology, she added, 'I hope you don't expect the kind of servants you're used to in St. Louis. Mattie's a good girl, but not always friendly. Her parents were slaves to some Cherokees before the war. They died, and she was brought up by the tribe. Call me if you need anything.'

Molly smiled. 'Don't worry about me, Kate. I'll be fine.'

Kate could see the shadows under Molly's eyes and guessed she hadn't slept well on the journey. If she had come to stay, as Kathleen guessed she had, how long would Molly retain her fresh appearance here? The wind and sun would soon dry her skin and hair, if she wasn't careful. Kate also wondered, as she looked into the brown eyes, what had brought Molly here? Did she have the same desire to conquer a new land that all the pioneers seemed to have? How much had Wendall told her about life in Indian Territory? And what did she plan to do here? Even if she and Wendall . . .

'I'll see you after you've rested,' Kate said, trying to summon the warmth she had first felt when her school friend had stood before her on the platform.

'Thank you. I'm sure I'll be in better spirits after I've cleaned up some.'

Kate shut the door and went down the stairs to the kitchen. While the pig was roasting, Kate instructed Mattie on how to prepare the trimmings and finished some household chores. She shook a rug out over the front porch and was replacing it in the hallway when she heard Wendall's heavy footsteps on the back stairs.

He now wore jeans, a vest, and a blue checked shirt, and he had knotted a yellow bandanna around his neck. Noticing that he had slipped a pair of ivory-handled six-shooters into his gun belt, Kate looked at him questioningly. He didn't normally carry his weapons. He slipped the gun belt off and slung it over a peg on the wall, so she refrained from asking why he had put it on.

Crossing the kitchen, he went to the pump and splashed fresh well water over his hands, neck, and face. Kathleen handed him a towel.

'Everything all right?' she asked.

Blotting his face with the towel, he answered, 'Hank and Tex did a good job of keeping an eye on things. Monty looks fine.'

Kate smiled at the reference to her horse. 'I rode a few miles every day.'

'Where to?'

'Along the river until the brush got too thick, then just across the near meadow so I could give him his head.'

'Talk to anybody?'

'On my rides? No.' She frowned. 'Why?'

'Just wondered.' He studied his sister. At nineteen, she should be able to take care of herself. But she had been unprepared for the wilderness when she'd first come here from St. Louis a year ago. He pulled back one of the wooden chairs and sat down at the kitchen table near the cook stove.

'Got any coffee, Sis?'

As she nodded and went to the stove to get him some coffee, Wendall realized how grown up she'd become. Her maturity had come with her ripening womanhood and with the blossoming of the spirit of a strong girl who'd had her share of

12

difficulties when they were young.

Kathleen poured coffee into a mug. 'How was St. Louis?' She tried to keep her voice conversational, knowing Wendall would tell her what Molly was doing here in his own good time.

He gave a low chuckle. 'They say I'm doing all right in Indian Territory. Of course, most people back east think the Indians here are savages.'

She lowered her eyes. *The way they were in Kansas*, she wanted to say. And she bit her tongue to keep the words back.

Wendall looked off toward the windows. Outside, dusk hovered. 'A city will rise out of these plains someday.'

'I find it hard to imagine a city in a barren place like this,' Kathleen said. She sounded more bitter than she had meant to, but she went on. 'I mean, how would you build a city out here?'

He put down his coffee cup. 'It'll happen, now the railroad's here. The mixed-bloods favor progress.' He frowned. 'I don't know, though. It'll be hard on the Indians.'

Kate wrinkled her nose. 'It isn't our land, and the Indians won't agree to the changes.' The way it was now, anyone could open up a business in town by getting a permit for the land. But when the proprietor died, the land

13

reverted to the tribe.

Wendall shook his head and looked at her. 'Some of them won't agree. Unfortunately, there are men who won't be stopped, no matter what the Indians want. More settlers straggle in here every day. Missionaries, railroad crews, cowboys looking for work on the range. Barges comin' up the Arkansas from the Mississippi, if they don't get caught in the sand bars.'

'It would be a good thing, wouldn't it?' Kathleen said. 'To civilize the place, I mean.'

Wendall frowned into the dark liquid in his mug. 'I don't know, Sis. 'Course I want to hang on to my land and get something for the improvements I've made. Everyone feels that way.' He put his elbows on the table and leaned forward, the lines on his face creasing deeply as he thought of their precarious situation. 'I respect these Indians, though. It wouldn't be fair to steal their land again. They've had that done once already.'

He looked into Kathleen's eyes, mirrors of inexperience even though she'd had to grow up more quickly than most young women. Set slightly wide apart, her eyes were clear blue and very serious. Her nose was long and straight, and her jaw was a little sharp, though it was less so when she smiled. His sister was on the serious side, he realized thoughtfully,

14

though he remembered some times when her eyes had sparkled and her white teeth had gleamed in laughter.

The Creek, Cherokees, Choctaws, Chickasaws, and Seminoles were advanced tribes, to the white man's way of thinking. But this was still a wild, untamed territory, and Kate was one of the few white women in these parts. Wendall didn't mind if good upstanding citizens like himself established homes here, but most of the men he saw moving into Indian Territory were not to be trusted — especially not with a woman like Kate. His thoughts troubled him.

He leaned back his chair, setting the mug down hard on the wooden table. Then he reached into his pocket, brought out a folded newspaper clipping and shook it open.

'What is it, Wendall?' Kate asked as she refilled his mug. Looking at the clipping, she saw a picture of the round, fair face of the woman upstairs. The article from the St. Louis *Star-Times* noted Molly's return from school in the East. Wendall was quiet for a moment, and Kate guessed what was coming.

'I have something to tell you, Sis,' he began, then cleared his throat again.

She waited.

'It's been more than a year since Amanda died.' He was silent for a moment. The only

15

sound in the room was the bubbling of the water in the pot on the iron stove.

'I need a wife, Kate. I don't mean to run the house; you do fine at that. But a man needs a wife.'

Kate kept her hands busy draining water off the cooked beets. 'Are you and Molly . . . ?'

She was suddenly nervous about the answer he would give.

A year ago she had been uprooted from all that had become familiar to her and transported to this untamed land where only the determined carved out a place to live. Now she had grown used to her life with Wendall.

She would never forget packing her belongings in a trunk and carpetbag and traveling by train all the way to Tulsa leaving civilization, as she knew it, behind her. She remembered the strenuous journey from the green hills of Missouri, across rivers wider than some lakes, out to the vast plains of waving wheat and rich grass where cattle grazed.

She vaguely remembered having lived out west when she and Wendall were children, but the memories were dim and tinged with horror.

If Wendall remarried, her whole world

16

would be turned upside down again. Not that there wasn't enough work for two women to do, but the thought of someone else running the house made her feel odd, disoriented.

'I called on Molly when I was in St. Louis,' Wendall said, clearing his throat again. 'I spoke to Frank Ladurie, asked his permission to court her. I explained my circumstances to him.'

Kate knew her brother was an attractive man. He was strong, his limbs as hard as iron from the life he led, his skin tanned from working outdoors. She should have guessed that he wanted a wife.

Kathleen swallowed hard. 'What did he say?'

Wendall folded the article about Molly and put it back in his pocket. 'Frank said I was welcome to try my luck.' Wendall smiled as he conjured up the memory, the skin around his blue-gray eyes crinkling. 'The first time I saw Molly, I was a gawky kid on my first trail horse. She was a little girl with long brown braids.' He shook his head. 'Thirteen years is a long time, I guess. I must've joined my first cattle drive about the time Molly was in grammar school.'

Kate took a loaf of bread from the oven and laid a cloth over it.

'So you're married?' she asked.

He paused. 'Yes, but this won't change anything, Sis,' he said. 'You can stay here for as long as you like. 'Course you might meet someone someday and get hitched yourself.'

Kate lowered her eyes, feeling the color creeping up her neck to her ears. She raised a hand to the buttons at the front of her dress. Then she turned to face him.

'You know I'm happy for you, Wendall,' she said. She rubbed her hands along the sides of the sturdy dress. 'Surely you'll want to throw a party to introduce Molly to our neighbors. We can use the church building. I'll be happy to help.'

'Thank you, Sis. I want Molly to get to know the people here. The sooner the better.'

Kathleen knew Wendall had loved Amanda deeply. He had been inconsolable when she died. But life on the prairie was lonely. Men and women put their strengths and talents together to carve out a life here, and Wendall obviously wanted his own family. He had lived through the hard times, and now he deserved some happiness.

Wendall thought about the prairie — the plentiful water, lush grass, and mild winters that permitted herds to live on the range, surviving on dry grass until early spring greened the prairies. But white settlement would change that. There would be more men trying to control the same amount of land, and they would all have different ideas about what the Indians wanted and needed.

Wendall rose and stretched, his blue checked shirt pulling tight across his chest. Then he went to the window and looked out.

'Men with ambition are coming here, Sis. Families who can farm and make things grow, and our cattle can support them. But I'm no fool, Kate. Greedy men will undermine the Indians' rights, and the whites'll fight to keep land they've squatted on. Times are changing. Even the Indians see that. They can't hang on to the old ways forever.' But he wasn't sure about all the results of the inevitable changes.

She walked to him and put a hand on his arm. 'Molly was always nice to me at school, even though she was in the class ahead of mine. I'm sure we'll get along fine.' She stopped talking before her voice began to tremble.

Wendall turned and put his hands on her shoulders, feelings of tenderness tugging at him. 'I know you will,' he said.

Wendall left to finish some chores while Kathleen checked on the big pot of beans she was cooking. Fixing supper kept her mind off herself. She was scooping flour out of a barrel when Molly appeared in the doorway. She looked much better after her rest and had changed into a practical cotton dress, a blue flowered print with a small white collar. Kate smiled at her.

'Molly,' said Kathleen, straightening. 'Wendall told me.'

'I hope you approve,' she said, the tinge of blush coloring her cheeks.

'Of course,' Kate said. 'Congratulations.' She wished she didn't feel so embarrassed. She would just have to get used to the idea that her brother now had a wife. 'Have you recovered from your journey?'

'Sufficiently to be of some use, I think,' Molly answered.

'No hurry.'

'Well, I'd better start helping as soon as I can. Otherwise I'll be accused of being a soft, good-for-nothing easterner.'

Both women smiled, and Kate felt less nervous about having another woman in the house. She knew Molly liked her, and she began to feel that her worries had been uncalled for.

'All right,' said Kate. 'If you really want to help, I'll show you where everything is. I'm afraid this kitchen's less convenient than what you're used to.'

Molly gave a rueful smile and shrugged. 'We had servants back home, but I'll manage.'

Kate nodded. 'We have only Mattie, and she doesn't talk much. Of course there're the hands. Hank and Tex will do whatever you need them to do. They're mixed-bloods,' she added self-consciously.

Molly nodded, but Kate saw the flicker that crossed her eye.

'I met them. They seem very nice.' Molly moistened her lips and looked around as if searching for something to keep her hands busy. 'I'll adapt,' she said, straightening her shoulders.

Kate smiled sympathetically. How like Molly she had been when she first came here a year ago. She shook her head. How strange life was.

'Molly, what made you decide to accept Wendall's proposal and come out west?' She blushed. 'You don't have to answer, if that's too personal a question.'

Molly pulled a chair out from the table and sat down, folding her hands in front of her. 'Oh, I don't mind, Kate. I know what you mean. Wendall told me how hard life is here. All those circulars about the glorious West — he said not to believe them. He knows, too, having been on all those trail rides, and having lived in Kansas when you were little — ' She cut herself off abruptly and pressed her lips together.

Kate sat down at the table and put a hand on Molly's arm. 'It's all right, Molly. You can talk about that. Wendall and I long ago accepted the death of our parents. But I'm glad he described some of the hardships here.' She glanced toward the doorway that opened toward the barn and the plains beyond. 'This can be a lonely place.' Not wanting to turn the conversation to herself, she asked again, 'So why did you come?'

'Well, Wendall was so enthusiastic. He said it's a good country, that there's opportunity here.' She frowned a little. 'He explained to me that the Indians won't own this land forever, even though by treaty they're entitled to it. He says there'll be legislation that will divide up the lands into individual allotments. Then each Indian will own land, and the remainder of tribal lands will be sold to the whites. He wants to be here when that happens.'

'You mean so he can buy the land the ranch sits on now?'

'Well, that. But he also knows there are other men, Kate, unfair men who'll take advantage of the Indians. He feels that if he stays here, he can help the tribes. He'll treat

22

the Indians fairly, give them a good price for their land.'

Molly shrugged as she continued. 'I guess I caught his enthusiasm. I wanted something new. The West needs women, too. It's our duty to help civilize the place.'

Then Molly blushed deeply. 'And, Kate, I've always had a crush on Wendall.' She sighed, and Kate saw a dreamy look in her eyes. 'It thrilled my heart to see him come walking into our parlor that Sunday. The way he smiled at me . . . ' She looked at Kate, unable to continue.

Kate had to admire the woman's spirit. Her own decision to come west had been made for her, but Molly could have married well at home. She must love Wendall very deeply.

Then a pang of grief threatened to overwhelm her, and she fought down her rising jealousy. She hadn't found anyone to marry, but that was no reason to be envious of Wendall and Molly. It made no sense to feel jealous just because Wendall would now rely on Molly instead of her.

'Well, then, I'll show you where we keep everything,' Kathleen said. She rose and set the coffeepot on the stove. Then she led Molly to the pantry and explained what was kept in each of the barrels.

'We get everything else at Dwayne's

General Store,' she was saying when Wendall came in.

'Well,' he said. 'I see you two are getting along just fine.' He gave Molly a look, and she glanced away, but Kate could see the blush that tinged her cheek. She suddenly felt like an intruder. She cleared her throat and moved toward the table in the center of the kitchen.

'I've shown Molly where everything is. She can run the kitchen just as well as I can now, I think.'

Molly laughed. 'Don't be too sure. I'll still need your help.'

Wendall hung his hat on a peg by the door. 'Well, I'll leave you two arguing over who's to fix my supper while I wash up.' With that, he went outside again, giving Kate a chance to tell Molly what had been foremost in her mind.

'I mean it, Molly,' she said. 'You'll have your own way of doing things, and I don't want to get in your way.'

'Don't be silly, Kate. I'm sure your way of doing things will be just fine. You've been here longer than I have, and I expect to learn everything from you about the ranch. I'll rely on your help.'

'Thank you, Molly, but no matter how generous you are, three is a crowd.' Tears threatened to brim over, for no rational reason, but Kate couldn't stop her feelings. She turned to check on the pig that was roasting in the oven. 'I plan to leave the ranch as soon as possible.'

Molly stepped closer and put a hand on her arm. 'But why, Kate? Unless . . . Has someone proposed to you, too? Oh, isn't that just grand! We'll both be newlyweds — '

'No, Molly,' Kate cut her off. 'But I might be able to teach at the mission school. I've been looking for a way to use my education. When I first begin, I can ride to the school every day. That way I won't be underfoot here all the time.'

'Oh, I see. Well, if that's what you want to do . . . ' Then Molly lowered her voice in sympathy. 'Kate, it must be difficult to meet suitable men out here.'

Kate stiffened. 'I'd rather not talk about that, Molly.' Then she shook her head. 'I'm sorry. I didn't mean to be rude.' But she couldn't bring herself to discuss the subject with another woman, especially when Molly was so near to the truth. It was true. There were few suitable men here. The railroad men and cowboys were a rough-and-tumble lot.

Molly remained silent as they set the table in the dining room. She had some knowledge of Kate's past, and knew how Wendall's and

Kate's parents had been killed in Kansas, so she didn't want to press her sister-in-law.

Wendall came in to supper. Kate carried the roast pig to the table on a large bone tray, and Wendall carved the meat. Molly cut the corn bread, and Kate served the fresh vegetables. As dusk hovered over Indian Territory, they ate silently, pursuing their own private thoughts.

Molly still looked refreshed in her blue cotton print, and Kate silently envied the other woman her looks. *I used to look like that*, she thought miserably. But out here there was always so much work to be done that she had just let her looks go.

When the meal was finished, Wendall pushed back his chair. 'I need a smoke,' he said.

Molly helped Kate clear the dishes. Kate took the plates outside and scraped off the leavings for the dogs. Then she poured water from the cauldron into a tub and washed the dishes while Molly put the other things away.

When everything was cleared away, the women joined Wendall in the parlor. The fire he had built sent sparks up the stone chimney. He took the newspaper clipping out of his pocket and placed it on the mantel near the framed photograph of their parents. Kate took a seat by the door so that Molly could have the rocker next to Wendall's. She cut out fabric patches for her new quilt and stitched them together. Later, she would pad the finished coverlet with cotton so that each colorful patch would stand out in relief. The work gave her time to think.

Wendall seated himself in his walnut rocker, his long legs stretched out, his feet resting on the stool, and reached for the newspapers he had brought back from St. Louis. Molly extracted a small book from her pocket and began to read.

Wendall felt around in his pockets murmuring, 'Now, where did I leave my tobacco pouch?' Both Molly and Kate started to get up. Their eyes met, and Kate lowered herself into her seat again.

'It's probably on the stand next to the bed upstairs,' she said. Molly nodded and softly left the room, and Kate returned to her work.

In a few minutes Molly returned and handed Wendall the pouch.

'You must tell me all about St. Louis, Molly,' Kate said.

'What would you like to know?'

'Did you visit our friends, the Wagners?'

'Of course. They send their love.'

As Molly described some of the people she had spent time with recently, the years rolled

27

back for Kate. She saw herself as a six-year-old girl, standing on the top step of their foster parents' house in St. Louis. Her brother was sixteen then, and he sat on a brown pony. He had looked at her solemnly as he said good-bye, for he was going to drive cattle up from Texas through Indian Territory to Kansas, where the cattle would be shipped by rail back to St. Louis.

In Texas he'd met and married Amanda, a beautiful dark-skinned Cherokee woman with rich black hair that hung past her shoulders. As Kathleen grew older, he and his wife had begun to ranch in Indian Territory. He had not come back to St. Louis until he had money to put in the bank. So Kathleen had grown up with Ned and Nana Wagner.

When his Cherokee wife died, Wendall had remained in Indian Territory, aware of his precarious right to reside here. A tenant rancher, he had made lease payments to the Cherokee Nation. Finally Kate had come to join him. She'd had nowhere else to go, and hadn't wanted to impose on her foster parents once she had finished school.

A small sigh escaped her as she listened to Molly describe the gaiety of city life — big homes, fancy dresses, and many people to talk to. She wondered if she would return to St. Louis someday. Life there seemed so much more permanent. Even though men built stores and houses or pitched tents in Indian Territory, they didn't own the land under them.

But there was a part of her that had learned to love the prairie — the constant singing of the cicada, the smell of burning twigs, the coyote cries at night. That part of her wanted to remain on this ranch sprawling over the vast plains.

She had grown used to the peaceful setting and the comfort of her brother's home, but now that he had a wife, Kate's position seemed more uncertain. She had depended so on Wendall's company. She wasn't sure she was willing to share him.

Finally she clasped her hands together and rose, her dress swishing softly around her legs. Walking over to the small rough-hewn oak table, she turned down the wick on the kerosene lamp she would carry upstairs with her.

Wendall rose to kiss her good night, and then she turned to Molly, who stretched out her hands. There was a tightness in Kate's chest, and her hands felt cold as she squeezed Molly's warm ones.

'It's nice to have you here,' she said. Her voice sounded far away, as if someone else were speaking. 'I hope you'll be happy.'

'I believe I will, Kate,' Molly said, giving her hands a squeeze.

Kate started up the narrow stairway to the second floor. The flame of the kerosene lamp fluttered as it lit her way. She turned toward the front of the house where her room overlooked the sloping porch roof. Finally alone in her room, she slid the latch in place.

Bright moonlight flooded the paned windows. The glass was another sign of Wendall's prosperity, for many settlers covered windows with greased paper.

Kate closed the gingham curtains and set the kerosene lamp on the small bedside table. As she sat down heavily on the quilted coverlet, a sudden chill swept over her, and she hugged herself, feeling like an outsider in her brother's house.

She knew Wendall didn't mean for her to feel pushed out, but she had gotten used to this being her home, and it really wasn't.

The sense of loss swelled in her heart. She had always wanted her own home, but until she married, she would not have one. And the thought of marriage to anyone she knew repulsed her. She thought about Jesse Smith, who clerked at Dwayne's store. Jesse had come to call several times, and she had been guilty of encouraging him a bit, just to relieve the boredom. He was quieter and better educated than the rough cowboys and half-breeds who worked for Wendall. And there was so little in Indian Territory to stimulate her mind that she enjoyed chatting with Jesse from time to time.

Unbuttoning her dress and letting it drop to the floor, Kate looked at herself in the full-length mirror that had been brought from St. Louis. The glass was imperfect, though, and her form seemed to shrink and expand as she stepped closer.

She stared thoughtfully at her light brown hair, serious oval face, her slightly bony nose. She did not consider herself a beauty, but she looked healthy enough, alive.

Turning away from the mirror, she examined her long arms. Her skin from the elbows down was tanned by the prairie sun. She unfastened her undergarments and stepped out of them. In the dim light of the kerosene lamp, she stared down at her lithe, pale body. Her narrow waist flowed into rounded hips and firm thighs. She had long legs for a woman of medium height, and well-proportioned feet. It was an odd sensation to examine her body so objectively.

It was a body that ran, worked, slept — a vessel for her spirit — and marriage would mean sharing it with someone else. For the first time she considered what it might be like to carry a child. As she placed her hand on her flat stomach, the thought of standing this way in front of a husband raised goose bumps on her flesh.

She picked up her clothing and draped it over the trunk at the foot of her bed. Then she turned the kerosene lamp all the way down and slipped into her nightdress.

The distant bark of a coyote made her step to the window. She drew in a breath and stood perfectly still, peering out the window.

On the horizon, against a bright moon, a rider and horse galloped along the rim of the plain. The horse's mane and tail and the man's long hair streamed out behind them as the horse stretched itself to its full length. She gazed at the captivating sight of man and horse racing the wind, her heart hammering in response. If only she could saddle her own horse now and give him his head. Racing across the plain behind the Indian, she could find release for the confused feelings that had been born within her.

She let the curtain drop and slipped into bed. Staring at the ceiling, she began to make plans for herself.

2

Kathleen was cooking grits and frying bacon when she heard Wendall's heavy footsteps on the stairs. She reached for one of the pewter plates they used for everyday meals.

The chair scraped on the wooden floor, and Wendall grunted, 'Good morning,' as he sat down at the sturdy kitchen table near the stove. Kate lifted the heavy frying pan and carried it to the table where she forked long strips of thick bacon onto her brother's plate. She wondered how long Molly intended to sleep, but she bit back the question. Molly probably wasn't used to getting up at five, the way they did on the ranch.

'I've been thinking, Wendall,' she said later, as she poured out some steaming coffee. 'I might like to do something new now that you've got Molly to help run the ranch.'

'We'll need you here. Molly won't know her way around, and you'll have to show her what to do.'

'Women like to run a household their own way, Wendall. You'll see.'

'Nonsense,' Wendall said between mouthfuls.

'Wendall, I'll stay on here, but I think it would be a good idea for me to get away from the ranch some of the time. I'd like to teach at the mission school in town. I can go see Joy today and talk to her about it. I'm qualified, since I graduated from the normal school in St. Louis, and I'm sure Joy could use me.'

The mission school, built three years ago, was run by the Presbyterian Home Mission Board in New York City. The pupils were mostly Indian children, but the settlers' children also attended.

Wendall frowned. 'I'm not sure I like the idea of your being in town so much. I'd feel safer with you on the ranch. Besides, Joy will have to write the Mission Board. It'll be months before you get an answer.'

'Well, then, in the meantime I'll just volunteer. I think I could help Joy a lot.'

After they finished, she picked up the dishes and placed them in the large tub. Wendall didn't say anything else. He didn't want to disappoint his sister, and he had enough on his mind now anyway.

'You'll stay here through the roundup, won't you?' he said as he went to get his hat.

Kathleen frowned. She hadn't really wanted to be underfoot that long. Still, roundup was a busy time, and she would be needed for all the extra cooking.

'All right,' she agreed. 'But I'm going to talk to Joy today. I've been wanting to see her anyway.'

'Good morning.' Molly stood at the kitchen door in a green and white cotton print dress. Although her eyes were still puffy with sleep, it was evident that she was ready to enter into the activities of the household.

'Good morning, Molly,' said Kate. She was glad she hadn't spoken her earlier criticism aloud. 'Would you like some breakfast?'

'I'd love some. Just show me what to do.' For a moment the women's eyes met, and then Kate indicated the bacon sizzling slowly in the frying pan. 'There's bacon cooking there, and there's coffee on the stove. Help yourself.'

'Thanks.' Molly paused only a moment to orient herself to the way the kitchen was set up, then went about the business of serving herself breakfast.

'I have some things to do upstairs,' Kate said. 'I'll be down later to show you where things are in the rest of the house.' She paused, then added, 'And in the barn.'

Kate went to Wendall's bedroom without thinking and started to smooth out the linens. Suddenly she felt a sting of embarrassment as she thought about Molly and Wendall sleeping in the bed together. She had never

35

given the intimate side of marriage much thought. Now she stood at the foot of Wendall's bed — their bed — staring at it, the blood rushing to her cheeks. Hearing Mattie's footsteps in the hallway, she quickly left the room.

'Please fold these linens, Mattie,' she ordered the girl. Handing her some freshly washed sheets, she fled down the stairs.

$$\star \quad \star \quad \star$$

Kathleen placed one booted foot on the driver's step and hoisted herself onto the wooden wagon seat. Tightening her grip on the leather reins, she slapped them on the horses' rumps, and the wagon jerked forward, away from the ranch house. Like many pioneer women, Kate was a skilled horse-woman who could handle horses and drive heavy wagons with little effort. Wendall had taught her well. Clucking to the horses, she guided them toward the road.

Dust billowed around her as she crossed the prairie and headed into town.

As she passed the small clump of trees where the road turned, she could see the collection of buildings in the distance. The horses swatted flies and snorted as they smelled the Arkansas River, west of town.

Since white men were not allowed to do business in the Cherokee Nation, traders had gravitated toward Tulsey Town across the border in the Creek Nation. Indian laws were more liberal there.

The town had been settled five years ago by J. P. Dwayne as a trading place for the Indians and the railroad men. Tulsa now had three stores, a post office, a small hotel, a livery stable, a smithy, and a saddle shop. The town was a curious mix of Indian and white, and Kate remembered her brother's comment about not wanting her to go there alone. The cowboys came to town to spend their money, and the gambling tents of the early years had fast given way to the Tulsa Hotel and Casino. Saloons were outlawed, but bootlegging was common. Except for the U.S. marshals who rode out from Fort Smith, Arkansas, there were only the Indian Lighthorse Police. One never knew when a stray bullet might fly, for every white man had to be his own law here.

In town, Indians unloaded ox-drawn wagons filled with venison, hams, wild turkeys, pecans, and dressed buckskin, and cotton, which they would trade for flour, coffee, sugar, tobacco, clothing, and other goods.

The Indians here were civilized. Most of

them dressed like the white men and the chiefs wore black suits like distinguished businessmen. Only their black hair and bronze skin and the Indian pride in their faces distinguished them from their neighbors. They lived in frame houses and log cabins just as the white settlers did, and on the outskirts of town, the tribal leaders had built mansions reminiscent of the plantation homes they had lived in before they were forced to leave the South.

Kate pulled the wagon alongside the railing in front of Dwayne's Store. Climbing down to the hard-packed ground, she secured the reins. She mounted the wooden steps and walked toward the store. There was a rowdy bunch inside, and as she approached she could hear their raucous laughter. Barry Hogan, one of the town's biggest jokers, was telling a story.

Hearing the men inside guffaw, Kate shook her head. As she reached for the door, it swung open before her. She looked up in surprise at the dark, handsome face of a full-blooded Indian. Black eyes stared out of deep sockets. Smooth burnished skin stretched over prominent high cheekbones. A finely carved nose led down to a firm mouth with evenly shaped lips. Straight black hair hung past broad muscular shoulders. He wore a black broadcloth suit, which accentuated his graceful but powerful stance.

Raven Sky faced her for a long moment. As their eyes locked, his gaze seemed to penetrate hers, and Kate stopped breathing. Then he stepped aside to let her pass. As she moved past him through the door, the sleeve of her calico dress brushed one of his sinewy arms, and he turned his head and once again looked down into her shimmering blue eyes. A tremor ran along her spine and spread through her legs, as if his eyes had penetrated the protective cover that had shrouded her feelings until that moment.

The corners of the tall Indian's mouth lifted slightly, and light flickered in his dark eyes. There was the merest hint of hesitation as he stepped onto the porch of the store.

Kate lowered her gaze, remembering him from the train station the day before. She could feel the warmth throbbing in her veins, and she kept her eyes down until she could regain her composure. Turning her back on him, she stepped inside.

She nodded to the other customers in the store. A few of the men lifted their hats to her, casting admiring gazes in her direction. But she knew she was safe enough here. There wasn't a white man or an Indian for miles around who didn't know and respect Wendall Calhoun.

Kate walked down the long aisle to examine the dry goods. Still recovering from the strange effect the Indian had had on her, she went through the motions of considering her list of supplies, exhaling two long breaths through puffed-up cheeks. She was barely aware that Jesse Smith was approaching her. From behind the counter, he beamed at Kate and straightened his bow tie. Finally she noticed him and whirled around.

'Afternoon, Kate. How is everything at the ranch?'

'Fine, Jesse. Fine. Wendall came home yesterday.'

'I know,' Jesse said, a slight blush tinting his pale face. 'I hear he brought back a new bride.' He shuffled his feet behind the counter. 'I reckon that'll mean some changes at home.'

Kate pulled her mouth back in an expression of impatience. She ought to have known that Jesse would already have heard the news. People didn't miss much here. She'd better make her business short and get on to the mission school. But before she could extricate herself, Jesse leaned over the glass-topped counter. She moved back a little, his wheedling tone annoying her.

'Will I be seeing you Sunday, Kate?' he asked.

Kate stared at him, hesitating. She was reluctant to let his Sunday calls continue. 'I don't know, Jesse,' she said. She studied his eager face. He was about her height, with a medium build. But as she looked at him, it wasn't Jesse's face she saw.

'Do you know the Indian called Raven Sky?' she asked on impulse, realizing after the words were already out of her mouth that she was making her curiosity too obvious.

'Who?' Jesse asked, annoyance dampening his enthusiasm.

'The tall man who just went out. He was with the Indian delegation on the train my brother came in on yesterday, but I'd never seen him before.'

Jesse frowned. 'You mean the town chief's second son.' A tightness across his face showed his displeasure with the direction of her queries. But his love of gossip was equal to his need for Kate's attention, and he found himself saying more than he expected.

'He's one of the better-known Creek Indians,' he said. 'I've heard it said he's noted for his leadership within the tribe.' Privately, Jesse felt a grudging respect for Raven Sky. He was admired wherever he went. 'They say

41

he's progressive. He's been to the East, went to college there.'

Kathleen nodded, her eyes darting around the room as she tried to avoid Jesse's gaze. 'I remember hearing of him now,' she said. Jesse stared at her oddly as a fresh blush appeared in her cheeks.

Kathleen ducked her head and reached into her pocket for her list. She didn't look at Jesse again as she ordered nails, a saw, sugar, white flour, and molasses. Wendall kept an account at the store, so she signed for the bill.

As she turned to walk to the door, she saw Jesse trying to catch her attention.

'Afternoon, Kathleen,' he said.

Feeling foolish, she let the door swing back in on her. 'Oh, afternoon, Jesse,' she said belatedly, then went out to the porch. As she shaded her eyes with her hand and looked down the street, she saw the lithe form of Raven Sky mount his beautiful red horse and move slowly down Main Street.

On the dirt street, several other Indians and their children were doing business or talking in groups, but her eyes were riveted on Raven Sky. Muscles rippled under the nankeen of his trousers as he sat astride the horse. She stood and watched until horse and rider were gone.

Something thrilled in her, and she

wondered at the new, strong sensations stirring beneath her skin after one brief contact with the manly Indian. This frightened her, for beneath her stirring emotions lay an old fear. She assumed it had something to do with her parents' death, but she could never quite remember that incident. And Wendall had told her over and over again that she had nothing to fear from a civilized Indian.

Holding on to the railing to steady herself, she walked down the steps to her wagon. Some of the Indians who worked at the store loaded her goods. When everything was secured, she walked to the mission school, a few blocks uphill on Fourth Street.

The barnlike white frame structure, with its wooden belfry, adorned the crest of the hill. Children's squeals and yells told her they were on recess. Joy Harrington, the young Irish widow from New York who had come out to teach at the school, might have time for a visit.

Now Kate saw her vivacious friend, her skirt billowing around her as small children tugged on it for her attention. Spotting Kathleen coming up the hill, Joy answered the children's questions, then waved them off.

What a pretty picture Joy made in her

simple green checked dress against the white mission school, thought Kathleen. Red hair, green eyes, and a wide smile showing her white teeth.

'What a surprise to see you, Kate,' said Joy, kissing her cheek. 'This must be a special occasion.'

'It is. I suppose you've heard my brother's gone and gotten married.'

Joy sighed.

'Lucky girl,' she said, and winked. Kate thought Joy had feelings for her brother, and she often wondered why the two hadn't gotten together, since they met often enough at church. But then, she thought, perhaps Joy's constant gaiety was too much for Wendall. He needed someone a bit more quiet and deferential. Joy was too filled with wit and unbounded energy for a man like Wendall. She needed someone with a sense of humor equal to her own. In any case, no romance had blossomed, and Kate knew better than to try to interfere with other people's feelings.

The two women linked arms and walked around the school yard. Joy stopped to nod toward pretty nine-year-old Courtney Dwayne, daughter of the town's founder. Tall and serious, with her braids neatly coiled around her head, Courtney was pushing a smaller Indian child in a makeshift swing that hung from the limb of a tree.

'Quite a young lady, that Courtney Dwayne,' said Joy.

Kathleen shaded her eyes from the bright sun to observe the child. 'Where's her little sister?' she asked, looking around for the five-year-old with blond curls whom she had seen so often with their mother at church.

'There she is.' Joy pointed to a clover patch next to the schoolhouse where Laura Dwayne was earnestly picking daisies. 'Laura and her sister like to weave daisy chains,' Joy explained as she and Kathleen continued to stroll around the yard.

From the hilltop on which the school stood, they could look down into valleys in all directions. To the north, the crude little settlement of Tulsa lay beside the railroad tracks. To the east, tall grasses waved in the dry wind. Noah Partridge's cabin nestled on the edge of a stand of oak trees to the south. Westward, a line of trees cut off their view of the Arkansas River. In the northeast, the new railroad bed wound its way over small hills and valleys on its way to Vinita, where the trains would connect with transportation to the East.

'Joy, I've been giving serious thought to becoming a teacher, like you,' Kathleen said.

'As you know, I'm qualified, and I want to work now that Wendall's new wife is on the ranch. I don't want to be underfoot all the time.'

'What does Wendall think?'

'He's not certain.' Kate shrugged. 'Oh, he wants me to do whatever will make me happy, but he's not anxious for me to be away from the ranch.'

'I think you'd make a wonderful teacher,' Joy told her.

'Could I work here at the mission school? I know you need help, and I thought perhaps we could write to the board and ask for approval. I'll serve as a volunteer until we hear from them.'

'That would be fun,' Joy said, squeezing Kate's arm, 'and you're right — I could use the help.'

'I can start right after roundup,' Kate said.

'All right. I'll write the board today. The children will love you, and heaven knows I'm overworked.' Joy gave a helpless shrug.

Kate's eyes sparkled. In truth, Joy was a very capable teacher. Nevertheless, Kate was sure she could make a difference by taking on some of the classroom chores. But she also knew that the work would be difficult. Most white teachers — Joy and Kate included — didn't speak the Creek dialect and had a difficult time teaching the full-bloods, whose parents didn't speak English.

'It's all set, then,' she said happily. 'I'll start after roundup. Oh, Joy, I'm so glad.' She kissed Joy on the cheek, feeling better than she had in days, then took her leave.

She turned and made her way back down the hill to the wagon. She'd have to hurry now. Clouds were gathering in the west. She didn't want to be out on the open prairie during a storm.

When she reached the wagon and untied the reins, the two horses, May and Jericho, were stamping and shaking their heads, excited by the coming storm. Shopkeepers had begun to close their windows and doors. As she pulled away from the rail and headed out of town, she noticed how fast the light was fading. Dark clouds now covered the sky. A strong, wet wind whipped Kathleen's hair around her and sent goose bumps creeping over her flesh.

'Haw!' she called out, urging the horses to a trot. The roiling skies looked ominous now, but Kathleen chided herself for being so nervous. It was only a storm.

Then she heard hooves pounding behind her — two horses, at least, coming up fast. Her heart beat faster, and she wondered who would be galloping along the road.

'Ho, there! Stop ahead.' The unfamiliar male voice was deep and authoritative. Her throat went dry as she thought about the many undesirables who frequented this road.

She drew back on the reins. She could never outrun her pursuers. It might be wiser to find out what they wanted.

Two men rode up to her, one on either side of the wagon. Fear pounded through her as she saw the six-shooters hanging from one horseman's belt. His hat covered his face, and in the dusky light she couldn't see his features. Then a streak of sunset reflected off a bright piece of metal, and she saw that he wore the badge of a U.S. marshal. The second man wore a badge, too. She sighed in relief.

'You all right, miss?' asked the man with the low-slung hat.

'Yes, sir, but you gave me a scare. You after someone?'

''Fraid so, ma'am. We're looking for a whiskey peddler we heard reports of. Been selling firewater to the Indians this side of the Missouri line.' He paused, looking over her wagon. 'Ain't safe for you to be traveling alone. Where you headed?'

'My brother's ranch, four miles out of town. I'm Wendall Calhoun's sister.'

The marshal nodded. 'Everybody knows Calhoun. He carries a lot of weight in the territory. He know you're out alone?'

'Yes, but I dallied too long over my errands, and I didn't know it would be getting dark so soon.'

'Deputy Jones will ride with you as far as your land, ma'am.'

The deputy touched the brim of his hat.

'Thank you,' said Kate.

The marshal turned his horse and then headed back toward town. 'I'll take the other road, Frank,' said the marshal. 'Fire into the air if you run into trouble.'

'Right.' Frank Jones turned to Kathleen. 'We'd better be getting along, ma'am.' He clicked his tongue to his horse and Kathleen slapped her team with the reins. The wagon creaked under its load as the horses strained forward at a brisk walk. They reached the ranch just before the storm broke.

3

Night descended as Kate washed the dishes while Molly dried them and put them on the shelves. One by one the ranch hands brought their empty plates in, saying, 'Thank you, ma'am,' for their grub. Wendall went to a neighboring ranch. Then Kate's thoughts turned to the endless sewing waiting to be done.

'Some of Wendall's shirts need mending,' Kate said to Molly as the two women finished their after-supper chores. ' 'Maybe you'd like to do them?'

'Of course, if you'll just show me where they are.'

Kate fetched the sewing basket and handed Molly several soft chambray shirts. Then they took their sewing into the parlor where Mattie had built a fire.

'It's so quiet here,' Molly said after they had taken up their work.

'I guess you get used to it,' Kate said. 'But there aren't many people around, except for the Indians.'

'How often do you go into town?'

'Sometimes not for weeks.'

It was true, Kate thought; she had gotten used to the loneliness. Occasional trips to town provided her with some human contact, but on the days when she saw only Indians, she felt especially alone. And before Molly came, she had had no one to talk to except Joy Harrington. There was no forum for ideas on the prairie. Watching Molly now, bent over her needle, she wondered if this woman would ever become a close friend. She struggled with her desire to enjoy her sister-in-law's company. If only Molly's presence didn't remind her that she hadn't found a husband and didn't have a home of her own.

If only she could stifle the feeling of panic that rose in her throat every time the thought of the future threatened her. But she couldn't. She didn't want to depend on her brother's charity forever.

Molly went upstairs early, and after another hour of sewing, Kate's fingers felt cramped. She put her work away and stretched her shoulders, longing for a breath of fresh air.

She stepped out onto the porch, shut the door behind her, and gazed out over the dark plain. The prairie solitude was complete at night, with no light from any other homestead and no sound except the howl of the wind across the plain. As she walked across the

51

porch, an unearthly shock ran through her. Astride his great red stallion sat Raven Sky, still as a statue. She wouldn't have seen him at all had it not been for a shaft of moonlight that spilled from behind a cloud and lit the surrounding prairie with a soft glow. Horse and man stood on a knoll, carved out of the glittering blanket of stars in the vast sky. The sight took her breath away.

Raven Sky neither moved nor spoke, yet his presence rooted her to the spot. Fear and admiration mingled in her at the terrible beauty of forbidden pleasure. The sight of him again aroused within her strange sensations that she didn't understand. But the dark figure also triggered some distant memory that disturbed her. Emotions warred within her. She was helpless to do anything but stand and stare.

As she watched him, her mind conjured up a new image: she saw herself behind the Indian, hair flying in the wind as the strong steed carried them across the plains. For a moment, she feared for her sanity. She wanted to flee, but stood rooted to the spot.

Then Raven Sky dropped to the ground and walked toward her, holding her gaze. She stood on the steps as he approached, each step closing the distance between them. Kathleen fought down an irrational urge to move toward him. She clenched her fists at her sides, to keep from reaching out to touch the finely chiseled chest, so clearly defined by his close-fitting buckskin shirt.

'I need to see Calhoun,' the Indian said. 'Tell your brother Raven Sky wants to speak to him.' His voice was deep and low, and she could sense the power in it, but he spoke softly so that the sound carried to her ears alone.

A sense of dread filled her now. She didn't want him to know that Wendall wasn't in the house. She told herself it was her own runaway emotions that frightened her. As the tall Indian watched her, she found her voice.

'He's not here,' she answered with a tremor. 'Shall I give him a message?'

Her heart pounded. His eyes seemed to drill right through her. Yet his expression was gentle and compassionate, as if he understood her fears. He stepped back a pace, still holding the reins.

'Your brother is a fair man,' Raven Sky said. 'The mixed-bloods trust him. They want him to talk to our people.'

'Talk to them about what?'

'Your government is talking of dissolving our tribal governments.'

'Yes. I've heard about this,' she said.

'Our people are divided. The conservative

full-bloods say this will never happen. They rely on our treaty, but the mixed-bloods talk of the white man's desire to own more land.'

'What can Wendall do?'

'He can speak to my people at the town meeting and tell them what the cattlemen want. He can help prevent bad feelings, even bloodshed. The cattlemen have long been our allies against white settlers. They only want to graze their herds on our land. The settlers want to take it from us.'

'I see.' She swallowed.

'The mixed-bloods look to men like your brother for advice and leadership, but the full-bloods say the white man's education has poisoned our minds. Calhoun can assure the tribe that the white men will deal with the Indians fairly.'

'But surely the tribal leaders must negotiate with men more powerful than Wendall,' said Kate. 'Isn't that why the delegation went to Washington? To discuss with the federal government the plans for the territory?'

Raven Sky nodded, placing his hand on his horse's muzzle, caressing it as he spoke. 'The leaders in Washington will make the agreements, but the businessmen in the territory will buy our lands, or steal them. Wendall Calhoun can persuade your people and mine to deal fairly.'

The implications were vast, Kate knew, but she was impressed that a man like Raven Sky had so much respect for her brother.

'Wendall will do what he can, I am sure,' Kate said.

She felt warmth creeping into her cheeks and lowered her eyes. 'He will be home soon,' she said.

No more was said. One moment Raven Sky stood still, a perfect masculine shape beside his beautiful horse. The next moment he leaped in one smooth motion onto the bare back of his horse, and the two moved out into the night. He seemed to be a part of the stallion, his hair streaming down his back. The flowing mane and rippling muscles of the horse seemed an extension of his own powerful body, the muscles in his limbs revealed by the soft folds of his buckskin suit. Kathleen watched his figure blend into the darkness. When he was gone, she reached for the porch railing to steady herself.

It was almost as if he had never been there at all. She wondered if she had imagined it, but his words echoed in her mind.

Her breathing slowed, and she retraced her steps into the house. Bolting the door behind her, she fetched the lamp and made her way, trembling, up the stairs to her room. She was glad to lock herself in there, feeling that she needed to place a barrier between herself and the outside world. Or was she perhaps erecting a barrier between two different parts of herself?

It was strange, her reaction to this Indian. On the one hand, she had had much casual contact with the Civilized Tribes since she had lived in Indian Territory. But now, after her encounter with Raven Sky, she realized how guarded she had really kept herself from the Indian people. Her upbringing in St. Louis had taught her that white women were morally and intellectually superior to Indians. It was the white man's duty to civilize the Indians, or so she had been led to believe. And yet the Indians she had met here were vastly different from the warlike Indians of the plains.

Perhaps the mixed-bloods who worked for Wendall had caused her to question what she had been taught about Indians. She did not know any of them well. But something about Raven Sky drew her to him, and suddenly the prejudices that had been hammered into her were being loosened in a way that confused her. Raven Sky held a fascination for her, and she wanted to see him again. Yet she was afraid of this strange new desire.

A shaft of moonlight found its way through the curtains, and she walked over to the window and looked out. In her mind she saw again the handsome, noble face, and she trembled with a newfound excitement. She dropped the curtain and lay on her down-filled coverlet, raking her fingers through her hair. She closed her eyes and pictures flitted across her mind.

The image of Raven Sky's blazing black eyes penetrating her own haunted her all night as she slept fitfully. Visions faded in and out of her dreams. Raven Sky's face was replaced by another, older face, first gentle, then horrified. Then there was blood, and fire crackled around her.

Kate screamed and sat up, clasping her cold, sweaty arms. It was the dream again, the one she'd had since childhood. She sank back into the pillows, drinking in the cool night air that wafted in from the open window. She stayed that way for a long time. At last she slept.

★ ★ ★

On the morning of the party, Kathleen donned a green satin dress she had brought with her from St. Louis more than a year ago. She'd made minor repairs to it and added a bustle. The high collar accentuated her oval face and thick hair, which she crimped with her curling iron, then pinned atop her head in stylish ringlets. She took her white kid shoes out of the trunk in which they'd traveled all the way here from St. Louis. Finally she donned a green bonnet trimmed with ribbon and feathers. As she inspected herself in front of the wavering glass, she hoped she'd be able to make as good an appearance as Molly undoubtedly would.

The other ranchers, the railroad men, and their families would come to the party at the church to meet Molly and wish the couple well. And the single men would come to gawk. Kate wondered what Molly would make of this wild town and its frontier welcome.

She went downstairs and found Wendall and Molly waiting outside. Wendall looked handsome in his best black suit, a green brocade vest, and a white shirt with a stand-up collar. He pushed his black felt hat back on his head and smiled at Kathleen, who grinned back at him. Molly, she noticed, was dressed in pink satin covered with lace. A pearl brooch shone at her throat, and a bonnet with pink ribbons and chiffon was tied under her chin. On her feet were white kid slippers.

'Oh, Molly, you look beautiful,' Kate said, returning Molly's warm smile.

Molly reached out to squeeze Kate's arm. 'I'm glad you think so, Kate.'

'You'll be the center of attention today,' said Kathleen. 'People will be coming from all over to meet Wendall's new bride.'

The three of them climbed into the buggy, and Wendall picked up the reins. The buggy jerked forward, and Wendall guided the horses away from the ranch house.

As they left the ranch behind, a flock of migrating geese approached a prairie slough, and the pond's resident geese responded dissonantly. Then the marsh, too, fell behind them as the creaking wagon carried them toward town.

Almost all the whites and a large number of Indians were headed for the church school on the hill. The crowd seemed nearly as excited as it had on that day when Kate had met Wendall and Molly at the depot. She remembered Raven Sky's words, and wondered if everyone here was aware of impending change.

Looking now at the people milling about the town, she was aware that more white men were encroaching here every day. But the territory was enormous, and the white settlers could teach the Indians a great deal. A lot of the men who were attracted to Indian Territory would not help civilize the Indians further, though. They had come here out of greed alone.

A chill passed through her. Would these undercurrents of animosity grow? No. Surely there was no real danger here, not from civilized Indians. Wendall would never let Molly and her stay in a place that might become dangerous. She shook herself, deciding it was only her nervousness getting the best of her.

As they pulled up in front of the whitewashed building, a cheer went up from the crowd. She glanced about self-consciously, remembering the last two times she had come to town. She half expected to see Raven Sky standing nearby. But he was nowhere in sight.

Wendall helped the two women out of the wagon, then raised his hands to quiet the crowd.

'My friends,' he boomed, 'I'm pleased that you folks turned out to wish us well. There'll be food and dancin' all night long.'

'Amen to that!' someone yelled. This was met with a loud 'Yeehaw!' Wendall leaped out of the wagon and joined his friends.

Long planks had been placed on sawhorses to make a table on the lawn. Joy and some of the wives of the railroad men had laid out a red and white checkered table-cloth. Sarah Dwayne hustled about, giving orders to the other women, who deferred to her because she was the wife of the town's founder. Sarah's daughters, Courtney and Laura, in their frilly Sunday best, ran delightedly around the table, their high tinkling laughter punctuating the air.

Kate led Molly toward the makeshift table, which groaned beneath its burden of food. The Indians had brought biscuits, honey, fried prairie chicken, dried fruit, and corn bread. Kathleen had delivered a large assortment of meats, pies, and cakes from the Calhoun kitchen the day before. Delicious boiled hams, homemade pickles, and crocks of hand-churned butter had come from the larders of the other ranchers.

Indians were dressed in black suits and cotton shirts. The women wore gingham dresses and long black braids hanging down their backs. Some wore striped blanket shawls with fringed borders, traded from the Osages whose lands bordered theirs.

One Indian girl came up to Molly and pointed to her bonnet. 'May I see hat?' she asked.

'Oh, all right.' Molly handed her bonnet to the girl, but Kate could see that she was disconcerted.

'They have a natural curiosity and don't mean any harm,' she said to Molly when the girl turned away to show her young friends the hat.

Kate could see in Molly's eyes the resentment and fear of a woman who had been taught to regard all Indians as ignorant savages. And yet she was surrounded by quiet, dignified adults dressed like white men and women, talking quietly among themselves. A few of them stared openly at her, but you could hardly call them savages.

The Indian girl, speaking a mixture of Creek and English, made much over the artificial flowers on the bonnet. She marveled that they looked real and yet did not smell like flowers. Sensing Molly's discomfort, Kate gently took the hat back and handed it to Molly. Molly stared at Kate with something like bewilderment, but there was something else in her eyes, too. Was it a flicker of admiration? Kate wondered. Perhaps, after today, Molly would be able to resign herself to a new and different life. Maybe she would decide that her place was with Wendall, no matter what that brought.

Kate put her arm around her sister-in-law's waist and led her inside. 'Let's go, Molly. The fiddler's just starting up.'

As the crowd began to go in for the dancing, Jesse Smith came up behind Kate and touched the sleeve of her dress.

'Hello, Jesse,' she said, releasing her hold on Molly as Sarah Dwayne came up and led her away.

'Will you join me for the grand march, Kathleen?' Jesse drawled. When he moved close to her she could smell the whiskey on his hot breath, and she turned her head aside. As he reached for her elbow, she had an over-powering urge to push him away. He apparently sensed her reluctance, for he tightened his grip on her arm and pulled her toward him.

'You go on, Jesse. I have to see about the food,' she said. 'I'll be there in time for the Virginia reel.'

'Now, Kate,' he slurred, 'you can't get rid of me that easy. You know we're short on women, so you're not allowed to sit out the grand march.'

Kate looked up to see Tex walk up to Joy Harrington, who smiled at him. He held out his arm and she took it, leading him inside.

As Kate started to follow them, Jesse grabbed her around the waist. With more whiskey under his belt than usual, he seemed unwilling to give up on his attempt at conquest. Kate gasped, the color draining from her face, as he pulled her back against him and brought his mouth near her ear.

'Kathleen, I've been courtin' you for some

time now. Since your brother's gone and got himself a bride, don't you think it's right time you found yourself a man? You can't stay out on that ranch forever.' He pressed his lips to her neck.

Kathleen hissed at him. 'Jesse Smith, you let go of me right now or I'll scream for help, and my brother will tear you limb from limb.'

She was livid with anger, and Jesse's whiskey breath made her feel sick. But as she struggled against him, Jesse only tightened his grip. Kathleen had become aware of a burgeoning hardness between Jesse's skinny thighs, and she found his arousal abhorrent.

'Jesse, let me go!'

'Aw, come on, Kate. Surely you don't begrudge me a little kiss. You ain't been leading me on for nothin', have you?' he grumbled. 'A man's got certain needs. Say you'll marry me. We'll announce it tonight.'

Kate's body was cold and rigid. She couldn't believe what she was hearing, nor could she believe what she felt next, as Jesse's right hand strayed up toward her breast. His fingers probed the soft curves, searching for an opening in the soft green satin.

In one fierce, desperate motion, Kate seized a cutting knife from the table and raised it high above her head. She screamed at the top of her lungs as she brought the blade down.

Jesse let go as the point of the knife caught his sleeve. He stumbled back, bumping into a keg as he fell. Kate threw the knife to the ground, then ran past the church without looking behind her, heading toward the river some distance away. Tears moistening her eyes, she was only aware of how good it felt to run, shedding the frustrations that had been building in her these last weeks. Through the tall grass she ran, her breath coming in gulps, snagging her dress in the brush.

A figure moved from behind a stand of trees just ahead, near the river, and stood watching her run. Her eyes watering from the wind, she didn't recognize Raven Sky until she was almost upon him.

A few feet from him, Kathleen slowed her pace. Then she sank to her knees, exhausted, her head in her hands, her heart pounding violently. She began to tremble as the tall Indian approached her, but she had no strength left to rise. Her mind was too befuddled to think what she might say to him, but even in her confusion, she felt an odd sense of refuge.

Slowly her breathing returned to normal,

and the warmth of the sun began to penetrate her limbs. Wiping her eyes with the back of her hands, sniffling loudly, she looked up to find Raven Sky standing over her.

4

Raven Sky knelt a few feet from Kathleen, but he made no move to touch her. He watched her with his calm dark eyes, his face relaxed and still.

She looked up at him, tears stinging her eyes. He slowly reached out to her, and she rose up toward him. Raven Sky's eyes were gentle, and his face seemed to radiate understanding. Her heart hammered, as if it had been activated by his gaze. Then his hand slid to her elbow, and he helped her to her feet.

She focused on his lips, soft and sensuous, then dropped her gaze to his chest. She could feel his warmth, and feeling overtook thought. Somewhere in a distant part of her mind confusion still raged. Her life had been overturned. She had been mauled by a man she wanted only as a friend.

Now she was standing so close to Raven Sky that she could feel his light breath on her hair. When she lowered her head, it touched his chest, and then she was in his arms. His strong presence seemed to surround her, offering comfort. She buried her face in the curve of his shoulder, incapable of coherent thought, knowing simply that she needed the solace this man was offering her. Some part of her mind warned her that he was an Indian, and that she must not trust him, but emotion swept away her fears, and for a few golden moments, she breathed in his warmth and his strength.

'Fear not, little one,' he whispered. His low voice was firm and melodious as his lips grazed her hair. His gentle hands stroked her, and she closed her eyes, glorying in his soothing touch. She clung to him, not caring what was happening inside her.

Raven Sky neither gripped her tightly nor held her away. Rather, his moves filled the needs he sensed in her. He had been blessed, like many Indians, with senses that ran deeper than most white men's. He was aware of feelings that could not be expressed in words. And he did not need words to know what this woman was feeling.

He caressed her face with his fingers, waiting until her heartbeat slowed. She melted against him, sliding her hands up over his chest. Tentatively, she felt his strong pectoral muscles through the soft buckskin of his tunic, and a thrill ran through her. She lifted her face to his as he pulled her closer, his hands around her waist, and she touched his straight dark hair. Their eyes locked. Blazing black ones looked into her blue ones, and the intensity of the contact shattered her. As she dropped her gaze to his full, sensitive lips, she was hardly aware that she was locking her arms around him.

The wind rustled in the grass at their feet. Shadows passed over them as clouds traveled across the sun. Deep desire began to burn within them as they stood together. His soft breathing fanned the embers in her heart, and the warmth spread downward through her body. The heat crept slowly over her as she burrowed deeper into the comfort of his arms.

'You are like a white dove,' he said softly. 'Something has frightened you. Tell me.' Then a menacing look came over his face. 'Has someone hurt you, my white dove?'

Though Kathleen hardly knew Raven Sky, she had an odd sense that he would go to any length to avenge her. Suddenly she knew that something terrible would happen to Jesse if she told Raven Sky what he had done to her.

'No, no,' she said. She held herself from him, trying to ignore the pleasure his nearness gave her.

Feeling her pull away, he released her, still holding her waist gently.

How could she confide her innermost

thoughts to an Indian? Yet she still had the uncanny feeling that he understood her. Awkwardness began to take the place of her runaway emotions, and she struggled for words. 'Raven Sky, I mustn't . . . ' Her voice trailed off.

'Hush, my sweet one,' he said in a soothing voice. He gently caressed her face with his fingertips.

But Kathleen was overcome with a sudden horror at her own behavior. How could she, a white woman, throw herself at this Indian? It was shameful. Wendall would be shocked.

The fact that Raven Sky was far better educated than she was did not still the irrational and uncontrollable fear that rose from some part of her. Her instincts and her eastern upbringing swept to the forefront of her mind. Her pale hand lying on his bronze arm reminded her of the white glow around the red flames of a prairie fire.

Raven Sky dropped his hands and studied her face, his expression solemn. When he spoke it was with firmness and understanding.

'Do not be afraid,' he said. 'I will not touch you if you do not want it.'

His kind, sensible words did something to calm her. But she still fought other thoughts. The old tales of Indian savagery and immorality warred with the emotions his nearness stirred in her.

She glanced away, unable to hold his gaze. 'I'm sorry. I didn't know what I was doing,' she said, finally looking back at him, her eyes pleading for understanding.

A ghost of a smile passed across his face. 'Little bird,' he said, lifting a finger to her chin, 'if something has frightened you, it is best to speak of it. The most fearsome thoughts are those lodged within the breast where they have no sun and air. You must name the thing you are afraid of. By confronting it, you will become master of it.'

She looked deep into his dark eyes, responding to his wisdom. 'You are right,' she said, her smile natural now. She breathed deeply, feeling better.

He turned and began to walk slowly toward the stand of trees above the river, glancing back in invitation for her to follow. From nearby a bobwhite called out. Kathleen walked beside him, the tall grass brushing her skirt as she moved.

'What was it that frightened you?' he asked again, this time not looking at her.

'It was a man,' she said, bitterness returning momentarily. Looking up at Raven Sky, she realized that she really wanted to unburden herself to this tall, perceptive

Indian. He seemed to have a depth of understanding that she had never before found in a man.

'He is a friend. But he became . . . aggressive. I was so frightened that I threatened him with a knife. Then I ran.'

At the mention of the knife Raven Sky's lip curved slightly. 'This man,' he said. 'He wants you to be his woman?'

'That's right.'

'And you don't want to be?'

'No. I don't love him.'

They were silent for a while. They had walked some distance up a rise, and Raven Sky sat down on a large outcropping. He stretched out his long legs on the warm stone and gazed out over the muddy river. Kathleen, too, watched the river. It was calm now, but capable of mighty floods.

'I was born here,' Raven Sky said, gesturing at the wide expanse before them. 'But my people's home is in the South, in the woodland you call Alabama.'

'I know,' she said, sitting next to him. 'I know about the trails your people walked when the white man's government took your land.'

'We call it the Trail of Tears,' he said. 'We walked all the way, carrying our fire without letting the flame die. We held our first council in this land right over there.' He pointed to a tall spreading oak some distance away. 'Council Oak.'

Kathleen had seen the dignified oak before and knew something of the history of the Creek Nation. She could almost picture the band of Lochapoka Creeks gathered around the tree, the flickering firelight and the silent valley before them, their faces dark and intent as they chanted in wild cadences the ritual that marked the founding of Tulsa. That was also the name of the Alabama settlement they had been forced to leave. Tulsa meant 'Old Town' in their language.

It was strange, Kathleen thought. She had grown up with the notion that the white settlers had had every right to any land that had not been 'improved,' even though the Indians had lived on it for thousands of years. The country needed to expand. The Indians had agreed to treaties, had sold their former lands.

But then she had come to live with Wendall, who knew Indians as men, not as lesser beings without souls. And as she looked at Raven Sky, a feeling of compassion overcame her. It surprised her that she could feel this way about an Indian.

'Your people were very courageous,' she said.

Raven Sky leaned forward, his elbows on his knees. He gazed at the river, his proud bearing a reflection of his heritage. Then he shook his head resignedly as he looked at her.

'We made many changes when the white men came,' he said. 'We learned from them.' He leaned down and picked up some of the soil, rubbing it between his fingers. 'We were hunters. But we learned to be farmers, confined to the land left us by your government.'

He narrowed his gaze. 'But then we were made to fight the white man's war, which divided the Indian nations.'

She knew he spoke of the recent war between the states. She listened intently but sympathetically as he continued.

'The white men would strip us of our heritage, our race. They would make us a soulless people. They do not understand that our heartbeat is the land they want to take from us.'

'But now you have this land. Your tribe lives on it and farms it.'

He shook his head. 'Not forever. The men in Washington talk now of dividing the land again. They do not understand our way. The Indian nations are a torn asunder race. They would make us a soulless people. They do not know our spiritual ties to the land our people were born onto.'

Kathleen gazed at the tall Council Oak behind them. A shiver ran down her spine as she thought of the Indians who used to roam these plains. They had been moved to the western part of the territory to make room for the Civilized Tribes.

She looked up to where the sun stood in the sky, suddenly remembering that no one knew where she was.

'I must be getting back,' she said, standing.

Raven Sky stood up and touched her hand, sending a tingling sensation down her spine.

'I will walk part way with you,' he said.

She nodded, not trusting herself to speak. They went down the hill and back through the trees. At the edge of the timber where they had met, he stopped and placed a hand on her shoulder.

'I leave you here,' he said.

She turned to face him. As she looked into his dignified face, the marks of responsibility already drawn in it, her heart missed a beat. Feeling the urge to raise her hand to his face, she controlled her breathing and smiled.

'I will see you again,' said Raven Sky.

The wind gusted and blew her skirt around her legs, and she raised a hand to brush strands of hair from her face. Then she gave him a gesture of good-bye and turned back toward the school, its white bell tower rising in the distance.

At the next rise, she turned to look back at the spot where Raven Sky had stood. He was gone. She touched her cheeks, embarrassment beginning to fill her. She was experiencing desire for a man such as she had never felt before.

She tried to control her turbulent emotions. Raven Sky was not the man for her. She needed a traditional home and family. The prairie and Wendall's ranch had been a temporary refuge, but life here was not permanent. She had come out to help Wendall with the ranch because he needed her and because she had had no place else to go. But now, she thought, tears threatening to choke her again, Wendall didn't need her anymore. Instead of teaching with Joy at the mission school, perhaps she would return to the East and make a home for herself there.

Perhaps she would write the Wagners and ask to stay with them for a few weeks until she found work and a respectable boarding-house. Surely there were some decent establishments in St. Louis where young women like herself could live while they taught school or worked in factories.

She turned back toward the party, but the

76

music, clapping, and hollering of the guests grated on her ears.

★　★　★

The party lasted until dawn. Those who weren't slumped against the wall sleeping staggered out to their wagons to go home when the sun rose in the eastern sky.

Dozing on a bench, Kate felt a hand shake her arm. Red-eyed, Wendall looked down at her. Molly stood behind him, her hair disheveled, nearly asleep on her feet.

'Oh,' Kate murmured, rousing herself, 'how long have I been asleep?' Her head was spinning, and she vaguely remembered being tossed from one dance partner to another.

She focused her eyes on Wendall as he said, 'Time to go home.' His breath stank, and his eyes were bloodshot.

Kate rose, trying to smile at Molly. Then the three of them stumbled into the blinding sunlight. Wendall got the horses from the stable where they'd been sheltered, swearing to himself as he fumbled with the harness.

Molly leaned against Kate, her eyes closing. Kate put one arm around her and helped Wendall lift her into the wagon, where she passed out between them.

As Kate held on to the side, the wagon

bounced wildly, making her head hurt even worse. Rocks crunched under the wheels as the horses plodded along. Oaks and elms along the road shaded them from the hazy morning sun.

They had passed out of town and were almost past a clump of trees and bushes, heading for open prairie, when Kate came fully awake. She neither saw nor heard anything, but she suddenly knew they were being watched.

She looked at Molly, who was sound asleep. Slumped in the driver's seat, Wendall held the reins loosely in his lap, for the horses knew their way home. But Kathleen's face radiated alertness as she sat up straight and looked around.

She knew Indians had an uncanny ability to stalk — to watch without being watched. Perhaps they were out there now. She had the distinct feeling there was no danger, however. Warmth began to invade her. Even though she could not see him, she knew Raven Sky was nearby. The thought made her tremble, but she held on to the feeling within her.

At the ranch, Kathleen and Wendall lifted Molly out of the wagon, and Wendall half carried her up to the bedroom.

Smothering a yawn, Kate went to her room and took off her party dress. Then she sat on the edge of her bed and slowly brushed out her tangled hair, a thousand thoughts crowding her tired head.

She envisioned the Wagners, her foster parents, standing on the doorstep of their house in St. Louis, waving goodbye to her. 'Be careful of the Indians,' they were saying.

The image clouded and faded, and in its place rose a worse one. There was the smell of smoke, a smoldering house, her brother pushing her aside.

Kathleen shook herself and held her head in her hands. It was all too terrible. Wendall mustn't find out she had been alone with Raven Sky. He would be worried about her.

Suddenly nauseated, she decided she needed sleep. At the party she had drunk some liquor, and she wanted the restful folds of unconsciousness to engulf her. She wanted the pictures to go away and, beneath the pictures, another disturbing memory that she couldn't quite reach.

Kate tossed back the covers and crawled into bed. Her curtains were drawn, and sleep came quickly. Blessed, welcome sleep.

★ ★ ★

Mattie fed the animals in the yard while the house slept, and the hands who'd made it

79

back to the ranch snored off their hangovers in the bunkhouse.

It was afternoon when Kate rose and freshened up with water from the pump in the kitchen. Wendall came downstairs, stripped to the waist in back of the house, doused himself with water from the well, and let his skin dry in the sun. Then, buttoning up his shirt, he strode into the kitchen, where Kate was rolling out some dough.

He took a seat, rubbing his forehead with his hand.

'I talked with Joy about working at the school,' Kate said, flattening the dough with the side of her hand.

Wendall grunted.

'She said I could start anytime.'

'How will you get there?' he asked. 'I can't spare the hands to drive you in every day.'

'I'll ride Monty.'

Wendall grunted again. 'You and Jesse not friendly anymore?' he asked. 'I noticed you didn't speak to him much at the dance.'

Kate was tempted to tell Wendall the truth about Jesse. If Wendall knew he had laid a hand on her, he would break Jesse's bones. But she felt her face warm as she remembered how near she had been to Raven Sky. Wendall would be furious about that, too, if he knew. So she didn't say anything about the incident. She didn't want to hurt Jesse as long as he stayed away.

Wendall gazed out the windows at the darkening prairie. His next words startled her. 'Hank told me that Indian, Raven Sky, was here.'

Kate swallowed before she could find words. 'He wanted you to speak at the town meeting, reassure people that the government will abide by its treaties. I told him you couldn't know what the government will do.'

Wendall shook his head, a look of concern passing over his face. 'The days of the Creek are numbered, I'm afraid. And there's nothing I can do about it, except to stay here and hope they are treated fairly.'

'What do you mean, Wendall?'

'The Creek population is on the decline. Already the whites in the territory are meeting secretly to find a way to buy the Indians' lands and let individual tribe members take their own plots of land instead of sharing communal property as they do now.'

Kate pressed her lips together, remembering what Raven Sky had said.

'The Indians have never understood the white man's notion that land can be bought and sold,' Wendall continued. 'It doesn't seem to make sense from their point of view. The land's there for using, and they share it communally. But it won't be for long.'

Kate greeted Molly as she came into the kitchen then, and the conversation returned to more comfortable topics. Still, Kathleen half listened. Wouldn't it be nice to have a home of her own, she thought, and a strong, loving husband like Wendall? The thought brought a stab of pain to her heart. She was shut off from her brother now. She would never be privy to the intimacies that would grow between him and Molly as man and wife, and she had no one with whom to share her private thoughts. Chilled as the new loneliness crept over her, she turned her thoughts to working at the school. It would be her refuge.

★ ★ ★

Several weeks after the welcome celebration, Kathleen walked out to the well and pulled up a bucket of cool water to douse over her head. It was a warm night, and dust and grime from the roundup had ground itself into her clothes and skin. She let the water run down over her hair, using her fingers to pull out the tangles and knots.

Cowboys from all the ranches in the

territory had joined in the roundup. Moving from one ranch to the other, they had rounded up cattle and cut out steers that belonged on other ranges, moving them to the pastures they had leased from the Indians. Wendall had gone out with the men and camped with them under the stars.

Women took no part in the roundup except to occasionally tend an injured or sick calf brought to the barn. Now, at the end of the roundup, the men worked nearer the ranch house, preparing to ship the cattle east. The distant mooing of the cows was a comforting sound. Tomorrow the last of the herd would be loaded into boxcars and bound for St. Louis and points east.

Somewhere out there, thought Kate as she looked toward the prairie now covered with cattle, Wendall and the other men sat around a campfire eating a meal prepared on the chuck wagon and served on tin plates. While Wendall was with the roundup, she and Molly took care of the ranch themselves.

She wrung out her hair and walked up to the house. Molly appeared on the porch to toss a basket of food leavings to the pigs. She leaned on the porch rail to rest.

'What are you looking at?' Kate asked as she approached Molly.

'You,' said Molly, with a sigh. 'I was

wondering how a woman keeps her looks with all this hard work.'

Kate shook her head. Molly did look a little worse for wear after only a few weeks on the prairie. She did the best she could with the toiletries she had brought with her from St. Louis. But the dry climate and the sun that climbed higher in the sky every day, were already having their effects on her delicate skin and hair.

Molly smiled at Kate, leaning her chin in her hand on the railing. 'You look so pretty when you pile your hair up in a knot or just let it stream behind you,' she said. 'My hair just stands out straight if I do that. It makes me look like a witch.'

The women laughed as water from Kate's hair dripped onto the dust at her feet. Kate mounted the steps, then dropped down into one of the rockers on the porch where she and Wendall had spent so many summer evenings. Molly sat beside her, dropping the pail beside her feet.

'What do you think about when you're alone out here?' Molly asked.

Kate shifted in the rocker. 'The same things you do, I suppose,' she answered vaguely.

'Do you ever want to go back east?'

'Sometimes. Why do you ask?'

Molly shrugged. 'I don't know. I just wondered if you missed it. I guess I'll always remember St. Louis. I wonder how long it will take me to get used to the frontier.'

'There are many things to like about it. Wendall thinks the land here has great potential. More and more people are coming to Tulsa to open up businesses.'

She smiled at her sister-in-law. 'And, Molly,' she said, 'it's good having you here.' Something caught in her throat as she said it. She couldn't help liking Molly, even though she hadn't wanted her here at first.

Molly reached over to squeeze Kate's hand. 'I'm so glad you said that. I was afraid I'd be a nuisance to you when I came out. I hope I haven't been just an extra burden. I've never run a household before, let alone a whole ranch.'

Kate looked into Molly's warm brown eyes. 'To be honest, I was afraid we wouldn't get along. But I was silly to worry about that. It's good having someone to talk to.'

'Aside from Sundays, it seems like you don't get to see other white folks much. It scares me a little.' Molly lowered her voice. 'You hear a lot of stories about women on the prairie going crazy.'

A feeling of uneasiness swept over Kate, but she said, 'Not that many, I don't think.

But you're right, we don't see our white neighbors except when we go into town.' She turned her face away. 'You get used to it.'

'Do you think you'll get married, Kate?'

Kate shifted her gaze toward the horizon. 'Someday, I suppose.'

Molly warmed to the subject. 'What do you want your husband to be like?'

Kate frowned, looking for a simple answer. 'Like Wendall, I suppose. I don't remember much about our father, so I've always looked to Wendall.'

'Well, I can see why,' Molly said with a grin. 'What about the Indians? Do they scare you?'

Kate looked away again. She didn't trust herself to look Molly in the eye. It would be nice to be able to confide in her, but Kate felt ill at ease telling anyone about Raven Sky. 'No,' she said, sitting a little straighter. 'They don't scare me.'

Molly rocked slowly back and forth, the quiet of the late afternoon lulling her. 'Late at night when I hear the coyotes call,' she said, 'I imagine waking up to find the house surrounded by painted braves on horseback, ready for war. Of course, I know they don't do that here.' Then Molly's face went pale, and she opened her mouth to say something, a look of consternation on her face.

Kate knew Molly must be thinking about the murder of her parents. She cut Molly off before she could apologize. 'No, the Indians don't do that here.' They were civilized, Europeanized.

Molly leaned closer, gripping the arm of Kathleen's chair. 'I'm sorry. I know how you and Wendall must have felt . . . about your parents, I mean.'

Kathleen felt her control slipping away from her. She stood up suddenly. 'No,' she said. 'I don't think you do.'

Molly turned white, as if she were afraid she had unlocked a deep-seated memory that would upset Kate.

Kate knew that Molly misunderstood her. She had not been much troubled by the death of her parents at the hands of Cheyenne Indians — not until lately, at least. She knew that talking to Molly might be a good thing, but she could not voice her feelings about Indians, about Raven Sky. Indeed, she could not even indulge in chitchat about marriage without feeling a surge of doubt and fear.

Then, too, Molly was Wendall's confidante. Until Kate was ready to talk to Wendall about her problems, she dared not reveal them to Molly.

Her thoughts whirled in her mind, and she felt the need to unburden herself. In the end the desire to share her feelings won out. She sat down, speaking slowly at first.

Though Molly already knew some of the story, she listened intently. She seemed anxious to understand more of what had happened to Wendall and Kate fourteen years ago.

★ ★ ★

As Wendall's laughter rang out over the dusty farmyard, Kathleen Calhoun, her hands outstretched, pursued a pet duck.

'You can't catch him,' jeered Wendall from the other side of the barnyard, where he whittled a whistle out of an old stick. Proving him wrong, she caught the squawking duck, held him in her arms, and sat down in the dirt.

Evidently deciding the chase was over, the duck settled itself in her lap but continued to quack. For a while both children were quiet. Only the scrape of Wendall's knife and the sound of the burro stamping flies off its legs broke the silence of the lazy Kansas afternoon. It was so quiet that Wendall — a lanky lad of fifteen left in charge of the farm while their parents were away — was getting bored.

'Hey, Sis,' he called to his five-year-old

sister, who was cooing at the duck. 'Let's go pick some strawberries.'

She turned her chubby face toward her older brother. 'Strawberries give me a tummy ache,' she said.

He laid down his whittling and came over to her. She looked up happily into his blue-gray eyes and freckled face. A mop of brown hair fell over his forehead. It was a face she loved and trusted. When their parents weren't here, Wendall took care of her.

He shook his head. 'Strawberries do not give you a tummy ache. Come on, I know a good spot by the river.' He leaned over and held out his hand for her.

The sun was high, and they had a couple of hours to hike over to the valley before their folks got home. Wendall called it *his* valley because no one else had ever mentioned it. It was thick with the most delicious wild strawberries he had ever tasted.

The first time he had found the valley, he had eaten so many berries that he had gotten sick. So Kathleen associated the red berries with his stomach ache.

She set the duck on the ground and straightened her skirt. When she stood, it was with ladylike deliberation. Wendall put his shoes on and slung his canteen over his shoulder. There was fresh drinking water on the way.

'Run in the house and get your basket,' he said, and she scurried across the dirt and climbed up the steps to the porch. When she had brought the basket, Wendall hoisted her onto his shoulders. They took the path behind the barn into the wooded area, leaving behind the sunny barnyard and dozing animals.

An hour passed. A huge cloud of dust, kicked up by horses, suddenly appeared on the western horizon. At the same time, Joshua and Mary Calhoun turned their buggy into the drive. They chatted easily about their new neighbors, whose house they had just helped raise.

'It'll be nice to have the Hoovers so near,' Mary said as Joshua got down and came around to his wife's side. She took off her bonnet and wiped away the perspiration that dampened her brow.

'We'll have to cut a trail to their land from here so you can exchange visits more easily,' Joshua said as he helped his wife down.

Just then he noticed a group of horsemen approaching fast. Indians — dressed for war with bright paint, carrying bows and arrows, feathers in their flying hair — came at a fast gallop. Mary's eyes widened and her hand flew to her mouth.

'The children,' she gasped, fear clutching at her throat.

'Quick, get inside,' said Joshua. He slapped the horse on the haunches, sending him galloping down the road, dragging the buggy behind. Then he hustled Mary inside. They bolted the doors, and he urged Mary to get into the cellar.

'No. You'll need me to load,' she said as he grabbed his rifle and she fastened the shutters on all the windows. 'Where are the children?' She ran to the back door and screamed. 'Wendall, Kathleen!' But there was no answer.

'Pray to God they've wandered off to a good hiding place,' Joshua said. 'I didn't see them anywhere when we came along. Don't worry. Wendall will know what to do.'

Joshua knew the Indians in this region were still bitter over the white man's encroachment on their lands and game preserves. Ever since hundreds of Cheyenne had been massacred by government troops at Sand Creek, Colorado, in 1864, Indian marauders had carried out a campaign of revenge against the settlers of western Kansas.

There was a piercing war whoop as the Indians bore down on the log house. Joshua and Mary huddled inside, firing the rifle, but the gun shots only enraged the Indians more.

'It's the end,' moaned Mary, trembling as she loaded the spare rifle for her husband. She prayed for the safety of her children. 'Wherever they are,' she said, tears streaming down her cheeks, 'keep them from being found, Lord.'

Suddenly a burning arrow crashed through the broken window and set the bedding on fire. Two braves kicked open the door, burst into the cabin, and aimed their spears at the couple, who now clung together in the center of the room, their eyes closed.

★   ★   ★

Wendall and Kathleen made their way home, swallowing strawberries with every step. The day had lengthened, and Wendall had lost track of time. He paused in the story he was telling his sister as they neared the top of the ridge. He smelled smoke, and his skin prickled. Something was not right.

'Kathleen, stay right here by this rock, you hear? I'm going to the top of the hill. Don't make any sounds, and sit very still.'

'Indians?' she whispered.

'Shush.' Assured his sister would not move, Wendall crept slowly up the hill.

When he neared the top, he dropped to the ground, crawled to the summit, and peered over the crest of the hill. At first he could not believe what he saw. Then a dull horror spread over him as he clutched his stomach and vomited.

Black cinders still smoked on the spot where their house had stood. In some places, the flames were not yet out. Only the house had burned. The barn was still standing, but all the animals were gone except for a few chickens, which screeched and wandered throughout the homestead.

He picked himself up and ran down the hill toward his home. He saw no one as he searched through the barn. He didn't need to look further. Some innate sense told him their parents were dead, but he slowly approached the burning house. Holding his handkerchief over his mouth he made his way across the fallen timbers. There he found the charred remains of their parents' bodies. He fell to the ground, choking and sobbing.

Left alone too long, Kathleen climbed the hill. When she saw the smoky ruins, she screamed and stumbled down the hill to her brother. Wendall grabbed her and smothered her screams.

'Indians, Indians,' he whispered. 'We've got to get away from here.' There was nothing left to take with them except the horse their father had sent running. Wendall carried

Kathleen to the buggy and climbed in beside her. Without a backward glance, he headed the horse toward the home of their nearest neighbor.

'Wendall got us safely to the neighbors' house,' Kathleen told Molly. 'They paid our fare to St. Louis and wired our friends that we were coming.'

Kate relived the scenes, as she had many times. 'The Wagners took good care of us. And Wendall was good to me, too. He spent hours with me at night, reading or talking. It was he who first got me to face up to what had happened.' She brushed a hand through her damp hair. 'He wanted me to understand it so that it wouldn't stay inside me and scare me all my life.'

A sympathetic smile touched Molly's lips.

Kathleen took a deep breath. 'I got over my parents' death as much as a person can, I suppose.' She paused. 'But I never wanted to see an Indian again.'

'What happened then?'

'Wendall had the frontier in his blood. He went off to drive cattle for a Texas rancher who had a Cherokee wife. He married their daughter. You know the rest.'

Molly nodded, the shadows of dusk hiding her face. 'But you never could accept that, could you? The fact that he married a half-breed. Have you ever forgiven him?'

Kate's eyes widened and she turned to stare at Molly. A surprising anger rose in her. Her reaction was unexpected, but Molly had unlocked a door that had remained closed to her. She repeated the question in her mind. Had she forgiven Wendall for marrying a half-breed?

'No, I suppose I haven't,' she whispered. Grief, anxiety, and guilt washed over her. If she had never forgiven Wendall, how could she forgive herself for being infatuated with a Creek brave? Was she capable of that kind of forgiveness?

She buried her forehead in her fists. *Will I always consider the entire Indian race guilty of the murder of our parents?* Her body began to shake as forgotten feelings began to surface. She loved Wendall and believed he could do no wrong, and she had a good understanding of the clashes of whites and Indian over disputed lands. But somewhere deep inside her lay a long-buried resentment. It was because of Wendall that she had come to live in Indian Territory. Had she been blaming him all along?

She looked up. Molly was silently watching, waiting. Kathleen knew instinctively that she was willing to listen. And so she began to talk again.

She talked about white and Indian relations as Wendall had carefully taught them to her. But now her own voice found its way through the carefully molded ideas of a young girl. Life on the prairie was hard. They had to get along with the Indians because they lived with them on the same land.

'We stole their land and killed their buffalo,' she whispered. 'There are treaties, but sometimes neither side lives up to its promises.'

Molly asked, 'Do you know the Indians here very well?'

Kathleen hesitated. 'Some.' Now that the emotional outburst was behind her, the air seemed less heavy.

'Wendall told me about the green corn dance,' Molly said. 'The white settlers are invited. Do you think he'll let us go?'

As darkness began to close around them, Kate thought of the green corn dance. Usually she enjoyed it. The Indians dressed in ceremonial costumes and invited the white settlers to watch and participate in the festivities. But something might keep her from going this time. She would have to see Raven Sky again. She pushed the idea aside and rose.

'Molly, now that the roundup is over, I'm going to start helping Joy at the school. I'll be going into town tomorrow.'

Molly rocked peacefully, gazing at dust clouds that blew along the horizon in the west. To the east a stand of trees tossed their branches as a breeze came up.

Kathleen went inside, passed through the kitchen, and went on up to her bedroom. It was fortunate that school would start tomorrow. It would keep her mind safely occupied.

She tried to put her conversation with Molly out of her mind. Maybe she did blame Wendall for bringing her here. But she would never say that to him. Wendall had been so kind. If it hadn't been for him, she would truly be outcast.

As Kate looked down at her long, slightly bony hands, an unaccountable grief pulled at her heart. Her hands were red from the work she did, and her arms were honey brown instead of lily white. If she went back east now, people would find her unappealing. But she wouldn't think about that. She had a job to do tomorrow.

★ ★ ★

Monday dawned bright and crisp. Kathleen dressed in a plaid gingham dress with ruffles on the sleeves and bodice. It was a practical

97

dress, and she would be able to ride in it, for she straddled her horse like a man.

By the time she got down to the kitchen, Molly had cooked eggs fresh from the hens. Hot coffee with fresh milk was waiting for her in a mug Molly had placed on the table. Wendall grunted a good-morning, his mouth full of hash-browns. Kathleen ate her breakfast, then stood up and started to leave the house.

'You be careful, Kate,' said her brother. He stood and patted her shoulder, but she flinched away from him.

'I've packed you a lunch,' said Molly, holding out bread, sliced beef, and fruit wrapped in cheesecloth.

'Oh, thank you, Molly. How thoughtful.' Kate kissed Molly good-bye and went down the back steps, where she found Monty already saddled and tied to the post. Hank was checking the cinch as Monty whickered at her approach.

'Thank you, Hank,' said Kate, 'but I could have saddled him myself. I don't want to create extra work for anyone.'

'Your brother said to saddle him, ma'am. Said you were goin' to the school every day from now on. You sure you don't want me to accompany you to town?'

'Don't worry, Hank. I'll be fine.'

He held the stirrup while she mounted. As she clucked her tongue to Monty, she felt the beginnings of excitement about her new adventure.

★ ★ ★

Joy, in a blue-checked dress, waved from the porch of the schoolhouse.

Kathleen dismounted and led her horse to a patch of grass where he could graze in the shade. The children, dark- and light-skinned, were beginning to arrive. Some of them smiled shyly at her. Others, silenced by the sight of a stranger, walked stiffly up the steps and into the schoolhouse.

'I hope I'm not late,' said Kate as she mounted the steps.

'Not at all. I just hope you know what you've bitten off.'

Joy led her into a large room where students were seated on benches.

'They'll do a geography drill on their tablets or slates. You can go around and see that they do it correctly while I teach from the blackboard. I'm glad you're here, Kate. We're going to have so much fun.' Squeezing Kate's arm, Joy looked earnestly at her. 'If we can get more children to come to school, the mission board can justify giving you a salary.'

'I'm sure all the children in the territory need the lessons, Joy. But it's not the money I want.' For Kate, teaching seemed to be the only way to keep her thoughts occupied and her hands busy just now. Of course, if she never married, she would have to make a living somehow. But for now, she steered her mind away from that avenue.

As Joy had told Kate, the shortage of books was a real problem. The white students brought whatever books their parents happened to have at home, like the McGuffey Reader or the Bible. And Joy had done a wonderful job of persuading the white children to share their books with the Indians.

Joy unrolled a large map that hung above the black-board. Then she announced that Kathleen would drill them on the state capitals. Kathleen hoped she was up to the task. As she spoke no Creek, she hoped they would be able to follow her English.

First, Joy had the children stand and say good morning to her and to their new teacher, Miss Calhoun. They mumbled the greetings, and then Joy asked Kathleen to lead them in a prayer. 'They know the Lord's Prayer,' she said to Kate.

'All right,' said Kathleen stepping up in front, looking at their upturned faces. At that moment, she felt deeply aware of the great responsibility she had undertaken. Without realizing it, she forgot herself as she became lost in deep concentration on the children.

'Let us pray,' she said, and began the prayer.

Some of the children spoke slowly. They knew most of the words, but Kate wondered if they understood the meanings. She suddenly hoped that the classroom contained a good Webster's dictionary.

The children sang a hymn, too, and Kate burst into a smile as she sang with them.

5

The morning passed quickly as Kate watched the children do their lessons on tablets and slates. At lunchtime, she and Joy ate while the children played in the yard. Then a dark cloud began to form in the east. The sun disappeared as the cloud seemed to blanket most of the sky.

Joy looked up. 'We'd better get the children inside,' she said.

While the children did arithmetic, Kate stood at the window and watched the clouds continue to gather. They did not look like normal rain clouds. Though still far in the distance, they rolled and changed shape as they advanced. She was so mesmerized by the clouds that she did not hear Joy call her name until she repeated it.

'Miss Calhoun, can you tell us which answer is correct?'

'Oh, yes,' she answered, startled and returned her attention to the blackboard.

The wind continued to blow as the rain started. Finally Joy walked over to Kate, who was standing near the door.

'I think we'd better dismiss the children.

They'll need to get home before the storm gets worse. She turned to the class. 'All right, children, school is over for the day. There's a storm coming, so I want all of you to hurry home.'

Pandemonium greeted the two women. The children — especially the Indians, who were used to running about in all weather — whooped and hollered and ran outside into the rain.

'Kate, you'd better spend the night with me. I think the storm is going to get worse.' Standing on the porch, buffeted by the wind, she had to raise her voice to be heard as Kate hurried to fetch an oilskin from her saddlebag.

'No, thanks, Joy,' Kate said, wrapping the oilskin around her. 'I know your room at the boardinghouse is small, so I won't impose. Monty is surefooted. He'll get me home before this blows up any more.'

'If you insist. Good-bye, then. I'm going to dash for it.' Joy picked up her skirts and headed down the hill to the house where she boarded.

Kathleen pulled on the oilskin slicker and hood and untied Monty. As she mounted and turned into the road, she could just see the last of the children running around the farthest bend.

As she left the town behind, the clouds became more ominous, tumbling and turning among themselves. She let Monty have his head. He would sense the oncoming storm and want to get home before it broke.

As raindrops spattered her face, the wind tore at her hood, throwing it back. The rain was coming down harder now, and the black clouds were directly ahead. They dipped downward as if pulled by some magnetic force. A chill ran down Kate's spine as she watched the whirling mass take on the shape of a funnel. Like a giant top spinning along the ground, the tornado careened to right and left and then came directly toward her.

She gripped the saddle horn convulsively, trying to see where she was, to see if there was any shelter. She knew she would never make it to the ranch before the twister caught her. Her heart beat wildly as fear gripped her. There was no escape. She had seen the work of a tornado before. This one would destroy everything in its path.

Monty, too, sensed the oncoming danger and laid his ears back. He began to run, wildly, uncontrollably. All she could do was hang on and pray that his animal instincts would lead them to safety.

Suddenly Kathleen felt the rhythmic beat of hooves behind her. Another rider was approaching at full gallop.

Glancing over her shoulder, she saw Raven Sky hunched low over the red stallion's neck, racing to catch up to her. Slowly his horse gained on hers, and he reached for her reins. Through the blinding rain she heard him speak to her horse. The two horses raced neck and neck until he finally was able to slow them to an easy canter. Then Raven Sky dropped the reins and flung his powerful arms around Kathleen's waist. The wind roared in her ears, but his voice rose above it.

'Hang on to me,' he yelled.

She reached for him, and in one swift motion he pulled her sideways onto his horse in front of him.

Then he turned his horse off the road and into a meadow, still holding Monty's reins. The tornado came on, but now they were racing out of its path.

As she watched the terrifying funnel approach, she wondered where Raven Sky was taking her. She could see no shelter. Even the trees bent to the ground as if flinching from the great storm. But she clung to his stallion's mane, her breathing shallow, her heart thudding.

They raced for the river where the water rushed madly before the wind, whitecaps tearing at its surface. They approached a thicket on a rise in the ground. Raven Sky slowed the horses to a trot and then halted by a low outcropping of rock. He flung himself off the stallion, then lifted her to the ground, holding her by the waist.

Then he bent aside some bushes and led Kathleen and the horses through a low opening between two large boulders. As they passed through the entrance of the cave, Raven Sky said, 'Follow the wall of the cave. You are safe here.'

It was pitch black ahead, and Kathleen moved slowly, letting her eyes get used to the darkness. She turned a corner and waited for him to catch up. There was more room above them. Both animals whinnied and snorted nervously. Raven Sky calmed them with his hands and voice, and they grew quiet. They were soothed by the Creek words he used.

When he was satisfied that the horses were all right, he joined her. 'I know the way,' he said. 'Come.'

He grasped Kathleen's hand and led her down a sloping passageway through several twists and turns in the large cavern. At last he stopped. He felt along the wall to a shelf at eye level and pulled down some implements.

'We can make a fire now,' he said.

She heard the friction of flint against metal, and soon he had a torch lit. The light flickered, throwing eerie shadows on the cave walls. They were in a large open area. Rough walls jutted out, and there were pools on the floor of the cavern. Above them, there was a small dot of light, an opening that let in air. Water dripped down the walls.

Kathleen listened, her eyes wide as the tornado raged outside. Gusts of air followed them into the cave, and she could hear a low distant roar. She looked upward.

'What will happen to the others?' she muttered, more to herself than to him. 'The ranch,' she murmured.

Raven Sky reached for her hand. 'Come,' he said. 'Sit down. You cannot do anything. Your loved ones will be all right. They have a root cellar, do they not?'

'Yes, yes . . . ' Like almost every home on the prairie, the ranch had a storage cellar large enough to provide shelter during a storm. Firm, heavy doors covered the entrance. Even if the entire house blew away, Kathleen told herself, those below would be safe. If only Molly, Wendall, and the hands had been able to get to the cellar . . . But Raven Sky was right. There was nothing she could do to help them.

She turned to look at him. 'I haven't thanked you,' she said, still shivering from the cold dampness and her fright.

Raven Sky looked into her clear blue eyes, which shone like water. As an Indian, he knew himself to be a spirit, and he knew he could share himself with another. He yearned for this white woman. He had not yet taken a woman from his own race, for he had dreamed of a goddess and had kept himself for her. This woman, he felt, was the one.

The fire in him burned for her, and he knew that she responded to him. Yet he often saw fear flicker across her face. When that happened, her whole body tensed and she pulled herself inward, away from him.

There was something in her, some evil spirit that must come out. He raised his hand to touch her forehead lightly. There was something he needed to know before they could share feelings as a man and a woman.

Kate closed her eyes at his gentle touch, but then she turned her face away. 'My family will be worried about me,' she said.

'Hush, hush, my little one,' he said. 'Let us sit down. The wind will die quickly, and all will be well. The storm will pass by your home.'

She hoped this would be so. In the strange way tornadoes had, it was just possible that this one would turn and pass by the ranch or cut a swath through some barren part of the range, away from the herds. As if he knew her thoughts. Raven Sky said, 'The herds will run before the storm. Do not worry. They know better than humans how to take care of themselves.'

Leading her to a dry place on the floor of the cavern, he spread out a deer hide that he had cured and left in the cave.

'Do you come here often? Alone?' she asked.

He smiled, the firelight reflecting in his dark eyes. 'Yes. It is my own place.' Kneeling, he indicated that she could sit beside him on the deer hide.

She sat down gratefully. 'Tell me about your life,' she said, smiling a little as she glanced at him.

Raven Sky gazed at the torch fire, and Kathleen's heart missed a beat as she caught his noble profile.

'The Five Civilized Tribes have become used to the ways of the white man,' he said. 'But in our hearts we know that our nations are dying.'

'How terrible for you.'

'There are prophecies that speak of the desolation of the land and of the abandonment of ceremonies and rituals.' He narrowed his eyes as if looking beyond the darkness that surrounded them. 'A cycle of history will end, and with it our religion, our power, our traditions. The people will change. The gifts of the earth will be used up. There will be a tremendous upheaval, and then a new heaven and earth will be created.'

Kathleen listened intently, moved by his words.

Then he seemed to relax. He bent one leg and rested an elbow on his knee. 'In the coming century, the Indian will have a new way of life.'

She gave him a sympathetic smile. Vague, frightening memories stirred in her, but she was mostly aware of the deep sense of calm he instilled in her. Here was a man to admire, she thought, but surely the beating of her heart spoke of more than admiration. 'Does it feel strange to you, having the white settlers here?'

His eyes darkened slightly, but he managed a sad smile. 'It is true the white man took away our homes and forced us into these alien lands, but no, it does not feel strange anymore.'

And now the white men were encroaching again, she thought. She felt suddenly self-conscious. The darkness could not hide the fact that she was white. She pulled her knees up to her chest as her skin prickled. She watched Raven Sky intently, tracing the lines of his face with her eyes.

He spoke of the sorrows of his tribe, sadness in his eyes, and her fear lessened as she perceived the gentleness in his voice. She allowed her eyes to travel over the length of him, feeling warm that she was sitting so near to him.

They were a strange pair, she realized. Both free spirits, perhaps, longing to be rid of the constraints that threatened them.

Silent now, he looked directly at her, moved his hand near her face, and held it inches away. She sat very still, responding to him, her awareness of his sensuality igniting something deep within her. Under his masterful gaze, confusion and desire began to torment her. She wanted him to touch her, to bring his face close to hers, yet she feared it.

Raven Sky studied the emotions that were reflected on her face. Then he narrowed his gaze to her mouth, certain that she wanted to be kissed.

Without knowing why, Kathleen parted her lips slightly to meet his kiss. He slid his hands around her waist, enclosing her thin form. Then he took her mouth in his, closing it over hers, tasting her sweetness.

She went willingly into his arms as he pulled her to him. The sensations that had been kindled when they had met before now spilled over her, causing her breath to come in short gasps. The full awareness that she was being held by a man overcame her, and she lost all thought.

She warmed to the feel of his body next to hers, answering his kiss, running her hands over his chest as he stroked her back. Every inch of her tingled at his touch, and she wanted more of him, wanted him to caress her as no other man had.

His hands, moving over her, were warm and liquid, and she found herself responding, opening her mouth wider as she felt his arms tighten around her.

Then, suddenly, awareness of her situation returned to her, and she turned her face to the side, gasping for air. She rested her cheek on his shoulder, clinging to his muscular arms as her breathing and heartbeat gradually slowed. She relaxed again as his hand slipped up to caress her hair.

Kathleen's feminine curves sparked life in Raven Sky's hands and desire in his heart. How badly he wanted to take her now, but he was not sure she was ready. He knew she wanted him, but he was afraid of making her do something she would regret.

When he took a wife, he would take full responsibility for her. And he only needed one wife — one woman to hold dear above all others, a woman he had worshiped in his dreams. A woman who was delicate and pure, but who would race the wind with him on a strong steed.

Kathleen moaned under his touch as his long fingers caressed her. She let her hands roam over his bronze skin. Firmly molded muscles rippled uder her fingertips. His mouth burned on hers as his tongue moved inside her mouth, asking, wanting, demanding.

Dizzying sensations grew and throbbed in the lower region of her body, spreading out to cause a hot blush that rose to the tips of her nipples, straining as his fingers fluttered over her throat.

And yet Raven Sky's gentleness continued to lull her.

'My beautiful one,' he said, kissing her eyes and forehead. With one hand he held her back firmly while the other hand moved slowly to her breasts.

'My white dove,' he whispered as both his hands cupped her breasts. Gently he unbuttoned her dress and bared her skin. His mouth sought their tender fullness. As he took the rose tip in his mouth, he heard her small fearful cry and felt her stiffen in his arms. For a moment anger and disappointment flashed in his eyes, but he controlled his emotions, reminding himself that she needed time.

Kathleen froze. Until she felt his lips on her breast, Raven Sky had been a refuge for her. Fear, chance, and latent desire had driven her into his arms. But now the reality of the situation terrified her. Suddenly the old fears began to surface. Before, she had thought of Raven Sky as only a strong, understanding man. Now she realized that she was being held in an embrace by an Indian, not one of her own kind.

Something caught at her conscience, forcing its way through the dizzying emotions. She tossed her head, struggling to free herself.

Instantly, his hand came up to cradle her face. 'What is it, my white flower?'

'I'm afraid,' she whispered. She stifled a sob as he rocked her gently against him.

'Hush, hush,' he said. 'I will not hurt you.'

She relaxed against his strong shoulder, feeling foolish, knowing he spoke the truth. She regretted having extinguished the fire that Raven Sky had lit within her, but at the same time, she was aware of the effect he had over her, and she was afraid of what she might do if she stayed with Raven Sky any longer.

The roar from outside had lessened. He stood up and lifted her gently to her feet. Then he kissed her forehead and smoothed her hair. She stood shaking in his arms, her breasts heaving under the thin gingham dress.

'Come,' he said, as she adjusted her hair and clothing. 'Let us see what damage the storm has done.' And he picked up the torch and led the way back to the horses.

As they neared the entrance sunlight began to force its way into the cavern. Emerging into the light, they surveyed the landscape. Trees were bent, partially uprooted. A half-mile away, a barn had been flung into the air and had landed in the middle of a field. Debris lined the riverbank, and the water still raced, threatening to overflow its banks.

'The cyclone did not pass here,' Raven Sky said. 'We were on the edge of its path.' He pointed across the river. 'See there, its path lay that way.'

Following his gaze, she could see a stretch of land on the distant horizon where everything had been obliterated. She trembled as she wondered if a house stood there before.

'Quickly,' she said. 'I must go home.'

He helped her into the saddle and handed her the reins. 'I will ride part way with you,' he said, 'to see that you get home safely.'

Her heart still thumped. She didn't want to risk being seen with him, but she did not argue. After all, he had saved her life.

Raven Sky mounted in a smooth, graceful

motion, dug his heels into the stallion's sides, and sent the great horse leaping forward. They rode swiftly back to the road that led to the Calhoun ranch. Hooves thundered over the ground as the two horses took the gentle slopes together. They turned onto the road and galloped along it, rocks flying behind them.

Riding hard helped release the tension in Kathleen. Now they were running free, spirits in the wind. If only they could go on like this forever. As they neared the ranch, she gave Monty his head, relishing his quick strides. Ahead of her raced Raven Sky, hugging his horse's neck.

Then, as they neared Calhoun land, they slowed, and Raven Sky pulled up. The two horses walked together for a moment, heaving from their run. The Indian sat tall and proud on the prancing red stallion, and something in Kathleen's heart turned over as she looked at him.

Memories of being in his arms assailed her, and she could not meet his gaze.

'I must go,' she said.

Raven Sky raised his chin in a gesture of farewell. Then she pressed her horse forward, anxious to find out how the ranch had fared.

Nearing home, she saw that the barbed-wire fence had been uprooted and tossed into tangled rolls on the ground. The gates to the property had flown off their hinges, and fence posts lay everywhere. Trees had been uprooted and lay on their sides.

When she reached the crest of the hill that would afford her a view of the ranch buildings, she saw to her immense relief that they were mostly intact. Debris was strewn about the yard, and the roof of a small outbuilding had been carried some distance, evidence of the high winds that had accompanied the storm.

As she cantered down the hill and into the yard, the screen door swung open and Molly ran out to her, crying, 'Kathleen, you're all right!'

Bringing Monty to a stop, Kate jumped down to hug Molly. 'Thank God you're safe. I was so worried.'

'And we were worried about you! Come into the house. Wendall just went out to the range to see how badly the herds were hurt. He didn't have time to round them up before the storm hit, and the tornado must have stampeded them.'

'I'm relieved to hear that's the worst that could have happened.' Kate nearly added that Raven Sky had said the animals would take care of themselves, but caught herself in time. Still, as Molly examined her closely, she felt that she would give herself away.

'Let's make some tea,' said Kathleen to change the subject.

'Yes,' said Molly, touching Kathleen's cheek. 'You're freezing.'

Kate walked through to the kitchen, relieved to see the house had not been damaged. The sturdy pine boards had stood up to the high winds that passed in the wake of the storm. The center of the tornado must have swiped through open grazing land. 'You had time to board the windows,' Kate commented.

'Yes, we were lucky,' said Molly. 'Wendall got everyone into the cellar. We prayed you were safe at school.' Then she regarded her sister-in-law curiously. 'Were you with the children, then?'

'No,' said Kathleen as she put the teakettle on the stove. 'We saw the storm coming, so we sent the children home early. I tried to get home, but when I saw the tornado, I sought shelter. Do you think it passed by the town?'

'I hope so,' said Molly. 'But where did you find shelter after you left the school?'

Kathleen's face reddened, and she hoped Molly would think it was the sudden warmth from the hot fire in the iron stove. She couldn't tell Molly about the cave, yet she had to say something.

'I was near Noah Partridge's farm. Raven Sky and some of the other Indians were close by, and they took me with them into a shelter they had dug into the side of the hill. We hid there with the horses until the storm passed.' She concentrated on steadying her hands so she could pour the tea.

Molly looked as though she thought there might be more to the story, but she didn't probe. Instead, she accepted the cup of tea Kate handed her, and they both sat down at the kitchen table. Just then, Wendall stomped into the kitchen.

'Thank God you're all right,' he said as he hugged Kate, lines of worry still creasing his face.

'She rode in just a few minutes ago,' said Molly. 'Some Indians gave her shelter.'

'I'm glad of that,' he said, splashing his hands and face in the wash basin.

'I'm so relieved to hear things are all right here,' Kate said. 'How does it look on the range?'

'The main herd is all right. Some fences are trampled down, and a few steer are trapped in the south ravine. I sent the men to round 'em up. We'll have to slaughter the ones that've been badly injured and butcher them for the meat and hides. We can save the ones with just a leg broke.'

'What can we do to help?' asked Molly.

'Make some bandages and boil water. We'll bring in any calves we find that need doctoring. Hank and the boys will have to mend what limbs they can over a fire on the range. I'll send a couple of wagons out for the carcasses.'

He wiped his face with a towel, then grabbed his hat. Kate threw herself into the work of cleaning up the damage the storm had done. The physical labor helped her forget the conflicts that threatened her. Some injured calves were bedded down in the barn, and Kathleen showed Molly how to feed them with a baby bottle, laughing as Molly struggled with the animals, spilling milk out the sides of their mouths into her lap.

The men worked late into the night, rounding up the cattle that had gotten caught in brush or ditches. It was past midnight before the Calhouns sat down to a well-earned meal.

Kathleen's bones ached as she carried a large pot of beans to the table. She wiped perspiration from her forehead and sat down, tucking a napkin under her chin, though her dress was mostly done for with sweat and dirt.

For a while the three of them ate in silence. Finally Wendall put down his fork and sat back.

'So,' he said, 'now that everything's under control again, tell us just what happened to you, Sis.'

Kathleen looked at her plate, composing her thoughts. She had to relate her story the same way she had told it to Molly earlier.

'We let the children go and I started to ride home,' she began, the same way she had before. 'Then I saw the funnel forming and looked for shelter. I remembered Noah Partridge's cabin, so I rode that way. Some Indians had gathered near a dugout near there, and they waved me in.'

Wendall nodded, waiting for her to continue as he poured himself some coffee.

'Raven Sky got the horses into cover, too,' she finished, hoping her voice wouldn't give away her secret. She felt uncomfortable deceiving them this way. She was nervous, too, lying to her brother. He knew her too well.

Wendall studied his sister, and Kathleen wondered if he sensed that she was holding something back. Surely he must find it curious that she had taken refuge with the Indians, for she usually avoided them.

He leaned forward. 'You sure you came through all right, Sis?'

Kate struggled against a blush. 'Oh, yes. I'm fine. 'Course it was scary, seeing that

121

funnel coming right at me, and after the storm passed, when I rode Monty on home, I saw the fences down on the way, and I didn't know what to think.'

Wendall couldn't miss the faint blush in her cheeks, but Kate hoped he would attribute it to all the excitement. 'I've never been so close to a tornado before,' she said quickly. 'There's really nothing like that weird funnel shape, gray and swirling, coming at you so fast across the plain. But it held a terrible fascination, all the same. I was compelled to stare at it, all the while knowing what destruction it could cause.'

'Well,' said Wendall, 'I think we'd better turn in. It's been a long day.'

'You two go on up,' Kathleen said. 'I'll clear up here.'

Alone in the kitchen, Kathleen slumped against the wooden counter and rested her head on her hands. It was hard to keep up a pretense. She felt ashamed — ashamed that she had lied, and ashamed of what she'd done with Raven Sky.

6

'The finger of the Lord reached down yesterday and guided the tornado away from this town for one reason: because we are here to do his work.' The Reverend Mr. Haworth paused and scrutinized his congregation, making sure his words had sunk in. 'We will show our gratitude by being even more fervent in our faith. Examine your souls,' he intoned, his voice rising. 'Is there anything there you would not want the Lord to see? He sees everything. If you have anything to hide, reveal it to the Lord, and ask him to cleanse your soul.'

Kathleen felt her face warm as she sat beside Wendall and Molly. Had the Lord been watching her when she was alone with Raven Sky? Shame began to wash over her.

No, she was not ashamed, she decided, only confused. She couldn't sort out her feelings about Raven Sky, and she couldn't talk to her family about him. Would divine guidance help? She closed her eyes and tried to pray.

If what I have done is sinful, she prayed silently, *please forgive me. Help me to understand my feelings, and please don't let Raven Sky think I'm a loose woman*. Then she opened her eyes. That last thought was ridiculous. Surely he didn't think that. Her heart beat rapidly as she remembered the emotion she had seen in his eyes when he held her. Then she dismissed the thought and scolded herself for her selfish prayer. God didn't intervene between men and women. He left them alone to work out their own affairs.

She raised her head to listen to the rest of the sermon, delivered in the same oratorical style. She grew restless, and after a while she began to feel that someone was staring at the back of her neck. She turned her head slightly. Jesse Smith sat some rows behind her, his starched collar turned down stiffly over his string tie.

She faced front again, wondering if he was still angry at her for going after him with the bread knife. Perhaps he was going to apologize for his drunken behavior.

When the collection plate was passed the preacher urged everyone to be generous. The extra funds would go to help those who had suffered during the storm.

Everyone stood and sang, 'Nearer My God to Thee' then filed out, forming into groups to talk about the storm.

Kate tensed as Jesse Smith approached her. He caught her eye briefly, then shook hands with Wendall and greeted her and Molly, his voice sounding unusually loud. Wondering if the others were aware of the new formality in his tone, Kathleen suspected he was trying hard to make up for his actions at the party.

'I'm glad to see you are all unharmed,' he said.

'Yes, thank goodness,' Molly said. 'We were worried about Kate, but some Indians took her in.'

Jesse looked at Kathleen oddly. 'How fortunate,' he said. 'Who were these Indians?'

'Raven Sky and Noah Partridge's family took her to their shelter,' Molly said. 'We're so grateful.'

A look of disdain passed over Jesse's face. Raising one thin eyebrow, he sneered, and she realized that he had no intention of apologizing for his behavior. His hands locked together behind his back, he looked ridiculously pompous to Kate.

'I hope I will be seeing your family this afternoon,' he told her. 'It has been my favorite pastime to visit your ranch on Sundays.'

Kate opened her mouth to protest, but Wendall clapped Jesse on the back. ''We'll expect to see you this afternoon, then, Jesse.

Come on out after dinner, and Molly will cut you a piece of apple pie.'

'Of course,' said Molly.

Kathleen clamped her mouth shut, not knowing what to say after that. Jesse was annoying her and he knew it. He only wanted to come to the ranch to harass her further. Turning her head, she noticed a group of strangers leaning on the railing across the road. One, standing with his foot on the lower railing, raised his hat to her. She didn't like the gleam in his eye. She glanced back at Jesse, feeling more pity then revulsion. With Wendall and Molly present, he could be no real threat.

'Let's go,' said Wendall. Ushering Kate and Molly to the buggy, he helped them up and then climbed up beside them. Clucking to the horses, he drove down the hill.

'Who are they?' asked Molly as they passed the darkly clad strangers.

'Don't stare, Molly,' Wendall muttered. When they were well away, he said, 'That's the Glass gang.'

Kathleen remembered hearing the name. 'Aren't they outlaws who live near here?'

'Outlaws?' Molly said, turning around to stare again in spite of Wendall's reprimand.

Kate had heard tales about the bank robberies they'd committed in distant towns, but the men had never harmed anybody here. She, too, turned back for another look, but the men were riding the other way, leaving a trail of dust.

Wendall shook his head. 'What I've heard about the Glass gang is mostly rumor, but I suspect most of it is true. They came here after committing crimes and hid from the marshals who were sent to track them down.'

At the ranch house, Mattie had dinner cooking, and it only took Kathleen and Molly a little while to oversee the finishing touches. The Reverend Mr. Haworth and his wife would join them for dinner.

The dining room table was laid with the best china and silver from the East, including some pieces Molly had received as wedding gifts. A damask linen tablecloth draped the table. Kathleen carried in piping hot potatoes and fresh greens, and the smell of rolls baking in the kitchen was overpowering.

'Everything looks lovely, Kathleen,' Molly said, surveying the sumptuous feast. 'I'm sure our guests will be impressed.'

The sound of a buggy told them the Haworths had arrived. Mr. Haworth helped his wife down. A wiry little woman in a somber brown dress, she had a brilliant smile and cornflower-blue eyes, which contrasted with her husband's severe countenance.

Kathleen started out to greet them, then caught herself. Molly was mistress of the house now. She would do the greeting. 'You go out, Molly,' she said. 'I'll wait here.'

Hearing the greetings, she felt a small pang of regret, but she struggled to push it aside. It felt odd to defer to Molly, but she would have to get used to it. She would try to be sociable and stop feeling sorry for herself. She stood in the parlor and waited until the Haworths came inside.

'What a pretty thing you are,' Mrs. Haworth was saying to Molly. 'Wendall is a lucky man.'

'Thank you, ma'am,' Molly said as she led the guests into the house. 'I believe everything is ready.' She indicated the way to the dining room where Wendall joined them.

'Lord,' the minister said when they had taken their places at the table, 'we beg your forgiveness of our many sins, and we thank you for the riches you have bestowed upon us. Please, Lord, forgive us our sins and make us worthy of your love.'

The words stung Kathleen. Surely she was the worst offender here. Was it possible that the minister knew she had been alone with the Indian? His every word seemed to stick a barb into her. Lost in self-recrimination, she remained motionless until Molly gently touched her arm. When she finally raised her head, she found the beady eyes of the minister looking right through her.

'I'll — I'll get the soup,' she stammered, and fled to the kitchen.

'Molly,' Mrs. Haworth said when the soup had been served, 'tell us about St. Louis.'

'My family has a lovely big house there,' Molly said, 'but now that I think of it, there are really an awful lot of people in St. Louis.'

Wendall laughed and squeezed his wife's hand. 'You see,' he said, 'I've already converted her to life in the wilderness.'

'Well,' said Mr. Haworth, 'this is hardly a wilderness anymore. The cattle drives and the railroad have made Indian Territory quite civilized, I'd say.'

'That's true,' said Wendall. 'I'm afraid our country is pushing westward at an amazing rate of speed.'

'That it is,' said Mrs. Haworth, nodding her head. 'Mr. Haworth says it's the country's progress that accounts for its sins.'

The minister cleared his throat. Sin was a favorite topic of his. He never resisted the chance to hold forth on the subject. 'The Indian Territory is in great need of salvation,' he said. 'The lawless find refuge here among the heathen Indians.'

Wendall leaned back in his chair and

129

cleared his throat. 'You mean the outlaws,' he said. 'The Indian governments have no jurisdiction over white criminals here, and the federal court for the Western District of Arkansas is responsible for seventy thousand square miles of territory.'

'Ludicrous arrangement,' said the minister. 'Unfortunately it has made this a lawless land.' He drew out his words in his preacherlike intonations. 'Only statehood will save us.'

'Tell us more,' Molly said. 'There's so much I don't know about politics here.'

Wendall frowned. He didn't want this minister scaring his wife, but he couldn't be rude.

'Gamblers, prostitutes, whiskey peddlers,' the Reverend Mr. Haworth went on. 'They've all followed the railroad and the cattle trade, though they're here illegally without a permit from the Indian government. They're a bad influence on the decent townsfolk.'

'Then again, the righteous among us are doing their share to put things right,' Mrs. Haworth said. 'And some of the Indians are true Christians. Think of the fine mission school in town. I hear you're teaching there now, Kathleen.'

Kate bowed her head in acknowledgment.

'That's right,' said Molly. 'Kate rode in

yesterday. That's how we almost lost her in the tornado.'

'Ahh,' said Mrs. Haworth.

'Praise the Lord you are safe,' said Mr. Haworth.

'Some Indians took her in,' said Molly.

Kathleen shuddered. Must they keep bringing it up? It perpetuated her lie. Out of the corner of her eye she caught the clergyman's glance, and she saw a glimmer of something there she could not quite name.

'There are many fine Christian Indians in the territory,' she said defensively.

'Yes,' said Mrs. Haworth. 'I've taught many of them the Bible. They are so like little children.'

Kate fiddled with her linen napkin, wishing they would get off the subject.

'Are there really many outlaws here?' asked Molly, shivering.

'Yes,' said Wendall, 'but you don't have to worry. They hide out here, but they know better than to do us any harm.'

'Why is that?' Molly asked.

'Because when the U.S. marshal came through, we'd know right where to lead them.'

Remembering the men congregated near the church earlier, Kate found this talk of outlaws nearly as disconcerting as talk of

131

Indians. She felt stifled in the stuffy dining room, but she forced herself to be polite until the long meal was over.

Finally, Mattie came in to take away the plates. China rattled in her hands. She seemed like a small black shadow hurrying away from the minister's intimidating presence.

'Come, Mr. Haworth,' said Wendall, standing. 'Join me on the porch while the ladies get the coffee.' As he led the man away, Kathleen cast a curious glance at Mrs. Haworth. How did this woman feel about her man, who was so determined to cleanse everybody's sins? A pang of guilt swept through her again, and she had to steady her hands to keep from dropping the cups and saucers.

Mattie scraped the leftovers into a heap for the dogs, and Kathleen carried the plates to the dining room for dessert. Everyone commented on the smell of the freshly baked apple pie, and Molly beamed at the compliments.

How happy Molly was in the role of wife and homemaker, Kathleen thought. She felt another wave of self-pity in spite of her resolve. Would she ever be so lucky? Molly was the center of the household now. Family, guests, servants, the entire home resolved around the woman of the house. Why couldn't it be that way for her? Why couldn't she love someone like Wendall, someone who could give her a respectable home like this one?

The face of Raven Sky began to materialize in her mind. Why couldn't she forget him? She could never marry an Indian, even if he asked her. No matter how respectable a man he might be, no matter how fine the frame house in which he lived, he was still an Indian. A white woman with her upbringing just did not marry a red man.

But she could not forget the effect Raven Sky had on her. Even now her skin tingled as she recalled his strong arms around her. But this was not love, she thought. Love was peace and comfort and the things Wendall gave Molly. Squelching her thoughts, she helped Molly serve the dessert.

The pie was delicious, and after both men had downed second helpings they all went into the parlor to finish the coffee.

'Are you having any other callers this afternoon?' Mrs. Haworth asked as she took a seat near the windows.

'No,' said Kathleen.

'Yes,' said Molly. They looked at each other. Kathleen had almost forgotten about Jesse Smith. She clamped her mouth shut.

133

'You're welcome to stay,' said Wendall. 'Perhaps you'd like to see some of my stock, Reverend. Mrs. Haworth might like to have a look at the calves we're nursing.'

'Oh, I'd be delighted,' said Mrs. Haworth. The three of them replaced their coffee cups on the tray Molly had brought in and filed out of the room.

Feeling no desire to accompany them, Kathleen and Molly sipped their coffee in silence. Kathleen leaned her head back against her chair and shut her eyes, wondering how much more of this Sunday-afternoon banality she could take.

Opening her eyes and looking out the window, Kathleen saw Jesse Smith ride up.

'Is that Jesse coming?' asked Molly. 'He seems like a nice man. Do you like him, Kate?'

Kate glowered. 'Jesse and I used to be friends.'

Molly cocked her head. 'What happened?'

'He started to talk about marriage, and I realized I'd led him on too far.'

'That's a shame.'

'For him or me?' snapped Kathleen.

'Well, I didn't mean . . . '

'I'm sorry if I sounded cross, Molly. It's not your fault. I simply didn't want him to think our friendship meant more than it did.'

'Did he ask you to marry him?'

'No, not exactly. He was in a drunken stupor the day of your party, and he told me what's been in his mind all along. He offended me, and I was rude to him.' Kathleen sighed. 'I suppose I'll have to be civil to him this evening, but if he's in search of a wife, he should look elsewhere.'

Kathleen felt like an animal in a trap. Wendall and Molly and the others wanted her to get married and be happy, but they were pushing her against barriers they didn't know existed, and she couldn't stand it much longer.

Jesse was wearing the same dark suit and stiff white collar he had worn that morning. He was carrying a bunch of dogwood blossoms. Rising to face the inevitable, Kathleen led him into the parlor, and Molly went to cut a piece of pie for him.

'These are for you,' he said stiffly, handing Kathleen the flowers. 'Please accept my apologies for the other day.'

She took the flowers. 'Thank you. Would you care to sit down?'

Nodding, he sat down and accepted the plate Molly handed him.

'Delicious,' he said, wiping his mouth on his napkin when he had eaten the pie. 'My compliments to you, Miss Molly.'

Molly bobbed her head and left the room.

'I brought a book, if you would like to read,' he said to Kathleen. 'It's Shakespeare.'

'That's nice,' she said, trying to relax a little. In the past, she and Jesse had often passed the time by reading aloud. She sighed and got up to fetch her copy, so they could take turns reading the parts.

There were few literate people in the territory, and Kate missed that.

'We were doing *King Lear*,' Jesse reminded her.

'Oh, yes.' She took her place and turned to the marker.

After they had read for a while, Kathleen began to stumble over the words. She put the book down in frustration. 'I'm sorry, Jesse, but I can't seem to concentrate today. I guess I'm not feeling very well.'

He glowered at her. 'I know you're still angry with me for the other day.' He scowled at her from behind his spectacles.

Kate saw the menace lurking in his froglike eyes. She turned her head stiffly. 'I'm afraid I'm not good company for you anymore, Jesse.'

'You mean you're tired of me.'

'Please let me explain, Jesse. I thought we were friends.'

He sniffed. 'We are friends, Kathleen.

Surely you realize how much we have in common. I've saved some money. I could give you a home like this one.' He cleared his throat. 'Well, smaller, maybe. Don't you want that?'

Kate clenched her fists. 'Of course I want that, Jesse,' she said. 'But I can't marry you.'

'Why not? I'm not as important and as powerful as your brother, is that it? I'm not good enough for the Calhouns? Well, at least I'm no half-breed like the ones who think they're running this town.'

'Jesse, you don't understand,' Kate said, fighting to hold in her temper. 'I can't marry you because I do not love you.'

Jesse leaned forward, still clutching the book.

'But you could learn to love me. What other choice have you? Marriage is based on mutual respect and trust. Surely you respect me.'

'That's not enough, Jesse.'

'You're being stubborn, Kathleen,' he said, getting up.

'No, you're being stubborn. I said no, and you just can't accept it.'

She stood. If she had once been mildly tempted by Jesse's offer of a home and companionship, the idea now left her cold. Now she knew now she could never marry a man she did not love.

'Please go, Jesse. It's no use talking.' Tears of frustration threatened. She tossed her book aside and rushed out of the room, colliding with Molly on her way.

'Is everything all right?' Molly asked.

'No!' Kathleen cried as she ran up the stairs.

7

Kathleen slammed the door behind her and threw herself on the bed. She could never marry Jesse Smith. The thought of intimate contact with him made her skin crawl.

She began to sob uncontrollably now, dimly aware that the rest of the household must think there was something wrong with her. She wished she were in the cave again with Raven Sky. She remembered his gentle touch, the warmth of his kisses.

The seed of desire for him had been planted in her breast, and she knew that no other man would ever satisfy that desire. Her mind told her to find someone like Jesse, someone of whom her family and her friends would approve, but her body and her heart cried out for Raven Sky. Her feelings and instincts operated apart from manmade laws and prejudices, even apart from her own conscience. Kathleen turned over on her back and stared at the beams in the ceiling. She wanted Raven Sky's arms around her again. Closing her eyes, she silently cried herself to sleep.

When she woke, it was almost dark, and

the ranch was quiet. She went to the washstand in the corner and splashed cold water on her face, then tiptoed downstairs. Wendall and Molly were sitting in the parlor. Molly stood and came to her.

'Kate, are you all right? I looked in on you, but you were asleep. Are you ill?'

'No, I was just tired from the storm, I guess.' She picked up her quilting basket, avoiding Molly's eyes, and sat down. 'I'm sorry if I made a scene. I'm afraid I've offended Jesse.'

'He'll get over it,' said Wendall, leaning back in the rocker.

'He wants to marry you, doesn't he?' asked Molly.

'I'm afraid so.'

'You could do worse,' commented Wendall, watching his sister carefully.

'But I don't love him.'

'That's important,' Molly said, patting her hand. She looked at her husband as if warning him not to force the issue.

Wendall was worried about Kate. There were few suitable men out here for a woman like her. He could hardly expect her to find a husband among the cowboys, the outlaws, or the Indians. The other ranchers in the area were either half-breeds or married men. Besides, Kathleen's breeding and education entitled her to something better.

A thought occurred to Wendall as he sat there looking at Kathleen. Now that he had Molly to run the house and look after him, maybe he should send his sister back east. She'd been so restless lately. The change might do her good. He would talk it over with Molly tonight, then suggest it to Kathleen tomorrow.

'Mrs. Haworth is nice, isn't she?' said Molly as she stuck her needle into her embroidery.

'Nice enough,' commented Wendall, studying an eastern newspaper.

'They sure do think this is a wild country.'

'I guess it is a rough place,' said Wendall. 'Every man's his own law. The U.S. marshals can't keep up with the crime in Indian Territory.'

'The Indians have their own law,' said Molly.

'The Lighthorse Police. But they've only got jurisdiction over the Indian Nations. They can't arrest whites.'

Molly laid her embroidery hoop in her lap, glancing from her sister-in-law to her husband. 'Are we really safe here, Wendall?'

'As I said before, the outlaws don't come here to rob us. They come here to escape the law. That might not be right, but it's the way

141

it is, I'm afraid. Only statehood can change all that.'

'Oh, that'll never happen,' said Molly, going back to her work. 'This land belongs to the Indians.'

'It's a sort of no-man's-land, as far as we're concerned,' Wendall said. 'You have to remember that.'

Molly stared out the window at the deepening shadows. 'What are the Indians really like, Wendall? Do they hate us?'

Wendall frowned, laying the paper down. 'They're good people. Most people don't understand that. They've made do with what they've been given. They're civilized, and they live like we do pretty much, what with their own laws and all.'

Molly spoke to Wendall in a sort of hushed voice. 'Mrs. Haworth said they go to church, but they also have pagan rites they follow.'

Wendall shrugged. 'I suppose some of them might be just paying lip service to Christianity.'

'I've heard that they're polygamous, too.' She drew her lips back in distaste. 'Is that true?'

'I suppose some of them still have more than one wife, but only one legal one,' Wendall said, laughing.

Molly blushed. 'That's sinful.'

'I suppose it is,' said Wendall, the amused look still on his face as he picked up his paper again.

Kathleen put down her quilting. 'Must we talk about the Indians?' Her face was pale.

'Sorry, Sis,' said Wendall. 'Of course not.' He cleared his throat and returned his attention to his paper. The room seemed suddenly stuffy.

When the embers had burned low, Kathleen said, 'I think I'll go up. I have to go to the school tomorrow, and I'll need an early start.' She said good night and went to her room, but the nap had rested her, and she wasn't sleepy. Perhaps some fresh air, she thought, so she went downstairs and out the back door toward the barn. Bobtail, one of their mongrel dogs, followed her.

Lanterns hung above the stalls where the calves were mending, and she lit one as she went in. They slept, tucked into the hay. The mothers had been found and brought in to nurse the babies. Kathleen petted the soft face of one of the cows.

As she turned to leave the barn she heard the faraway sound of a coyote. Long and mournful it cried. She waited for the answering cry of its mate. There was none. *How odd*, she thought. The call echoed in her mind as she stepped out into the night and looked over the moonlit plain.

Along the horizon an Indian rode a wild stallion. The horse was stretched out in full flight. Naked except for a breechclout, the Indian clung to his mane. Together they flew across the ground.

Kathleen leaned against the barn, breathless. She recognized the figure of Raven Sky as he and the red stallion fled through the moonlight. Her heart pounded wildly, and she stifled a cry, wondering where he was going and why he rode at night in only a breechclout.

Quickly she ran into the house. She knew there would be no sleep for her this night.

'Molly, I can't possibly eat all this,' Kathleen protested the next morning as Molly put a plate of pancakes before her.

'You're a working girl now, and you have a long ride ahead of you.' Molly tweaked her sister-in-law's cheek, and Kathleen warmed to her. They had grown close in the short time Molly had been here. How she wished she could simply relax and enjoy her company. If only she didn't still have ambiguous feelings about her place on the ranch.

'I hope you're feeling better today,' Molly said, 'but if you don't mind my saying so, Kate, you haven't seemed yourself lately. Is there anything you'd like to tell me?'

Kathleen lowered her coffee cup, the blood beginning to warm her cheeks. 'I wish I could talk about it, Molly,' she admitted. 'I don't know what's happening to me.' She shook her head. 'I just don't know.'

'Did something in particular happen to upset you?'

Kathleen stared at her plate. Visions floated before her: her parents, her brother, the girls' school, Raven Sky. 'Not *one* thing. *Many* things. I don't know where it all begins or ends. I don't understand my fate.'

'I wish I could help you.' Molly's voice was full of concern, and her eyes looked a little alarmed.

'Thank you, Molly. I wish you could, too. But I guess this is something I have to work out for myself.' Gulping the last of her food, she went out of the house.

Molly watched her gallop away, waving at Wendall as he rode toward the house. He cut across the field to join Kate, and Molly watched them talking as their horses pranced about.

★   ★   ★

It was a relief to be back in the schoolroom. Kathleen worked with the children all day,

145

helping them with their reading and arithmetic. Once, as she gazed into the big black eyes of a lovely little girl who spoke no English, Kathleen felt her heart contract. She wondered if her people and Raven Sky's would ever understand each other.

At the end of the day, she and Joy sent the children on their way, then started to tidy up the classroom. Joy was rolling up the map of the world and Kate was wiping off the blackboard. Suddenly Joy turned and stared at the door.

Kathleen whirled around. There, silhouetted by the afternoon sun, stood Raven Sky. He was dressed in denim jeans that hugged his muscled thighs. The sleeves of his yellow cotton shirt were rolled up to his elbows, exposing his forearms. Around his forehead he had tied a bright blue bandanna to keep his shoulder-length black hair out of his eyes.

Kathleen stood still, her heart missing a beat. Hands on his hips, Raven Sky stepped into the room, his boots sounding loud on the wooden floor.

'Can I help you?' asked Joy, moving forward and dusting off her hands.

Raven Sky shook his head and looked at Kathleen. When he spoke, his voice was low and even. 'I've come to see Miss Calhoun.'

Joy looked from one to the other.

146

'It's all right, Joy' said Kate. 'Raven Sky and I are friends.'

Joy nodded. 'I'll finish up here. You go on.'

Kathleen put down the eraser and followed him out to the porch. Not knowing what to say, she leaned her back against the post.

His lips curved in a smile, and his eyes glimmered as he said, 'Do you like me this way?'

'You look . . . ' She turned away, unable to finish.

He moved to stand in front of her, forcing her to look at him. 'I want you to think of me as a civilized Indian. That is what we are.'

'I know,' she said, biting her lip. She caught the hint of bitterness in his voice, but his eyes were sincere. She took a deep breath, trying to control her racing heartbeats.

'I will see you home,' he said indicating the wagon he had brought. 'Your horse can follow behind.'

Unable to do otherwise, she nodded. 'All right.'

He walked her down the steps, then reached out to help her into the wagon. As she took his hand, she felt the heat burn into her own. She seated herself in the wagon, but Raven Sky still held her hand, looking up at her. Then gently, slowly, he raised her trembling hand to his lips. He turned it over

147

and kissed her palm, and Kathleen closed her eyes as a shock jolted through her.

Quickly she pulled her hand away, eager to prevent prying eyes from seeing what had passed between them.

He walked around the horses and climbed up beside her, graceful as a cat, his hair bouncing behind him. Glancing over her shoulder, she saw Joy walk out onto the school porch to watch them depart.

As the wagon clattered down the road, Raven Sky sat proudly beside Kathleen, feeling that it was right to have this woman at his side. After all, he was as much at home in the white man's world as in his own, and he was determined to make Kathleen see that. It did not concern him that he wanted to take a white woman for a wife. Many white men took Indian maidens, so why not?

As a full-blood, he was privy to the respect of his tribe. It saddened him to see the tribal purity lost as the white man's world encroached, but he had been born into a hard lot and had learned to adapt. It was the only way, if a sad one. The old ways would not last.

Still this was a serious decision. If he took Kathleen Calhoun for a wife, his children would be half-breeds. But soon there would be many other half-breeds. The next generation would have to meld the white man's ways with their own. It would not be easy, but it was the only future the Indians had. His people had fought to hold on to their lands in the Southeast more than a generation ago. They had lost. They would always lose against the white men. The only way to survive was to take what the white man offered, make the best of it, while still remaining an Indian.

He looked down at the white woman beside him. She seemed serene, but her eyes hid something in their depths, some mystery he couldn't quite understand. Still, though, when he looked at her, he knew love. His heart pounded with his feelings for her. He returned his attention to the road. He would combine Indian tradition with white man's ways when he courted her.

As they approached the gate to the Calhoun ranch, Raven Sky slowed the horse.

'Shall I take you all the way home or do you want to ride your horse now?'

Kathleen gazed at him wistfully. Part of her wanted to take him to the house so her family could meet him, but another part reminded her that he was an Indian and would not be welcome in her home. She twisted her skirt in her lap. Would this difference always have to come between them?

'I want . . . ' But she couldn't finish the thought. She looked at his smooth skin and full lips. Impulsively she put a hand up to his hair.

He smiled at her, then slowly pulled her to him, kissing her full on the mouth.

Kathleen closed her eyes and relaxed against his strong body, feeling his hard back and muscular chest. His silky hair fell over her face as she answered his kiss with her own. Her mind went blank as she gave in to sensation and feeling. Sensing his desire for her, she was unable to hold her emotions at bay.

He bathed her face with tiny kisses and moaned her name. His swift hands roamed over her body, finding her seductive curves. This was his woman, his instincts told him; he must make her his forever.

When he cupped her breasts with his hands, she felt the warmth spreading through her. It was as if they were floating on a cloud together high above the ground. Yes, yes, Kathleen cried silently.

Raven Sky sensed her surrender and had to summon all his strength not to take her right there in the blazing sunlight. He wanted her with all his heart. His body cried out for her. But he would wait until he had made her his wife. He wanted her to know how much she meant to him.

'My love, my love,' he whispered to her.

'You were meant for me. I read it in the stars.'

She rested her head on his chest, listening to the beating of his strong heart.

'You have not yet given me your answer, Kathleen.'

Realizing how rarely he said her name, she forced her mind back to the present. She was due home.

As she looked down the long drive, her emotions churned. What would they think if she took him to the ranch? Even though it was beyond her wildest imaginings, she had lost her heart to Raven Sky, yet she didn't know exactly what he wanted from her. Did he want her to be his woman? That might not mean the same thing to him as it meant to her. Hadn't her brother just said that some of the Indians took more than one wife, even though their law forbade it?

Perhaps it would be better to tell Wendall and Molly first, then bring him to the ranch. She pulled herself upright. She could no longer deceive her brother and sister-in-law about this man.

'No, I'll go alone, Raven Sky.' She looked into his eyes to make sure he understood her feelings. 'It is too soon.'

He smiled down at her, holding her head with his hand. 'Very well,' he said. 'You go alone. But I will come to see you. I believe you have visitors on Sunday?'

'Yes,' she said.

He jumped down from the wagon, helped her to her feet, and kissed her once more, making her change her mind. The urgency in them both made her want to retract her words, to bring him home now, today.

But he was already moving her away from him and leading her to Monty, who shook his head and chomped at the bridle. Kathleen put her foot in the stirrup and Raven Sky lifted her up. He held her gaze for a moment, then he slapped Monty's flank, urging him off.

Kathleen turned to look back at him. 'Sunday,' she called.

How magnificent he looked, standing there, his weight on one leg. All of the wild landscape behind him seemed to complement his solitary, proud figure. She turned forward and raced toward the ranch.

8

Each time Kathleen tried to tell Wendall and Molly about Raven Sky, the words stuck in her throat. Her hesitation made her remember all of her own doubts. With a start, she realized Wendall was addressing her.

'Kathleen, I've been thinking,' he said. 'That is, Molly and I have been thinking. How would you like to go back east?'

She looked up, surprised. Not long ago, she had thought such a trip would be her salvation, but now the thought made her stiffen. Were Wendall and Molly trying to get rid of her? Was this their way of getting her out on her own? Her voice trembled as she questioned her brother's intentions. 'Why now?' she asked.

'Now's as good a time as any. Maybe better. It's almost summer, and the territory's in for a dry spell. Might be cooler back east. And it's time you were with people your own age again, Kate.'

'It's generous of you to offer,' she said, her throat constricting. 'I know I'm underfoot here.' Tears formed in Kathleen's eyes.

'It's not that at all and you know it,' said

Molly. Laying her sewing aside and folding her hands in her lap, she looked very much like a stern little mother. 'It's your own happiness we want.'

'You don't want me to turn into a spinster.' Kathleen couldn't help the note of bitterness that crept into her voice.

'We want what's best for you,' said Wendall as he concentrated on lighting his pipe.

'You mean marriage and a home?'

'Kathleen Calhoun, this is your home. But can you deny you'd want marriage if the right person came along?' Molly asked.

She had to tell them, Kathleen thought. 'I think the right person already has come along.' Her words were so soft she wasn't even sure she'd said them aloud.

Wendall stopped rocking. 'Who is he? Not Jesse?'

'No.' Her throat tightened; she could hardly breathe.

'Who, then, for heaven's sake? Don't keep us in suspense.'

'Well, I'm not sure.' Kate stood up and walked across the room, then turned to face Wendall and Molly.

'I thought you said — '

'I know, but it's confusing,' Kate admitted.

'Do you love him?' Molly asked, sitting forward, the thought of romance lighting her eyes.

'I feel' — Kate searched for words — 'attracted to him, but I don't know if I love him. I don't know if I can.'

Wendall read the conflicting feelings on his sister's face. 'Why not?' he asked.

Kate turned to face the fireplace. 'He's an Indian, a Creek.' She covered her face with her hands and rested her forehead on the mantel. There was a great clatter as the framed photograph of their parents fell to the floor, shattering the glass. For a moment, Kathleen stared at it in horror, then she looked at Wendall and saw the expression in his eyes. A feeling of cold dread swept up her spine as she looked again at the ruined picture. Suddenly she raised her hands and covered her ears. From somewhere in the dim recesses of her mind, old fears swept forward. She fell to her knees, listening to a maddened scream that seemed to come from somewhere far off.

Molly's face went white. As Kathleen's scream pierced the air, Wendall leaped to his feet and pulled her up, trying to smother the scream in his chest. But she struggled in his arms.

'Help me, Molly,' he said. 'Let's get her upstairs.' Between the two of them they carried Kathleen upstairs and put her on her bed. As Wendall held her, she mumbled deliriously, her whole body trembling while sweat broke out on her forehead.

'Send Hank for Doc Johnson,' he ordered Molly.

Molly ran down the stairs, fear gripping her. So this was what Kathleen had been burdened with all this time. She had fallen in love with an Indian, and her conflicting feelings were driving her mad. Molly felt hysterical sobs rise within her, but she forced herself to remain calm as she ran to the bunkhouse and thew open the door. The men looked up in surprise.

'Where's Hank?' she cried.

'Right here, Miss Molly. What is it?' said the ranch foreman, coming toward her.

'Run into town, Hank. Get Doc Johnson. Hurry — it's Kathleen!'

Hank grabbed his hat from the hook by his bed and started out after her, lifting a lantern down from beside the door. 'What's the matter?' he asked.

'I don't know, Hank. I don't know. Tell Doc she's awful sick, and to come quick.'

As Molly ran back to the house, it occurred to her that what afflicted Kate might not be a disease the doctor could cure, but they had to try to help her somehow.

Wendall was sitting beside the bed where Kathleen lay moaning and tossing.

'Fire, fire,' she groaned, her face damp with perspiration. 'Don't kill him. He didn't mean to hurt them.'

'She's delirious,' Wendall said as Molly approached. Molly drew a chair up on the other side and took one of Kathleen's thrashing hands.

As soon as they heard horses outside, Molly went down to let the doctor in, hoping he could do something for Kathleen.

His calm demeanor was somehow reassuring as he nodded to Wendall and sat down to take Kathleen's pulse.

'You can leave me with her now,' he said. 'I'll call you if I need anything.'

Molly sat with Wendall in the parlor. Neither spoke as the tall clock in the hall ticked away the minutes.

After half an hour, the doctor descended the stairs.

'She's sleeping,' he informed them.

'What is it, Doc?' asked Molly.

The doctor lowered himself into the nearest chair. 'To be honest with you, I don't know. Her heart is in good condition. There's no sign of an illness. In fact there's no sign of anything wrong with her except nervous hysteria. Tell me, has something upset her?'

'Yes,' said Molly, eyeing her husband.

'Tell me about it,' said the doctor.

Wendall related what happened, including Kathleen's mention of the Indian. He also told the doctor about their parents' death.

Doc Johnson listened carefully. 'I see. Does she talk about the murder of your parents?'

'No,' said Wendall. 'I encouraged her to face the truth when we were young. I hope that wasn't the wrong thing to do.'

'No, it wasn't.'

'Is she well enough to travel, Doc?' asked Wendall.

'Yes. In fact, a change of environment right now would be good for her.'

'It's settled, then,' Wendall said. 'She must leave for St. Louis as soon as possible.'

'Let her sleep. In the morning you can tell her about your plans for her. That should take her attention off her troubles. It's best if she gets exercise and stays busy.'

'Thank you, Doctor,' Wendall said. He sighed, but the muscles in his face were tight with worry. 'I knew something was bothering her, even before she told us about the Indian. It's probably all my fault for bringing her here to Indian Territory in the first place.'

'No, don't blame yourself. We can't run from life, can we? The best thing is to confront it. Our fears remain ghosts that haunt us only as long as we don't look them full in the face. I'm sure she'll be fine. Now, you two get some sleep.'

After seeing the doctor out, Wendall and Molly went upstairs, arms around each other for support. An illness of the body was easier to face, because one knew what to do. It was harder to deal with Kathleen being troubled by an experience only she could know about.

'Don't worry, Wendall,' Molly said, trying to smooth the worry lines out of her husband's face. 'I know it's hard.'

He shook his head exasperatedly, but he looked with love at this woman whose inner strength could help him. 'She's so alone right now.'

'Yes, but that girl has strength. I've seen it, and she'll win her battle. I know it.'

Wendall looked into his wife's eyes, her certainty helping him. They went into their bedroom and blew out the lamp.

★　★　★

Kathleen awoke to sun streaming through her window. Thinking she had overslept, she threw back the covers and sat up. Then the memory of last night came back to her, and she slumped back down in the bed. She remembered seeing the picture of her parents on the floor, then a horrifying scream. The rest seemed dreamlike.

She thought she remembered seeing Doc Johnson, and then she recalled a lot of dreams. She felt her forehead, wondering if she was ill. Standing, she felt slightly unsteady. Maybe she would send word to Joy not to expect her today.

Just then Molly came in with a breakfast tray.

'How are you feeling, Kate?' she asked, setting down the tray.

'I feel all right. Just sleepy. Was Doc Johnson here?'

'Yes. He said you should rest as long as you needed. Then, when you're up and around, he wants you to get some exercise.'

'Oh, did he say what's wrong with me?'

Molly wrinkled her brow. 'In a manner of speaking. Sit down, Kate, and eat your breakfast. Wendall will explain it.' Molly left the tray on the bed and slipped out.

After she ate, Kate felt better. When Wendall came in, she was struck by the look of love and concern on his face. She noticed something else, too: there were tiny worry lines around his eyes she had not seen before.

'Good morning, Sis. How're you doing?'

'Fine, brother, fine. I hear you're going to tell me what's wrong with me.' Wendall sat on the foot of her bed and stretched out his long legs.

'Doc Johnson said a change of environment might do you some good, Kathleen. There's still that trip to St. Louis we were discussing. Would you like that?'

Kathleen's eyes, which had been bright a moment ago, now clouded over. 'You still want me to go?'

'Only for your own sake.'

The image of Raven Sky began to materialize in front of her, bringing with it all the confused emotions she had about him. 'I'd love to see St. Louis again,' she finally said.

'Then it's settled. I'll write to the Wagners. I'm sure they'd love to see you.'

'I'll send word to Joy.'

'One of the boys will ride in and tell her. I'm sure she'll understand.'

'Thank you.'

'When would you like to leave?'

'I'd like a few days here first. I'd like to tell Raven Sky . . . ' She looked quickly at Wendall. 'I hadn't told you who . . . ' She looked away.

'He's a good man,' Wendall finally said. But Kathleen knew that conflict tore at him. She was sure that he had never expected her to be attracted to a red man, even one as cultured as the Creek chief's son. 'Do you think it's wise to see him?' Wendall asked.

'He deserves that much.'

'Not if it will upset you.'

The protectiveness in Wendall's eyes reminded Kate that her brother would break any man who harmed her.

'No, please, Wendall, I know how you feel. I've invited him here Sunday. Please let him come. He deserves to be treated fairly. He . . . saved my life, you see.' She bit her lip and glanced down. 'The storm . . . '

They were silent as Wendall realized what she was telling him.

'I see,' he said quietly. Then he squeezed her hand. 'A man like Raven Sky is always welcome here. If you're sure you want him to come.'

'I'll be all right, I promise. Then I'll leave for a while.' She sighed. 'I guess the change of scenery would do me some good. Give me some time to sort this all out.' The brightness returned to her eyes as she looked at him.

'Thanks,' she said. 'For everything.'

He looked down at her, the love between them strong. They shared a bond few siblings knew, perhaps because they'd been on their own for so long. 'You know I'd do anything for you, Kate. That's how it's always been, and that's how it'll always be.'

'I know.' Her lip trembled as she fought her tears.

162

Later that day Kate dressed and saddled Monty. She told Molly she was doing as the doctor ordered and going for the exercise, but by the time she had crossed the ranch boundary and followed the river for about a mile and a half she knew that the exercise had just been an excuse.

She rode slower now, pushing through the brush, trying to locate the cave where she and Raven Sky had hidden during the storm. At last she saw the stone that covered the entryway.

She dismounted and tied Monty to a low branch, then made her way toward the cave. Branches cracked beneath her feet, and she slid through the opening into the cavern. With the opening uncovered, there was enough light for her to go in part of the way.

She smiled as she ran her hand along the moist walls. A warm feeling tingled inside her as she recalled being here with Raven Sky. She imagined him coming up behind her, placing his strong hands on her shoulders.

The thought of him warmed her very being. Accompanying the grief in her heart was the knowledge that she was dangerously close to being in love with him, but with that knowledge came fear. The fear was too much to bear right now, and so she must leave the love alone.

At dusk, Raven Sky rode near the cave. Gazing at the surroundings, he turned toward the river to smell the fresh breeze. He paused some distance from the cave, noting crushed twigs and bent leaves where someone had recently passed. Dismounting he saw small footprints, followed their trail, and entered the cave. Lifting a thread from the corner of a jagged rock, he smiled.

So, she had come here. He closed his eyes and held the thread over his heart. She desired him. This had been her sign.

'Oh, my little white flower,' he said to himself. 'You are the sun and the moon to me. I will play for you the song of the dove on my flute. You will be mine. I will make you mine.'

He returned to his horse and mounted. Then he threw back his head and let out a wild, piercing yell. It was a cry of joy, triumph, and pure emotion. The red stallion reared and danced on his hind legs, Raven Sky clinging to his back with his knees. Then the stallion bounded across the plain in exhilaration, celebrating its wildness.

9

Sunday dinner was barely finished and the dishes cleared when Molly cried breathlessly, 'Kate, he's coming! Hurry!' Molly's face was flushed as she followed Kathleen onto the front porch.

The red stallion approached slowly, bearing Raven Sky, who was dressed in the handsome black suit he'd been wearing on the day he stepped off the train and into Kathleen's life.

Kathleen walked down the steps toward him. He dismounted and bowed over her hand, her skin burning under his touch. Then she turned and led him up onto the porch.

Wendall extended his hand. ' 'Welcome to the Calhoun ranch, Raven Sky,' he said. 'This is my wife, Molly.'

Raven Sky bowed over her hand, and when he raised his eyes, she smiled at him. Kathleen suspected that even Molly was not unaffected by the masculinity emanating from him.

'Come in, please,' she said, looking into his handsome face as he held the door open for her.

'I'll get some coffee,' Molly said, disappearing into the kitchen.

Kate had led Raven Sky into the parlor. Wendall followed them and sat down in his rocker.

Kathleen had gotten so used to Raven Sky in buckskins or jeans that she had forgotten this was the way she had seen him first — as a tribal leader who had met with government officials in Washington.

'How do your people feel about the upcoming tribal elections?' Wendall asked.

'It is hard to say. Many of us fear the factions within the tribe. We cannot afford a rebellion. My hope is that the people will accept whoever is elected chief.'

'Even if it is not you.'

'Of course.'

Kathleen could see the approval in Wendall's eyes. Raven Sky spoke with confidence. He was a natural leader, and people would always look up to him.

'Have you spent much time at Okmulgee?' Wendall spoke of the capital of the Creek Nation.

'With my father, yes. I have tried to learn the intricacies of government. My tribe needs educated leaders to bring them into the new century.'

How elegantly he spoke, Kathleen thought, glancing at Molly, who was serving coffee.

'You have heard of the petitions that have

been circulating among the settlers who want to buy the town of Tulsa from the Creeks?' asked Wendall.

Raven Sky's eyes darkened. 'I have heard.' He set his coffee cup on the table near him. 'Even though the whites do not really want us to know. I am sorry about it.'

'I take it you would be against allotments if the U.S. government wanted to settle more whites on unalloted Indian lands?'

'I am opposed to the U.S. government stealing any more of our land than it already has,' Raven Sky said evenly. 'There are some who think it would be good for tribal economy, but I believe they are wrong.'

Kathleen stood up. 'Would you like to see the ranch, Raven Sky?' she asked.

'Yes, I would.' He stood.

She glanced into his face, and he returned her gaze. 'This way,' she said, leading him out through the kitchen and down the back steps. Outside she took a breath of fresh air as Raven Sky walked beside her.

In the barn she showed him the calves. Some of them were mended and on their feet already. As they stood looking down at one small calf, Raven Sky leaned close behind Kate.

'I do not want to look at calves, Kathleen. I want to look at you.' He picked up a strand of her hair and let it slide through his fingers.

Kathleen's heart pounded against her chest. She tried to organize her thoughts, but his nearness overwhelmed her. Something stirred deep within her, and as she turned to him, he brought his mouth down on hers. She started to pull away, but his firm hold on her shoulders prevented her from moving. Slowly his arms slipped around her, and he pulled her against him.

Kathleen's thoughts became ragged, and tingling sensations began to spread over her body. In spite of herself, her arms went around his neck, and she arched her body to his. She had never known such a virile man before, and he aroused feminine responses in her that were far beyond her control.

She moved against him, opening her lips to his demanding tongue. Within moments, she was lost in a sea of responses, wanting him, needing him.

Then, deep in a corner of her mind, a tiny warning penetrated the haze of pure sexuality she felt. It was a cold, deadly feeling that sprang from some part of her mind she did not control. She tried to focus on what the warning was telling her. She was aware of Raven Sky's male hardness as he pressed between her thighs. His hand was on her breast, and she breathed heavily.

'I know you want me, my dearest,' he said. 'I know you came to the cave.'

She pulled her mouth from his in sudden fright. 'No,' she said, turning her face to the side and trying to pull away.

'Raven Sky, I must tell you something.'

'What is it, my dearest one?' He eased his hold on her only slightly.

'I have to go away for a while.'

He grasped her chin in his hand and turned her to face him. 'What is this?'

'To St. Louis.'

The look in his eyes was fearsome, and she wished she didn't have to tell him this way.

'Why?'

'I need time to think,' she said, pulling away from him. 'I need to visit my home.'

He glared at her. 'Are you running away from me?'

'No, Raven Sky, I am not. I have strong feelings for you.' She blushed as she said it.

'And I for you.' He put a finger on her cheek. She almost turned to him again, but the warnings kept their hold over her.

'No, you don't understand. It is something in me. I must sort out something in myself before I can do anything about these feelings I have for you.'

His eyes narrowed, and he turned her face,

forcing her to look at him again. 'What is this thing in you?'

As she looked up into his black eyes, she wanted to cry out. She was helpless in his grasp, yet she was so afraid of the thing gnawing at her.

'I do not know. It is something I do not understand.'

'And in St. Louis you will understand it better?'

She looked down, her lashes hiding her eyes. 'Perhaps. I must try.'

'Look at me.'

Her eyes flew open.

'You must tell me, Kathleen. I can help you.'

'No, you cannot.'

His grip on her tightened. He wanted to reach inside her and kill the thing that stood between him and the satisfaction of his desire for her.

Kathleen started to panic. 'Raven Sky, please let me go. You're hurting me.'

'I am patient, Kathleen. But you must help me.'

'You can do nothing. I must do this myself.' Anger began to burn in her when he did not let her go.

'Tell me, Kathleen. What is it that troubles you? Perhaps together we can conquer it.

170

When you look at me, sometimes I see fear in your eyes. What is it that frightens you? Surely you know I would never hurt you?'

Kathleen started to cry. 'No,' she whispered. 'Not you.'

He pulled her against him, holding her gently now. 'Shh, shh. Do not cry. I want you, Kathleen. And I do not understand why you keep yourself from me. I am driven with passion. I do everything for you, and I want you to give yourself to me. I want to marry you.'

She leaned against him, pressing her cheek against his chest. The same burning desire for him still flowed within her, but the fears haunted her, too. She could never be an Indian's woman. The gentleman's suit he wore did not hide the fact that he was not her kind. His habits and way of life would be strange to her, even if outward appearances did not make it seem so. She could never be a member of an Indian tribe, even one of the Five Civilized Tribes.

'I know it sounds mad,' she said, trying to breathe evenly. 'You must be patient. Right now I need time to think. I need peace and quiet.'

'I will show you peace if you let me.'

'No, no,' she shook her head. 'I must go away.'

'Why?'

'I must go where I won't see any Indians.' There, she had said it.

Anger flashed in Raven Sky's eyes. He dropped his hands from her and took a step back.

'So, you are like the rest. You whites, you run over our land; you try to 'civilize' us. We go to your schools, your churches. We become like you, and still we are not good enough for you.'

He pushed Kathleen away from him, and she stumbled backward and fell into the hay. He stood over her glaring. His muscles flexed as anger and desire flooded through him. Who was this woman to promise so much and then reject him? No one rejected Raven Sky. He moved toward her as her eyes widened in terror. Then he held himself back. He must get away from her. She was a demon. If she stayed in his sight, he might do her damage. He must leave this place before he did something he would later regret.

'I will go,' he said and turned on his heel.

Kathleen lay on the floor, prickly strands of hay piercing her dress and hair as tears ran down her cheeks. She wanted to go after him, wanted to explain. But she watched him stride away. A moment later, she heard hoofbeats as the stallion galloped off.

'Raven Sky,' she whispered through her tears, 'I'm sorry. I didn't mean to hurt you.'

She lay there until the sound of hooves pounding the earth faded in the distance. As she pulled herself up, Molly came running through the door. When she saw Kathleen on the ground, she gasped.

'Oh, my God, Kate, did he hurt you?'

'No, no. I'm all right. I'm afraid I hurt him, though.'

'What do you mean?' she asked, helping Kathleen up.

'I told him I was leaving.'

'Was he so angry?'

'I told him I didn't want to see any Indians.'

'Did he strike you?'

'No. He just pushed me down on the hay. He was insulted. I don't blame him.'

'Don't worry, Kate. It's you we've got to think of.'

Kathleen leaned on the other woman for comfort. Tears stained her cheeks. 'Oh, Molly, what am I to do? I've got to go away. I can't stand this any longer.'

'You can leave tomorrow. Wendall's got your ticket. I'll help you pack.' Molly tried to sound comforting, but she was frightened. She wanted to get Kathleen out of Indian Territory before something terrible happened.

★ ★ ★

Kathleen, dressed in a navy blue traveling suit, hugged Molly good-bye.

'You take care, now,' Molly said, her lip beginning to tremble. 'We'll miss you.'

'I'll miss you too, Molly,' Kate said, looking at the woman she had been jealous of not long ago. How wrong she had been. Molly only wanted to bring happiness, whatever she did. Kathleen hugged her tightly then climbed into the wagon next to her brother.

She gazed at the passing landscape on the way to town. The dogwoods were in bloom now. The cicadas screeched noisily among the high grasses. Dust stung Kathleen's eyes, and the low hills in the distance pulled at her heart.

At the depot, Wendall helped her down. A gust of wind caught her skirt, and it billowed around her. 'A few months ago, it was I who met you here.'

Wendall looked as if he wanted to say something, then thought the better of it. 'I'll miss you, little Sis.'

'I'll miss you, too.'

He crushed her to him in a bear hug. 'But I

want you to have a good time.'

'I will.'

He shifted his weight and took her hands in his. 'Kate, your home is with us, but if you decide to make your home back east, you know I'll be happy for you.'

The locomotive pulled up to the station, and passengers began to climb aboard. Kate turned to kiss Wendall good-bye. 'I'll write,' she said.

Kathleen found a seat across from an elderly couple, then leaned her head out the window. She shaded her eyes from the sun and waved, watching the little station as the train pulled away. Soon the town became nothing but indistinguishable buildings huddled in the distance. The train picked up speed, barbed wire flew by, and trees rushed past. It had been hot, and now the land looked dry.

They passed a farm where an Indian stood on the roof of the house, a rifle in hand, watching the train pass. There was a somberness in his gaze that chilled Kate. Remembering a lone rider on a red horse against the moonlit prairie, she thought her heart would break.

Half a mile out of the station the train whistled its signal to the lone prairie for miles around. Wendall scuffed a boot in the dust then walked slowly to the wagon and watched the train disappear in the distance.

Clapping his hat on, he climbed into the wagon and sat for a moment wondering if Kate would ever come back.

10

St. Louis was noisier than she remembered. As Kathleen walked along the busy sidewalks, horses pulling hansom cabs clip-clopped along, men and women whirred past on bicycles, and an occasional trolley clattered by. But she enjoyed the excitement of the city as she strolled along, twirling her new pink and white parasol.

The Wagners had been overjoyed to see her. They had made her comfortable in her old room in their big, well-furnished house and assured her she was welcome to stay as long as she liked. She had fallen asleep between percale sheets in the comfort of the familiar bed with its cherrywood posters and ruffled canopy. And this morning she had awakened refreshed and eager to tour the town. She had gone out by herself and had taken a horse-drawn streetcar to the shopping district, where she was to meet Nana Wagner at a tea shop.

She passed a young gentleman who tipped his stovepipe hat and smiled at her. She had nearly forgotten what it was like to be so formally admired by elegantly dressed men and ladies. She turned down Elm Street and approached the tea shop. Nana, a plump woman with gray hair pulled back in a neat bun, was sitting at one of the outdoor tables. Green eyes peered out from behind her tiny spectacles, and when she smiled dimples appeared at the corners of her mouth.

'Did you have a nice morning, dear?' she asked as Kathleen approached. Nana was cooling herself with a peacock-blue fan, but Kate found the weather pleasant, compared to the dusty heat at the ranch during the summer.

'Oh, yes, it was lovely.' She sat next to Nana on an ornate white iron chair.

'You do look flushed. I hope you have not been overdoing it.'

'No, Nana,' said Kathleen, using the name she had called Mrs. Wagner ever since she was a little girl. 'I was so excited to see everything.'

'News of your arrival has spread fast,' Nana said. 'Already there've been callers and invitations from many of your old friends. I don't think you had any idea you were so popular.'

'Now that I think of it,' said Kathleen, 'there are a great many people I would like to see.'

'We could arrange a little party for you.'

'Oh, I'm afraid that would be too much trouble.'

'Not at all. The house has been needing the sound of young people's voices and laughter since you left. I would love a party. Say, Saturday after next — that is, if you feel up to it.'

'I'd love it,' said Kathleen, warming to the idea.

'I'll make a list of refreshments,' Nana Wagner said. 'It will give me an excuse to try out a new recipe.'

'Nana, you're making me hungry. Shall we order?'

'Now tell me about Wendall and Molly,' Nana Wagner said after they had ordered. 'How are they getting along?' she asked.

'Just fine. I think they're very happy.'

'Molly doesn't mind living out there?'

'She seems to have the same sense of adventure I did when I left.' As she finished the sentence, it occurred to Kathleen that she was here now because she had lost her sense of adventure. Was it cowardly to have come back?

If Nana noticed any change in Kate's countenance, she did not comment. She continued the conversation. 'It must take a great deal of courage to face the wilderness. I remember when Henry brought me to St.

Louis years ago. It was a much smaller city then, but growing. Manufacturing had overtaken fur trading, and the city was still rebuilding after the fire. Still, it was civilized.'

As the waiter set their food before them, Kathleen looked out over the street. 'That building looks new,' she commented, gazing at a four-story structure on the opposite corner. The heavy granite seemed so solid compared to the wooden structures she had grown used to. She smiled to herself, remembering Wendall's comment that a city would someday rise where Tulsa now stood.

'Yes, it's a new office building I believe. St. Louis is growing, but I think I liked it better when it was smaller.'

Kathleen patted Nana's soft hand. 'Perhaps we all like things best as we remember them. But you have a lovely home here now.' She sighed.

A look of concern passed over Nana's face. 'Is that why you came back? Were you unhappy out west?'

'I don't know, Nana,' Kate said, speaking frankly. 'I was very happy there with Wendall. Then he got married, and I began to feel uncertain about my place in the household.' She shrugged and directed her attention to the luncheon. 'My thoughts turned to St. Louis. It would be so nice to marry and have a home here, though I'd miss Molly and Wendall, of course.'

Nana smiled. 'But, my dear, you haven't mentioned the main ingredient.'

'What is that?'

'The man you will marry.'

Kathleen blushed.

'My dear,' said Nana, trying to ease her embarrassment. 'I am the closest thing you have to a mother. Someone must talk to you about the things a girl should know.'

'I suppose you are right, Nana. And I appreciate your interest.' She looked down at her plate.

'Now, it's possible that you will meet someone while you're here. In my day, of course, people married for convenience. If a girl was lucky enough to get a good man, she might learn to love him. But the best marriages are those based on love from the beginning. It's my hope that you'll have such a marriage.'

The two women turned to less serious subjects, chatting pleasantly as they ate their meal. Then, finishing her dessert, Nana seemed to remember something. 'Oh, I nearly forgot to tell you,' she said. 'Lori Banfield sent word that she would call this afternoon with her mother. You mustn't let those two wear you out.'

'Don't worry, Nana,' Kathleen said, laughing. 'Just being back in St. Louis gives me the energy I need.' She finished the last few bites of her meal, and they hailed a hansom cab.

The residential neighborhood where the Wagners lived had spacious lawns and large homes set back from the curbings. Shady trees overhung the brick streets, and lilacs scented the air. The cab pulled up in front of the house, and the two women got out. Kathleen stood gazing at the big white house with its delicate tracery, light blue trim, and ornamental details. It looked peaceful and inviting in the spring afternoon.

There was the big oak she had climbed as a girl. The lawn, which wrapped around the entire house, was green and soft-looking, enclosed by a white picket fence. She held the gate open for Nana, and they walked up the flagstone path to the front steps. It had been here on these steps that she had told Wendall good-bye so many years ago.

She drifted back in memory. That had been the start of it, when Wendall went on the first cattle drive and wound up in Indian Territory. Now here she was in St. Louis again, and so much had happened in between.

They stepped inside the cool vestibule, where high ceilings and elaborate woodwork bespoke warmth and grandeur at the same time. She followed Nana into the parlor, a comfortably furnished room with a love seat, wing chairs, and inlaid tables.

Kathleen smiled. She would have to practice on the upright piano if she was going to entertain. She hadn't touched a keyboard in over a year. Nana went on to the kitchen at the back of the house, leaving Kathleen to wander through the familiar rooms. She passed through the hallway, with its curving walnut staircase that rose to the bedrooms above, and entered the library. How well she remembered taking books down from the tall shelves, curling up in the well-worn over-stuffed chair, and losing herself in a fictional adventure.

But her favorite place was the veranda where she had so often sat in the chain-hung wooden swing and enjoyed the cool breeze drifting in from the river.

Kathleen stepped onto the veranda now and sat down on the swing, feeling it move with her weight. She tried not to think about Raven Sky, but his face forced its way into her mind. She saw the anger fill his dark face as he pushed her into the hay. She didn't blame him for being angry. But she was here to forget about that complication, or at least to sort out her feelings, and the best approach was to relax and take in her surroundings.

She would have time enough to delve into her feelings later on. She wasn't ready just yet.

Her thoughts were interrupted as a young woman with blond hair appeared on the veranda.

'Kate, is it really you?' The young woman ran across the distance that separated them and flung herself at Kate.

'Lori Banfield!' Kate returned the hug and kissed her cheek. 'You look wonderful.' Indeed the girl was a vision of freshness with her peaches-and-cream complexion, the yellow stripes of her calling costume accenting her blond curls.

'I was just thrilled when I heard you were coming home. Is it for good or are you just on a visit?'

'I don't know, Lori. I think I am here to find out that very thing. But here, sit down. You must have lots of news to tell me. I'd love to hear some nice old-fashioned gossip.' Lori had been with Kate in the lower grades at school, but she had not gone on to normal school and so was not trained for anything except marriage.

'Well, I do have some gossip, as a matter of fact. I hope you're going to invite everyone over. Then you can see and hear it all for yourself. I don't know where to begin.' Lori sat in a wicker chair near the swing, tapping her foot on the wooden boards of the porch

184

in her excitement.

Nana came out with a tray of ice-cold lemonade. 'I heard you two out here talking, and I decided you'd need something to cool you off.'

'Thank you Mrs. Wagner, I am thirsty. Please join us. I was just about to tell Kate all the latest gossip.'

'No, thank you, my dears. You enjoy yourselves. There's more lemonade in the kitchen if you run out. And I hope Kathleen has invited you to her party next Saturday night. I'm going to make some of my favorite dishes. It will be so nice to have young people about again.'

Lori pressed her hands together. 'I'd love to come,' she said as Nana disappeared into the house. Turning to Kathleen, Lori said, 'You see? I was just saying there should be a party. It's the perfect thing.'

'Now, tell me the gossip, Lori. I know you're just dying to.' Kate leaned back in the swing, and the loquacious Lori settled into her wicker chair.

'Well, you remember Gerald Lange and Meryl Miller?'

'Yes, they must be married by now. Those two were promised to each other while they were still children. Did you go to the wedding?'

'No, and that's just the point — they didn't get married. Meryl ran off with a trapper who was in St. Louis selling beaver pelts. He took her away with him to Colorado.'

'You don't say.' Kathleen wondered vaguely if the match was successful. Meryl was an only child and had always gotten what she wanted. How would she fare with a trapper out west?

'And what happened to Gerald?'

'He is the most eligible bachelor in St. Louis now. You should see him, Kathleen. He is just back from Europe, and he's so handsome. He's filled out, and his dark hair falls across his forehead in the most devilish way.'

Kate smiled. 'You couldn't possibly be interested in him yourself, could you?' she teased.

'Oh Kate, you have the same dry humor. I adore him, but he won't even look at me. Still, one has to try. Say, will Nana ask him to the party? His family is acquainted with the Wagners, I believe.'

'I think it can be arranged.' Kate laughed. It felt good to indulge in such girlish scheming again. She gave in to merriment as she listened to Lori's account of who was doing what.

'Donald Orr is studying to become a

doctor. He's home for the summer now. Wendy Spring has a baby. Oh, Kate, he is so beautiful. But I'm being selfish. You haven't said anything at all. You must be the one with stories to tell. What's it like living out west? Is it really like the tales we hear?'

Lori squirmed deeper into the wicker chair, geting comfortable, and Kate saw her slip her shoes off. Kathleen didn't want to disappoint her friend, so she tried to tell her the better stories about life on the prairie.

'The West has its own kind of beauty, Lori. It isn't always green like the countryside here, but even when it gets hot and dry, the prairie holds a beautiful power. You can get lost in the wide open spaces. Sometimes I didn't see a soul except Hank and my brother for a whole day.'

'Who's Hank?'

'He's the ranch foreman. He handles things when Wendall's gone.' Kate remembered that Lori hardly knew Wendall. He had spent only a year in St. Louis, and had only met her friends when he'd come to visit.

'Are there wild Indians?' asked Lori, bringing a stab of pain to Kathleen.

'There are Indians, but they're not wild,' she explained, trying to be patient. She would have to expect that sort of question. Young

187

ladies of Lori's class thought all Indians were savages.

'Indian Territory is the home of the Five Civilized Tribes. They're educated, and they look and dress just as we do, for the most part. They've lived in log houses for many years, and the wealthier members of the tribes live in fine homes like we do.'

'How odd. When did they get civilized?'

Kathleen frowned at the ignorance of the question. Still, she herself hadn't learned much about Indians when she was in school, either. All she had known was that the Indians signed treaties and ceded their lands to the federal government, not that they were harassed into signing agreements they did not want. She never knew that they had educated themselves in white man's law, to fight him better in court. But she had learned such things from Wendall and from Raven Sky.

She swallowed, a muscle in her cheek twitching. 'Some have a natural talent for leadership and government,' she went on. 'From their negotiations with our government, they adopted our way of governing.' She paused, her stilted words pushed aside by powerful emotions. Then she said more slowly, 'In Indian Territory they had to learn how to be farmers like white men. There aren't very many buffalo and wild animals left to hunt in the lands they're restricted to.'

'How fascinating,' Lori said. 'Do you know any Indians?'

'Yes,' said Kathleen, feeling she could not go on, the tremor in her voice giving her away. 'I know some very brave ones. One in particular is very sensitive, and he is so handsome, Lori. You should see him.'

She shut her eyes and pressed her lips together, squeezing back tears.

Lori watched her friend silently, and after a moment she gracefully changed the subject. 'Who will you invite to the party, Kathleen?' She leaned forward and touched Kathleen's knee.

Kate took a deep breath, then wiped her eyes with her handkerchief. Was she going to spend every minute telling people here about Indians? Was she never to be allowed to forget? If so, why had she come here at all? She squelched the anger that threatened to rise in her, and smiled at Lori.

'You can help me with the guest list. I might forget someone. Let's go into the library and work on it now.' She stood and led Lori in to the desk where she knew Nana kept paper, pen and ink.

11

Kathleen sank down onto the love seat in the parlor and looked around the room at her guests. Lori Banfield, looking lovely in white cambric and lace, was playing 'Nellie Was a Lady' on the piano. Several young men leaned over her, attempting to harmonize as they competed for her attention. Among them was Frank Conway, who liked showing off his strong tenor voice.

Kathleen was dressed in a blue and silver satin dress, the ruched lace over the low neckline hiding the curves of her breasts. A delicate tiffany overskirt fell to the floor over the satin skirt and bustle. She had been right to leave the dress here, she thought. She would have had no occasion to wear it in Indian Territory. It still fit her slim figure and complemented her blue eyes and light brown hair, which was now coiled and wrapped around her head, with tiny curls springing around her face.

'Glad to be back, Kate?' asked Johnny Church, a tall young man with brown hair.

'Yes, it's very nice.'

'Great to have you among us again, Kate,'

said someone else, passing by on the way to the punch bowl.

'You're not going to deny me a dance with you, I hope,' Frank Conway asked, walking away from the piano, where he had left the singing to the other men hovering over Lori.

'I'd love to dance, after a rest,' she said. Surreptitiously, she slipped her shoes off to flex her toes in their white stockings. A flurry of activity made her glance toward the door. Gerald Lange had come in, fashionably late, and was at once surrounded by chattering friends.

Kate noticed how handsome he looked in his perfectly cut dark frock coat and silk tie. Lori was right. His face had filled out nicely, and his smile was relaxed and confident. She would greet him later. No one would miss her now if she slipped out to the veranda for some fresh air.

With the guests surrounding the new arrival, Kate slipped on her shoes, tiptoed across the polished wood floor and drifted out the door to the veranda. There she kicked off her shoes once again and breathed in the lilac scent of the evening air and eased herself into the swing. Closing her eyes, she inhaled the sweet scents from the garden, trying to identify the plants by smell, as she had done when she was a girl working with Nana among the flowers.

'Hello, Kathleen,' said a deep voice out of the darkness.

With a start, she jumped up to face Gerald Lange, who stood in the shadows before her. He seemed even taller than she remembered him until she realized that he was wearing stylish European-cut shoes while she stood barefoot, exaggerating the difference in their height.

'I didn't hear you come out. It's good to see you, Gerald.'

He grinned at her in the moonlight, the smile lighting up his angular features, and bent to kiss her hand. As he did, a lock of his dark hair fell forward and brushed her skin.

'You look lovely, Kate. I think the frontier must agree with you.'

'Thank you.' She motioned for him to sit down, and he sank into a rattan chair. 'I hear you've been in Europe.'

'Yes. My father gave me the trip as a present for finishing law school. I tried to see as much of the Continent as I could. Once I start practicing law, I'll probably be working for the rest of my life, and I won't be able to get away.' He cleared his throat in mock seriousness. 'I'm at the age where one takes on responsibility.'

'I'm glad you enjoyed your trip,' she said,

pushing the swing lightly back and forth.

He looked at her intently. 'While I was in Europe, my mother wrote that you had gone to join your brother in Indian Territory. I was disappointed that I wouldn't be able to see you when I returned home.' He lowered his voice slightly. 'I thought of you often, Kate.'

'Really? But you scarcely knew me.'

'You were very young.' He smiled, his teeth gleaming in the moonlight, the sparkle of merriment in his eyes. 'I had watched you grow up, and I wondered what kind of woman you'd turn out to be.'

'Well,' she said, the satin of her skirt swishing against her legs as she took a more comfortable position, 'what is your verdict?'

'I would say you've turned out very well indeed.' He raised a dark eyebrow at her. 'But tell me, how did you like living out there on the prairie? I would very much like to see the frontier one day.'

She turned away, looking out at the silhouetted shapes of the shrubbery next to the house. There was that awful question. She knew she would have to answer it again and again. Everyone wanted to know what the West was like, what exciting adventures she had had. People would not understand her reluctance to talk about her life on the prairie.

'Everyone wants to know about it,' she said candidly. 'But I came here to forget it, and no one seems to understand that.' She shut her mouth, having spoken with more vehemence than she'd meant to.

Sensing the change in her, Gerald dropped his bantering tone. 'I'm sorry. People only mean to be polite. And we're all very interested in you, Kate.' His tone softened. 'You were well liked here.'

She nodded in acknowledgment. 'It's kind of you to say that. I'll just have to learn how to talk about my life.' She sighed, finding it easy to unburden herself to Gerald. 'I have strong feelings connected with Indian Territory. I need to sort them out.'

'Anything an old friend can help out with?' He leaned forward.

She stopped the movement of the swing. 'No, I just need to experience life here again. It's possible that I won't return to my brother's ranch. He doesn't need me anymore, now that he has a wife.'

'He married Molly Ladurie, didn't he?'

'Yes,' she said.

'I knew Molly,' Gerald said, smiling, 'but she, too, was younger than I. She must be all grown up by now.'

'I'm afraid we all are,' said Kate, and Gerald laughed again.

'I remember one Christmas when Molly followed me out of her parents' house after my family came to call,' he said. 'She threw snowballs at me and I got angry. I chased her until I tripped and fell. It was embarrassing.'

Both Kathleen and Gerald laughed softly, envisioning the scene. How pleasant it was to sit here in the cool darkness and talk. She turned to study him. His strong features were set in a pleasant expression as he enjoyed the memories. She was conscious of the squeak of the chain as she began to move the swing once again.

'Shouldn't we go in now?' she asked. 'All the guests expect to spend some time with me, and we've been out here for quite a while.' *People might talk*, she started to say, but the words died on her lips.

As she slipped on her shoes and rose, she saw a smile of pleasure dancing on his lips, and she grew flushed when she realized his glance was resting on her breasts.

'Whatever you wish,' he whispered as she moved past him.

Back inside, the guests were gathered around the refreshment table, where Nana was busy ladling out punch.

'Here, let me do that,' said Kathleen, moving behind the dining room table and taking the punch ladle from her.

'All right, dear,' Nana acquiesced. 'I'll bring in the deviled eggs.'

When the food had been served, Kathleen sat next to Johnny Church and Brad Marlow, neighbor boys she'd grown up with. But she noticed the intent looks coming her way from Gerald Lange, who sat across the room.

After they'd all eaten, a group drifted back to the piano, but Gerald remained where he was. Legs crossed, he watched Kate entertain her friends.

It was late when the guests filed out, thanking Nana and Kathleen for the party, many of them insisting Kathleen visit soon. Kate was appreciative of their desire to sweep her up in their social life again, but the thought left her less excited than she had expected it would. It was one thing to see old friends again. It was another to imagine a constant round of parties and gossip, seeing the same people again and again.

Lori Banfield came to say good night, looking wistful as she squeezed Kate's hand. 'Thanks for inviting me,' she said. 'And thanks for doing that other favor.' She rolled her eyes in Gerald's direction, where he stood talking to Ned Wagner. Lori leaned forward and whispered in Kate's ear. 'I guess it didn't do any good.'

196

Kate gave the girl a wry grin. 'You mean he wasn't attentive?'

'He seems preoccupied. Oh, well . . . ' She gave a little shrug. Johnny Church was waiting for her on the porch. She hurried out to take his arm, and they clattered down the steps.

A short time later, Gerald shook hands with Nana and complimented her again on the food. Then he took Kathleen's hand and held it, looking into her eyes. 'It's been wonderful seeing you, Kathleen. Will you invite me again?'

'Yes, of course,' she said. 'You're always welcome.'

'May I call tomorrow afternoon? I'd like to take you for a ride and show you the town.'

She hadn't expected to see him again so soon, but she did want to see all the changes in St. Louis since she'd left. 'All right. That would be very nice.'

'Tomorrow, then, about two?' He turned to Nana. 'And of course Nana will join us.'

Gerald left them, his long strides carrying him down the walk to the gate. Watching him, Kate noticed the confident set of his broad shoulders. He was a debonair and attractive man, and the fact that he was still single must cause many young women a great deal of excitement. But she felt only friendship for him, and she hoped he would not call on her too often. She needed friends to take her mind off her problems, and she wanted to have fun with people her own age. But she realized, with a sudden panicky feeling in her chest, that she was far from ready for romance.

After helping Nana and the maid clear up, she went to her bedroom. As she undressed and prepared for bed she felt grateful for the comfort of her room with its chintz curtains and yellow-flowered wallpaper. The room brought back so many pleasant memories. Here she could wrap herself in a cocoon of pleasant thoughts.

But as she lay down on top of the chenille bedspread, her earlier unsettling feelings returned. She felt as if she had left her heart on the sweeping plains. By day, she might pretend to be the St. Louisan she once was, but by night, the prairie claimed her.

Having the two homes had done nothing but split her in two. And it seemed she would have to give up one for the other. Thoughts and images tormented her, and she was afraid to fall asleep, for fear of her dreams.

She stared at the ceiling, wishing she were still the child who had once slept in this room, wishing Wendall would come in to talk to her, the way he used to, making sure she was all right, trying to comfort her.

She sat up and wiped the tears from her cheeks. Wendall was married, and she was on her own now. She had to face whatever was troubling her and work everything out for herself.

She finished undressing and put on her nightgown. Then she lay down between the soft percale sheets, watching the moonlight spill in through the open casement window. Outside, crickets chirped. The wind played with the curtains, making shadows dance on the rug beside her bed. Slowly the comfort of her big canopy bed and the quiet summer night calmed her.

She was determined to bring things to rights. Tomorrow would be a new day. She would start over. She would enjoy Gerald's company. Perhaps she should let herself get to know him better. Certainly he had every qualification for a fine husband. Perhaps if he really was interested in her, her feelings for him might grow. She couldn't imagine feeling the wild passion for him that she had experienced when Raven Sky touched her, but she didn't need those feelings with a man like Gerald.

Thinking of those feelings now, she felt ashamed. Surely it was wrong to allow her body to burn that way for a man's touch. A man like Gerald would be patient and kind. He would make a good companion. She tried to think of him as she drifted to sleep, wondering if she could learn to love him.

* * *

Sunday dawned warm and sunny, with fleecy clouds drifting across a china-blue sky. After church, Kathleen and the Wagners sat down to dinner in the polished Queen Anne chairs around the rosewood table. Kathleen could not help but compare these surroundings with Wendall and Molly's sturdy but practical pine and oak furniture. The ranch was luxurious for a frontier home, but compared to this house, cluttered with knickknacks, it seemed spare indeed.

Ned presided over the meal, his white whiskers accentuating his puffy cheeks. 'Nana tells me you're going to see the sights today.'

'Yes,' Kate said. 'Gerald Lange is very eager to show us all the new sights.'

'Are you sure you want me to go along?' asked Nana.

'Yes,' Kate said, speaking quickly. 'You might think of things I'd like to see that Gerald wouldn't. And besides, I want you to enjoy the ride, Nana.'

The older woman seemed pleased, but

Kate knew Nana wasn't fooled. She probably knew Kate wanted her along to serve as a buffer between Kate and Gerald.

The doorbell rang, and Sissy, the maid, answered it. A moment later, she came in to announce Gerald's arrival.

Kathleen rose. 'I'll entertain him until you're ready to leave, Nana.' She smoothed her fitted green linen suit, picked up her lisle-thread gloves from the side table, and went into the parlor. Gerald was looking out the window, rocking on his heels. As Kathleen came in, he turned and smiled.

'Good afternoon,' he said, reaching for her hand. 'Have you recovered from the party?' He was wearing a navy reefer jacket and cream-colored duck trousers.

'Yes, and you?'

'Very much so. And I'm ready to treat you to an afternoon of entertainment. Will Nana be joining us?'

'Yes,' said Kathleen. She noticed a trace of disappointment in his dark eyes, but as Nana entered the room, he bowed gallantly over her hand.

'Gerald,' teased Nana, 'you don't need to be so debonair with me. I've known you since you were in knee britches, remember?'

He straightened and laughed. 'And I probably broke a few of your windows at that.' He offered the older woman his arm, then stood back for Kate to lead the way.

Outside, Gerald's driver, Billy, opened the small halfdoor of the carriage so the ladies could climb in. Gerald signaled Billy to start, and the horses' shoes clattered on the brick street as the carriage pulled away.

'Could we see the river?' Kate asked. 'I always loved the Mississippi so.'

'Of course,' said Gerald. 'No tour of our city is complete without a drive along the levee.'

After passing out of the residential areas, they drove toward the waterfront, passing warehouses and shipyards on the way. As they came nearer the water, they could see the barges and steamboat landings under the Eads Bridge. The great bridge crossed the Mississippi in three graceful spans of five hundred feet or more, bringing the Illinois coal fields closer to the city's manufacturing.

They turned down Washington Avenue and drove through the center of town. Smoke from the brewery stacks blew across the sky, and the wind carried it away. Later, driving along Third Street, they passed the Merchants' Exchange. Still not used to seeing so many people about, Kate smiled, remembering the smallness of Tulsa.

'Tell us, Gerald, what are your plans, now

that you're back from Europe?' asked Nana.

'I don't know,' he said, throwing Kate a glance. 'I've not yet decided where to open my law practice.'

'Surely your father would like you to stay here,' Nana said.

Gerald turned his head to look out at the passing scenery. 'Yes, he would like that, but I have not yet decided what I'll do.'

'I understand,' said Nana.

Kathleen glanced at him, thinking of his broken engagement. He must have suffered a deep heartache when Meryl eloped with another man. Perhaps he felt a pain similar to hers. If so, she and Gerald had more in common than she had thought.

Gerald turned to her. Shifting his weight closer to her, he signaled the driver to start back to the house.

'Perhaps you could drop me off and continue your outing,' Nana said. 'I'm sure there are a great many things you've yet to see.'

Gerald's brown eyes lit up. 'I would like to take Kathleen to Forest Park, if that is all right with you.'

'Well, I don't know,' said Kate.

'Of course you must go,' urged Nana. 'It's so good for you to get out of the house.'

'All right,' Kathleen agreed. She was silent

the rest of the way back to the house. After Nana left them, Gerald had Billy drive on slowly. Gerald leaned against the side of the buggy so he could look at Kathleen.

Her profile had not changed since she was a young girl. Curls fell across her forehead, and thick brown lashes curled up from her sparkling blue eyes. She had a slightly turned-up nose and soft lips, which were now slightly pursed. Her chin was firm, and her coiffure revealed her long smooth neck.

'You look well, Kate,' he said. Then he couldn't resist teasing her. 'Your skin is more tanned than is fashionable, you know.'

She glared at him. 'I know it's not attractive, but on the ranch I didn't have time to worry about such things.'

'On the contrary,' he said, capturing her gloved hand, 'I like a healthy, hardworking woman.'

She resented his flippant remarks and snatched her hand away. 'Then it's a good thing you didn't marry Meryl Miller.'

Then she looked quickly at him. 'I'm sorry. I didn't mean to say it that way.'

'Don't be sorry on that account,' he said.

'Did you love her?' Kate looked down, hoping he wouldn't think she was being too personal. But she was curious. She wanted to know if other people suffered from heart-break, and if they did, how they recovered.

He studied her, lifting a finger to touch one of her curls. 'I'd known Meryl all my life, and I thought we could make a satisfactory marriage.' He paused, letting the curl drop. 'I could have loved her.'

She turned back to meet his gaze, wishing she had never asked. 'I see,' she said.

Kathleen swallowed the lump in her throat and returned to contemplating her surroundings. She was pulled back from her daydreams when she felt Gerald's arm slip around the back of the seat.

'Did you think about St. Louis while you were away?' he asked.

'Occasionally' she answered.

'I suppose you never once gave me a thought,' Gerald said.

'To be honest with you, that is nearly true. When I first went west, I spent almost every waking minute working. I was exhausted at the end of a day. Sometimes in the evenings, when we sat on the porch or by the fire, we would speak of home.'

'What did you talk about?'

'Wendall read the newspapers. When we saw an article about someone we knew, he would show me.'

'Yes?'

'There was a piece about you when you finished law school. I remember it said you were leaving for Europe.'

'What did you think?'

Kate shrugged. 'I thought that was nice for you, and that you would probably make a very good lawyer.'

'I'm glad you thought so,' said Gerald.

Kate turned away, embarrassed. Then, feeling the heat of his gaze, she faced him again. 'Gerald,' she said, 'there's something I want to make clear.'

'Yes?'

'I've always counted you as a friend. I hope it is only friendship you want from me now, for friendship is all I can offer you.' She looked forward, unable to meet his gaze.

Gerald raised an eyebrow and removed his arm. 'I've always admired you, Kathleen, even when you were in pigtails. You've become an attractive woman, and I'd be a fool not to notice it. But we can remain friends, if that is what you want.'

'That is what I want.'

The carriage stopped before a large expanse of green lawn and overhanging oaks and elms. The 1400-acre park offered cool shade along curving walks and wide road-ways. Here were 1100 acres of forest. Black, white, and water oak, horse chestnut, blackberry, butternut, ash, tulip, and magnolia trees abounded. Gerald took Kate's arm, and they walked toward a bandstand in the center of the green, where they sat on a long wooden bench and listened as the band played a rousing march.

A boy passed selling popcorn, and Gerald purchased a box. When the band finished the number, Kathleen and Gerald made their way down a gentle slope to a large pond where several ducks swam. Near the opposite shore, a graceful swan floated in front of an ornate pagoda.

'Oh, how lovely,' said Kathleen, looking at the swan.

'Beautiful,' remarked Gerald. 'The swan's loveliness reminds me of you.' He stood near her, and she could feel his gaze, though he made no move to touch her.

'Gerald,' she said, 'you promised.'

'A man can give a lady compliments, can't he?'

She sighed. 'As long as you understand how I feel.' She took a step closer to the bank to put distance between them. 'Gerald, I know you must think me rude.'

He shrugged and returned to contemplating the swan. 'Not at all. If I didn't enjoy your company I wouldn't be here.'

'It's been a lovely afternoon, Gerald. I

haven't thanked you.'

'You're quite welcome.'

A feeling of melancholy stole over Kathleen. Since she had made her feelings clear, she supposed Gerald wouldn't waste any more time on her. She wasn't fooled by his offer of friendship. Men didn't spend time with women just for friendship. She knew she wouldn't see him again except at large social gatherings. It was a shame. He was not unattractive. If she had never met Raven Sky, she might even have considered marrying Gerald. But visions of the lean figure astride the wild red stallion haunted her memory.

She turned away from him to admire the lily pads floating in the water so he couldn't see the struggle that must show in her eyes. Perhaps in time she could marry someone like Gerald. But she wasn't ready for that yet, and she couldn't lead him to believe she was.

Gerald threw some popcorn at the ducks, watching them scramble for it. In his navy jacket and duck trousers he looked cool and relaxed. She knew how many woman must admire him, and she was flattered that he had singled her out. Then she thought of Lori and felt slightly guilty. She had forgotten until that moment how desperately Lori had sought Gerald's attention. Perhaps she could do something about that.

'Did you see Lori Banfield last night?' she asked.

Gerald frowned. 'Oh, yes,' he said. 'She wore a bright yellow dress with ribbons, did she not?'

Kathleen was pleased that he remembered the way she looked. Perhaps she had caught his eye after all. 'Yes. She looked very pretty. I've always envied her for her blond hair.'

Gerald frowned at her. When he spoke it was with some irritation. 'You have no reason to envy another woman's beauty, Kate.' He threw the last of the popcorn at the quacking ducks and took her arm. 'Let's go,' he said and propelled her up the hill. He didn't speak another word all the way home.

'Won't you come in?' Kathleen asked when he had walked her to the door.

'No, I don't believe I will.'

Knowing he was offended, not wanting him to leave this way, she said, 'Thank you for a lovely afternoon, Gerald.'

Taking her hand, he held it lightly, without the warm squeeze he had given it earlier. Then he turned on his heel and left.

Kathleen let herself in, then shrugged out of her linen jacket. She found Nana and Ned on the veranda.

'How was your afternoon?' asked Ned.

Kate smiled at the bald man who had been the only father she had ever really known. 'It was very pleasant.'

'But not thrilling?' Nana smiled, looking at her over the rims of her spectacles.

'Oh, Nana, you read me like a book.'

'It's easy to see when you want something and when you're not interested.'

'I'm afraid you're right.'

Ned put down the tool catalog he had been looking at and got up. 'If you ladies will excuse me,' he said, 'I've got to attend to those rosebushes.'

After Ned left, Kathleen said, 'Nana, I'm going to need something to do here. As I told you, I started to teach at the mission school before I left the ranch. I really enjoyed it for the few days I was there, before the tornado interrupted things.' She told Nana about the storm.

'Was anyone hurt?'

'No, but there was a lot of property damage.'

Kathleen suddenly wanted to tell Nana the whole story of Raven Sky. She wanted so much to share her excitement and her fears. But she held her tongue in check. Nana would be sympathetic to her feelings, perhaps. But she wouldn't approve of the

210

circumstances in which they had occurred, and she probably wouldn't approve of Kate's feelings for a Creek Indian.

Kathleen clenched her hands into tight fists. 'I'll see if I can help Sissy in the kitchen.'

12

Summer turned into autumn, and Kathleen fell into a routine of household duties and social calls, none of it stimulating. It dulled her mind, but there was a certain solace in not having to think about what she did, merely following the expected behavior.

Much to her surprise, Gerald Lange was still attentive. He occasionally escorted other young ladies to social events, so that no undue rumors would be created about whom he was seeing. Lori gave up on him and set her sights on a reporter at the St. Louis *Post-Dispatch*.

Late in October Gerald asked Kathleen to attend the Oktoberfest with him. The annual festival was given by the large German community of St. Louis, and there would be much drinking and merrymaking in the streets. It was a time people could get away with doing things they would not normally do. Kate was nervous about going. But Gerald had promised to bring her home whenever she asked.

Now she awaited his arrival, wearing a burgundy satin dress trimmed with black fur.

When the doorbell rang, she opened it herself to admit him.

Gerald looked dashing in a blue cutaway coat with white ruffled shirt. 'My, my, my,' he said, 'don't you look lovely!'

He handed her a bouquet of gladioli. Laughing in spite of herself, she took the flowers to the kitchen, where Nana assured her she would place them in a vase on the piano in the parlor. Kathleen and Gerald left the house and descended the steps, and Gerald said, '*Mademoiselle*,' as he held the gate for her.

'You mean *Fräulein*,' she corrected, trying to affect a heavy German accent.

'My mistake,' he said. 'I had forgotten my German.'

Their laughter intermingled as they stepped out to the carriage. Gerald threw his arm over the back of the carriage seat, establishing an atmosphere of easy camaraderie. Kate smiled, remembering an earlier day when she had resented his doing so. Had her feelings changed since then? she wondered.

Not really, she decided. She still thought of Gerald as just a friend. But she had begun to trust him. He had lived up to his word and had made no further advances. The community buzzed with gossip about which young woman this eligible bachelor would finally wed, and Kate was flattered that he often chose to escort her.

The festival took place in one of the German neighborhoods. People crowded the gaily decorated street. Booths had been set up where ale and beer were served along with bratwurst, bauernwurst, and other German foods. At several booths, Hummel figurines were sold, and artists displayed their wares.

Gerald and Kathleen got out at the end of the street. Deciding his servant deserved a little fun, Gerald sent Billy on his way. Billy nodded, and the horses clopped away.

Gerald took Kathleen's arm and steered her into the crowd, where a German band was playing polkas. When they reached the first booth, Gerald bought two steins of beer and handed her one.

'Oh, Gerald, I don't think I can drink this much,' Kate said, staring at the large stein.

'Bottoms up,' he said as he tossed the beer down. Kate did her best, but handed him half the mug to finish for her.

'Ah,' said Gerald, draining her stein, too. He guided her deeper into the crowd to a pavilion where several accordian players were offering lively German music.

'Dance with me, Kate?' he asked. There was a sparkle in his eye, and his hair fell rakishly across his forehead as he led her to the dance floor and swung her in his arms. They danced until Kate begged for a rest, laughing at the gaiety of the rambunctious polka music.

'I've worked up a thirst,' Gerald said, and led her down several steps to a basement beer garden decorated with colored lanterns. They found an empty wooden table and sat down. Kate caught her breath while Gerald ordered beer. A group of musicians played concertinas on a small stage, and a blond tenor sang of wanderlust followed by a return to hearth and home.

A plump waitress, dressed in a colorful Bavarian costume with a fitted bodice and fluffy white sleeves, served the beer. Gerald pinched her cheek as she set down the steins. She blew him a kiss as she departed.

'Enjoying yourself, Kathleen?' he asked as he drank.

'It's very colorful,' she said. Just then she noticed Lori Banfield sitting with a young blond man several tables away. Kate wondered if this was her new flame.

'Oh, look, there's Lori,' said Kathleen.

'So it is, so it is,' Gerald said. 'Let's invite 'em to join us.'

He raised his stein and intoned, 'Hops and malt, God bless 'em!'

Gathering her skirts, Kate got up and went

over to where Lori sat, looking very pretty in pink ruffles and white lace.

'Why, Kathleen!' Lori smiled, then glanced wistfully at Gerald, who was humming along with the entertainers.

'Lori, would you and your friend like to join us? Gerald has requested the pleasure of your company.'

Lori's eyes lit up as she accepted the invitation, then introduced Kathleen to her escort, Mark Phillips.

Mark rose and bowed to Kathleen. He was so blond and had such blue eyes that he might have been related to Lori. The two of them followed Kathleen back to her table.

Gerald rose to shake hands with both of them. 'Sit down. My favorite waitress will bring us a round of beers.'

As he held Lori's chair, Mark eyed Kathleen's plunging neckline.

'Nice to see you, Lori. Where've you been keeping yourself?' asked Gerald. He didn't wait for her reply, however, but turned to Mark and began a conversation.

Kathleen shrugged at Lori. She was glad her friend didn't show any resentment at her being with Gerald, only mild disappointment.

'Gerald, don't you think we should get some air?' asked Kathleen finally. She was beginning to feel the effects of the stuffy beer

216

hall, filled with smoke from pipes and cigars. Gerald scraped back his chair and rose, taking one last swig from his mug.

' 'Scuse us, please,' said Gerald, bowing to Mark and Lori. 'The lady wants some air.'

On the street, Gerald threw an arm around Kate's shoulders, and she turned her head to avoid his beer breath. Glad to be outside, though, she let Gerald steer her along the street between the booths, narrowly avoiding colliding with other couples.

'Let's get out of this crowd,' he said, loosening his collar. Then he turned abruptly down a side street, making Kathleen stumble. He tightened his grasp around her waist to keep her from falling, and she clung to him to catch herself.

They swung around the corner near a high brick wall. Before she realized what he was doing, Gerald had swung her against the wall and pinned her there.

'Gerald, what are you doing?'

'Kissing you, Kathleen Calhoun,' he said. 'I think it's time.' He bent his head and opened his lips to taste her mouth.

She moved her head so that his mouth landed on her chin. She wasn't afraid of Gerald in the least, but she resented his behavior.

'Gerald, please, let me go,' she gasped as

she felt his hand on her satin-covered breast. His other arm held her still, so that she couldn't wriggle away, and his fingers began to explore her décolletage.

She froze in shock as Gerald gazed down at her breasts.

'Tempting getup you're wearing, Kate. And it's a night for celebrating. Gives a man ideas. You're driving me crazy,' he muttered. 'I can't stand it when I see you like this. Surely you haven't been spending all this time with me for nothing.'

His mouth found hers, and his fingers had reached her nipples. A feeling of dread came over her as he pressed himself against her, still holding her roughly against the wall. She heard him moan as he pushed against her thighs, and she felt the burgeoning of his desire. She didn't struggle, knowing that would be futile, but she clenched her teeth and spoke in a threatening voice, 'Gerald Lange, let me go this instant, or I will scream for the police!'

'Not if you're kissing me, you won't.'

When he attempted to cover her mouth with his again, she pretended to relax so that he would let down his guard. Then, as he slid both arms around her and leaned against her, she moved. In one coordinated effort, she raised her knee, bit his lip, and pushed him away. As he stumbled backward, catching his balance, she ran free of him, racing up the street toward the lights.

She elbowed her way anxiously through the crowd, looking toward the end of the street for a hansom cab. Gerald caught up with her just as she was hailing one.

'Kate, don't leave me,' he said.

'You're perfectly capable of taking care of yourself,' she snapped, climbing into the cab.

It was a relief to let herself in at home. She shut the door and walked into the parlor, finding Nana still up, waiting for her. As the older woman put down her spectacles and got up, Kathleen noticed a pallor about her face.

'What is it, Nana?' she asked as she moved toward the sofa where Nana had been sitting. 'Is something wrong?'

'Sit down, Kathleen. Someone came here to see you.'

'Who?'

'A man. He said he knew you in Indian Territory.'

Kathleen's heart thudded. Who could have come all the way from Indian Territory for her?

'His name is Raven Sky,' said Nana.

Kathleen's knees gave way, and she sank into a chair.

'Where is he?'

'He's staying at the Lindell Hotel.' Nana peered curiously at her foster daughter, and Kate could see that she wanted to ask a great many more questions about Raven Sky. But she only said, 'Who is he?'

'He's a . . . a very important leader of the Creek Indians.' Kathleen's face flushed.

Nana shook her head. 'I never expected to see an Indian like that . . . here. He was dressed in a handsomely tailored suit.'

An odd smile played about Kathleen's lips. 'Are you surprised that he is so civilized?'

Nana shrugged, adjusting her spectacles. 'Well, I didn't know what to expect.'

'When will he return?'

'He wants you to send word as to when would be a convenient time.' She smiled gently at Kate. 'Perhaps you'd better tell me about him. If you want to, that is.'

'Oh, Nana, I don't know what to do. I want to see him,' she said slowly. 'But I'm afraid to.'

Nana looked at her over the rims of the spectacles. 'I see. Well, perhaps things will seem clearer in the morning. Did you have a nice evening?'

Grimacing, Kathleen said, 'No.' Then she rose, kissed Nana good night, and went up to bed, hoping she would be able to sleep. But she lay wide-eyed, staring out the window at the moon.

Why had Raven Sky come here? It surprised her that he would walk unannounced into her St. Louis life. She wondered how long he would stay and what he wanted.

Perhaps he was angry with her. That thought frightened her. What if he had come to exact his revenge on her? She couldn't stop the thoughts from spinning around in her mind until finally, in the wee hours of the morning, she drifted off into a restless sleep.

★ ★ ★

The Lindell Hotel stood on Washington Avenue three blocks west of the Eads Bridge. Kathleen left the cab and walked into the lobby, pausing to orient herself. To her right, on a thick, sculptured carpet, stood several tufted wing chairs with nailhead trim. Velvet-covered love seats sat in groupings of two and three for the convenience of the guests. Tall, slender red-marble pillars lent majesty to the room, which was lit by electric light bulbs set in brass chandeliers.

Kathleen, dressed in a navy blue linen suit, crossed the marble floor to the mahogany front desk, where a sleepy-looking clerk was sorting mail. He looked up when she approached.

'I'm looking for Mr. Raven Sky,' she said. 'He is staying here.'

The clerk consulted the ledger, then glanced at the pigeonholes behind him. 'He left this morning and he hasn't returned yet.' He looked at Kate speculatively. She thought he might be wondering what type of woman she was, alone in a hotel asking for an Indian man who was obviously traveling by himself. But he kept his opinions to himself as he cleared his throat and returned to the ledger.

'Thank you, I'll wait,' she said, and walked across the lobby to a burgundy velvet love seat. The fronds of a large potted palm brushed her cheek as she sat down.

Waiting for the coming interview, she reflected on the two sides of Raven Sky's nature that she had come to know. He rode the plains and rolling hills like part of the natural life there. He was swift as a deer, stealthy as a fox, strong and certain as a lion. Part of him was as wild as the savage tornado that had thrown them together. When she was near him, she could feel that same wildness of spirit in herself, and it frightened her.

But he was also a gentleman, a leader of his tribe. An expert in government affairs, he moved in the white man's world. If he was angry with her for leaving, surely he would not call on her in this civilized manner.

222

Suddenly she saw his tall figure stride through the glass-paneled doors. He was dressed in a fitted cutaway, the deep blue color contrasting with his burnished skin. A white shirt with a stiff front accented his dark complexion, making his eyes seem blacker and his hair smooth and glossy. The fitted trousers accentuated his thighs as he took long strides across the lobby.

She stood, trembling, all thought banished, as he came toward her. Then he was in front of her, his masculine scent fresh. Even in these formal surroundings he had the power to arouse feelings she thought she had succeeded in burying. As he looked down at her, his eyes drinking in her face, everything came back, all the longings she had felt in Indian Territory. For a moment there was no one, nothing else, only Raven Sky and herself.

'Thank you for coming,' he said.

She nodded, not trusting her voice. All she could do was look at him, realize again the beauty of his firm chin, his angular features, his penetrating eyes that held so many expressions, some of which she had learned so well.

'Can we sit down?' she asked, feeling she couldn't stand without support much longer.

He crossed to sit next to her, angling his body so that he could look at her beside him.

He watched her silently, broodingly, as if assessing her mood.

She bit her lip, wondering if he still desired her. Could he see the desire in her own eyes? She tried to still the beating of her heart.

When he spoke, his voice was deep and low. 'When are you coming home?' he asked. She saw the accusation in his eyes.

She looked away from him. 'This is my home.'

'But is this your spiritual home?'

'You of all people ought to understand that people want to live where their ancestors lived,' she began. 'My family was born here, raised here, until my parents decided to go to Kansas.' *And they never came back*, part of her screamed.

She sat still, not facing him, avoiding his black eyes, which pierced her like arrows. Her heart was pounding and she was losing what small grip she held on her emotions. She had so wanted to appear cool-headed. She forced herself to speak evenly. 'Why are you here, Raven Sky?'

'I am here on business for my tribe.' She glanced a his profile as he turned to watch passers-by. Then he leaned toward her again. 'But that is not my real reason.'

He had looked angry before, but now his gaze softened. He regarded her silently. 'Is it because of me?' he asked.

'What?'

'The reason you have not returned to your brother's home.'

She lowered her head. How could she answer that? She might have returned before now if it hadn't been for Raven Sky, yet when Wendall had married, everything had changed. A chain of events had led up to her flight and to her reluctance to leave St. Louis. But she must be honest with him, for he would detect deceit.

'Partly,' she said, still looking down.

His voice was softer but more intense now, and he moved nearer. 'I have to know, Kathleen. My heart longs for you. You do not understand the power you have over me. I have never experienced this before. I had a dream when I was a very young man. A vision told me I would love a white woman, a goddess, that she would come to me from her people's home just as my people had come from their home, and that she would live with me. I have to know if you are that woman.'

'I am not a goddess, Raven Sky. I am a person, and I don't know at this moment where my roots are. I need to find that out.'

'You are a woman, I know, but you can be a goddess as well.'

'You flatter me, Raven Sky. I am not

worthy of these thoughts.'

'I will decide if you are worthy.'

'Raven Sky, I must try to make you understand something. My parents were killed by Indians. I can never forget that.' She swallowed. 'I know you. Your people would never do such a thing. Your tribe is peaceful. You are . . . ' She hesitated.

'We are civilized,' he said. And the way he pulled his mouth back in a mocking sneer when he said it made grief tear at her.

'That is what you want in a man, is it not?'

'Yes, of course, but . . . ' She searched for words. 'My feelings and my mind are not the same.' She hoped he would understand.

He placed his hand over his heart. 'You mean you feel something here, but your head tells you it is dangerous to feel such things.'

She nodded, becoming misty.

'It is often that way for us,' he said, 'for my people. As tribal leaders, we must often do what is wise for the tribe, even if it breaks our hearts to do so.' Then his eyes narrowed. 'But we are not talking about a nation; we speak about a woman. If your heart tells you to feel something, then your mind must be wrong. Your heart knows. It is only your demon thoughts that are not right. The Indian knows about troubled spirits, and there are ways to deal with them.'

Kathleen looked into his face — his high cheekbones and graceful nose emphasizing his Indian heritage, silky black lashes lowered over intense eyes. She wanted more than anything to reach out and touch his face, run her hands over his smooth skin. But she clenched her hands tight to prevent herself from doing so, trusting her sense of propriety to keep her from doing something foolish.

'Raven Sky, I . . . ' Her voice drifted off, and she raised one hand. He took the hand and lifted it to his cheek. Then he closed his eyes and pressed his lips against her gloved hand.

'I want you,' he said, opening his eyes.

She could feel the desire throbbing in his veins as he sat next to her, taut as a leopard ready to spring. That desire leaped between them, and her heart beat faster, as if they were alone.

Then slowly, consciousness of their surroundings returned, and he slowly withdrew her hand.

'Do not slip away from me,' he said. 'I must see you alone. Come to my room.' His voice was husky.

'I couldn't,' she breathed, her eyes widening.

'You needn't be afraid.' She saw sudden irritation in his eyes.

'Please, Raven Sky. I need time. I need

solitude. Surely you can understand that I need to be alone.'

He regarded her with veiled eyes. This he could understand. He himself had spent many days and weeks alone when he'd had the need, but he had sought solitude in the wilderness, not amid the clatter of streetcars. 'You do not come to a city to be alone,' he said, his voice heavy with irony.

'There is a house,' she said, 'a big house. You were there last evening. There is a garden behind the house. I stay in my room or sit in the garden. It is very peaceful. I have much time alone.'

'But in your room, how will you get over the death of your parents? You cannot do that by running away from Indian people. If you come back to Indian Territory, you can roam the hills. If you commune with nature there, surely you can confront your fears and absolve your demon feelings.'

'No, Raven Sky. I must be here where I grew up. Please believe me, it is necessary. I would come back with you if I could. I cannot.'

'Do you have feelings for me, Kathleen?'

She looked down. 'Yes, I do. But I am not ready.' She twisted a handkerchief in her lap. 'I cannot promise you that I will ever be. You must not wait for me.' She looked at him, tears glistening in her eyes.

His features hardened. He could be patient, but only if he knew the true reason, and only if he knew how long. 'I can wait for what I want, but I must have some word from you.' He grabbed her hands roughly this time. His words were harsh, impatient. 'You want me, too. You have said so. I have seen the look in your eyes. I have felt your body's response to mine. You cannot deny it.'

'Please,' she said. His anger frightened her, and she stood up.

'I will wait,' he said, rising. 'I will wait two more days for you to give me a sign.'

'No, you mustn't wait. I can't tell you how long it will take.'

Suddenly he grabbed her arms and pulled her close to him, glaring down at her. 'Is there another man? You must tell me if there is another man.'

The pressure on her arms hurt her.

'Tell me,' he demanded.

'No, no. There is no one else.'

Satisfied, he let go of her arm. 'I will wait two days. If you do not give me a sign by then, I will leave.'

She nodded, a lump in her throat, her arm still stinging.

'Now I will take you home.'

'No!'

'You do not want to be seen with me.' He pressed his lips together.

She shook her head. 'It's not that. I simply do not want to cause my hosts to worry. I do not want to bring my problems into their home. Do you understand?'

He regarded her through eyes that had narrowed to slits, but he did not speak.

'Besides,' she said, 'I am not going home.'

'Where are you going?'

She averted her head. 'That is not your concern.'

'You know I could follow you if I wanted to. Even in a city.' His lips curled slightly, and she knew he was referring to his skills as a tracker.

'Yes, you could follow me, but you would be wasting your time.' There was no reason why he should not visit her in the Wagners' home, but she did not want to prolong the painful encounter. It frightened her that she was tempted to surrender herself completely to this man. It made her want to run from him.

'Please, Raven Sky, go back to Indian Territory. You do not belong here.' The words slipped out of her mouth before she realized she'd uttered them.

Rage swept over Raven Sky. For a single moment the two sides of his nature stood in delicate balance. His instincts demanded a savage response. But he had been educated and civilized by his enemy, the white man, and he knew what would happen if he behaved like a savage in this formal setting.

Kathleen felt him tremble on the brink of rage. She summoned her strength. She had to remain in control. If the day ever came when she gave in to him, she would do so willingly and with her whole heart. She did not want to be forced.

'I will send word if my feelings change,' she said.

His eyes met her challenge, and he seemed to restrain the fire that burned in him. She knew she could push him no further, and she suppressed the urge to throw herself into his arms, to press herself against his powerful body. He must meet her on her own terms or not at all.

'Good-bye, Raven Sky.' Her last look at him was one of love. If only he could understand how it made her suffer to leave him.

She walked quickly to the door. Outside she leaned for a moment against the building, fanning herself. Then she jumped nervously as a dirty little street Arab asked her for a penny. Then the hotel doorman helped her into a hansom cab. She glanced back at the little urchin, who was now watching a wealthy-looking couple.

Seeing Raven Sky had brought back all of the old sensations. She never felt so alive with any other man. She thought of Gerald's advances and laughed ironically. She was tempted to turn the buggy around and run back to Raven Sky and say, 'Yes, yes, I am yours.' It would be so easy to throw caution to the wind.

And yet doubts nagged at her. How long would the thrilling feelings last between them? Was their fire enough to sustain a marriage? She still couldn't bring herself to say she wanted to live with an Indian. It would mean spending her life on the frontier, and she was afraid of that. Would just being with Raven Sky make up for everything else she would miss? She didn't think so.

A scream of desperation had begun to build inside her as the cab pulled up before the Wagners' house, and she forced it down. No one was about as she went inside, so she was able to go to her room and be alone.

Once Raven Sky left St. Louis, he would no longer be hers to think of. He would return to Indian Territory and marry someone else. It wouldn't be fair to ask him to wait forever. She had to decide now, for his sake as well as her own.

She sat looking over the garden where rosebushes climbed on trellises, pain gnawing at her. Visions floated before her — visions of the West when she was a child, the death of her parents, coming to this house, Wendall growing up and leaving, Wendall and his new wife, her life at school, then going away. She relived it all as she sat there watching the sunlight fade. Finally there was a knock on the door, and Sissy's small voice called to her.

'Dinner, ma'am. Miz Wagner wants to know if you'll eat something.'

'Yes, Sissy, tell her to set a place for me. I'll be down.' Kathleen rose to change into a lighter gown for dinner. She hoped she could compose her features as easily.

13

Gerald Lange strode out to the garden, where Kathleen was examining a rosebush.

Kathleen raised her head and was about to speak when she saw his angry expression.

'Kathleen Calhoun, I want an explanation.'

She glared at him, stunned. She thought he might have come to apologize for his behavior during the Oktoberfest. Instead, he seemed ready to vent his rage on her. 'What are you talking about?' she demanded.

'Mrs. Wagner told me about this man who came to see you, this Indian. What does he want?'

She opened her mouth to protest, but Gerald began to shout at her.

'Who is this man?' He came closer and grabbed her arm. 'Look here, Kathleen. I haven't been spending all my time hanging around here for nothing.'

'I realize that, Gerald, but I told you how I felt. I've been honest with you.'

'I want to marry you, and I have to know where I stand.'

'Well, this is hardly the way to find out. Are you planning to endear yourself to me by breaking my arm?'

He dropped her arm. 'Can it be possible that this Indian is my rival?'

'Gerald, I told you I only wanted friendship from you.'

His brows drew down in an angry knot. 'I had hoped your feelings would change.'

She shook her head. 'I'm sorry if I've wasted your time, Gerald. I have not changed my mind.'

'It's this Indian, isn't it? I knew there must be someone, but because I didn't see any evidence of another man I let myself believe I had no competition. You are a marriageable woman, and I didn't think you'd refuse me forever. You have to marry someone.'

'Oh, do I?'

'You do if you want a home and family of your own.'

She turned her back on him and walked through the garden to a tall elm tree, pressing her hand to its rough bark. What he said was true, but she hated hearing it.

He took a step toward her, shaking his head in exasperation. 'Kathleen, I don't mean to insult you. If I've made you angry, I'm sorry. I seem to be sorry for a lot of things. I came here to apologize for my behavior the other night. Now I'm not sure it isn't you who should apologize to me.'

She spun around. 'What for?'

Gerald clenched his fists. Just then Nana opened the back door, crossed the veranda, and walked hesitantly down the steps toward them.

'What is it, Nana?' asked Kate, walking toward her.

'I'm sorry. I wouldn't interrupt . . . only he's come. Your visitor. He's in the parlor.'

Kathleen emitted a little gasp, and her eyes flew to the house. She turned and stared in horror at Gerald. The timing couldn't be worse. Gerald stood, his feet braced, his fists clenched.

'I'll go in,' she said. 'Gerald, please wait here.' She hurried up the walk. 'Nana, please wait with Gerald while I speak to Raven Sky.' She stopped and turned, attempting to explain the unexpected visit. 'He is leaving tomorrow. He has probably come to say good-bye.' Then she fled into the house, hoping Nana could keep Gerald occupied.

She slowed her steps as she approached the double doors to the parlor. Raven Sky stood with his back to the open doors. He was dressed in a handsome brown frock coat, his legs slightly apart, his hands locked together behind him.

She took a breath and lifted her chin as he turned. She braced herself. He didn't speak.

His eyes roamed over her, assessing her mood.

His face was relaxed. The only departure from his city dress was the strip of leather he wore around his forehead. He dropped his arms to his sides and took a step toward her.

'I wanted to see you.'

'Yes, Raven Sky.' Her voice was uneven and breathless.

'Have you thought about what you want?'

'Yes.' She looked away.

'Will you come back with me?'

She shook her head, leaning on the doorjamb and looking at the hook rug under his feet. 'I am not ready.'

'Do you want me to wait for you?'

'No, Raven Sky, do not wait for me.'

She raised her head, and as he moved closer, she imagined she could hear the beating of his heart. Or was it her own? He lifted her chin with his fingers.

'Do you mean it?' he asked gently.

There were tears in her eyes when she spoke. 'You wanted my answer. I cannot go with you. You must return to your home.'

His handsome features hardened. 'It will be hard to go back without you.'

His lips were close to hers, and before she knew what she was doing, she had placed her hand on his chest. His eyes flickered, and he slowly bent his head closer, brushing her lips with his. A warm coil of desire began to unfurl itself in her, and in spite of what she knew she should do, she parted her lips, awaiting his kiss — one last treasure to remember him by.

Suddenly footsteps sounded on the parquet floor behind them, and a hand grabbed Raven Sky's shoulder and flung him away from Kathleen. Before he could regain his balance, she rushed forward.

'Gerald!' she cried. She rushed between them, but Gerald pushed her aside, into the love seat.

Raven Sky lunged for Gerald, seizing his lapels. With one powerful thrust, he brought Gerald to his knees, and within seconds the two men were rolling across the floor into the hallway.

Gerald got up on his knees again and twisted Raven Sky's arm behind his back. The Indian grunted and rolled beneath Gerald, tossing him over his head and toward the front door. Gerald landed on the porch, grunting loudly.

'Oh, my God,' Kate muttered, running after them.

Outside, the fight continued. Gerald aimed a fist at Raven Sky's stomach and seemed surprised to encounter a taut, muscular torso.

Gerald's wrist twisted under the impact, and Raven Sky hooked him under the chin and sent him flying across the yard.

'God in heaven!' cried Nana, coming up behind Kate on the porch. 'They'll kill each other!' A small crowd had gathered on the other side of the picket fence.

'Not if I can help it,' Kathleen muttered between clenched teeth. She ran down the steps to try to move in between the struggling pair.

'Gerald, stop!' she screamed. 'There's no reason to fight him.'

Gerald was bruised and out of breath by this time. Raven Sky had sent him sprawling on the ground and was pressing one knee into his chest.

'He was kissing you!' Gerald shouted, trying to break the other man's hold on him. Then, some of his strength returning, he forced Raven Sky off of his chest.

'He's leaving today,' Kathleen yelled to Gerald. Then she stood in Raven Sky's path. 'Please don't hurt him anymore,' she pleaded. 'He is foolish.'

'Who is this man?' sneered Raven Sky, wiping the blood from his lip with the back of his hand.

'He is a friend, that is all.'

'A strange friend.'

'He's upset right now. Please forgive him.' She turned to Gerald, who was pulling himself up. 'Gerald, that's enough. Shake hands, now!'

The two adversaries glared at each other. Gerald clenched a fist. Then, seeing Kathleen's determined glance, he warily extended his hand.

Raven Sky took Gerald's hand in a brief grasp. He stared into the other man's dark brown eyes, assessing him.

Gerald turned deliberately to Kathleen, straightening his shoulders and nodding to her. 'I am at your service, should you need me,' he said. Then he turned on his heel and left, salvaging what pride he could. If Kathleen was going to sully herself with this Indian, it was no concern of his, he thought, grudgingly admitting to himself that the man had been a formidable opponent.

Kathleen wiped her hands on her skirt. 'I'm sorry,' she said, her humiliation complete.

Raven Sky stared down at her, his expression hard. 'You said there was no other man. I cannot believe you would lie to me.'

'There isn't another man. He means nothing to me.'

'Then why was he here?'

'He came to apologize to me for some rude

behavior the other evening. There was a celebration . . . ' She gestured helplessly.

'Did he hurt you?'

'No.'

Raven Sky raised his chin, and Kathleen thought she detected a touch of humor in his eyes. 'He is very jealous.'

She could not help but smile. If she had thought Raven Sky would behave jealously, he surprised her. Obviously he was confident of his own superiority. The thought amused her, in spite of how miserable she felt.

'I suppose he is,' she said. How nice it would be to throw her head back and actually laugh, she thought, to forget everything that had happened and enjoy Raven Sky's company. But she squelched these frivolous feelings. Something deep within her stopped her.

Raven Sky brushed himself off. 'I am weary of the white man's world. I long for the open plains.' He looked at Kathleen almost pityingly. 'You should come home with me. Your brother would be happy to see you.'

'I must stay here. I'm sorry,' she said, shaking her head.

He took her hand and kissed the palm and then her fingers. Kathleen felt pain in her heart and fought to keep the grief back. She loved him. Why couldn't she tell him?

As he turned and walked out the gate, Kate's heart stood still. She ran to the gate, watching him go, feeling suddenly that she would never see him again.

She stood there until he was out of sight in the suddenly quiet yard. Then Nana's footsteps behind her reminded her of what her two suitors had done to the house.

'Oh, Nana, I'm so sorry,' she said, 'I feel so humiliated.'

'My dear, come inside, and don't be sorry. It wasn't your fault.'

Together they went into the house and upstairs to Nana's sitting room, where Ned stood at the doorway.

'That's the way, Kate,' he said. 'You got two fellows knockin' each other down for you. Reminds me of my own youth.' He gave a chuckle.

'Ned,' admonished his wife, 'can't you see the poor girl is upset?'

Ned shook his head and left them, and Nana closed the door.

'Now, my dear,' she said, 'I think we should talk.'

Kate sank to an ottoman next to an overstuffed chair. 'I know, Nana, but I didn't want to burden you with my troubles.'

'It's no burden for me. Sometimes a second viewpoint can help. If an older woman can get over her own desires and prejudices, that is.'

Kate looked at her ruefully. 'I've tried to resolve it alone, but perhaps it would be better to talk about it. What am I to do?'

'You must consult your heart.'

'That's what I have been trying to do, with little success.'

'Don't worry, my dear. Perhaps we can sort it out. But you must tell me all that troubles you. I only have the vaguest of notions.'

'Isn't it obvious? I'm in love with Raven Sky.' She looked down at her hands, blushing. 'But I cannot marry him.'

'Because he is an Indian?'

'Yes.' She looked up. 'Even you were shocked when he first came here, were you not?'

'That I was. But I think I see that there is more to this man than first meets the eye. But what of Gerald? You seem to enjoy being with him. too.'

'I feel as if I ought to love him. He is so eligible, and I'm the envy of all my friends because he pays so much attention to me.' She shrugged. 'A home with Gerald would be lovely, I know. I would have everything.' She shook her head. 'But I cannot marry him either.'

'No?'

'I don't love him, Nana, and I don't think I ever can. I suppose I could have once if . . .' She pressed her lips together.

'If you'd never met Raven Sky?'

She nodded. 'I'm afraid so.'

'Has Raven Sky proposed to you?'

'Yes.' She clasped her hands together. 'But I'm frightened of him. I know it's not rational, but when he comes near me, some instinct within me vibrates with fear.'

'Is it not just the fear of the feelings he creates in you? Perhaps you have never been in love before. It can be a little frightening, dear.'

'It's not just that,' she said slowly. 'I think it's something else. It could be because of the Indians who killed my parents.'

'I see.'

'But there's more. A hazy picture, something I've begun to see recently in my dreams.'

She shut her eyes and conjured up the memory. A man stood over her, a look of concern on his face. As he bent closer she could see he had red skin and black hair. She felt dizzy as if she had fallen, and she felt a pain in her head. She raised her hand to her head.

'There's an Indian,' she said. 'He's picking me up. I'm afraid.' She opened her eyes and looked at Nana.

'Nana, why can't I remember what it is that

frightens me? When I'm near Raven Sky the same fear overcomes me. I don't understand it.'

'Don't worry. You will probably remember it in time. Some memories go very deep. I can see that something holds you back from Raven Sky. I can also see that you love him.' Nana patted her hand.

'Oh, Nana.' Kathleen threw herself into her foster mother's arms. 'I didn't think you and Ned would approve of my loving an Indian.'

Nana smiled gently. 'Perhaps we are not so prejudiced, after all.'

'I feel relieved, Nana, just having talked about it.'

'Of course, dear. You can't keep your fears all bottled up inside you. If you can confront them, they don't hold the same power over you.'

Kate looked at Nana with rounded eyes. 'He said that,' she said softly.

'What's that?'

'Nothing, nothing,' she said, shaking her head.

'Everything will come right in time. I'm sure of it,' Nana said.

'Thank you, Nana. I hope you're right.'

14

November was cold. Icy rain poured down on the city every day for nearly two weeks. Carriages splashed through large puddles, and pedestrians hugged the buildings and fences to keep from getting wet.

At the end of the second week of rain, Kathleen dressed warmly and prepared to leave the house.

'I wish you didn't have to go out in this,' Nana said.

'Don't worry, Nana. It will do me good. I can't stay in the house forever. I need to get out.'

Holding her skirts high to keep them out of the water, she left the house and was just stepping into the waiting hansom cab when a familiar voice called her name.

Gerald Lange was running toward her along the wet sidewalk, holding his hat in the cold wind. The door to the carriage was still open and he caught hold of the edge.

'I was just coming to see you,' he said. 'May I get in? I don't like standing in this drizzle.'

Kathleen moved over. He stepped in, and

the buggy lurched forward.

'Where are we going?' he asked. She could see that the anger of their encounter three weeks before had left him. He was his usual charming self again. Evidently, he had not held a grudge.

'Well, I don't know about we, but I was going downtown to do some shopping,' she said.

'Will you think me impertinent if I come along? I had to see you and apologize.'

Kathleen gave him a half-hearted smile. It wasn't hard to forgive him. She couldn't blame Gerald for what had happened. She had been melancholy since Raven Sky left, and she was almost glad to have Gerald for company again.

'I don't mind your coming along,' she said.

'I wasn't sure what my reception might be,' he said, brushing a hand through his damp hair. 'I don't know why I persist in seeing you, Kathleen. You never offer me any encouragement. But I'm so disappointed in the other women I meet. There's a deeper quality about you that I find compelling. I just can't go away and forget you.'

'You are flattering me, Gerald.'

'I am sorry for the other day. It seems all I do is apologize to you. Will Nana ever forgive me for brawling in her house?'

She laughed. 'I'm sure she will, but I've begun to think that I bring out the worst in you, Gerald.' Then she felt sorry she had teased him. 'I don't think ill of you, if that's what you're afraid of. I know you don't have a bad nature. If it's my forgiveness you want, I accept your apology, but this changes nothing between us.'

'You cannot keep me from hoping, Kathleen. I know you don't love me now, but surely in time you'll see my good qualities.'

She swallowed, wishing he would stop talking of marriage. 'You will be a good husband for someone, but not for me.' She pressed her lips together, hardly understanding why she kept refusing him. She had determined to forget Raven Sky. Why not accept Gerald's proposal?

'Won't you marry someday? You're not meant for a convent,' he said.

She blushed, thinking how her own body responded to Raven Sky's advances — but not to Gerald's. 'No,' she said, 'I am not meant for a convent.'

'I presume that Indian has returned to the hinterlands.'

She turned on Gerald. 'His name is Raven Sky, and he lives in the Creek Nation, Indian Territory. I would appreciate it if you referred to him by name.'

'I'm sorry. I didn't mean to offend you. He and I were never properly introduced, you know.'

Gerald appeared miffed, but Kathleen could not stay angry. She sat in silence, watching him. His dark hair fell across his forehead. The expression in his brown eyes was sincere. His lips were firmly shaped and sensual, his chin firm. Could she love him? Certainly marriage to Gerald would be comfortable, if not exciting. And he did not frighten her the way Raven Sky did. She looked away from him.

She would have to bear his children, and the thought of making love with Gerald did not stir her. It would be a duty, not an act of passion, as she knew it could be. Tears appeared at the corners of her eyes, and she squeezed them shut, trying to make the hurt go away.

When they reached Broadway, Gerald paid the driver, then helped Kathleen out of the cab. Taking her arm, he guided her around a puddle and along the sidewalk. His panache returned as he commented on the displays in shop windows. They walked to the upholstery shop, where Kathleen examined some fabrics Nana needed to cover a pair of wing chairs. She placed the order Nana had given her and asked the shopkeeper to send his wagon for the chairs. Gerald amused himself by running his fingers over the different fabrics lying about. With her errand finished, she turned to him.

'I have to go to the pharmacy now,' she said.

'Very well, and then we shall have some lunch, if you will allow me.'

'We'll see,' said Kathleen.

Outside, Gerald took the curb side to protect Kathleen from splashing mud. He held her elbow to guide her through the crowd.

At the pharmacy, Kathleen ordered medicine for Ned and some herbs and bath salts. Gerald insisted on carrying her packages.

'Now for lunch,' he said as they left the pharmacy.

Kathleen gave in, realizing she was hungry, and he led her along the street until they turned into the dining room of the Southern Hotel, where they checked their coats and packages and followed the headwaiter to a secluded corner. A red rose in a thin crystal vase graced the linen-draped table.

The menu was large, but Kathleen settled on baked chicken, and Gerald ordered roast beef smothered in gravy.

'Gerald, I really should not let you entertain me. You are wrong if you expect anything to come of this.'

'I am patient, Kathleen.'

She relished the food when it came, and after lunch, while they drank coffee, she said, 'Perhaps I should continue my errands alone, Gerald. I don't want to waste your time.'

'You do not waste my time. But if you'd rather be alone, I won't force myself on you.'

'I'm sorry, Gerald. It's just that I feel so hopeless about everything right now. I'm not very good company. But thank you for lunch.'

Gerald paid the check, and they went outside. The rain had stopped, but the sky was still cloudy. He took Kathleen's hand and bowed over it.

'I shall take myself off,' he said in mock sadness. 'But I am at your service. I hope you'll allow me to call every so often. My only other companions are my law books — frightfully boring. I'll take these packages back for you, so you won't be burdened with them.'

'Gerald,' she protested, but he lifted a hand to silence her.

'I insist,' he said. He tipped his hat and left her.

Kathleen continued along the street, feeling even more melancholy. Now she had sent another suitor away. What was wrong with her? Gerald was right. She couldn't avoid marriage forever.

She crossed the street, entered a large dry-goods store, and made her way toward a young woman who stood behind the counter where petticoats and lace drawers were displayed and where mannequins wore complicated bustles made of cotton and metal.

'May I help you?' asked the clerk.

'Yes, I need some new underthings. Perhaps you could show me something in a medium price range.'

The clerk held up a pair of drawers made of silk covered with ruffles and lace. Kathleen ran her fingers over the material, imagining it next to her skin. The sensuous fabric made her skin tingle. Her own cotton things seemed plain by comparison.

'Yes, I'll take these,' she said feeling daring, and gave the woman her size.

'Petticoats are over here, if you'd care to examine them.'

Kathleen spent the better part of an hour selecting delicate frilly underclothes. She was glad Gerald had not accompanied her here. She would have had to make him wait outside.

Thanking the saleswoman for her help, she had her packages wrapped and left the store. Remembering her final errand, she walked toward a bookshop on a side street. As she opened the door, a little bell tinkled overhead. She stood at the door of the little shop where floor-to-ceiling shelves were filled with books.

'Well, well, Miss Kathleen Calhoun.' Herbert Goodmanson rose from his desk and hurried to take her packages from her. 'What can I do for you? How are Ned and Mrs. Wagner? I haven't seen them in some months.' He was a pale little man with a bald pate, lively eyes, and a kind face. He had known Kathleen since she was a child, and the Wagners were among his favorite customers.

'They are both fine,' she said, dropping into the chair he offered her. 'In fact, Ned sent me here to pick up the volume of Wordsworth he ordered.'

'Yes, yes, I have it in the back. Can I offer you some tea? It will take me a moment to locate it.'

'No, thank you, Mr. Goodmanson, I've just had lunch. I'll just browse if you don't mind.'

'Of course, of course, help yourself, and if you find anything else you'd like, just let me know.'

He hurried off to the rear of the store to find the book Ned had ordered, a first edition that would make a handsome addition to the family library.

Kate loved the cozy little shop. Books covered three walls. The front window looked out onto a quiet street lined with elms. She eyed the shelves, divided by subject categories, then got up to examine some of the titles. Her eyes drifted idly over the volumes of poetry, romance, and classics. A section on the American West caught her eye. There were several journals telling of explorers' travels, and there were some early diaries.

She picked up a collection of photographs of the frontier and flipped through the pages. It all looked so familiar. There were pictures of wagons loaded with goods and families traveling west. There were many pictures of California during the great gold strike. In another section, outlaws posed for their portraits with their weapons. She recognized some of the names of some men who hid out in Indian Territory, among them the Indian bandit, Sam Starr.

Kathleen paused, struck by the photograph. The sober-looking Indian outlaw seemed to stare out of the portrait at her. Something about him held her attention. Then the association clicked in her mind. The foggy image she had seen so often in her dreams suddenly returned. Sam Starr's face disappeared before her eyes, and the hazy memory took its place . . .

An Indian looked down at her, an expression of concern in his eyes. He spoke in an Indian tongue. When she cried out, he comforted her. Then the picture was gone, leaving her puzzled. She could remember nothing else.

'That's a fine collection of photographs. Would you like it?' Kathleen was jolted out of her reverie.

'No, no. It just made me think about something else.' She replaced the collection on the shelf, and the bookseller handed her the package for Ned.

'Thank you, Mr. Goodmanson. Ned will be pleased.'

'Give my regards to him and Nana.'

'I will.'

She left the shop in a daze. What was this strange picture she saw in her memory? She was almost certain it wasn't all imagination. The picture persisted as she walked into the street to find a cab.

As she rode home she started to recall other things — events that had taken place when she was very young. She saw her parents laughing and playing with her as she toddled on the wood-plank floor, making sounds that approximated words. She became so lost in the world of the past, that she was only vaguely aware of the carriage as it jogged along.

The scene changed, and she saw flames — tall, shooting flames that seemed to leap up into the sky. Against the fire, dark trees stood like black sentinels trying to halt the advance of the rushing inferno. Men ran about and shouted. Kathleen was alone in the room. The front door stood open.

Kathleen had been taught as a child that a prairie fire was one of the greatest threats to the Kansas pioneers. Dried grasses in summer burned like tinder. Countless times her mother would get up in the middle of the night to look at the horizon, trying to detect the light in the distance that preceded the licking flames.

Kathleen was too young to understand the threat, but she was terrified by the flames and by the blast of heat that burst through the open door. Wendall, who had been left to tend her while their parents fought the fire, had run outside to haul buckets of water from the nearby stream.

Kathleen took a step forward and fell over her trailing nightgown. Hitting her head on the floor, she let out a wail.

A band of friendly Indians had gathered near the house. They had come to the Calhoun house to offer their help. An old warrior, hearing the child cry and seeing the open door, went inside to investigate. He moved toward Kathleen and reached to comfort her.

Just then Kathleen's mother appeared in the doorway. Agitated by the fire, seeing the breech-clad Indian hovering over her child she thought the worst. Mary Calhoun had no second thoughts. She reached outside the door for the ax, swung it over her head, and let it fly.

Only the warrior's last-second sidestep kept his skull from being sliced in two. The razor-sharp ax sliced at his ear with a mighty blow, and he screamed, dropping Kathleen to the floor.

Blood dripped on Kathleen. Screams erupted everywhere. Wendall rushed inside, pale and horrified. Her mother reached for her, and then all was darkness . . .

Kathleen leaned against the inside of the carriage, trembling. She looked down at her gloved hand on the door handle and realized that the motion of the hansom cab had stopped.

Sissy ran down the walk to carry the packages to the house. Kathleen, still trembling, went to her room and splashed cold water on her face. She raised her head and stared at herself in the oval mirror, shocked by her agitated, pale look.

The photograph of the Indian outlaw had

triggered the recollection that had been so long hidden from her. She shuddered, recalling the violence, but the memory of the incident was important. She toweled her face dry and sat down on her bed, staring at the yellow print wall paper, feeling as if a burden had been lifted from her.

Raven Sky's words came back to her. 'If you could name your fear, you could master it.' Nana had said the same thing, reminding her that if she could confront her fears, they couldn't hold the same power over her.

Now it was clear how she had become afraid of Indians. As a tiny girl, she hadn't known what was happening. All she could see was blood, all she heard was screaming, when she had looked into the Indian's face. But he hadn't been trying to hurt her. He was there to help. The fear and pain she had experienced had stayed buried in her memory all this time.

Relief swept over her. Her childhood fears and the savage murder of her parents were falling into proper perspective for the first time. And all this had a great deal to do with her feelings for Raven Sky. She could see clearly for the first time how her fear of Indians had kept her from him. She had grown up with the prejudices against Indians common among women of her class. And the violence she had experienced on the prairie had only reinforced those values.

But times were changing. The Civilized Tribes had spawned many men like Raven Sky, leaders of their nations, men with strong individual personalities. She felt she was seeing Raven Sky for the first time — as himself, without the ingrained fears and prejudices that had forced her to judge him not as a man who loved her, but as an Indian. The word itself had triggered deeply buried memories every time she saw him.

No longer afraid, she felt suddenly stronger. She saw the Creek Indians for the first time as the peaceable people they really were, unlike the warring Cheyenne.

Nana tapped on the door and came in. She looked at Kathleen in surprise.

'Nana, I've decided to go home.'

Nana had thought the tears at the corners of Kate's eyes were from grief, but she saw now that they were tears of relief.

'If that is what you've decided, dear, then you must. Of course, I'd love to see you settled in St. Louis, but I will never stand in the way of your wishes. You must go where your heart is.'

'Yes, Nana. Oh, yes.' She sat on the bed and took Nana's outstretched hands. Her eyes sparkled as she said, 'I know where my heart is now. It's on the prairie.'

'Then you should return there. I know Wendall and Molly will be glad to have you back.' Nana left her alone with her thoughts.

Sitting there, Kathleen realized something else. She had missed the comforts of St. Louis and the trappings of civilization, and certainly the Wagners' house had provided a retreat from the wilderness. But now she felt another longing, one that would never be satisfied in these surroundings. She had become attuned to the wide open spaces, the cries of animals on the prairie, the music of the cicadas.

Life here was civilized, but she would grow tired of it eventually. How many parties could she attend without growing bored? How much of Lori's chatter could she take? Marriage to Gerald Lange? Pleasant perhaps, but it would not be enough for her. Not nearly enough.

The spark within her had been kindled by life on the prairie. It would not be extinguished by a return to the old life she had known here. In a rush she realized that she had grown up. Life had raced on, and she had to keep in step. Face flushed, heart beating quickly, she began to pack, needing to act on her decision immediately.

She didn't allow herself to think about the

fact that she had sent Raven Sky away. She did not consider the possibility that he might not wait for her. She packed her dresses and personal belongings. Then she took the new underthings out of the brown paper packages and laid them carefully in the suitcases.

A sliver of a thought flashed through her mind: if she married, dark strong hands would remove these delicate underthings from her body. Trembling, she disciplined her mind to stop such thoughts, kept her herself busy with the packing.

15

December brought harsh weather to Indian Territory. The cold spell began with a snowstorm which was followed by icy rains and sleet. Water froze on the ground and on the trees. Icicles hung from barbed-wire fences. It was the worst storm ever, and Wendall was worried about the thousands of cattle in his grazing lands.

Kathleen and Molly kept the fires burning in the stone fireplaces. Hank and Tex had their hands full chopping and drying wood when they weren't riding out in the snow in search of the cattle. The kitchen was the warmest room in the ranch house, the center of activity.

Kathleen stacked the warming pans by the fireplace. Later in the evening she would fill the pans with hot coals and use them to warm the ice-cold sheets before they went to bed.

Molly came into the kitchen just as Wendall stomped onto the porch and shook off the snow. She held the door for him. 'How does it look?' she asked.

'Bad. Most of the cattle can't find shelter.

Some of them are huddled in the vacant log cabins. The rest are in danger of freezing to death, and we can't get the feed to 'em.'

'Have you heard from any of the other ranchers?' asked Kathleen.

'Jack Carlton lost some of his horses in the ravine east of the Brady Hotel,' he said. 'The herds on Osage land can't get any food. Their owners were counting on winter undergrowth to keep 'em alive. I doubt a thousand of 'em will pull through.'

'How many cattle on the Osage land?' asked Molly.

Wendall sat down by the fire and pulled off his boots. 'Maybe five thousand.'

'How are things in town?' asked Kathleen. Neither she nor Molly had ventured off the ranch since the storm began a week ago.

'The stores are doing a landslide business in overshoes,' he said. 'But the trains can't get through. They're digging out the tracks now, but it looks like we're in for more snow.'

'Any danger of our supplies being cut off?' asked Molly.

'We're all right for a while. I doubt this will last more than another week.'

Kathleen had been back on the ranch for nearly a month. She hadn't written ahead, figuring she could travel as fast by rail as a letter could. So when she had arrived at the

263

little Tulsa depot, there had been no one to meet her. She had borrowed a wagon at the Dwayne Store and made the long, cold ride to the ranch, where Molly had cried at the sight of her. When Wendall came in from the range that day, he had beamed at his little sister.

It felt wonderful to be back on the ranch. Above her the big sky stretched on forever, and the fresh smells reminded her she was no longer in the crowded city. She enjoyed a certain freedom here that she didn't feel anywhere else.

But Raven Sky was nowhere to be found. She'd sent a message to his father's home and had later learned that he had not yet returned home after transacting the business in St. Louis. He had sent his family word that he was going on a journey.

She had been very disappointed, although she knew better than to hope he had waited for her. Slowly she had told Molly and Wendall everything that had happened. Molly had listened wide-eyed to the account of the fight between Gerald and Raven Sky. Kathleen could read the mixed feelings that registered in their eyes.

Molly said, 'I'm glad you've resolved your feelings, Kate, and you know we're glad to see you back on the ranch.' She'd glanced at

264

Wendall quickly. 'I'm sure Raven Sky is a fine man, Kathleen,' she went on, 'if you're sure it's what you want.'

Kathleen had shrugged helplessly and gazed at the black night outside the parlor windows. 'It doesn't matter now, does it? I've lost both of them. First Gerald, now Raven Sky. I must be determined to throw my life away.'

'Oh, Kate, don't say that,' said Molly. 'Raven Sky will return when he learns you're here.'

'How can he know that?'

'Well, you sent word to the tribe, didn't you? The chiefs will let him know you've asked for him. He'll know why, won't he?'

Kathleen shook her head. 'I don't know about that, Molly. But thank you for looking on the bright side.'

Molly had given her a sympathetic look. Then the corner of her mouth had turned up in a grin. 'I remember Gerald. He was the kind of beau every girl dreamed about.'

'He remembers you throwing snowballs at him,' said Kathleen, smiling, thinking of Raven Sky. She couldn't blame him. She had sent him away, and he might not accept her now. His pride had been hurt, his feelings trampled on. But, with a shred of hope, she would wait for him to return. Surely he would come back to his home. It might be too late, but the love she carried in her heart drove her to seek him out. She had come all this distance. At least she wanted to talk to him. But she would have to wait until she heard news of him. Once again, she remembered his telling her that if she could name her fear she would become master of it. He would surely understand that she had finally done so.

Meanwhile, the storm raged on. The Calhouns did what they could to help the others in the area, but as the days dragged on, it was clear that the smaller ranches would not survive. Even after the snow stopped, the ground remained frozen for several weeks. As cattle died, ranchers around them went broke, threw in their lot. It looked as if only Wendall and Jack Carlton, both of whom had plenty of money in St. Louis banks, would pull through.

Kathleen wondered where Raven Sky could be in this cold. The clever Indian knew how to survive the elements no matter where he was, and he might be far away, out of the reach of the storm. Still, she worried and wondered if he knew she was here. Perhaps he just didn't want to see her anymore. Maybe he had given up on her and decided he would be better off with a woman from his own tribe.

The joy Kathleen had felt as she returned home was slowly eroded by doubt and finally turned to sorrow. Each night watching Molly and Wendall comfort each other, she envied the warmth they shared. Kathleen felt lonely in her cold bed. The coals of the warming pan did not warm her heart. Only the strong, tender hands of a Creek could do that.

The cold months dragged on. Each day was much the same as the next. Kathleen dismissed the idea of teaching in this weather. Though she was an excellent horsewoman, she could not face the hardship of the ride into town and back every day.

Kathleen stayed on the ranch through January and most of February. Then, late in February, the snow and ice melted enough to allow Wendall to drive Molly and Kate to church, where they greeted townspeople they had not seen for weeks and eagerly caught up on the news. Illness reduced the numbers of the congregation, and the harsh storm had claimed at least one life, but many voices rose in the echoing room of the little whitewashed building.

Kathleen joined the others in singing a hymn of thanksgiving, but her mind was only half focused on the sermon. She kept remembering Raven Sky standing in the doorway of the schoolroom. She saw him in her mind's eye, in his tight denim jeans and the white shirt that accented his dark skin.

'Purify your hearts,' the preacher's voice intoned, jolting Kathleen back to the present. 'Beware the heathen influence.' The Reverend Mr. Haworth was delivering a particularly bitter sermon today. Having recently become more alarmed than usual at the laxity among the native Indians, he had started a campaign to stamp out their old religion. Many Indians still practiced their ancient beliefs while pretending to accept Christianity, and Mr. Haworth was afraid for their souls. 'The heathen Indians mouth Christianity because to do so is politically advantageous,' he lectured. 'But I fear greatly that in their hearts they do not accept Christ as their Savior.'

He also feared for the rough little community of Tulsa. Isolation from federal authorities had increased lawlessness. Cowboys and railroad men coming into town invariably gambled and fought. More and more private citizens had to take cover from the random gunfire that erupted in the street. Tulsa had become a rough town, and the Reverend Mr. Haworth feared he wasn't doing his job well enough.

Thus, the accusing sermon this morning. He admonished the whites to serve as examples for the Indians. 'When the Indians, who are children of our civilization, see white men behaving in a reckless manner, they brand us hypocrites, and rightly so,' preached the minister. He leaned forward on his lectern as if his beady eyes could reach into the conscience of every person present. 'Study the Ten Commandments and live piously,' he reminded them.

The sermon over, the Calhouns rose and went to shake hands with their neighbors, and Kathleen sought out Joy, for they had seen each other only once since Kate's return.

'Oh, Kate, there you are,' said the vibrant Irish woman. 'How is everything at the ranch?' Her red hair gave off highlights in a winter sun that was doing its best to brighten the windy day. Joy was thinner, probably a result of the work she'd done helping the Indians whose livestock had suffered in the storm. She'd helped gather supplies for volunteers to take on horseback to those who couldn't get to town and had run out of food.

'We're all right, Joy. We've been luckier than some.'

'Do you think you'll be able to return to the school soon?'

'I hope so, Joy. Maybe when the weather gets better, I'll be able to ride into town again.' Kathleen hoped so, for her mind longed for a challenge, and her heart grieved.

Noting Kathleen's pallor, Joy asked, 'Are you getting enough rest? You look pale.'

'It isn't rest I need.'

Joy lowered her voice. 'There's no news of Raven Sky, then?' She looked anxiously at her friend's drawn face, for Kathleen had told her how things were.

'No.' Kathleen looked away. 'I suppose I shouldn't expect to hear. I'll probably never see him again.' She had been too overcome by the loss, and by her own bad timing, to allow pride to keep her from talking about it to Molly and Joy. It had become harder and harder to maintain hope.

She tried to turn the attention from herself. 'How do you manage to look so well, Joy, after all you've done here?'

The other woman shrugged. 'I learned the hard way, Kate.'

Kate squeezed Joy's hand. She knew the pretty teacher could remarry if she wanted to, but working with the children seemed to be enough reward, for the time being.

'I have my job,' Joy said. 'I went through great sadness when my husband died. I'll never forget the loneliness of that first year, Kate, but at least I was able to open my heart to others. Out here you can't isolate yourself.' She spoke so low that only Kathleen could hear. 'I knew long ago that you loved Raven Sky. I could see it in the way you looked at him. But . . . ' She paused, pressing her lips together. 'If he doesn't return, don't shut yourself off from life.'

Kathleen smiled in appreciation. 'You're right, Joy. I'll remember your words. And as soon as the weather breaks, I'll come to teach again.'

The women separated to talk with other neighbors. Then Kate rejoined Molly and Wendall to return to the ranch.

It was a slow ride, as the roads were still muddy. Kate remembered riding home this way after Wendall and Molly had been feted at the church. She had known that Raven Sky was watching. Her feelings now were as frozen as the ground under the carriage wheels. She knew that Raven Sky was nowhere near, for if he were, she would have felt his presence.

She looked out over the cold countryside. The river ran high because of the melting snow and ice. Many of the farmers already feared flooding. Here and there the surviving cattle dotted the landscape, a small scattering compared to the large herds that usually covered the grazing land.

Along the road, branches had fallen under the weight of snow, and the trees looked

271

barren. Kathleen shivered. The landscape was stripped of all warmth and so was she.

One day led to the next, and the ranch struggled to recover. Every day the sun shone a little longer, giving the hard ground the energy it needed for growing things. Gradually life was returned to earth, and in late March, plants and grasses began to turn green. Molly, too, shared in the renewal of life, for she discovered she was pregnant.

One afternoon Kathleen and Molly were working in the vegetable plot some distance from the house. Wendall had planted trees around the garden to provide shade in the summer when the sun parched the land.

The ground was damp from the wet spring, so the seeds they planted would grow fast. The women bent over their furrows, pulling out weeds and refuse to make room for the little seeds, talking to relieve the tedium of the work.

'I'm so glad the winter's behind us,' Molly said. 'I wonder if we'll ever have another as bad as that.'

'I've certainly never seen the likes of it,' Kate commented. They were both silent for a moment, tugging and digging as they worked their way along.

Molly straightened, leaning on the rake to catch her breath. She gazed at Kathleen, still bent over the ground. 'Have you heard from Gerald Lange?' she asked. She knew Kate corresponded with him irregularly.

Kathleen rose and retied the bandanna that held her hair back out of her face. 'I've heard from him,' she said, shaking her head. 'I don't understand why he still writes, although I suppose I'm guilty of encouraging it. His letters are entertaining, and answering them gives me something to do. Still, he ought to forget me and marry someone else.'

'I guess he can't forget you,' Molly said.

Kate shook her head. 'How oddly things turn out. I like Gerald as a friend, but that is all.' She looked out over the land. 'I've no word from Raven Sky, but I can't forget him, Molly.'

Molly observed her sister-in-law silently. Finally she asked, 'So you still feel the same?'

'Yes, Molly, I'm afraid I do. Why?'

Molly frowned at the ground and said. 'I heard a rumor about him. They say he's returned.'

'Molly, why didn't you tell me?' She wiped her hands on her calico dress.

'I know I should have. I guess I wanted to be sure it was true.'

Kate had a queasy feeling beneath her ribs. 'When did you hear it?'

'After church yesterday.'

He was back in Indian Territory. Yet he had not come to see her. To Kathleen that meant he did not want to see her anymore.

She had insulted him by refusing him, and he would not give her a second chance. She glanced at Molly, who looked as if she wanted to say something else. 'What is it Molly?'

'They say he is betrothed.'

Kathleen felt as if someone had hit her full in the face. 'It can't be,' she whispered, slumping to her knees, the seeds in her hands rolling helter-skelter on the ground.

Molly dropped to her side. 'I was afraid to tell you. I guess I'd half hoped you'd gotten over him. Your letters from Gerald sound so nice, and life has been so hard for you here. Oh, dear, now I've made it worse.'

Kathleen's face was white, and she felt as if someone had wrapped a hand around her heart, cutting her off from her surroundings.

'You've done nothing wrong, Molly,' she said when she found her voice. 'I'm the one to blame. I lost my chance. How cruel fate is. If I'd accepted Raven Sky when he loved me, I wouldn't have lost him. Now I've ruined everything for myself, and he'll never look at me again. Oh, Molly.' Tears spilled over. 'Why is love so hard?' She sobbed into Molly's shoulder unashamedly while her sister-in-law held her. Finally she took a few deep breaths and sat up.

'When will he marry?' she asked.

'I don't know.'

Kathleen stared blankly about her. How would she live here now? How could she stay where the very ground and sky reminded her of the man who permeated her heart and mind. She wanted to scream and pound her fists on the ground. Covering her face with her hands, she let the tears spill forth. Finally she raised her head and looked at her sister-in-law. 'I'm sorry for behaving this way, Molly. Thank you for telling me about it. You may have saved me from some embarrassment. I'll try to get over it.' She dried her tears with the hem of her dress. It would be hard to lock up her broken heart. She could not even hope that it would mend, but she could shut it away in a secret part of her where it would not be revealed to anyone, least of all to Raven Sky, if she ever saw him again.

She leaned down and began gathering the seeds that had spilled. Forcing a little laugh for Molly's sake, she said, 'We'd better straighten these seeds. If the rows are crooked, the plants will choke each other when they grow.'

Molly looked despairing, and Kathleen

knew she felt sorry for her. She didn't want her pity. She was tired of being a burden to everyone. She would have to take her personal problems off the ranch — even if that meant marrying Gerald, if he hadn't given up on her.

She clenched her fists. Every time she looked at Molly and her brother, she would be reminded that she had not found happiness in the arms of a husband. She threw herself into the gardening with renewed vigor. She needed to clear her mind. Then she would decide what to do.

Slowly her impulse to run away receded, and she realized that she needn't act hastily. Molly and Wendall had made it abundantly clear that she was welcome on the ranch. But she wouldn't make a lifetime of it. She'd developed a habit of running away from things, and she had decided not to do that again. She would see this through, somehow.

After a while, she remembered that Molly had only heard a rumor. What if it wasn't true? She would first have to find out if Raven Sky really was betrothed. If he was, she would reconsider Gerald Lange's offer of marriage. She did not want to marry him, but she didn't feel right imposing on her brother or the Wagners forever. She needed a home to call her own.

Of course, she could work, like Joy, and board with someone, but the thought of living in Tulsa and seeing Raven Sky was too painful to consider at the moment. At least if she married Gerald, she would live in St. Louis, and eventually she would have children. She felt a slight dryness in her throat as she considered it.

She wanted children. She knew that now. She wanted to see life passed on to the next generation. She hoped that her children would grow up to be pioneers, too, to carry on what she and her generation had started in building the country.

'It's noon,' called Molly, coming back along the row she had planted. 'I think we should go in. The men will be wanting their meal.'

The sun had climbed in the sky. Though it was March, the day felt warm with the promise of spring.

They went in to prepare the meal. Wendall rode in from checking fences and came up the back steps and into the kitchen. Molly's silent glance told him that she had told Kate about Raven Sky.

Wendall gave his wife a slight nod and went on into the dining room. He trusted that Kathleen's feelings for the Indian would eventually fade. Time healed. He had only to look at his beloved Molly to know this. He had loved Amanda, his first wife, but his heart had mended and he had learned to love again.

★ ★ ★

After leaving St. Louis, Raven Sky had wandered far and wide. He was reluctant to return to Tulsa. Pride at having been unsuccessful in bringing back the wife he desired kept him on the move. He traveled northwest, into the mountains of Colorado and Wyoming Territory. He wintered alone, relying on his skills as hunter and tracker. He cleansed his soul and strengthened his body. He came down out of the mountains a man who could live close to nature, the way his people had in the generations before him in the hills of the Southeast, before the white man had taken their land.

He returned home because his people needed him. It was time for him to take an Indian wife. His heart still belonged to Kathleen, but he would not show his feelings again. He must master them instead. His tenderness had turned to bitterness as he built a shell around his love. He had hardened himself to the disappointment.

He had wanted to share himself. He knew

that man and woman could become one, and he was ready to give of himself physically and spiritually, but Kathleen had rejected him. He would not let himself suffer that humiliation again.

No one would ever know his pain. He would marry a suitable maiden, perhaps sealing a political relationship with another clan within the tribe.

Deciding what was the best avenue, he paid a visit to an old friend of his father's, Jno Loughridge of the Euchee Creeks. These Indians had isolated themselves from the rest of the Creek Nation. They spoke their own dialect, and almost no English. Raven Sky communicated with them through sign language and the few words of their dialect he knew.

Jno welcomed him to the farm where his family raised corn and hogs. Raven Sky spent nearly a month in the settlement, finding it a comfort to be in a real Creek community after living near Tulsa, with its cowboys, outlaws, traders, and gamblers. Here life was carried on in the traditional manner. The Euchees rigidly observed the old unwritten laws. Their language cut them off from outside influences, and they could refuse for a while longer to accept the notion that the Indians of this land were a conquered people.

Raven Sky walked with Jno among the

brush arbors that enclosed the village square. In the background was the log hut where sacred utensils were stored. Raven Sky was considering the older man's suggestion that he marry his daughter, a pretty olive-skinned maiden of sixteen.

'She is docile and trained in the ways of a homemaker,' Jno said.

The girl had caught Raven Sky's eye as she served meals in Jno's home but in spite of his plans, he was not ready for a final commitment. Not wanting to insult his elder, he said, 'I have not yet decided to marry.'

'It will strengthen the relations between our people,' the old Indian said. 'You are a young man. You need a wife for your home. You cannot rely on aunts and cousins to take care of your homemaking needs forever. They cannot warm your bed. My daughter will get you many sons.'

Raven Sky glanced at the perceptive old man. 'It is true that I want sons to pass on our heritage.' It was also true that his sexual nature cried out for a mate. He was not meant to be celibate.

He raised his chin, gazing along the logs laid lengthwise under the arbors for ceremonial meetings.

'I will consider what you have offered,' he said.

16

Kathleen pinned her hair up, donned a freshly ironed cotton dress, and tied her straw bonnet under her chin. Then she climbed into the wagon and headed for Tulsa to pick up supplies for the ranch.

As the horses jogged down the road, the wild cacophony of fowls gathered at the slough told her that spring had arrived.

She sat straight as the wagon rumbled past the shacks at the edge of town. Children scattered before her, and she drove past a shabby-looking old-timer leaning against the corner of a building. Even though it was early in the day, the tinkle of the player piano drifted toward her from the Tulsa Hotel.

Jesse Smith, who had been cool to her since her return from St. Louis, was shelving merchandise in the rear of Dwayne's General Store when she entered. He looked around at her and apparently decided to let her wait until he had finished his task. Then he dusted off his hands and approached her.

Mr. Dwayne came up to her at the same moment. 'Morning, Miss Calhoun,' he said, sorting through a stack of mail and handing her a white envelope postmarked St. Louis.

'Thank you, Mr. Dwayne,' she said. 'And how are Mrs. Dwayne and the girls?'

'They're just fine, ma'am. I'm sure Sarah would like to see you any time. You just stop by the house.' He smiled, proud as always of his family.

'Thank you, I'll do that.'

She turned to the window for light, opened the letter, and scanned its contents briefly. Seeing it was only a newsy letter from Lori Banfield, she started to fold it up again.

Jesse came up behind her and was straining to see what she was reading. She dropped the letter to her side.

'News?' asked Jesse, rocking forward.

'A letter,' she said, trying to control the irritation in her voice. 'Jesse, I've come for some supplies.'

'Of course, Miss Calhoun. What may I help you with?' She ignored his formality, knowing he was only trying to annoy her.

'I need some honey, a half-dozen sacks of flour, and some sewing needles. If you'll show me what you have, I'll choose the needles myself. Then I want to look at a new saddle for Monty.'

Jesse moved about the shelves getting the honey and locating some needles to show Kathleen. While he busied himself, she drifted near some Creek women who were browsing through the store with their children. It was a small chance, but she might hear some gossip about Raven Sky. The women — dressed in prairie clothes like herself but wearing long braids and moccasins — spoke a mixture of English and Creek, punctuated with much laughter. At the end of the conversation, she heard one woman giggle and say something about the town chief's son. Kathleen moved closer, but she caught nothing more.

She went over to the saddles, inhaling the strong scent of leather. When the warm weather came she would be able to ride out farther on her own, and she needed a new saddle. She rubbed the smooth, hard leather of the seat, wondering if there was a way to find out what she wanted to know.

'How is business, Jesse?' she asked when he came near.

'What do you mean?'

'Since the thaw, has the store been busy?'

Jesse shrugged. 'Usual.'

'Much trading with the Indians?'

'Usual.' He frowned at her. 'Why all the questions? You haven't been this interested in my business since . . . ' He stopped.

'Since I saw Raven Sky here that day,' she finished for him bluntly. She knew what Jesse thought about her behavior, but it didn't matter. She could easily suffer a little hurt pride if it meant getting the information she wanted.

'Yes,' Jesse said, averting his gaze.

'I just thought the Creek community might be very busy now,' Kate persisted.

'Why?'

She summoned her courage. 'Because I heard that Raven Sky has been betrothed.'

'Oh, I see. Well, for your information, Miss Busybody, I know nothing about it. If Raven Sky is betrothed, no one would bother to tell me. And I'd appreciate it if you didn't come here just to snoop around and pick up gossip.'

'I'm sorry,' said Kathleen. 'If that's the way you feel about it, I'll pass the time of day elsewhere. It's clear you've got better things to do than waste time with me.' She picked up her purchases and walked out the door, calling over her shoulder, 'Charge this to Wendall's account.'

Jesse hurried toward the door, then he stopped and shook his head. He didn't follow her out.

Outside, history repeated itself. As Kate stepped outside the store, she halted, heart in her throat, and stared into the face of Raven Sky. He stood tall and proud at the edge of

284

the boardwalk, near the spot where she had tied her horse.

Kate stood stone-still, unaware of anything around her. She had hoped for news of Raven Sky, but she had not expected to see him like this. It had been nearly five months since she had set eyes on his face, but she had memorized every part of it. He had not changed, except for an even haughtier lift to his chin and a new coolness in his dark gaze.

Raven Sky had seen Kathleen's wagon tied up in front of the store. He knew she had returned to her brother's ranch, but he had not tried to see her.

Staring at her now as she emerged from the store, he realized he might as well never have gone away. Here in the living, breathing flesh was the woman he had tried to forget.

The long, cold months of indecision, disappointment, and frustration all surged through his mind at once, and when she stepped into his path, she became a ready target for his anger. Her fresh beauty further angered him. He assumed that she planned by now to marry someone else, and he stared at her with lips tightly drawn, his face a mask of suppressed violence.

'Raven Sky,' Kathleen murmured, her voice trembling with the shock of seeing him after the long, lonely winter. There was anger in his eyes, but the sight of him still jolted her senses in the same old way. A rush of feeling coursed through her, making her want to reach out and smooth the anger from his normally gentle face.

'Why did you come back here?' he said, his lips still tight, the tone harsh.

She lowered her eyes, stung by his rudeness. Even her small hopes were dashed. 'Raven Sky,' she said, 'I am sorry for what I said to you.'

'You mock me, woman.'

'I am not mocking you.' She dared to take a step closer. 'I want to talk to you. I have heard that you are betrothed.'

Raven Sky had observed her downcast eyes, her surprise at seeing him. Even now she looked uncomfortable in his company, embarrassed at seeing him again. Some vengeful part of him wanted to hurt her as she had hurt him. He had to see if she had any feeling for him left.

Raising his chin he said, 'I have been offered a Euchee princess for a wife. The union would benefit our people.'

His words cut Kathleen to the quick, but she fought down the fear in her stomach and stood straight. His arrogance and harshness left no room for doubt that he did not care for her anymore. Daggers cut into her when she remembered his tender touch, his lips on hers. The thought that he would make love to another woman filled her with jealousy and pain. She had to end the interview quickly. Looking at him now only reminded her of what she had lost.

Fearing her own actions, she ran down the steps and threw her packages into the back of the wagon, then rushed blindly up the street.

Seeing her turn her back on him enraged Raven Sky. He had spoken harshly, but his native instincts told him she should be punished for her behavior. How much she had promised with her eyes and her body. But she had run back to St. Louis, that evil city, and betrayed him. Now, shamelessly, she had returned to his territory to torment him.

Kathleen walked briskly to the edge of town, her chest heaving and tears staining the front of her dress. She leaned on a sycamore tree and gave vent to her tears out of earshot of passers-by.

Hearing thundering hooves, she turned quickly.

The red stallion was bearing down on her, its furious whinny seeming to echo Raven Sky's own runaway emotions. Kathleen cowered near the peeling bark of the sycamore, steadying herself against the sturdy trunk. The stallion reared, its hooves thrusting before her.

Raven Sky stared down at her white face, her hair tangled by the breeze, her heaving breasts beneath the thin fabric of her dress. His turbulent emotions bested him. He would have her now. No woman would dare do to him what she had done. He thought of her being bedded by some future husband, and he cursed. He would take her first. She would not reach her wedding night a virgin. She still belonged to him, for his soul claimed her.

He leapt off the horse and strode toward her. Seizing her in his arms, he picked her up and threw her across the back of his horse, then leaped on behind her. He touched the stallion's ribs and the horse sped across the open countryside.

Nettie Dawson, wife of a railroad clerk, was hanging laundry in the backyard when she saw an Indian in buckskins throw a seemingly lifeless form over his horse and ride away.

Gasping, she ran inside and yanked her son off his chair.

'Run to the store, Jimmy! Get Mr. Dwayne. Tell him to raise a posse. The Indians have just run off with a white woman. Now, run!' She pushed him out the door, then got her husband's shotgun and sat down to pray. She had always feared an Indian uprising against the whites who were invading their territory. Oh, merciful heaven, she thought, they should never have come to this godforsaken place.

Jimmy ran to town, not stopping until he located Mr. Dwayne. Breathless, Jimmy blurted, 'Mr. Dwayne, my ma says the Indians just took off with a white woman!' He pointed in the direction he had come. 'That way.'

J.P. rubbed his chin and considered. Then his glance fell on Kathleen's wagon. 'That's Miss Calhoun's wagon,' he said. Heavy boots thumped on the porch as men came to see what was the trouble. 'Wonder if there could be somethin' to this.'

Jesse emerged from the store. 'If it's Kathleen,' he said behind J.P., 'she's been askin' for it. I wouldn't bother to go after the likes of her.'

'Might get ourselves into a peck of trouble,' said Ray Farnsworth, a railroad man. No one wanted to start trouble with the Indians if it wasn't warranted.

'We might just have a look-see,' another trader offered. 'If Miss Kathleen's in trouble, her brother'd be mighty mad if we didn't find out.'

Within seconds, a group of men had

gathered in the middle of Main Street. On their way out of town they stopped at the Dawson house to question Nettie, then moved on.

Kathleen was nearly senseless by the time Raven Sky stopped near the cave, still beyond thought and determined to spend his fire on her.

He dragged her off the horse and into the cave, leading the stallion in behind him. He carried Kathleen deep into the cave and laid her on the ground beside the pool. He stripped off his buckskin suit, and stood over her naked except for his breechclout. Then he splashed cool water from the pool onto his skin to wash away the perspiration. The water had a soothing effect, and he trickled some on Kathleen's brow.

He wanted to enjoy this woman, willfully, controlling every move, but he would make her enjoy it as well. He would make her regret rejecting him.

Kathleen opened her eyes and stared at Raven Sky, a mixture of surprise and fear tingling along her spine. But the fear was different now. No longer fearful of Indians, she feared only this man's anger.

'Raven Sky, listen to me,' she pleaded, but he came to her and made her lie back, his expression silencing her.

290

Her heart raced from the exertion of the ride, and now his nearness stirred her senses to a fever pitch. She could only emit a small sound in her throat as she felt the shock of his touch. Before she realized what he was doing, his nearly naked body lay over hers, his hands on her shoulders.

'Ah, my little bird, you look at me in surprise,' he said. 'But I see passion in your eyes. I see that you cannot hide it. That is good, for I want to you to feel me as I take you.'

She was too surprised to struggle as he pulled her clothing to her waist and then lower. He exhaled a sharp breath as he gazed at her white, rounded breasts, and she felt him tremble. He quickly bent to taste her nipple with his mouth. Her mind seemed to disconnect from her body and the feeling of his skin against hers devastated her.

Against her will her body was aroused, and she could not stop him. It angered her that he wanted only to use her, that his words of love and kindness had meant nothing. She had found him again, but his only thought was to ravage her. She had been right. He was nothing but a savage, for all his pretensions.

The slow circular motions of his tongue on her breasts jarred her nerves, and she threw her head back, arching her body toward him.

Thoughts were lost in sensation as his hands explored her. She writhed against him as passion overcame reason. Suddenly she wanted a release from the craving she had for him. Nothing would stand in the way of the desire that raged between them, neither anger nor the knowledge of his treachery.

He pushed her clothing away from her legs and sought her smooth thighs. A tingling sensation stirred in her lower regions, more intense than she thought possible. She reached for him hungrily, bringing him closer. She knew she was behaving wildly, but she was lost. She could not stop herself from becoming a victim of the same madness that claimed him.

He tossed her dress aside and sought her moist center. In one impatient motion he tore away the remaining clothing that separated them. Once he had dreamed they would be together like this, but only after the purifying rites of marriage. Now his body and his mind could not wait for that. The desire for possession was strong, and his need for release more urgent than anything else.

She lay naked under him, and he relished the sight of her loveliness — she was his and his alone. The thought renewed his vigor and he removed his breechclout, revealing the long hardened evidence of his desire. His passion pent up inside him, he prepared her to receive him.

Kathleen shrank in sudden fright. Though she was innocent of sexual experience, she knew what he was about to do. Her body still craved him, but she saw him now as a savage who was taking her for his own pleasure, uncaring of her own. He would ravage her and forsake her, and leave her with nothing. She pulled herself out of his reach and huddled on her discarded dress.

His eyes narrowed to slits, and he poised himself to spring after her. Then the red stallion whickered softly, breaking into the sphere of desire that possessed Raven Sky. He looked at Kathleen's face and saw that she trembled. Her eyes were filled with tears, and he remembered the old fear she had told him about. For a moment he was confused. Some sense of balance returned to him. His savage nature was now tempered by his civilized one, and in that instant, mercy claimed his heart. He did not move.

The horse pawed the ground, and Raven Sky looked in the direction of the cave entrance, remembering that he had been too aroused to remember to pull the stone over the entrance. He had not even bothered to cover his tracks.

As he stood, Kathleen stared at his lithe

naked body. Her gaze was drawn to the male sexuality she saw before her, and the sight of him sent new waves of wonder through her. Her own body was still wet with a strange new surge of desire for union with Raven Sky. Irrationally, she wanted to forget the last few moments. She wanted him to come back to her and complete the act he had begun.

But he turned and looked down at her, his long black hair falling over his shoulders. 'Get up,' he said. 'Cover yourself,' and he hastily tied his breechclout and pulled on his trousers and buckskin shirt. Then he crept along the walls of the cave toward the entrance.

The posse was heading toward the cave, led by farmers who had seen Raven Sky on his mad ride. Where a white woman was involved, the white community was only too quick to aid in the search.

'We'll hang that no-good Indian,' Ray Farnsworth muttered as they rode doggedly along. There was no process of law except the Indian Police, and enraged whites would not wait upon a cumbersome system of enforcement to punish an Indian who had committed an offense against a white woman. Finally they came upon the entrance to the cave.

Raven Sky perceived the danger at once.

Only if Kathleen protested his innocence would he be saved from the white men's wrath.

He must act quickly. He could face the posse, overcome them, and make a fast getaway, or he could drag Kathleen deeper into the cave where the white men would not dare to penetrate. But they could not stay in the cave forever, for they had no food. If only he knew what Kathleen would do. She had once cared for him. But whatever affections she had once had for him, he had now destroyed.

Though outnumbered, he had a better chance against his pursuers now before they penetrated the cave and stationed themselves along the way. He would have to make his move.

Pain wrenched his heart. He had punished Kathleen, led her to the point where she had almost been ruined, had his revenge. Now, though, his love for her, a love that refused to die, surged through him and his heart was sundered.

He had been foolish not to cover his tracks. Passion had made him reckless. He would have to pay by facing the white men and making his getaway.

He walked stealthily back to where Kathleen sat. He knew he could take her with him, on his flight, but he would not do so if she did not want to go. He would be a fugitive, and it might be a long time before he was able to return here. He would not force Kathleen to accompany him.

She was dressed, her tangled hair and wrinkled dress the only evidence of the near rape.

He choked down the emotions that threatened clear thought. She would hand him over to the posse if he let her, yet his love for her drove him to speak a final word. He knelt beside her. He was gentle now, but he could see that she had not recovered from his violent display of emotion, and he had to speak with haste.

'Look at me, Kathleen,' he said in a low voice. When she did, he saw that the look in her eyes spelled certain death for him.

Kathleen could not see the man who had once loved and courted her. She saw only the hatred and fears of her past. They had been there for a reason, perhaps to warn her that all Indians were savages if you delved deep enough into their nature. She should never have trusted Raven Sky. She was foolish to think she could ever live with such a man. She wished they had never met.

'I am sure that the white men have come looking for us,' he said. 'They know you're here. They will show me no mercy, for I have touched a white woman.' He pulled a neckerchief out of his pocket.

'I do not want to hurt you,' he said as he held the neckerchief in his hand. 'There is one chance for me to face them, and that is if you will defend me.' He peered into her eyes, but he saw only confused emotion. 'Can I hope that you will speak for me? You must answer me. I must hear it from your own lips. Will you swear that I have not touched you?'

The full impact of what he was saying hit her. How could she defend him against a posse of white men? He had touched her. Exploring a body intimately was just as serious a crime as rape in their eyes. She hunched her shoulders, grief assailing her. If he had loved her, she would have done anything for him. But clearly he did not.

Raven Sky could wait no longer. The men were entering the cave. He gripped the cloth that would bind her mouth and moved toward her.

'Well?' he asked.

Seeing the threatening movement, Kathleen made her decision. 'No,' she snapped. I will not defend you.'

He tied the cloth around her mouth. Tears burned her eyes. Hating himself for what he had to do, Raven Sky quickly bound her hands and feet. He felt that he was destroying himself. As he located the rope he had left in the cave months before and used it to bind Kathleen's wrists and ankles, he knew that he would never be the same again.

He hated her, and hated himself because he loved her. His tears fell to her cheeks as he leaned over and kissed her tenderly on the forehead.

'Good-bye, my love,' he said. 'You were the only thing pure in my heart. Now there is nothing.' Then he was gone.

Kathleen understood none of his actions, her inner pain greater than her bonds. She struggled with the constrictions then gave up, falling back and resting her head on a cold rock.

Raven Sky led his horse along the twistings and turnings until he neared the entrance. The posse had just found the courage to venture into the cave; he could hear their voices. Leaving his horse behind an outcropping, he leaped up to a ledge that ran along the passage and crawled forward until he was almost on top of his pursuers. Then he gave an ear-shattering war whoop, and the red stallion, responding to his call, clattered forward, startling the men. Raven Sky leaped off the ledge, landing lightly on the stallion's back. Lying low on the animal's neck, he dug his heels in as the horse lunged toward the posse.

Kathleen heard the ear-splitting cry from somewhere near the entrance, and then she fainted.

The men flung themselves against the wall of the cave to avoid the clattering hooves, and Raven Sky rode out of the cave. He crossed the meadow and rode at full speed toward a small stand of trees and disappeared into the shadows. He did not stop until he was well away and sure he was not being followed.

17

The posse stared after the specter that exploded out of the darkness. After the dust had settled, Frank Owens said, 'Reckon we ought to see what's in there.'

They all stared into the ominous depths of the cave. No sound emerged.

'The girl wasn't with him,' someone said.

Jesse Smith stepped forward, his face even paler than usual. 'She might be dead,' he said and, in spite of his earlier recriminations, summoned his courage to look into the dark cave.

'As long as the matches hold out, we'll be all right,' Frank said.

'I say we go back for torches,' said Ray.

'No, listen,' said Dwayne. There was a stir and a slight groan. They forged farther into the darkness.

Following a curve in the wall, they finally found the chamber where Kathleen lay. There was enough light coming from the opening far overhead so that they could see her prone form.

'Oh, my God!' Jesse screamed, rushing to her side. The other men surrounded her.

'Don't move her. She might be hurt,' Jesse said. Frank Owen took his knife and removed the gag.

'Are you hurt?' J.P. asked, helping Frank Owen untie her wrists and ankles.

'No,' she gasped. 'I'm all right.' She rubbed her wrists where the rope had burned them.

'Which way did he go?' Frank asked her.

'I don't know,' she said, shaking her head.

'The posse will follow him.'

'No,' she said. 'I'm all right, really.'

Jesse screwed up his face in a look of apprehension. 'Did he . . . ?' He couldn't bring himself to continue, and the other men were too embarrassed to hold her gaze.

The indelicate question hung in the air. If she said he had raped her, she knew they would hunt him down and hang him. No stone would remain unturned until they found him. Remembering Raven Sky's question to her and what she had answered, she saw him in her mind's eye, fleeing from their vengeance. She could send them after him if she wanted to. In her anger, she might have done so, but something stopped her now. Some part of her was still loyal to him, for she remembered the time when he had been kind to her, when he had loved her.

'No,' she said, looking at Jesse. 'He did nothing.'

'Well, then,' said Farnsworth. 'That's different. But we'll put the word out. If he knows what's good for him, he won't show his face around here for a good long time, Creek or no Creek.'

She could see the relief in their eyes, and she knew that every man there would think twice about taking on Raven Sky here in Indian Territory where they were subject to the red man's justice. No one needed trouble with the Creeks.

Jesse could not hold Kate's gaze. In those few moments of crisis, he had let his feelings for her get the better of him. But now that the worst was over a thought nagged at him. If Raven Sky had done nothing, what had Kate been doing with him in this cave and why was she bound and gagged? He frowned at her.

'Why did he tie you up?' Jesse asked.

'He knew you would never believe him,' she said. 'He had to get away.' It was the truth. She wasn't going to tell them what he'd almost done. 'Even though he didn't do anything, it would look like he did. And,' she added biting her lip, 'he knew I wouldn't defend him.'

Frank Owens cleared his throat. 'Were you here against your will?' he asked. Her honor still might need defending.

Kate looked at him. If she said yes, they

might launch a search for him and punish him anyway, unbeknownst to her. No matter how Raven Sky had hurt her, she had no wish to see him dead.

If she said she wasn't here against her will, her reputation would be ruined. She would have to try a compromise.

'I insulted him,' she said. 'He was angry with me. He brought me here so we could settle it, but by the time we got here, his anger had cooled. Then he heard you coming, and he knew he was in danger. He feared what I would tell you about him.' She fought the emotion that surged in her. 'I gave him no choice. He had to tie me up so I wouldn't give him away.'

'But he left you like this, tied up?' Jesse's high-pitched voice was evidence of his own precarious emotional state.

'He knew you'd find me.'

'What if we hadn't?' Jesse said petulantly. 'What if we'd chased him instead, thinking there was no one here? You would have died here.'

Kathleen's spirits were beginning to return to her. 'I don't think I would have died, Jesse, but I appreciate your concern.'

Jesse stuck out his chin. Frank Owens helped her up, then led the way out of the cave.

'We'll take you home, Miss Kate,' volunteered Ray Farnsworth. 'See that no harm comes to you.'

'I'll be all right, really,' Kate protested. She was beginning to feel foolish about having caused so much uproar.

'You left your wagon in town. We'll at least take you back there.'

Realizing that they were right, she said, 'I'd be much obliged.'

Jesse almost offered to let Kate ride with him, then thought better of it. She rode behind Frank Owens instead. She tried to maintain her dignity, but she could feel her face burning all the way back to town. The situation would be equally hard to explain to Wendall and Molly, and it would be a while before she could show her face in Tulsa again. Thoughts of Raven Sky made her tremble with anger.

A glimmer at the back of her mind told her it was not over yet. She wished never to see him again, but she knew there would be future meetings. There was still so much between them that hadn't been resolved.

As soon as Frank Owen helped her dismount in front of the general store, she climbed into the wagon and drove swiftly out of town. Indians and whites followed her with their eyes as she passed along Main Street.

She did not slow the horses until she was well inside the confines of the Calhoun ranch. Then she took time to think. It would do no good to evade the family's questions. Wendall and Molly would hear about the incident soon enough. She might as well tell them the truth and hope they would trust her.

But could she trust herself? She could not throw all the blame on Raven Sky. She had encouraged him from the very beginning. She had wanted him to touch her intimately, and she had responded to him in a way that must have driven him wild with desire. She felt deeply ashamed, and she was uncertain how to handle her confusing feelings for Raven Sky.

No matter how long they were apart, it was always the same when they were together. Their strong feelings for each other had led them to that dark and desolate cave. It would be best, she decided stoically, if she never saw him again.

Chickens squawked and fluttered as she pulled the team up in front of the barn. She jumped to the ground, leaving the horses with Hank, and went inside the house.

'What happened to you?' Molly said, straightening as Kathleen entered the kitchen. 'Are you all right?'

'I'm fine, Molly. But I'm afraid I had a

run-in with Raven Sky.' She looked out the window, searching for her brother. 'Where's Wendall?'

'He'll be out till suppertime,' Molly said. 'Can you tell me about it?'

Kathleen sank into a chair and leaned on the wooden table. 'I suppose I'd better.'

Molly drew up a chair and sat down at the table with Kathleen. 'It's true, then, he's back?'

'Yes.'

'Did you . . . ?' She let the question fade, then tried again. 'Did you find out anything?'

'He said his marriage to a Euchee woman would benefit the tribe.'

'So it's true,' Molly said, drawing in her breath.

'I was so angry and upset that I ran away from him. Oh, Molly, it was awful. I have never hated anyone so much in my life. I don't understand what happened to me. This harsh, ugly feeling rose up from my stomach, and I had the strongest urge to strike him. It was . . . primitive.' She buried her face in her hands.

'Oh, Kathleen.' Molly reached out to brush Kathleen's hair away from her forehead.

Kate took a breath and went on, 'I ran away, but he followed me. He pulled me up on his horse and took me to the cave where we . . . ' She stopped, letting her voice drift off. She had told no one about their first encounter in the cave. Luckily, Molly didn't notice her hesitation.

'To a cave! I can't believe any of this.'

'I must have passed out. He carried me in. He was so angry!'

'My God, did he hurt you? Wendall will see him dead.'

'Molly, no! By the time we got there, I guess his senses had returned to him.' She felt in her pockets for a handkerchief, hurrying over the next part. 'He didn't do anything to me. Then a posse arrived. Raven Sky knew I would hand him over to them. I was still hurt and angry, so I told him that if they found us together I wouldn't defend him. He had to get away, so he tied me up and left me there.'

Molly's eyes were like saucers as Kathleen continued.

'When the posse found me, they assumed the worst, but I told them nothing had happened, so they didn't go after him.'

Molly lifted her eyebrows. 'I wonder what Wendall will do.'

'I don't know, but the story will be all over town by tomorrow.' She sat up straighter, attempting to shrug off her lost reputation. 'I'll have to go away again, Molly. I wouldn't want to bring humiliation on the family.'

'Don't worry, Kate. Wendall will know what to do. I'm just glad Raven Sky didn't touch you.' She hugged her sister-in-law. 'Is there anything else you want to tell me?' asked Molly.

Kate felt an instant pang of guilt. 'What else is there to tell?'

Molly stumbled awkwardly over her words. 'I — know it was hard on you when you heard — when I told you he was to be married. I just . . . well, I thought you might feel . . . well . . .'

'I don't know, Molly. Something in me has died. I thought I could trust him. Then he destroyed that trust. But it's my fault, too. He wanted me. He courted me.' The tears started again. 'He was such a gentleman then. He got tired of waiting. I can't say I blame him. How could he understand?'

'You're very generous,' Molly said.

'I can afford to be generous,' Kathleen said bitterly.

Kathleen bathed, then pinned her hair up and donned a fresh dress. She peered into the mirror and saw that the flush had left her cheeks and the redness was gone from her eyes.

There was a knock on her door, and Wendall entered. She felt her jaw clench. She could tell by his expression that Molly had told him. She stiffened, waiting for his words.

'Are you all right, Sis?' he asked, his face drawn into lines that she'd seen only when he faced an opponent. For the first time she felt what it must be like to stand up to her brother's anger.

'I'm all right, Wendall,' she said, taking a seat on the bed. He moved to the chair by the window and sat down, leaning forward. 'I want to hear the story from your lips,' he said.

Kathleen told him what happened, leaving out only the fact that Raven Sky had stripped them both of their clothing.

The muscles in Wendall's jaw had grown taut, and when he spoke, his voice was raw. 'If I ever see that Indian in this territory again. I'll have his scalp.'

'Wendall, I tried to explain it was partly my fault.'

'Doesn't matter. He ruined your reputation and left you alone in that cave instead of standing up to the posse. No man does that to my sister and gets away with it.'

'It was that, or hanging. He knew I'd be safe when he left me.'

The muscles twitched in his jaw, and his eyelids were drawn low over his eyes. He was holding something in. He stood and paced around her room in a small circle, his shoulders tense.

'I want to know what really happened in that cave, Kathleen.'

Her mouth jerked in agitation and her heart pounded. She straightened her spine. 'I told you what happened. He didn't damage my honor, if that's what you mean.'

Her face burned, and Wendall stopped in front of her, forcing her to look him in the eye. She held his gaze, hoping he couldn't see the way she was trembling inside.

'I'll kill that Indian if he laid a hand on you,' he said in a low, tight voice. 'There was a time when I believed Raven Sky to be one of the most civilized of his people, but he's no better than a common savage if this is the way he treats women.'

She jerked her chin sideways. 'I wouldn't know how he treats women.' Her lip trembled, and she turned around, not wanting Wendall to see her cry.

She closed her eyes, facing the window. She could never tell Wendall how badly Raven Sky had hurt her.

'I just want to be sure,' Wendall said. He looked at his sister's bent shoulders, trying to decide just how much the Indian had done. He believed Kate when she said Raven Sky hadn't raped her. For that he was thankful. It was possible that he had tried to, that only the posse's intervention had stopped him. But

Wendall would probably never know.

The fact that the Indian had run away gave Wendall a bad feeling. If he had been innocent of harming Kate's virtue, he should have faced the posse.

'I mean it, Kate,' he said. 'If I ever find out that Raven Sky laid a hand on you, I'll tear the man from limb to limb.'

Wendall's anger flooded him, and he grasped the back of the chair so hard his knuckles whitened. But he restrained his angry words. Looking at his sister, hugging her arms to herself, he felt sorrow temper his anger. He took a deep breath, walked over to her, and put an arm around her shoulders.

In a gentler voice, he asked, 'Do you want me to go after him, Sis?'

She shook her head, leaning against his shoulder. 'No, Wendall. I don't.'

He was silent, staring out at the vast blackness of the plain before them. Then he muttered, 'All right, if you say so. But he'll know better than to show his face around here ever again.'

'This is his home, Wendall. He can't stay away forever.'

Wendall shrugged. 'Our kind don't cotton to Indians treating white women that way. He'll stay away if he knows what's best for him.'

Finally Wendall left her, and she prepared for bed. Alone, she asked herself why Raven Sky had left. Of course, he was outnumbered. He could hardly have defeated a posse of armed men.

Then, with a dull ache in her heart, she remembered the truth. She had sent him away. She had said she would not defend him. But why should she? He was betrothed to another woman, and his treatment of her had been abominable. Deep in her heart she knew there was a time when he would have shown valor . . . but all that was in the past now.

'Raven Sky, where are you now?' she whispered, remembering the way he used to ride across the plain under the moon. Then another sweet, tantalizing picture came to her mind — the way he had looked standing naked beside her.

She wanted to reach out and touch that nude form, and it shamed her to think such thoughts. Jesse was right: she was becoming wanton.

She turned over, hugging the pillow to her, clenching her fists. Raven Sky had awakened desire in her, then given her up. Resentment, deep and powerful, festered in her as she lay there.

Finally she rose, pulled on a bed coat, and

tiptoed downstairs. As she approached the open door to the parlor, she heard Molly's low voice.

'I hate to see her like this.' Molly sounded so sad.

'She should marry and settle down,' said Wendall.

'Pity there's no one around here to ask her except that funny little clerk at the store. The other men coming out here seem to have families back home, for the most part.'

'Oh, Jesse's all right in his way. Thrifty, too. I bet he'll build a big house in town one day.'

'But, Wendall, you know that's not all there is to marriage.'

Kathleen heard Wendall get up and move over to his wife. 'Well, then, who shall we find for our sister that will please her?'

'What about Gerald Lange? He and Kate have been corresponding, and I have it on the best authority that they saw a lot of each other in St. Louis.'

Wendall expelled a breath. 'I had hopes there myself.'

'If only she could love him,' Molly said.

'Well, you know how it is when a woman makes up her mind.'

Kathleen fled up the stairs to her room and bolted her door. There it was again. She was a problem for everyone. Could she ever love any man other than Raven Sky? Why must he rule her thoughts and feelings so? He had not ravaged her, but he had ruined her for wanting anyone else. In that, she was his prisoner.

Pounding her fist on the bed and moaning, she cried, 'Damn you, Raven Sky, damn you!' Her tears soaking the pillow, she cried herself to sleep.

18

Summer came. Far away in Wyoming Territory, Raven Sky wandered, making his home under the stars, occasionally accepting the hospitality of friendly Indian tribes. They were grateful for his skill as a hunter and tracker, and he was welcome almost everywhere he went.

Turning his back on the white man's world and on his own civilized nation, he lived close to nature. He regained a certain freedom that he had lost while living in Indian Territory. He hated the inevitability of the white man's rule of the land, and his regret that the Creeks were a conquered people deepened. He saw how land and gold had made the greedy white men move westward. They had already depleted the plains of buffalo. The Indian way of life was perishing. His sons and his sons' sons would live like the white men, and he grieved for them.

Their only hope would be to fight with the white man's weapons — education and money, earned as the white man earned it. But that would be an alien way to live, and many of his people did not want that.

Already the mixed-bloods were adapting, but the full-bloods clung to the old ways.

He had learned to live the white man's way because he knew it was the only way to survive. But it was an expression of self to be able to roam the hills. He regained his strength from living off the land as his ancestors had done. He relished this way of life.

He turned more and more to spiritual practices in an effort to cleanse his troubled soul. He did not take a wife, but remained celibate. He sent word to Jno Loughridge of the Euchees that he was not ready to marry, that he was purifying himself.

Raven Sky needed only one woman, and he had destroyed his chance of winning her hand. He would not have been able to live with her in wild freedom in the wilderness, but if he had her, he would have been willing to make the kind of home she wanted, among people of her kind.

At night he slept alone on the hard ground. He still saw her face in his dreams. The vision of her would come again and again until he thought it would drive him mad. He hunted and rode and shared meals with families of the Cheyenne and the Nez Percé. Though their ways were different from his own Creek ways, he proved himself among them and was accepted.

Slowly, after months in the wilderness, the dreams of Kathleen went away. At first, he could go for a day without thinking of her. Then several days. Finally, he could live most of the time without thinking of her. But sometimes without warning the thoughts would come back. At times she seemed like a demon he would never get rid of. But he learned to tolerate the occasional feelings of loss, and he lived his life.

The women of the tribes looked at him with longing. The young ones yearned for him, and the older women harbored the hope that this virile man would invigorate the lifeblood of their families. Many desired him, but he was oblivious of them. He explained to the tribal fathers that he was considering becoming a holy man after his hunting days were over. And no one argued his decision.

★   ★   ★

Summer in Tulsa was a wild time. The number of gambling tents increased, and several illegal saloons went up. Wendall tried to keep the women at home on the ranch, afraid for their safety. Gunfights erupted when cowboys went into town with their pockets full of money after the spring roundups, eager to enjoy the social gatherings.

On Sundays, however, the sinners dressed in their best clothes, and families came in from ranches and farms to attend church and exchange social visits.

Wendall persuaded Kathleen to go to church every Sunday. He told her to hold her head up and face the sniveling gossips. She had nothing to hide.

She went through with it, though it was a terrible embarrassment. Finally the gossip died down, the townspeople stopped snickering behind her back, and she seemed to be on the fringes of respectability again. She was, after all, Wendall Calhoun's sister, and everyone stood in awe of his reputation as a man of honor and of his ability to use his gun.

In June Wendall had another chance to prove his superiority in the territory.

Every day herds from surrounding ranches were loaded onto railroad cars to be shipped to Kansas City. The cattle bawled and milled as the cowboys moved them out. The cowboys had driven them to the stockyards near town where they awaited transport.

One day as Hank and Tex slid the bars into place behind the cattle in the holding pens,

Wendall shaded his eyes against the sun and counted the cars he and Jack Carlton had ordered for the day.

'Six cars,' said Tex as the train chugged to a stop. 'Ain't enough for our head and Carlton's, too.'

Wendall had realized the same thing. Jack Carlton's hands were just now moving the last of their herd into the pens, from where they would be loaded onto the cars. Between the two herds there were two thousand head, too many for six cars.

'Go find out where the extra cars are. We'll start loading our cattle into these cars. I can't have my herd standing around here another day.'

Tex turned his horse to check the train. Someone had not followed orders. There should be at least twice as many cars.

Wendall cantered his horse over to the chutes where Jack Carlton's men had slid back the freight-car doors. Hank approached from the other end of the train. Already some of Wendall's men were arguing with Carlton's over whose herds would be loaded into the cars.

Carlton stood at the head of the train, and Wendall rode up to him. 'Mornin', Jack,' he said, dismounting, his face not giving away his thoughts.

'Mornin', Wendall.' Carlton pushed his hat back and hooked his thumbs in his belt as he turned to Wendall. 'What're we gonna do 'bout these cattle cars?'

Wendall leaned forward in his saddle, resting his wrists on the saddle horn. 'Believe those cars are mine, Jack. I need those cars 'cause my herd's been waitin' since sunup.'

He could see a muscle twitch under Carlton's eye as he took a step forward. Wendall didn't move, but he was conscious of the weight of his six-shooters in their holsters within easy reach.

'Now, just a minute here, Wendall. I ordered six cars. Looks like maybe the railroad messed up.'

'I ordered six cars, too, Jack. But my herd got here first. Those cars are mine.'

'Who says?'

Wendall carefully surveyed the position of his men around the yards in relation to Jack's. They were equally matched. From his perch on horseback a little distance away, Hank watched his employer, sensing something was up. Wendall raised the brim of his hat just slightly, and Hank freed his right hand, letting it rest on his thigh. Tex emerged into the sunlight near the railroad station and stopped where he was, watching Wendall and Jack.

Then he took himself over to the holding pens and leaned on the crossbar, eyeing the hands who were moving cattle into position. Then he eased his elbows back onto the railing and jerked his head up, watching Wendall.

'Sorry, Jack,' said Wendall, reaching for his gun as if he had all the time in the world. 'But I say.'

'Damn you, Calhoun.' Carlton reached for his gun, but he was too late. He heard pistols cock behind him even before he saw that Hank had covered his men from his position at the other end of the cars. Tex had his gun directly on him.

Wendall's other hands, getting the message, pulled their guns, and Jack's men threw their hands up. Wendall still spoke in a lazy drawl. 'Why don't you and your men wait over there?' he said, gesturing to the end of the pens nearest the station.

For a moment no one moved. But Carlton's men had been caught off guard, and it only took a second for them to realize that Wendall had the upper hand. Jack Carlton's eyes flashed daggers, but he turned and walked where Wendall wanted him to go. Soon the other men followed. Tex brought up the rear, his gun trained on the men who scuffed through the dirt, their

321

hands over their heads.

Wendall kept his gun on Jack until all the men were at the railing by the end of the platform, their hands on the top rail.

'Okay, men,' he called to his hands. 'Load 'em up!'

Wooden doors slammed back on the six cars, and the men prodded the cattle forward, their bellows accompanying the clack of hooves on wood as they lumbered up the ramps. Wendall waited patiently, watching Carlton and his men standing in the sun. Tex never moved from his watch over the rival cattlemen. No one had to say that a false move would have cost Carlton something. Tex was a straight shot.

Wendall had not thought about the fact that he and Jack were friends. It was simply a matter of survival. If the other cars were a day late, Wendall would lose too much money. If Carlton had gotten his herd there earlier in the day, Wendall would have tried to work something out. He was firm when it came to business. That was how he had gained his muscle in the territory. You needed that to survive.

When the cattle were in and the train ready to leave, Wendall holstered his gun.

'All right,' he called to Tex, 'let 'em go.' Then he dismounted and walked to where

Jack was wiping his brow with a red handkerchief.

'Sorry I had to do that, Jack,' he said over the hiss of the engine. 'Buy you a drink to show there's no hard feelings.'

Jack spit in the dirt, then squinted at his opponent. Wendall took his time removing his hat and wiping the sweat from his forehead, letting Jack settle his anger. But he knew Carlton would come around to his way of thinking. It was important that they shake hands in front of the men, so no fights would break out.

Carlton knew what had to be done, even if it meant acknowledging Calhoun's supremacy. He didn't want a fight. His cattle would just have to be a day late. He wiped his hands on his denims and stuck out his hand.

The other men stood around as the two bosses shook. 'No hard feelin's, Wendall,' Carlton said. 'I reckon you can afford to buy me and my foreman a drink.'

'Reckon I can, Jack. You go over to the hotel and tell Wiley to set us up in the back room there. I'll be along soon as I take care of a little business with my men here.'

Jack turned to his hands. 'All right, men, ship 'em out tomorrow.'

The hands disbursed, and Wendall clapped Tex on the back. 'Good work,' he said, appreciating the alertness of his two foremen.

'Just doin' a job,' said Tex.

Hank rode up, and Wendall gave him the thumbs-up sign. The other man nodded, the pleased look in his eye showing his pride at being part of the Calhoun contingent. It paid to work for a man who didn't have any second thoughts before he acted. In the West, split-second timing could save a life or a fortune.

★   ★   ★

The Calhouns were proud of their position in the territory. Kathleen was comforted by the fact that her brother was always there to depend on, and she didn't know what she would have done without Molly's support and friendship. She envied Molly, seeing the renewal of life in her, but she was regaining confidence, and she tried not to regret that she didn't have her own child growing in her.

Joy Harrington had gone home to Missouri for the summer months, so there wasn't any school now, but Kathleen thought she might teach again in September.

One Sunday afternoon Molly, Kathleen, and Wendall picnicked near Bird Creek, shaded by trees. Nearby the sweet melody of the western meadowlark was punctuated by the chirping of vesper sparrows and red-winged blackbirds.

Wendall leaned his back against a strong elm, his legs stretched out before him, and Molly watched her sister-in-law eating roast beef between thick slabs of bread. She'd been turning something over in her mind, and she finally decided to speak.

'Have you heard from Gerald, Kathleen?' she asked.

Kathleen shrugged. She no longer cared what they thought about her situation. Once she might have settled for marriage to Gerald, but now she didn't want to marry at all. This hadn't been a conscious decision. It had just grown in her.

'No. I haven't answered the letter he sent me in March.'

'Have you thought of visiting St. Louis again, Kate?' Wendall ventured.

Kathleen shook her head. 'I have you two here. I don't need anyone else. I have my teaching to think about.'

'Oh, that,' he said.

'It's important.'

'I didn't mean it wasn't. I just meant it might not be enough for you.'

'It is.'

They were silent. There was no arguing with her. Wendall knew how she was when she had her mind set on something.

'The green corn festival's in a couple of weeks, Molly said, changing the subject. 'Can we go, Wendall?' They had not gone to the last one, but now there was no reason why they shouldn't join in the celebrations the way the other settlers did.

'I suppose,' Wendall said after a while. He looked at Kathleen, who was concentrating on a chicken leg now. She didn't appear to be listening to them.

'It's settled, then,' Molly said.

Kathleen lay on her back in the warm sun. The rays felt good on her face and limbs. She had pushed her sleeves up above her elbows and kicked off her shoes and stockings, feeling that she could let the sun get to her calves with only relatives present.

She had struggled to put Raven Sky out of her mind, and she had begun to succeed. Nothing mattered anymore. Her frayed emotions were patched together, and she was healing. She was calm. She had locked her love away in her heart where no one could approach it. She did not put herself into vulnerable situations anymore. That was one reason she would not go to St. Louis. Suppose she did meet someone who wanted to marry her, as Gerald had? That would only lead to endless misunderstandings. And so she had not written to Gerald. She knew he would wait for her no longer. He would marry someone else, which was just as well.

It would be better to live her life without a man than to go through all that pain again. She was content.

She relaxed and drifted off into a nap.

19

The corn ripened in the Creek nation, and the green corn festival approached. The chief summoned his people, as in days of old, by sending out bundles of sticks to individual Indians. Each day the recipient threw away one stick, and when no sticks remained, the people gathered for the dance, camping in the woods near the meeting place. The green corn festival had a deeply religious meaning for the Indians, but the whites were invited to watch. During the festival grudges were forgiven, for this was the new year.

On the third day of the festivities, Wendall and his family attended. Their wagon rolled through the woods, passing Indian campsites along the way. Nearing a square of hard-packed earth that had been swept clean for the occasion, they heard the beating of a drum made of rawhide stretched over the end of a hollow log. The same drum that beat the dances in the Creeks' eastern homes, it had come with them all the way during their unhappy wanderings.

The Calhouns heard the shaking of gourd rattles and the clattering of the dried terrapin shells filled with pebbles, which the Creek women wore on their legs as they danced. The odd-sounding tunes and the wildly beautiful rhythms filled the woods as the Calhouns approached the gathering.

As of old, brush arbors had been erected on three sides of the square where the sacred fire burned. Creek officials sat in the west arbor, the central shed. The warriors sat in the north arbor. Leaders seated in the south arbor rattled gourds during the dances and kept up a continuous chant. The rest of the people sat according to clan. Each clan was made up of the descendants of a single female ancestor. The white visitors were allowed to watch from outside the square.

Gone were the denim, cotton, and duck clothes that the Indians wore for their daily work. Their ceremonial costumes cast them in the mold of an ancient people who had attempted to make a new home here in this land but whose hearts remained in their centuries-old homelands to the east. Many of the men wore bright blue or green calico hunting shirts trimmed with scarlet fringe and belted with broad beaded girdles. Gaily colored handkerchiefs bound their heads, turban-style, with one end hanging beside the ear. Their leggings were made of buckskin and green or scarlet cloth, with embroidered knee bands and tassels. Their embroidered moccasins were brightly ornamented with beads and silk.

Wendall helped the women down from the wagon. Nearer the clearing where the fire flickered they could see the ring of men and women, some with feathers in their long braids. The leader called out in his tribal tongue, and the dancers answered him. Already some of the Indians and whites lay in a drunken stupor at the edge of the woods, for bootleg whiskey flowed at such events.

The female dancers who had been circling the fire returned to the outer edge. The buffalo dance was about to commence. Young warriors came forward, stripped to fighting attire — breechclouts, moccasins, bone necklaces, and eagle feathers in their hair. Their bodies were decorated with paint, their arms and legs bloody from the scarification ceremony. One dancer wore a buffalo mask and tail.

To the beating of the drum the buffalo dancer began slowly, wandering aimlessly toward the center of the dance area. He turned his masked head from side to side and made grazing motions. Then the hunters entered, carrying colorful shields and feathered lances, dancing faster than the buffalo. Paint covered their features, and their bodies glistened with sweat in the flickering firelight.

Suddenly the dancers seemed to discover the buffalo and turned toward him. As they came near the Calhouns, who stood amid the ring of people circling the fire, Kathleen gave a start.

Molly turned to her. 'What's wrong?'

Kathleen didn't speak. She was staring at a tall, virile Indian, bent over in the dance, and stepping quickly. The buffalo dancer seemed to see the hunters and stamped his feet, tossing his head from side to side to the beat of the drum. He began to charge the hunters.

As the dancers circled again, Kathleen whispered to Molly. 'That's Raven Sky. I'm sure of it.' She did not need to see his face. She knew his lithe, muscular body. The two women stood rigid, knowing that if Wendall saw Raven Sky, he might kill him. Kathleen was silent.

The hunters thrust their spears at the buffalo dancer. Kathleen stood rooted to the spot, watching Raven Sky as he twisted and turned his body, wild and uninhibited. Her heart beat to the rhythm of the drum, and she could feel the blood throb in her veins as the firelight cast an eerie spell on the watchers.

The hunters reeled around the buffalo dancer. Raven Sky thrust his spear at the buffalo, who staggered about, wounded and angry. The rest of the hunters danced back, watching the duel between this bold hunter and the buffalo, cavorting, hunching over, then leaping, twisting, and falling around the fire. Several times the dancers came so near the edge of the circle that Kathleen could have reached out and touched them.

Emotions she hadn't felt in months tumbled inside her. She thought she had exorcised Raven Sky from her consciousness, but the sight of him nearly naked, his muscles rippling in the firelight, reawakened sensations she thought had died. Then fear struck her heart, as she hoped Wendall didn't recognize him.

The hunters danced toward the fallen buffalo. He struggled to raise his head, then finally slumped on the ground, motionless. Now, at a signal, the dancers dropped to one knee and brought their upright spears down in unison with a single thud. The buffalo was dead.

Raven Sky kneeled close to Kathleen, his head bent like the others in a silent prayer of thanksgiving to the Great Spirit for their good fortune, asking the buffalo's forgiveness. The night was still except for the droning chant and Kate's beating heart.

Suddenly the hunters leaped up and danced madly around the buffalo, then lifted him above their heads and carried him out of the ring.

Emotions tore at Kathleen as she followed Raven Sky with her eyes.

'Kathleen,' whispered Molly. 'Do you think we could sit down now?'

Kathleen looked at Molly's features and noticed how red her face was. The warmth from the fire must have overheated her.

Wendall had spotted some other ranchers and gone off to join them, so Kathleen led Molly to a log near the edge of the woods behind the clearing.

'I'm sorry,' Molly said. 'It's just that I feel dizzy. Let's sit down here.' Molly looked flushed, and Kathleen was too busy looking after her to notice where Raven Sky had gone. She looked around for Wendall, but he was nowhere in sight, so she led Molly away from the crowd and asked one of the Indian women for some water. She had been so overcome at finding Raven Sky here that she had not thought of Molly, and now she worried that Molly might have had too much exertion.

'I'll be all right in a minute,' Molly said. 'I think the excitement of the dance just got me overheated.'

'Just rest here. It's cooler away from the fire.' They sat quietly at the edge of the woods. On the other side of the ring, where the white men were sharing their whiskey with the Indians, boisterous jokes could be heard. When the Indian woman brought a pitcher of water, Molly drank. Then Kathleen bathed her face.

She did not hear the soft breaking of twigs behind her as someone approached.

But she sensed Raven Sky's presence. She stopped bathing Molly's face, and Molly opened her eyes to stare up at the dark countenance of the man who stood behind Kathleen. Silent, she stared at Kathleen.

Leaving Molly in the care of the Indian woman, Kathleen lowered the pitcher of water. She stood, straightening her back before she turned to face Raven Sky. Slowly, she raised her eyes from his shoulders and neck to his firm chin, his full lips, and long straight nose, looking at last into the black eyes, her heart sounding a deafening thud in her ears.

If she expected to see hate or lust in his eyes, she did not find either. She saw desire, muted by something else. That he had suffered was clear, but there was also a new sense of calm and resignation. And in the depths of his eyes was a look that made her heart fill again with all the feeling she had always had for him. For she saw his need to be forgiven.

Raven Sky stood still in this moment of revelation. He had thought himself cleansed of her, but seeing her now he felt a stab of love so great he thought his heart would burst. He could not comprehend how they had come to such an impossible pass. Never before had there been such difficult obstacles between himself and what he wanted. That this white woman had caused him so much grief was unforgivable.

Yet, seeing her standing there, he still wanted her. He could not stand the thought that another might someday possess her, might already possess her. His vision had told him she was his, and he felt again the same urge that had made him sweep her onto his horse and carry her to the cave.

Her eyes were wide, her lips partly open as if she wanted to speak, but no words came. Her face was bright. How he longed to hold her in his arms. It was sheer madness to want her still, yet he could not reason with his heart or suppress the urgency he felt. He could not speak.

For a long time they stood there. Then Molly made a movement, afraid of what might happen if Wendall saw Raven Sky with Kathleen. Kathleen understood the look Molly gave her and whispered to him, 'It's not safe here.'

His heart beat fast. He understood. If Wendall Calhoun or the other white men recognized him, he would be in great danger. The Creeks knew that he had lost favor with the whites. They protected him, but he did not know how long he could keep his presence unknown. He much preferred his life in the western mountains. He had come back only because his people needed him.

He knew he should not stay here, in view of others. But Kathleen hadn't moved. He allowed himself a brief gesture. Reaching out to touch her face, he felt a tear slip down her cheek to his finger.

Kathleen dared to take a step toward him. Seeing the rising and falling of her breast, he felt an ache in his groin that challenged his vow of celibacy. Her lips were still parted, her hair loosened from the ribbon at her neck. Her blue eyes blazed into his. She seemed completely unaware of their surrounding.

The dark night, the flickering firelight, and the eerie chants coming from the circle of Indians around the fire combined to warm his blood. The atmosphere of rejuvenation and celebration drew Kathleen and Raven Sky together to acknowledge what they felt, what they had always felt for each other.

Though Kathleen could not reconcile all her anger, and mistrust, all the abandonment and silence that had come before this moment, she knew that she wanted Raven Sky more than anything. Now that she stood before him, her body cried out for his touch. She wanted to explore the naked body she had seen but had not come to know in the cave on the day he had left her.

She hardly knew what she did as she stepped toward him, lips parted, eyes questioning. When he lifted his hand again, she reached for it and felt it close around her own.

His black eyes reflected light from the fire, and he brushed against her thigh, his pulsing manhood evidence of his desire. Gently, he led her out of the light and deep into the woods.

'Raven Sky,' she breathed as she followed him.

'Hush, my white bird,' he said as he swung her into a hidden clearing far from the crowd of celebrants. He covered her mouth with his, his tongue darting in to explore hers. He encircled her with his strong arms, pulling her nearer his full maleness. Kathleen arched to him and moved her hips in an unconscious rhythm, twisting in his arms as her own need built.

Tiny warnings tried to insinuate themselves through the swell of sensation she felt, but she pushed them back. She had fought against this for too long. Now her passion was demanding to be spent.

'Ah, my little one,' he said, as his tongue left her mouth to taste her ear. 'You still drive me mad with desire. How I have longed for you. How I tried to forget you. But I could not.' Thoughts of purification and celibacy were banished from Raven Sky's mind. Months of unsatisfied love built in him to the breaking point.

He captured her hand and held it over his male hardness, loosening his breechclout as he did so. Kathleen curled her fingers around his straining flesh. Her breathing was quick and uneven, and though he wanted to please her he didn't know how long he could control his need. Reason had left his mind. His sensuous nature had burst its confines. There was no moment but this one. He would seize it.

He cradled her back with one arm while he reached under her knees with the other, sweeping her up off her feet. Carrying her out of the clearing and deep among the trees, he gently put her down on a bed of leaves.

She threw her arms around him and pulled him closer. Then his hands were on her breasts, struggling to unfasten her bodice. Her heart pounded as she helped him bare her breasts, the nipples erect to his touch. Then, with a soft moan, he lowered his head and tasted the firm point of one nipple, caressing the other with his fingers.

Wrapping her arms around him, Kathleen stroked his sinewy back, thrilling at the smooth skin and hard muscles. She lowered her hands to his hips, then pressed them against his firm buttocks.

Quickly he removed her dress and tossed it aside, then slid her underclothes off, baring her body. She raised her hips as he peeled away the last of her underthings. Then he ran his hands up over her smooth thighs to the silky mound of her womanhood.

The intensity of his lovemaking heightened as his tongue darted in and out of her mouth and his fingers worked their miracles. Tiny explosions began to go off within her as his fingers kneaded her gently, exciting her to a fever pitch. She responded by opening herself to him, inviting the fulfillment she had thirsted for. Her body began to move to the distant sound of the drum, picking up its sensual, ancient rhythm. She shuddered as his long hardness found its way over her smooth skin, seeking the entrance she offered.

Raven Sky gripped her shoulders as his throbbing manhood penetrated deep inside the haven that had been forbidden to him for so long. He held still for a moment, nearly mad with desire, making sure she was all right. Then, seeing the joy and passion in her face, he began to move within her, thrilling to her wild response.

She ignored the prick of pain as he pushed through her maidenhood, holding him inside her, fitting her hips to his as she met his rhythm. Time was suspended, and the night sounds faded into a blur of pleasure. United with Raven Sky at last, she held him tightly, matching his passion, until he tumbled her over the brink of reason and into a realm of pure sensation she hadn't known existed. Then he relaxed above her, and she shut her eyes and floated. For a long time, they lay in each other's arms.

Slowly, consciousness of time and place returned, and Kathleen breathed deeply, her heartbeat steadying. She felt the weight of his body on top of her and became aware of what they had done.

As he lay limp inside her, she began to feel a vague apprehension. She had given herself to a man who was not her husband. A flush crept over her, and she began to pull away.

Raven Sky felt Kathleen grow tense beneath him, and he became aware of his own indiscretion. He had used her to satisfy a lust he could no longer control. She had wanted him, too, he could tell. Her body's responses were undeniable. But now he feared the consequences for her.

It was not the white man's way to let a young woman of Kate's position give herself to a man before marriage. He would be hunted down and punished for molesting her a second time. His body was at long last satisfied, but his heart was filled with regret. Kathleen, too, had been filled with pleasure, but when she regained her reason, she would be frightened. Already he felt the anguish of losing her again.

Kathleen pulled out of his arms and reached for her clothing. 'We must part,' she said, afraid to look at him. How humiliating that he finally knew she could not keep herself from him. How shameful that her love for him had led to this forbidden coupling. And yet she had had no choice. She was obsessed with him.

He raised himself to his knees and touched her chin with his finger. 'I am sorry if I have hurt you.'

Her agitated state showed him that she regretted their act of love already, and that saddened him. For even if he could never have her as a wife, their lovemaking had been an act of beauty that he would hold in his heart forever.

'Don't be sorry,' Kate said, her voice tight. 'I, too, wanted this. But you must go. Run, quickly. My brother must not find us together.' She dressed hurriedly, unable to meet his gaze because of the deep shame she felt. Surely he had lost all respect for her. She understood his desire for her body, just as she acknowledged her need for his. But their carnal passion did not mean that he loved her. If he had, he would have said so when she first came back from St. Louis. She knew she had to get away from him.

She brushed the leaves from her hair and stood up, straightening her clothing. If only he would give a sign that he felt something for her other than lust, she might be able to face him again, but he did not. He merely stood there in all his magnificent nakedness, lit by the moonlight, staring down at her.

Raven Sky searched for words, but they would not come. He had lost all opportunity to show her his feelings except by demonstrating his physical need for her. Passion had overcome them both, and he had seized on her own desire to satisfy them both. He could not hope that she loved him. She had made that clear when she had said she would not defend him that day long ago. She would not defend him now. He could see that in her manner, as she smoothed her hair and her

342

clothes, as if to rid her body of his love. He wanted to hold her and gaze into her eyes, but she would not even look at him.

He had not spoken, and she did not dare risk being seen with him. With her family's help, she had mended her reputation last time. But she would have no excuse now. What could she say or do to deny that they had been together in the woods?

She turned away, not wanting him to see her tears. She stumbled, and a branch caught her hair, but she followed the sounds of the singing and the drums back toward the clearing. When she reached a circle of Indian women, she stayed among them until she felt calm enough to face Molly and Wendall.

Raven Sky went to the other side of the circle, weaving in and out among his people, watching Kathleen. Finally she returned to where Molly sat. She knew she could not hide the fact that she had been with Raven Sky, but she hoped Molly would not ask what had occurred. She watched Raven Sky until he finally disappeared into the darkness of the forest.

Molly touched the hem of her skirt, reminding her that people were watching, and Kathleen sat down.

20

'Are you all right, Kate?' Molly asked, touching her arm. They spoke in low voices so as not to draw attention to themselves.

'Yes,' Kathleen said, not looking Molly in the eye, 'but this is dangerous for him. He shouldn't be here.'

Molly watched Kathleen's face. 'You love him very much, don't you?'

Kathleen nodded, reddening at the memory of what she had just done. 'Oh, Molly, what am I to do? Will I ever get over him? Please don't tell Wendall I was with Raven Sky. I'm afraid of what he might do.'

'I won't say anything. Wendall's temper is likely to explode. He and the other men have been drinking. They could shoot up the place any minute.'

Kathleen peered into the gloom for a sign of Raven Sky, her feelings in turmoil. What would happen now? She wouldn't dare try to see him again. If he showed his face now, he'd be punished by some drunken white men who remembered the day he ran off with a white woman.

A sudden commotion across the circle

attracted them. Two men's voices were raised above the din of chanting and the yells coming from outside the circle. The liquor had had its effect. Two half-breeds were wrestling on the ground while the white men took sides and placed bets. Kate heard some of their words. Two of the heaviest bettors were hurling insults at each other. A punch was thrown, and voices were raised to brawling pitch.

An Indian let out a war whoop as he brought the side of his hand down over the back of a white man's head. The man let out a scream and stumbled toward his cronies, who laughed and threw him back at the Indian, who was poised for another blow.

Wendall had had his share of liquor, but he was deeply concerned about his pregnant wife and his sister. He extricated himself from the brawl and pushed his way through the crowd, stepping over a log to reach Kate and Molly.

'Some of our neighbors have had too much to drink,' he said. 'I've got no stake in this argument. Let's get out of here.' He took Molly's arm and led her away from the crowd. The stomp dance could carry on without them. Kate followed them back through the woods to their wagon. She glanced furtively about for any sign of Raven

Sky, but there was none.

Kathleen was silent on the way home, still overcome by what had occurred and afraid of her thoughts. She had tried to forget Raven Sky, and now a part of her was angry that he had come back to remind her of her own vulnerability. All she had to do was look at him and her feelings would lurch out of control. Now she had shown him the power he had over her. But how would she ever survive if she never saw him again? She clutched the side of the wagon until wooden splinters dug into her fingers.

Alone in bed that night, bittersweet grief and longing overcame her as the tenderness between her legs reminded her that, in one way at least, Raven Sky had finally made her his. Over and over she saw his face in her mind, and she tried to decipher all the emotions she had seen there. Some small part of her thought there was a hint of love in those eyes, but she chided herself for thinking that. One thing was certain, she must never speak of their union to anyone. If anyone knew what had happened tonight, the outraged white community would seek revenge.

★ ★ ★

The weeks passed with no word from Raven Sky. Rumor had it that he had gone to the Euchee Creeks in the south.

In September, Kate went back to teaching. Her life fell into a routine of serving others, which helped her to forget her guilt. Every day she got up early, breakfasted, and rode Monty into town. She and Joy helped the children with their ABC's, and Kathleen learned a little Creek from some of the students. The two women divided the class into higher and lower grades. Besides teaching grammar, history, and arithmetic, they led songs and played games. On nice days, they took hikes. Once they passed by the Creek Council Oak, and Kathleen sadly remembered being there with Raven Sky as he solemnly recounted his people's removal to Indian Territory.

October came, and the grasses yellowed. Leaves turned, and the harvest was rich. Farmers reaped profits that would see them through the hard winter ahead.

Since the green corn festival, there had been a new restlessness in the air. One Thursday evening Frank Owen rode out from town to see Wendall. The two men spoke in low tones on the porch.

After a long time, Frank left. Wendall

returned to the parlor and heaved himself into the rocker.

'Frank says there's to be a meeting in town tomorrow night,' he told Molly and Kate. 'All of the whites are supposed to attend. I don't like it. Something's afoot. It's to be in the room above Dwayne's Store. The Indians aren't supposed to know about it, but those men are fools if they think the Indians won't know. Can't keep something like that under wraps for long.' He shook his head, his worried expression showing his disapproval of the men of his own race who were muscling their way into Indian Territory, many of them illegally.

'What's the meeting about?' asked Kathleen.

'The townsmen want to present a united front. Can't say as I'll go along with them, but I'll have to see what they propose. I don't mean to stand in the way of progress here, but you have to go about it gradually. If we persuade the Indians to sell us more land, we'll have to pay them a fair price for it. We all know some of the whites in this country just want to take it away from them.'

'As long as the sun rises and goes down . . . ' Kate murmured.

'What's that?'

'Oh, nothing.' She remembered Raven Sky

telling her what the U.S. government had promised them when they had removed the Indians to the territory — that they would be protected and offered a new way of life, and that they would be treated as separate Indian nations forever. But now there was a plan to allot the Indian lands to individual members of the tribes instead of allowing them to live on their lands communally, as they always had.

White speculators thought the way to bring Indians into the next century was to teach them how to manage their own lands, whether they desired it or not.

'Will we be attending the meeting with you?' Molly asked.

'No,' he said.

'I'd like to go,' said Kathleen, then swallowed hard. She hoped Wendall wouldn't ask her why. She hardly knew herself, except that she felt she had some stake in the issues.

Wendall rubbed his chin. 'All right. You can come with me, Sis, but I don't want Molly there in her condition.'

The next night when Kathleen and Wendall arrived in town, they saw that several wagons were parked along Main Street and a crowd had gathered in front of the store. Kate wondered how they thought they were keeping this meeting a secret from the

Indians. She followed her brother upstairs to the smoke-filled room above the store. Wendall and Kate nodded to the cowboys, railroad men, and businessmen standing around in the room. The faces of the men told Kathleen that some of them were less interested in the issue of the meeting than in a good fight.

Judge Tollett, his black suit and vest straining over a portly paunch, pounded a gavel, and one of the cowboys pulled a chair forward and offered it to Kate.

'Meeting come to order,' Judge Tollett bellowed. 'The business of this meeting is to discuss the fact that some speculators here have been trying to buy this here townsite from the Creeks and turn around and sell lots to the white businessmen, makin' 'em pay higher prices.'

'Here, here,' said a voice in the back of the room.

'Now, you men know that for several years we've had petitions before the Creek Council, trying to get the Indians to set aside a certain number of acres for a townsite in each town in the Creek Nation. All you men would get your lots at cost. The remaining property in the townsite would be disposed of subject to any agreement reached between the Creeks and U.S. government officials.'

'There's been a rumor,' said Frank Owen, taking the floor and gesturing with his corncob pipe, 'that someone here wants to take advantage of us. We heard that one of us went to St. Louis to get the money to pay the Creeks and finance those of us who couldn't pay them. Then we'd have to pay interest on the financing. I call this unfair.'

A loud protest broke out, and Judge Tollett pounded his gavel again.

J. P. Dwayne stood up and said, 'I believe you are suggesting that I am using my influence to buy the town and finance the other businessmen here. That is not true.' His voice grated in anger. 'If I find out who started this rumor, he'll have to face me.'

Roars rose up from the crowd.

Judge Tollett's bushy gray eyebrows met. 'Order!' he shouted.

'I propose a motion,' Frank Owen shouted above the din. 'Let's draw up a petition and go to the Creeks. We want to buy the town on our own terms.'

Cheers followed, and the judge again pounded his gavel to silence the rowdy bunch.

Pete Moss, a man who liked his liquor, stood on a chair. 'All those in favor, say aye,' he said. 'All those opposed, go home.'

Just then a crash resounded. Ray Farnsworth had let loose a string of insults and then upended his neighbor's chair. 'Indian-lover,' he yelled as the man he'd knocked to the floor struggled to his feet.

Six-shooters clicked all over the hall as hammers were pushed back. There was a rush for the stairway, and Wendall stood in front of Kate, his own gun drawn.

'I knew it'd come to this,' he muttered between clenched teeth. 'Let's make a run for it, Sis. Stay low.' He quickly pulled Kathleen to the stairs, and they wasted no time getting down them. They ducked their heads, making for the buckboard as the argument erupted into a brawl.

Bullets flew through the street, several landing in the walls of the stores. Patrons of the Tulsa Hotel dropped to the floor to avoid being hit by stray bullets. One bullet struck a gas lantern, and flames from the small fire danced in the dust as the lantern rolled. Horses in the fire's path screamed and reared, flailing their hooves. Two horses broke loose and raced down the street, eyes wild and teeth bared. Someone ran forward to stamp out the flames and calm the horses.

'Hurry up, Sis,' Wendall called as he picked up the reins. Kathleen leaped in just as the buckboard started to move, falling back against the seat as the horses lurched forward and raced out of town. A mile down the road, Wendall slowed the pace, letting the horses catch their breath.

'Scheming against the Indians won't do any good,' Wendall said. 'Those men will get nowhere.'

'Will they be cheated if these men buy the townsite?' Kate said.

'It'll take someone smarter and more sober than that bunch to cheat those shrewd Indians.'

'What do you think will happen to the Creek Nation, Wendall?'

He shrugged, shifting his position. 'It's bound to be absorbed as the country moves westward.' Growing more serious, he added, 'Someday there'll be no distinction between Indian and white. They're dyin' out now. What's left of 'em will be assimilated. All except the stubborn full-bloods who live in the hills. Some of them don't even speak English.'

Kathleen sat in silence, thinking of Raven Sky.

Wendall grunted. 'But that's the way of it, I suppose. We're the conquerors, even though most folks don't see it that way. The Indians used to roam the land. Now our kind want to use it for farming and grazing cattle. The two just don't mix.'

She lifted her hands helplessly. 'Why does it have to be this way?'

'The whites need to grow food for a hungry country. They need to take the minerals from the ground to make industries run. The wilderness isn't safe from the progress now that we're here.' He shrugged. 'That's regrettable, maybe, but it's the truth. The sooner everybody faces up to that the better off we'll be. But we have to live with the Indians and do the best we can by them.'

Kate felt saddened. She couldn't imagine the day when the prairie would be crowded with humanity the way it was back east. It would be a shame to bring industry here, she thought, looking up at the wide sky and the twinkling stars. In the densely populated cities in the East, you couldn't see the stars as you could here, where they seemed to shine down with great purpose. The Indians, she knew, needed to feel close to the heavens.

Wendall delivered Kathleen into the house and tended to the horses. Then he stood alone on the porch for a long time, smoking a cigarillo and looking out over the ranch he was so proud of.

He wondered about the wisdom of remaining in the territory. His ranch was doing well now. He controlled the cattle trade in these parts, something he would not easily give up. The way he saw it, he could continue his relationship with the Indians easily. But more and more whites were coming all the time, and already the other farmers were crowding him. The cattle could no longer roam the open range. They were fenced into the property he leased from the Indians. Profits were less than they had been in the days of the cattle drives, when cattle could graze where they chose.

And he worried about the women's safety. Molly was about to have their child. Would it be safe to bring a child up here? Wendall sighed. The frontier was all he knew. There was no other way for him to make a living. Both Molly and Kathleen were courageous women. They had survived all the dangers that had come to them. He hoped it would continue that way. But an increasing number of bad men roamed the territory in spite of the U.S. marshals sent out from the Western District of Arkansas, which had jurisdiction over whites in Indian Territory. 'Hanging' Judge Parker had as his goal to rid Indian Territory of white criminals who had set out to exploit the Indians. Parker was zealous in his work, and his marshals and deputies left no stone unturned. Still, it was a wild territory, too vast for anything but organized law to prevent the lawlessness that reigned in

70,000 square miles of outlaw-haunted terrain.

There were only the Indian Lighthorse Police in their high leather boots, military jackets, and trousers with a stripe down the side, with their long braids and their felt hats with rounded crowns and flat brims. Although they carried rifles, they had no legal authority over the white settlers.

On the trail that passed through Tulsa to the Sand Springs settlement that had sprung up west of the Arkansas River after the war, wealthy Creek landowners had built large, sturdy white houses — more evidence of their acceptance of the white man's way of life. But the down-trodden full-bloods who clung to the hills refused to move forward with progress.

Wendall knew that the Calhouns somehow were a part of this territory. If they could stay here, and if he could buy his land from the Indians one day, he would pass all this on to his children.

About the Indians' fate he was less sure. Those who adapted would survive the many changes that were forced on them. Still, he had seen some poverty-stricken Indians who hated what the whites had taken from them. Many had suffered at the hands of the federal government. That, Wendall feared, would be a lasting burden for both sides to carry.

21

Molly's baby was due in another month. Kathleen found that she both looked forward to the event and dreaded it. Molly had made it clear that she would rely on Kathleen's help, but Kathleen began to feel like an outsider again. And seeing Molly almost ready to produce Wendall's heir made her want a child of her own.

The long ride home from school every day invigorated her and helped her forget her troubles. One afternoon as she returned to the ranch, Wendall came out from the barn to help her dismount.

'Thanks,' she said as she dropped to the ground. 'Hard day?'

'All right.' As they walked Monty to the stables for his rubdown, Wendall was silent, and she could tell there was something on his mind. He unstrapped Monty's saddle for her, and Kate led the horse into his stall and gave him a lump of sugar. Then she walked with Wendall slowly toward the house.

Finally he said, 'Molly's due soon.'

She smiled at her brother. 'Is that what's on your mind?' Seeing a nervous flicker in his eyes she realized that, tough as he was, he was unsure about becoming a father. She put her hand on his arm and squeezed it, remembering how Amanda had died and, with her, Wendall's unborn child.

'Molly's in good health,' Kathleen said. 'She'll do fine. And Doc Johnson's delivered dozens of babies since he's been out here.'

'I know,' Wendall said, scuffing a boot in the dust. 'But I've been thinking about having you take Molly home to St. Louis to have the baby. What would you think of that?'

'Oh.' She glanced down and then back at Wendall. 'I hadn't thought of it. But of course, if that's what you want.'

'I've talked to Molly. She'd like her parents to see the child, and I can't leave the ranch just now. She'd have better medical care than she can here.'

Of course, women had babies here every day, but she could see why Wendall would want Molly's first baby to be born back east.

Wendall jerked his chin up. 'A trip might be good for you too, Sis,' he said.

She cocked her head, looking up at him. She supposed Molly and Wendall still harbored hopes of her marrying someone back east, but she wasn't going to waste time arguing about it. 'That'd be fine,' she said. 'When do you think we should leave?'

On a brisk Saturday morning, Wendall drove Kathleen and Molly to the station. The train was crowded with passengers going east. As Wendall bade them good-bye, he took his sister by the shoulders and hugged her.

'Don't worry, brother,' she said. 'I'll take good care of Molly and the baby.'

'I know you will, Sis,' he said, leaning down to kiss her on the cheek. Then he embraced his wife, holding her gently. 'I just hope you don't have such a good time in St. Louis that you decide to stay.'

'No chance of that,' Molly said, her eyes swimming with tears. Unspoken communication passed between husband and wife. Kate could see that they were so much in love it was hard for them to see anything else around them.

Tears stung her eyes, and she fought the unexpected feelings that gripped her. She had managed to keep herself in a sort of limbo ever since the green corn festival. Now that she was about to board the train, though, she had to acknowledge that Raven Sky had sent her no sign. Though she couldn't blame him, it broke her heart. She wondered at the last moment if she might tell Wendall, beg him to search for Raven Sky. But of course she knew she couldn't.

Suddenly Kathleen thought of a reason why Raven Sky had not sent her some word. He might think she did not want to see him. She had never apologized for not standing up for him in front of the posse. He probably reasoned that she did not love him, but sought only to shame him. Slowly it came to her that perhaps Raven Sky had feelings for her, just as she had for him. They had just never had a chance to understand each other.

Wendall stood back from his wife. Though she would only be gone for a couple of months, he found it hard to let her go. It was right that her parents should be on hand for the birth, but he had to remind himself that he was doing the right thing.

The women boarded the train and found their seats in their first-class reserved compartment. Wendall noted an unusually large number of guards on the train, more than he had ever seen on his many business trips east. He stopped the conductor to inquire about this.

The conductor eyed Wendall. Then, recognizing him, he said, 'Gold shipment aboard.'

Guards sat at either end of each passenger car, grimfaced, rifles pointed at the ceiling. Kate peered out at them, then pulled her head back into the compartment. She didn't say anything to Molly, but she exchanged glances with Wendall, aware of the worry in his eyes. He gave Molly one last hug, then left the car.

The train moved at its usual lackadaisical speed, making stops along the way for the convenience of passengers. The sun shining in the window made Kathleen sleepy, and she began to doze, her head against the side of the compartment. She was dimly aware of the jolting and rumbling as the train made its way northeast. Molly, too, had settled in and was gazing dreamily out the window.

Suddenly Kathleen was jolted awake by gunfire. At first she thought it was merely passengers shooting prairie chickens. Then she heard glass shatter, as one of the guards at the end of the car broke a window with his rifle and blazed away.

'What is it?' asked Molly, clutching her stomach, her eyes wide. Kathleen bolted upright and looked out the window. A group of horsemen bore down on the train, which jerked to a dead stop. Some of the outlaws dismounted and boarded the train while their leader covered them from horseback midway down the train. Scarves covered the men's faces.

'Get down,' Kathleen said as she helped

Molly down onto the floor for cover. Some of the passengers were attempting to return the fire. She heard the outlaws barking orders. Above them, glass tinkled and crashed as a bullet flew through the window of the compartment.

As heavy boots stomped through the car, Kathleen peered out of the compartment. The bandit on their car brandished six-shooters. The guard at the front of the car lay sprawled on his seat, and another outlaw at the other end of the car had the second guard covered. Kate crawled across to the door of their compartment to see more of what was going on.

'Toss your rifle out the window,' ordered the taller of the two bandits. His voice was muffled behind the scarf, but she could see steely gray eyes beneath the brim of the black felt hat that rode low over his forehead. The rest of his features were obscured by the scarf. He wielded his guns with confidence, making Kathleen tremble. She moved back to Molly as the man barked at the other passengers.

'We don't intend to hurt any o' you folks. All we want is the gold on this train. If everyone cooperates, no one will get hurt.'

His words did nothing to reassure Kate, and when she looked at Molly's white face, her stomach clenched in fright.

The tall bandit continued as if he had all the time in the world. 'I want every man here to hold out his hands so we can see 'em.' He started down the aisle, past the compartments, examining the hands held out to him. He passed by most of them, then stopped and leaned on the door of the compartment across from Kate's and Molly's. He stared at a rounded man with a bald pate who was dressed in a tailored suit and wore a gold watch chain and spectacles. Kate recognized the unfortunate man. He was a banker from St. Louis.

'I said hold out your hands,' said the outlaw, nudging the man in the ribs with his gun. Sweat poured down the fat man's face as he reluctantly held them out.

'The hands of a woman,' snorted the bandit, then raised his voice to the other passengers. 'Hardworking men with calluses on their hands, they work for their money, and we got nothin' against 'em. This one here gets his money soft and easy.' He poked the barrel of his gun into the fat man's stomach. 'Hand it over.'

He motioned to the other outlaw, who had searched the guard and taken his pistol. The second outlaw was shorter, but with broader shoulders.

'Take his money.' The tall outlaw proceeded through the car.

'Who are they?' whispered Molly, trembling as she stared after the cocky bandit who sauntered past.

'I don't know,' Kathleen said. But for some reason he looked familiar. 'I'm sure I've never met him, but I think I've seen his eyes before.'

'I wish they'd hurry,' said Molly. 'What are they doing?'

Outside, more orders were roared. Suddenly the train jolted forward, moved about fifty yards, then stopped.

'Stay down, Molly,' Kathleen risked peeking out the window. The gang had detached the express car that carried the safe. When the rest of the cars were a safe distance away, they heard a loud explosion and Kathleen ducked, holding her ears. Then she looked again. The men had apparently blown the safe open with dynamite, sending currency wafting through the air. Passengers leaned out of the train to watch. Outside, the outlaws filled their hats with money and, loaded the gold bars into their saddlebags. They moved more quickly now, as if anxious to get away. Kate watched in fascination as the gang members rode up and down the train, still holding the conductors and engineer under guard.

Some of the passengers were even cheering the outlaws now.

Then the tall outlaw returned to their car. He walked slowly up and down, looking at the passengers again, and Kathleen saw that he had a slightly uneven gait that she had been too nervous to notice before. Either he was limping from a recent wound or a break that had not healed right. His stiff leg did nothing to lessen his bravado.

'Now, I don't want you folks to do anything foolish till we get away. We'll need a hostage to guarantee our safety. He looked around the car and then said, 'You.' The masked man was looking directly at Kathleen.

'Get up.' He walked over and gripped her arm. She rose, wincing, as he increased the pressure on her arm until it hurt.

Kate struggled to free her arm from his grip. Molly screamed, but the outlaw made a gesture as if to hit her with the back of his hand.

'Leave her alone,' Kate yelled, throwing herself between Molly and the man.

'Shut up,' he said to Kathleen, pulling her back to her feet. 'I don't hit pregnant women.'

Glaring at the outlaw, Kathleen said in a controlled voice, 'It's all right, Molly. He won't hurt us.' Her look dared the man to lay a finger on Molly. If he did, she thought, she would tear his eyes out with her fingernails.

The masked man twisted her arm behind her and thrust her forward, rendering her powerless. He pushed her ahead and out of the car, and she stumbled down the steps to the rocky ground beside the tracks.

A third man walked over to them. Much shorter, with a wiry build, he spoke in a higher-pitched voice. 'All right, let's go,' he said.

Before Kate could open her mouth to protest again, they tied a red scarf around her mouth, gagging her. Then they flung her onto a brown mare. Once she was mounted in the saddle, they tied her hands to the pommel. She struggled at first, but saw it was useless. She searched for a look at Molly on the train, as the rest of the gang relinquished their posts.

Fear and panic replaced her initial shock. No one would move to stop the outlaws, because they held a gun on her. She finally saw Molly. She was leaning out of the car, her face dead-white. Another passenger pulled her back in.

The outlaw who had claimed Kathleen held the reins of her horse. At a signal from the wiry little leader of the bunch, he jerked Kate's horse forward. As the horses set off at a gallop, Kathleen twisted her hands within the confining ropes and hung on desperately.

The gang crossed open prairie for about a mile, then ascended a ridge. Kate jounced along with them, afraid she would fall and not be able to protect herself. They followed open country for several hours, passing through groves of cottonwood and birch, fording streams. Checking the sun, Kathleen could tell they had gone south into the Cherokee Nation.

Kate was a good horsewoman, but after several hours in the saddle, with the scarf nearly choking her, she began to weary. Wondering how quickly the train would get word out to look for the outlaws, she looked at her hard-riding captors, slouched back against the cantles as the horses made their way down a rocky incline. Shivers ran up her spine. There seemed no escape, so she bent her efforts toward keeping her seat.

A line of trees loomed ahead, and they approached a river crossing. Kate tried to figure out how far east they'd come. She speculated that this might be the Canadian River. Her throat felt parched, and she wished they'd stop for a drink, but the outlaws turned and descended into a narrow box canyon before they reached the river. The trail narrowed, twisted, and turned until they passed through an opening in some rocks and came out on sloping ground. Still they rode downward into the valley, keeping cover in the thick trees.

The leader raised a hand, and they halted. From a cliff that rose directly in front of them, she saw a flash of light. Then they rode ahead, but at a slower pace. The ground leveled, and they passed a plum thicket, entered an alfalfa patch, and crossed a grassy field dotted with sycamores.

Approaching a ramshackle log cabin and a corral with several good-looking horses in it, the outlaws halted and dismounted.

Kate was surprised to see a woman emerge from the cabin. Wearing a long-sleeved dress with fringe on the bodice, she carried a gun. The men seemed to defer to this leathery-faced dark-haired woman. She motioned to Kathleen's captor. 'Bring her in, Billy,' the woman said.

'Okay, Belle,' said the tall man who still held Kate's reins, and he cut her hands loose from the pommel. Weapons were in evidence everywhere as the men tied up their horses. She got down docilely and followed as she was directed into the cabin.

Inside, the woman sat on a chair as the other outlaws poured the loot out of their saddlebags onto the table.

'Look at that gold,' said one of the bandits as they counted out shares under the supervision of the woman, who appeared to be the leader of the gang.

Finally Belle turned her attention to Kate. 'Let's have a look at her,' she said as she sauntered over to the hostage. The woman was not pretty, but she had a certain bravado that commanded the respect of all the men. She circled Kathleen slowly, rocking her weight from one foot to the other in a rough gait. Kathleen averted her face.

'What d'ya aim to do with her, Billy?' Belle asked.

Kathleen glanced at the man who had brought her here, now that he had removed his mask and hat, she had a chance to see his face. A slight upturn of his lip formed a perpetual smirk, and he had a square jaw. A scar ran down his left cheek to his chin. His skin had a sallow tint to it, and his eyes were bloodshot.

'Maybe I'll keep her, Belle. What do you think?'

'You know we don't keep women. Too much trouble. They always try to run away and squeal. I say we blindfold her, ride her out of here, and leave her somewhere. If we keep her, they'll come lookin' for her. If we give her back, maybe they'll be less anxious to come after us. No one will want to mess with Belle Starr on this, 'specially if we give them back this hostage soon as we divide up the money and go our separate ways.'

Shocked, Kathleen realized she was in the presence of the famous outlaw who had ridden with the James-Younger gang and had championed rustlers, horse thieves, and bootleggers in Indian Territory. Kate had heard of Belle Starr, but she certainly had never thought she'd meet her face to face. A man approached. He held a long knife and had greasy long hair.

'What say we have a little fun with her first?'

Billy stepped in the other man's path, blocking his approach to Kate. 'I picked her, and I brought her back. I decide what happens to her. You slime keep your hands off her till I say so.' He touched the butt of his gun. 'Anybody says different, step outside.'

There were no challengers. Kate slowly exhaled in relief, trying to be calm. The idea of them all pawing and mauling her threatened to shake the sanity right out of her, and she needed her presence of mind. If she could reason with Billy, she might have some hope of escape, but she didn't know where they were. She could wander for days in the wilderness without seeing another human, even if she escaped. *God*, she prayed, *send someone after me now!*

Billy strode over and looked down at her. She could smell his foul breath as he leered at her through hard gray eyes.

'Over there.' Indicating a door on the other side of the room, he yanked her to her feet, shoved her roughly in front of him, and pushed her through the doorway.

Inside the smaller room she saw a seedy mattress lying on the floor and a small wooden chest standing to one side. Billy closed the door behind him, and she went instantly rigid as he came up to her and put his hands on her shoulders. She looked around frantically for a way of escape, but there was none.

She started to protest Billy's clumsy advances, then made herself stand still. Perhaps she could trick him into leaving her alone until she could think of a plan. By then there might be a posse after the outlaws, and she would be rescued. She had to think of something to say. Steeling herself to defy the evil-smelling man, she jerked her shoulders backward and walked quickly away from him.

'You're not going to waste your opportunity in the daytime are you?' she said, imitating the hard voice and the rough swagger of Belle Starr.

371

He looked at her suspiciously. 'What d'ya mean?'

She summoned her courage. 'Well, if you enjoy me now, all those men out there will want their turn.' She gave him a teasing smirk, struggling not to choke on her words. 'I'd much rather stay with you.' Her stomach churned but she tried to sound convincing. She cocked her head, and looked into his lustful, bloodshot eyes.

He stared back at her, licking his lips. 'I getcha, honey. We'd be better off at night, with nobody watching.'

'That's right, Billy.' She placed one hand on his chest and began to walk her fingers up his shirt buttons, choking down the bile in her throat. 'You keep those other animals outta here for me.'

He put his arms around her waist, and she made herself accept his embrace.

'You a married woman?' he asked.

Kathleen hesitated. She didn't want him to think her innocent, or he would not believe her promises. On the other hand, she wanted to lessen the outlaw's fears that an angry husband might bear down on the hideout. She had to get him to let his guard down.

She kept her eyes on his as she said, 'My husband's dead.'

'That so?' He swayed back and forth.

Kathleen thought she would be ill, but she forced herself to look directly into his hard eyes. If she could keep her wits about her, she might be able to get away. Everything depended on what she said and did now. If there was one thing she was certain of, it was her intelligence. She was sure she could think better than these halfwits.

'It's hard for me to wait,' he said.

'I'll make it worth your while,' she said, still looking him in the eye. Her heart pounded with the fear that he would decide to take her now. She would rather die than give her body to this man.

'You better live up to your promises.' He grasped her arm and tossed her onto the mattress. 'I need a drink,' he said. 'I'll be back.' He left the room, and Kathleen heard a key turn in the lock.

She sat up wearily on the shabby mattress. Feeling lost and scared, she wondered how she had summoned up so much bravado. The fearful ride away from the train and the sight of Molly's frightened face had been enough to tear her apart.

What if a posse did find them? The outlaws would shoot her before she could be rescued. She had to think of a way to save her life. The idea of that filthy man molesting her was unthinkable. Briefly, Raven Sky's face flashed through her mind, but she forced the image away. It only reminded her that she had experienced sensual love with a man she desired. As sinful as that might have been, it made the thought of rape by these beasts all the more impossible to endure.

22

As soon as the outlaws had disappeared over the hill, pandemonium broke out on the train. Horses were brought out of the freight car, riders dispatched back to Tulsa with haste. Molly sent word straight to Wendall. The train got up steam and continued east.

That night two men pounded on the door of Wendall Calhoun's ranch house.

'What is it?' Wendall said, jerking open the door.

'Train's been held up. Your sister's been taken hostage,' panted one of the riders. 'The outlaws got away with thirty thousand dollars, too. We're getting up a posse in town.'

'My wife?' he asked, the hair standing up on the back of his neck.

'You're wife's all right. She's goin' on to St. Louis.'

'I'll get my men and leave immediately.'

Wendall picked up his holster and his rifle then strode to the stables and saddled his mount. Slipping his Winchester into its sling he checked his saddlebags for extra ammunition.

'Hank,' he called to his foreman, 'you and

the boys find out where the outlaws were last seen. I'll ride into town and join the posse. They'll need as many men as they can get.'

At least Molly was safe, he thought. He prayed that Kathleen would keep her head and not do anything foolish. In one smooth motion, he flung the reins over the saddle horn and mounted, the horse stepping sideways as he took his seat. Then he dug in his heels and rode hell-bent-for-leather into town. Word of the robbery had already reached Tulsa, and he found horses and riders in front of the Dwayne Store. Some of the men who had ridden after Kate when Raven Sky had swept her away had now gathered to ride again.

'We were just comin' after you,' said Frank Owen as soon as Wendall reined in.

Wendall yelled, 'Let's go, men. We've got a hard ride ahead of us,' and they rode out of town.

Behind them, in the shadows of the buildings, on a motionless red stallion, sat a tall Indian dressed in dark blue hunting shirt with green fringe. Raven Sky. He had been alerted by Indians who heard the commotion in town and brought news of the train robbery to his father's house. A white woman, they said, had been taken hostage.

376

She was the sister of the rancher known as Calhoun.

Raven Sky had crept silently into town, keeping to the shadows, watching the white men as they made noisy preparations, furtively listening to their conversation until, finally, he knew what he had to do.

As soon as the posse left, he slipped out of town and rode hard across the prairie, following trails that he knew, stopping only to rest and water his horse. He was headed for a hill he'd heard the white men mention — the hill over which the outlaws had disappeared with Kathleen. From there he could easily track them.

The white outlaws who roamed Indian Territory were careless and easy to track. It would be a simple matter to find them. He didn't even think about Kathleen being his tormentor. He did not question his need to rescue her.

★　★　★

Kathleen awoke to sunrise. At first she couldn't remember where she was, but everything came back to her when she saw the fully clothed man sleeping nearby on the shabby mattress. Feeling a wave of nausea, she squirmed away from him and huddled on the floor. Her temples throbbed as she remembered what had happened last night.

The gang members had celebrated their success by getting drunk. The outlaws had forced her to act as their servant, pouring their liquor and refilling their glasses. Whenever one of the men tried to touch her, Billy had stuck a gun in his face, so the others had left her alone. He had danced clumsily around the room, then sent her to the flea-bitten bedroom to wait for him. When he had finally entered the bedroom, though, he had simply collapsed on the bed in a drunken stupor and passed out.

When Kathleen crept to the door and looked through the keyhole, she saw that Belle had placed a guard at the table in the outer room. The woman outlaw, evidently too smart to allow all of her men to get drunk at one time, must have kept some of them sober enough to act as sentinels. Kathleen had known at once that the only way to get past the guard was to threaten him with Billy's guns, but he had left them outside the door.

Hoping that the guard would fall asleep, she had kept watch through the keyhole for hours, listening to the even breathing of her captor as the alert guard played solitaire in the next room. Finally, drowsiness had overcome her, and she had fallen asleep.

Now Kate tiptoed to the window to look out, praying that Billy would not wake. No one was about. Crossing the room silently, she looked through the keyhole and discovered that the guard at the table had been replaced by Belle herself. She was drinking coffee from a tin mug and staring straight at the door behind which Kate watched. Kate's heart leaped to her throat, and she stumbled backward and caught herself, nearly tripping over Billy's sprawling form on the mattress.

★　★　★

Raven Sky reached the canyon early in the morning. His progress was slower now. He found it difficult to track his quarry over the rocky ground but he had located the opening through which the outlaws had left the canyon. Raven Sky sat still on his horse and watched Wendall's posse pass over the ridge and enter the canyon. He hadn't thought the white men would get this far this fast. But Wendall Calhoun was a sharp man, driven to find his sister. For the first time, Raven Sky considered letting the white men know of his presence.

He had no doubt that he could find and release Kathleen himself. But if she was still angry with him she might turn him over to

379

the posse as soon as she got the chance. However, if she saw him coming with her brother, she might understand that he wished her only good.

But could he trust this white man? If he could talk to Calhoun alone he might be able to reason with him, offer his help as scout. If he aided the rescue of Kathleen, he might be free of their suspicion of crimes against her. Working with the white men might win him favor on both sides. And where Kathleen was concerned, he was involved. He knew that without question. He would love her forever, even if she never returned that love.

The posse made its way down the trail toward Raven Sky. The Indian needed to act wisely, to gain their confidence quickly without getting shot in the process. He decided to raise a flag of truce and trust that Wendall would honor it and hear him out.

Raven Sky dismounted and pulled a white piece of linen from his saddlebag. Then he took a knife from his belt and cut a long branch from a sapling. He tied the white cloth to the branch and hoisted it above him. Then he walked to a spot on the trail that was visible for some distance and planted the flag.

The white men came on, moving faster now. Suddenly Wendall saw the white flag waving in the slight breeze that blew in the canyon. He signaled his men to stop, and they pulled up behind him.

'Might be a trap,' one of the men said.

He edged the horse forward slowly, coming closer to the flag. He was keenly aware of the six-shooters in his holsters, in case he had to make a fast draw. Still, he did not touch his guns, wanting to see who was waving truce. Approaching the flag he called out, 'What do you want?'

Raven Sky came down from the rocks to where Wendall could see him but the rest of the posse could not. He raised his hand in a gesture of peace and walked forward, shoulders thrown back. He was not armed. He held Wendall's gaze, his eyes unflinching.

'I want to talk,' said Raven Sky.

'I have no time for this. We're hunting outlaws.'

'I can help you.'

'Talk fast or get out of my way.' Wendall could not keep the sharp edge out of his voice.

Raven Sky stepped forward, strength evident in his muscular form, a haughty arrogance in his eyes. He had no difficulty convincing Wendall Calhoun that he was facing his equal.

'I can help you track the outlaws,' said Raven Sky. 'I will find their hideout. I want her safe as much as you do.'

'I know what you want from her.'

Raven Sky stiffened at the insult. 'I want your sister for my wife, Calhoun, but she does not care for me.' His eyes flashed his anger.

Wendall paused. He did not fully trust the Indian, but something made him listen to what Raven Sky said. He had never understood the relationship between his sister and this man, but he had thought they cared for each other deeply.

'If I help you, we'll find her sooner,' said Raven Sky.

Wendall narrowed his eyes, and his horse sidestepped on the rocky terrain, snorting and rearing his head. Perhaps that was true, he thought. Perhaps Raven Sky had had a reason to run off with Kathleen to that cave. A reason he didn't yet understand.

'We will accept your help,' he said. 'What do you want from us in exchange?'

'A chance to prove myself to you and your men.'

'It is agreed, but you must find her. If my sister gets out of there unharmed, I will ask her to treat you fairly. Until then, you have my word no one will string you up. Come.' He turned his horse around and Raven Sky called softly to the red stallion. He leaped onto his horse and followed Wendall back to the waiting men.

'Hold your fire,' Wendall shouted. 'It's the Indian, Raven Sky. He's with us.'

'I'll be durned,' said Frank Owens, shaking his head in amazement and putting his hand to his gun.

Wendall saw the gesture. 'Don't,' he said. 'I gave Raven Sky my word that you wouldn't harm him. He'll lead us to the hideout. We might find out that we've been wrong about him. Kathleen will tell us the truth when we find her. We need his tracking skills. Every minute counts now, and if he can lead us to Kate quicker, he'll earn his reprieve. Come on, men, let's go.'

Raven Sky rode ahead and waited for them on the floor of the canyon. Then he turned his horse and led them single file through the small opening in the rocks. The men had to dismount to get their heavily laden horses through. Cursing and swearing, they followed the Indian.

On the other side of the pass, Raven Sky examined the ground and the surrounding brush. Then he pointed out the way they should go.

23

As the posse passed through the opening in the rocks that led out of the canyon, a lookout signaled with a mirror to the outlaw camp guard, Chet Hardin, a tough-looking rustler recently befriended by Belle. As soon as he saw the signal, he dashed into the sleepy camp.

'Belle!' he shouted as he ran up to the cabin and burst through the door. 'Posse comin' down from the canyon. There's an Indian tracker with 'em, too.'

Belle walked across the room, thinking. She had to decide whether to fight it out or run. The outlaws stumbled to their feet and buckled on their gun belts.

Kathleen, still huddled in the cramped bedroom, heard the commotion. At the outlaw's words, 'Indian tracker,' she bit her lip, stifling the cry that rose to her throat. Did she dare hope that Indian was Raven Sky? Someone from the train could have hurried back to Tulsa and alerted Wendall, she reasoned, but surely her brother and Raven Sky would not have ridden out together in search of her. Unless . . .

She shook her head, refusing to believe in pipedreams. It was beyond hope and reason that Raven Sky might be traveling with a posse of white men from Tulsa. After all, he was the enemy of her brother's friends. No, she told herself, it was not possible. They must have hired another member of one of the tribes to lead them to the bandits' hideaway.

The knock thundered on the door, and Billy grunted in response.

'Get up, Billy,' came the grating voice of Belle Starr through the wooden door.

Billy sat up, holding his head, and struggled to his feet, a dazed look in his unfocused eyes. 'What's goin' on?' he muttered.

Kathleen shrank back against the wall as Belle pounded on the door again.

'Come on, Bill. Posse's comin'.'

Kathleen could hear the other outlaws gathering in the adjacent room.

'What're we gonna do, Belle?' one of them asked.

'I say we stand and fight,' said another outlaw. 'We outnumber 'em.'

'Shut up, everybody,' Belle said. 'I can't hear myself think.' She fell silent for a moment, evidently considering their predicament. 'I don't need another run in with

Hangin' Judge Parker right now. As I see it, there's only one way out.'

Billy pulled on his boots, unlocked the door, and kicked it open. Kate watched and listened in silence as Belle and the gang hatched their plan.

'I wasn't anywhere near that train,' Belle said. 'Far as they know, the men who held up that train had nothin' to do with Belle Starr.'

'What're you sayin', Belle?'

'You all can make a getaway, while I stay here and talk to that posse.'

'You can't do that, Belle.'

'They can't prove nothin'. I'll tell 'em they're trespassin'.' She picked up her rifle and gestured to the men. 'Now, you all saddle up and git. Don't come back for a month.'

The men collected their gear, and Belle turned to stare at Kate.

'What about her?' asked Chet Hardin.

'Get her out of here fast,' Belle said. 'She's your charge,' she barked at Billy. 'Get her on a horse.'

Billy glowered at Kathleen, then lumbered out of the cabin toward the corral, muttering about women being more trouble than they were worth.

Kathleen thought frantically, trying to find a reason to stay here until the posse arrived. She eyed Belle, who was looking at her, leaning on her rifle, one foot on a chair. For a moment, they assessed each other — two women on opposite sides of the law.

Billy returned and walked over to Kate, grabbed her arm, and yanked her toward the door. Outside, he pushed her toward a brown and white spotted pony. Grumbling, he shook the neckerchief Kate recognized from the day before and began to curl it into a gag.

'I don't need that,' she told Billy, looking him in the eye. He continued to prepare the gag, evidently not believing her. He took a step closer to her, but she put up a hand.

'I promise I won't disappoint you. Let me ride with my hands and mouth free, and I won't give you any trouble.'

Suddenly she thought of a further way to trick him. She walked up to him, leaned close to his ear, and whispered, 'I didn't disappoint you last night, did I Billy?' She gave him what she hoped was an innocent smile.

Billy looked confused, but he put the gag back into his pocket.

Kate's heart was pounding violently. If she could convince this hateful man that he had enjoyed her favors during his drunken stupor, if she could endear herself to him, maybe she could gain his trust. She had to be free on the ride to make her move.

Billy eyed her slyly. 'All right. But let me warn you, girlie, you make one false move and you'll have a bullet in your back.' He put his hand on his gun.

Kathleen nodded.

'Hurry up,' he said, jerking his head toward the pony, and Kathleen put her foot in the stirrup and mounted. The pony shifted its weight slightly as Kate settled herself, and she gathered her skirt around her hips to accommodate the saddle. She peered through the trees, hoping to catch a glimpse of the posse, but there was none.

Bill pointed his gun at Kate, and she sent the pony forward. In single file the gang moved away from the hideout, in the opposite direction from the way they'd come.

'Where are you taking me?' asked Kathleen when they came out of the woods and onto a grassy meadow.

'Away from here,' growled Billy. 'You be quiet now. We have to move fast if we're to outrun that posse.' He slapped the reins across his horse's neck, and the gang took off.

Kathleen squeezed her knees to the saddle as they raced over the countryside, heading west, nerves taut, her heart beating rapidly. The posse had almost caught up with the outlaws, but they had escaped again. Kate felt sure Wendall was with the posse. If only there were some way she could let them know where she was.

★ ★ ★

When the posse rode into the outlaw camp, they found Belle Starr in front of her tumble-down cabin. She was sitting in a rocking chair with her feet propped up on a wooden crate and her eyes closed. Smoke curled up from the stone chimney where she'd lit a fire, as if she had no reason to hide her whereabouts. Across her knee was a Winchester .44 carbine. No one else was about. A scrawny mongrel lazed in the sun at her feet. The dog raised its head and growled at the posse, but Belle spoke sharply to it and the dog put its mangy head back between its paws.

Raven Sky looked at the ground and surrounding brush as Wendall dismounted and strode up to the woman.

'You always greet strangers with a rifle, ma'am?'

'I do when they're trespassing. What d'ya want?'

'We're looking for the robbers of the Frisco bound for St. Louis yesterday. You wouldn't know anything about that, would you?'

'Sure wouldn't. Been right here all the time.'

Wendall eyed the infamous woman with suspicion, taking in her leathery skin, dirty teeth, and the .44. He knew she was lying. 'Anybody pass by here? A gang of about six men riding with a woman hostage?'

'Haven't seen a soul. Just me and my son. Jim!' she called. A lanky adolescent came out of the house and leaned on the door. He carried a lethal sawed-off 12-gauge shotgun. 'We ain't had no visitors, have we?'

'Nope,' the kid answered, clamping his mouth shut.

Raven Sky was examining some hoof prints that Jim and Belle had not been quite successful in covering. Then he put his ear to the ground. He stood up and joined Wendall. 'A group of men have ridden off recently,' he said.

Belle pointed her rifle at him. 'No one calls Belle Starr a liar to her face,' she said menacingly. 'Now, you ride out of here the way you came in.'

'What if we ride out the other way?' asked Wendall.

'You get a load of buckshot in your back. This here is my land, leased nice and legal from the Cherokees, and while you're on my property you do what I say.' She stood up and leveled the rifle, but Wendall only glared at her.

'They left here not long ago,' said Raven Sky. 'And your sister is with them.' Belle aimed the rifle at Raven Sky's head. His blood boiled, but he knew about Belle Starr. She would shoot. They turned back to their horses and mounted. Wendall signaled to the men to go back the way the had come.

When they had passed through the forest, Raven Sky motioned for them to stop. 'The outlaws headed west,' he said pointing in past Belle's house. 'We'll circle around.'

'Won't she have a lookout?' Frank Owen asked.

'They're riding too hard and fast to bother with signals,' said Raven Sky.

'Can we catch them?'

'We will catch them.' Raven Sky's black eyes looked into Wendall's blue-gray ones. In that moment, they knew they could trust each other. They would not rest until they knew Kathleen was safe.

The men watered their horses and drank from a stream, then mounted up. Wendall rubbed the back of his neck and stretched his shoulders. His eyes had a sunken, tired look, but there was no time to rest.

Frank Owen rode up to Wendall and spoke

in a low voice. 'You think this Indian knows what he's doing?'

'You got any better ideas, Frank?' he asked the other man.

Frank shrugged and fell back.

Wendall and his men rode out of the valley and ascended a ridge. Standing on a butte and looking over a wide stretch of country-side, they saw no sign of the outlaws. But Raven Sky's eyes were sharper then theirs. He sat very still, watching. Then he raised a hand and pointed at the horizon.

Far in the distance, tiny moving figures approached the horizon, leaving a cloud of dust behind.

'They're half a day ahead of us,' said Wendall. He wheeled his horse. 'Let's go.'

Raven Sky shut off his thinking, directing all of his attention to tracking the gang. He could not allow himself to think about the fact that Kathleen was with them. She had been with them in Belle Starr's cabin last night, but he didn't think about that either. He had seen the tracks in the dirt. One horse bore a lighter load — Kathleen.

Wendall's train of thought was similar. The thought of his sister at the hands of those vile creatures made him see red. But he, too, concentrated on the job at hand. The horses would soon be too tired to travel, and they would have to find fresh animals.

Wendall was beginning to feel a grudging admiration for Raven Sky. He had thought him one of the finest men in the Creek Nation until he had unleashed his savage instincts on Kate that day. But Wendall had had time to quell his anger. Kathleen had said little about the incident in the cave, and Wendall acknowledged that he knew nothing of Raven's Sky's side of the story.

At first his fury over the Indian's treatment of his sister had blinded him to all else. But now, as he watched Raven Sky riding his powerful steed, he felt his respect growing. He was nearly ready to admit that perhaps he had misjudged this man.

Raven Sky was an expert tracker with razor-sharp senses, and Wendall could see his dogged determination. Perhaps this man truly loved Kate. Wendall remembered his own first marriage — to the beautiful half-Cherokee Amanda — and he could well imagine how Kate might feel about Raven Sky.

He turned his thoughts back to the job at hand. They had to find Kate. His expression grim, he hoped that she was still safe. He looked at the strong back of the Indian riding ahead of him. How would Raven Sky react if Kathleen had been hurt? Wendall hated to think of what he might do.

Kathleen was beginning to feel the effects of the long, hard ride. By evening, even the outlaws had begun to look exhausted. They finally stopped under a cliff in a grove of willows, and Kate leaned over the saddle.

'Please, I've got to rest,' she said to Billy, who rode close to her. The scout circled back to see if there was any sign of their pursuers.

'That posse's gotta rest, too,' Billy grumbled. 'We might as well camp here.' They drew the horses close to the cliff and spread out blankets. One of the men split off and took another trail, to try to confuse the posse.

Kathleen felt more weary than she'd thought possible. Every muscle ached, and she was bruised and saddle sore. She was hungry as well. She gladly accepted the beef jerky and bread that Billy offered her.

'Is that all the food we have?' she asked after she'd eaten it.

'Can't risk a fire,' he told her. 'We'll be up before dawn, anyway. I've got half a mind to wait here and pick off your friends from ambush.'

She stiffened. 'What makes you so sure they're my friends?' she snapped at him.

'Well, now, they ain't no friends of ours, but they're mighty anxious to catch up with us. Can't imagine what they want with us, lessen it's you.'

'Maybe,' Kate said. She had to try to prevent a shoot-out unless she was sure the outlaws would lose. Perhaps, if she could stay awake, she could steal a gun.

Billy took first watch while she tried to rest. But soon her weariness defeated her resolve to stay awake, and she fell asleep on the hard ground.

★ ★ ★

At nightfall, Raven Sky led the posse to a Creek settlement comprising several log cabins, one large stone building, and a few business establishments. The Indians came out to greet them, and Raven Sky told the town elders that the posse was hunting white robbers and kidnappers. The Creeks fed and watered the horses and offered the men a meal and a place to rest.

'We appreciate your hospitality,' said Wendall when he was introduced to the town chief, a muscular older man dressed in finely embroidered hunting shirt and fringed leather jacket.

'Friends of Raven Sky are welcome here,' the chief said. 'You will be refreshed for your journey. We will lend you fresh horses, and our warriors will accompany you on your hunt for the outlaws. The woman they have with them, she means much to Raven Sky.'

'To me, also,' Wendall said. 'I am her brother.'

The old man nodded. 'We will help you. These bandits that roam our lands, we would be better off without them.'

Wendall rejoined his men, who were glancing around nervously. These Indians seemed much like the ones in Tulsa, but they were awfully friendly with Raven Sky, and the men had not forgotten their recent encounter with him.

The chief invited them to eat with him, and the men followed him to a large frame house at the edge of the town. They found the place spotless. The chief's wife bade them sit at a long wooden table, where she served a meal of venison and corn.

Raven Sky sat silently at the end of the table in a straight-back cane chair, hardly tasting his food.

After the meal, the men slept on mats and blankets in front of the fireplace. With warm food in their bellies the exhausted search party slept soundly while Raven Sky ventured out into the darkness alone to continue his quest in the pale moonlight.

In the morning, when Raven Sky touched

him on the shoulder, Wendall sat up quickly and roused the other men. They stumbled out to a well in the center of the yard to splash water on their faces.

Hearing the soft clop of hooves on the road, they looked up to see six young Creek braves riding toward them. Wendall remembered the chief's promise of help and extended his hand to each of them. The posse mounted up and together the party rode out of the settlement, following Raven Sky.

★ ★ ★

The scout rode into camp at first light. He poked Billy and the other outlaws. Kathleen woke to find she had pulled the blanket entirely over her face, for the night had been very cold. Her first thought was that she had not succeeded in staying awake long enough to try to escape.

'Get a move on,' Billy said, rolling out of his blanket and getting to his feet. He stretched, yawned, and went to saddle the horses.

'We're gonna need fresh horses today, Billy,' said Clem Ennis, a ratty-looking man who looked to be about ten years Billy's senior. He was smaller, and his whiskers seemed to stick out in all directions.

'Can't risk making a trade around here,' Billy said. 'We'll have to get far enough out of these parts so no questions'll be asked. We're still in Creek country, I reckon.'

Kate was given one slice of stale bread, which she accepted gratefully and ate with silent concentration, knowing she would need nourishment to keep up the grueling pace for another day.

The bandits rode all morning. At noon they stopped outside a small village. Clem and Chet went into the town to trade the horses for fresh ones while Billy and two other men stayed with Kate. She was allowed to rest in a grove of tall oaks, free from undergrowth. She ate some apples they had picked in a nearby orchard. Apples had never tasted so good to her.

She wondered idly how far they had come, but she was too tired to worry about it much. All thought of escape was submerged below the immediate necessity of surviving. If she could just get her strength up, maybe she would be able to think better. Right now the thought of outrunning these men seemed impossible, and she didn't relish the thought of a bullet in her back.

Billy chewed an apple and stared at Kate. She tensed, wondering what he was contemplating. Then he dropped the core of his apple into the dirt and walked over to her.

He grabbed her arm and pulled her up. Then he placed his dirty mouth over hers and forced a kiss, which made her shudder. She struggled in his arms, but he just raised his head and laughed at her.

'Don't think you're off the hook yet, little miss. Soon as we get where we're goin', you can live up to all your promises,' he said.

'Where are we going?'

'Ah, you'd like to know, wouldn't you? Then you'd leave a sign for your friends. You just go with us, and you'll find out when we get there.'

He released Kate roughly and she staggered backward, away from him. She had to leave a sign for the posse, she thought, so they'd know she was still with the gang.

The two men returned from the village with fresh horses. Kate's pony was replaced with a reddish mare with a white star on its forehead. The red horse caused a pang in her heart. It reminded her so much of Raven Sky's stallion that it could have been its offspring.

'Mount up,' Billy said. As she passed him, he reached out and squeezed her bottom, making her flinch.

At nightfall the outlaws stopped at a broken-down farm to ask for food. The old farmer, a wizened black man who looked as if he'd seen days with a gun himself, looked over the men sitting on their horses in front of his house. He didn't know who they were, but he seemed to sense that he'd better not refuse them. He went to his potbellied stove and prepared a meal.

Billy posted a lookout and joined the rest of the bandits in the house. They ate beans and stew in silence, their shotguns propped up beside them. Once or twice the old man eyed Kate, who was sitting beside Billy on an upturned crate. She hadn't bathed or combed her hair since she left the ranch and she felt she must look as seedy as the gunmen.

When the men had finished eating, they plunked down some of the coins and currency they had stolen from the train. Billy laid down some extra money and said to the farmer, 'Anybody comes lookin' for us, you ain't seen nobody, you hear?'

'I ain't seen nobody,' said the old man, pocketing the money.

Kate frowned. She hoped the old man was lying, and would point the posse in the right direction . . . if they were still on the trail, she thought with despair. She tried to catch the farmer's eye, but he knew better than to look at her.

The gang mounted up and started on their

way again. A few miles from the farm they approached a nearly barren hill tufted here and there with scrubby brambles and short brown grass on it.

'We'll split up here,' said Billy. 'Hutch and I'll take the girl and ride south. Clem, you and Pete ride due west, then circle back. Chet, you take the high road. If no one follows you, meet us in three weeks back at Belle's.'

Kate looked about. How could she indicate her direction to the posse? She tugged at the tattered ruffle on one sleeve of her dress, pretending to be loosening it for comfort's sake. Slowly and silently, she managed to tear the ruffle loose nearly all the way around. One quick jerk would sent if drifting to the ground.

The other men took off, leaving the big brawny man named Hutch with Billy and her. Billy waited until the others disappeared, then turned to face his companions.

'We'll go southwest. If the others are caught and talk, they won't know which way we went.' Pleased with his clever decision, he spurred his horse forward. Before she fell in line in front of Hutch, Kathleen dropped the ruffle, praying that Hutch wouldn't see it. Then she trotted forward.

★   ★   ★

Raven Sky, Wendall, and the posse kept up with the gang by riding hard, resting and changing horses only when necessary. Raven Sky found it easy to track the careless outlaws, who left a trail that a ten-year-old Indian could have followed.

They came to the farmhouse where the outlaws had paid for their meal. The old black man was wary until Wendall showed him some money.

'We're looking for a gang of outlaws traveling with a white woman. Anyone like that pass by here?' Wendall asked.

Raven Sky had already told him that the bandits' horses had turned into the rickety farmyard, where skinny hens scratched in the dirt.

'Outlaws, you say?' said the old man.

Wendall nodded. 'Which way did they go?'

'There were some men rode by. Can't say as they were outlaws.'

'We don't have all day,' Wendall said. He knew when a man was stalling. He also knew the outlaws had probably paid the old man for his silence. But the greed in the old codger's eye told him that he could loosen his tongue by paying more for it. He started to put his money away.

'Near as I can recall, they went north.'

'How many of 'em were there?'

The old man squinted at his fingers, trying to count. 'Half a dozen of 'em anyway.'

Wendall handed him the money. 'Much obliged,' he said and led his horse back to Raven Sky, who was still examining the ground.

Raven Sky looked at the assortment of tracks, deciphering which horses came in and where they were led. He set off on the trail, motioning for the posse to follow him.

24

Billy's trio made better time without the rest of the gang to slow them down. They rode hard for several days, and Kate felt as if her body could not take much more abuse. Even her good horsemanship could not withstand the grueling paces Billy put her through. With the posse on his trail, he would never let her go now, she surmised, since she could give a very accurate description of him that would lead to his capture by U.S. marshals. She had begun to lose hope of escaping with her life, and she didn't even know if the posse was still behind them. Whenever she could, she left signs for the pursuers — pieces of cloth draped over brambles, strands of her hair tucked between two rocks near a stream where she drank. It was a small chance, but perhaps worth something.

Now they pushed through a straggling forest of post oaks and blackjack. It had rained, and the horses hooves sank in the spongy turf. Billy could do little to cover their tracks, so he pressed them forward, looking for firmer ground.

The posse came to the fork in the trail

where the gang had split up. Seeing the hoof prints in the dirt, Raven Sky got off to examine them. It was clear that several horses had circled and changed directions. He studied the ground carefully. The party had split up into three groups, but he could easily see the directions they had gone. He strode over to Wendall.

'We'll have to split up,' he said. Wendall looked north where a trail led into some low hills. Trees thinned out in the direction of Creek Territory. Raven Sky considered the tracks that led due west over open prairie. This was flat land that made for easy tracking. But another set of tracks took off southwest.

Raven Sky pointed to the ground. 'Three horses went that way,' he said, pointing southwest. 'One of the three horses was carrying a lighter load than the rest.' He looked at Wendall, who nodded and turned to the other men.

'I think it's time the rest of you men turned back. You've done more than your share, and by now the U.S. marshals ought to be looking for this gang.'

'We'll follow the north road, see if we get any closer to 'em,' said Frank Owen.

'Much obliged, Frank,' said Wendall. 'You've all done more than your share.'

'No more than you'da done for any one of us,' said Frank. He turned to the rest of the men. Though loyal to Wendall's cause, they would be glad to turn toward home. They bade Wendall good-bye, gave one last wary look at his Indian colleague, and turned their horses northward toward the low-lying hills.

'They might catch up with the ones who went back that way,' Wendall said. Then he turned to Raven Sky who had leaned down behind a boulder at the side of the road. He picked something up and brought it back. He stared at the piece of cloth, now mottled with dirt. Its color registered on his mind and he quickly handed it to Wendall.

As Wendall took the cloth, he could read the expression in Raven Sky's eyes. The piece of cloth was a sign, a cry for help, and an affirmation of Kathleen's belief that someone was trying to rescue her.

Raven Sky gazed intently to the southwest. Then he walked back to the Creeks who had been riding with them. Wendall did not hear what he said, but after an interchange of words, the Creeks bade Raven Sky farewell and turned their horses for home.

Wendall looked west over the open prairie while Raven Sky mounted. For a moment they sat in the cool autumn sunlight. Wendall's horse snorted and shook his head, and Raven Sky's mount pawed the ground and flicked its ears forward, eager to be on the move again.

In the distance a small ridge broke the flat landscape. 'You're sure there's no use trying that way?' Wendall said, jerking his head to the west.

'I am certain,' said Raven Sky. He met Wendall's gaze. 'We'll make better time now.'

'I'm with you,' Wendall said. The two men galloped down the road, headed southwest.

★ ★ ★

Kathleen was beginning to think her captors would never stop. They had ridden for days and nights now, through lands that belonged to the western tribes that had been settled in Indian Territory. When they needed fresh horses now, Billy didn't bother to trade. He simply stole them. She felt filthy. They stopped at out-of-the-way farmhouses to buy meals, and only once had she washed in a stream, not daring to take her clothes off because of the watchful eyes of the two bandits nearby. She had no idea where they were. She still thought of escape, but she was worn out during the day, and one of the men stood guard during the night. She knew there were many problems connected with escape:

she had no money, for example, and she would not survive for very long on her own. Occasionally they met up with Indians, but she had no chance to make a sign. Billy kept his hand on his gun, making sure she saw it. She doubted she could make the Indians understand her, anyway, and she wasn't sure she could trust them.

As the days passed, however, her stamina increased, and she began to feel more alert during the hard rides. Also in her favor was the fact that Billy, exhausted from the frantic pace, didn't touch her. But she never let her guard down. The way he sometimes looked at her made her suspect that he would not leave her alone for much longer. Then what? she wondered. Would he kill her because she could identify him if he was brought to trial. But then, she thought, he didn't intend to get caught. Maybe she should try to convince him that she might become an outlaw, too. She began to plan what she would say to him the next time they stopped to rest.

They had slowed down their pace and were riding through a belt of forest that gave onto a wide plain. The land sloped downward gently as far as the eye could see, but vegetation was sparse and she was beginning to feel thirsty.

'Gonna get somewhere safe soon,' Billy

said, and she saw a devilish gleam in his eye. She tried to shrug as if it didn't matter to her.

He laughed, pleased to hear the sound of his own voice. 'Think I'll dress you and show you off. We'll go to dinner in one of them big hotels. Get you all dolled up in a pretty dress. Clean you up, too. You're not so appetizin' in yer present state.' He laughed again at his own cleverness. 'Then you'll be my luck at the gamblin' table.'

She looked over at him, and the way his eyes lit up at the thought of money gave her a further clue to his character. She lifted her eyebrows and said, 'Fine, Billy. Maybe I'll help you get lucky.'

He never told Kate where they were going, and she acted as if she didn't care. Billy seemed to be taking his time with her, perhaps because there was a third party to consider. Hutch was big and dumb, but he was also strong, and Billy might not want to share her with him. If he took his pleasure from Kate, Hutch would probably want to do the same. Billy must have figured there would be time enough to romp later on.

The thought also crossed her mind that he might be all talk. Maybe he was the sort of man who didn't often need a woman. Liquor and money seemed to bring more of a gleam to his eye than his ideas of what he would do with her.

Kate pulled listlessly at her tangled hair. Soon it would be too cold to camp under the stars, and Billy would have to head for civilization. In a town or a city, surely she could get away from him. Meanwhile, she would keep flattering him. He was stupid and vain, but she would act as if she liked him. She had to be careful, though, for if he saw through her deception, he wouldn't hesitate to put a bullet in her back.

She rode up beside Billy. They were crossing a vast plain. Tall dry grasses rustled lazily, and on the horizon a large herd of longhorns grazed.

Affecting a pout, she said, 'When you gonna show me a town? I'm getting pretty tired of all this country. You gonna spend any of that money?'

Billy smirked. 'Matter of fact, that's just what I had in mind. Reckon it's time you and me did a little celebratin'.'

'Where might that be?'

'Ha, that's for me to know and you to find out.'

'I could use a bath — a real one, I mean.'

He wrinkled his nose. 'Wouldn't mind one of those myself. Oughta get dressed up right smart and have a night on the town.

What do ya say, missy? We can afford it.'
He let out a guffaw, just to impress
himself.

'Depends,' she said.

'On what?'

'Well,' she said, affecting a drawl, 'I'd need
some new clothes.'

'Oh, I got everything planned. Just you wait
and see.'

She smiled, trying to look pleased with his
vague promises. 'I've waited this long,' she
said. 'I suppose I can wait some more. How
far've we come, anyway?' She wanted Billy to
think she could never find her way home,
even if he set her loose.

'Far enough' was all he said.

They rode in silence for some time. Then
Kate prodded him again. 'How much longer
before we come to this town?'

'Maybe two days.'

Kate tried to think what town might lie
two days from here in the direction they
were headed. She looked around her, trying
to get her bearings. They were on a low
rise from which she could see miles and
miles of country broken up by small groves
of cottonwoods. The blue sky stretched
endlessly. The buffalo grass here was coarse
and wiry, and for some days now they had
seen a haze in the distance, probably from

a prairie fire. She tried not to let the vast space increase her sense of loneliness.

★ ★ ★

Following a half a day's ride behind Kathleen, Raven Sky and Wendall spoke little, concentrating on the trail. They stopped everyone they met to ask if two men and a woman had passed by. With increasing frequency, they received an affirmative answer. After a conversation with a cowboy, Raven Sky pulled back his lips in a sardonic grin. 'The outlaws have grown overconfident,' he said. 'They don't think we're still behind them.'

Heartened, the two men pressed forward.

As the days passed, Wendall's admiration for Raven Sky increased. Living with the Indian gave him a chance to appreciate his qualities. Surely his dogged determination to rescue Kathleen did not come from only a sense of duty. It had to be something deeper than that.

Thinking of Raven Sky and Kathleen made Wendall miss his own wife. At a town in the Texas panhandle, he had telegraphed St. Louis and received word back that Molly was safe with her parents.

As they rode, the two men sometimes

talked to relieve the tedium and anxiety. Wendall learned more of Raven Sky and his people. He already knew that the Creeks had once had homes, Negro slaves, farms, plantations, trading establishments. In some places in their southeastern lands, Christian churches and mission schools had flourished. Raven Sky spoke with sadness of how the federal government had uprooted them from their homes and moved them beyond the Mississippi. Their only hope for the future, he said, lay in the patents issued to them and the other Five Civilized Tribes, guaranteeing them their western lands. It was with a great deal of irony that Raven Sky spoke of the promises made by President Andrew Jackson.

Wendall listened solemnly. Raven Sky cherished his people and knew of the changes to come. He was a man caught in a dilemma, at the mercy of the white man.

'And yet you ride with me,' said Wendall after listening to Raven Sky for a time. 'And I make use of Indian land for my ranch. Would you not rather all men like myself left your territory?'

Raven Sky eyed him, no malice or judgment in his eyes. 'It was written in our prophecies that this would occur,' he said. 'We are forever separated from the white man, and yet he shapes our world. We must learn to survive.'

'And yet you have no love for us.'

'That is true.'

'Will it always be so?' Wendall wondered.

'For some it will always be so,' Raven Sky said, looking into the distance. 'But those of us who can live in the white man's world will survive. Already many mixed-bloods have adopted the white man's ways.'

As they traveled westward, Wendall wondered how Raven Sky knew they were still on the trail of the outlaws and Kate. But Raven Sky knew.

They crossed dry lands with deep rifts and gorges in the soil. Then, pushing through canebrake, they came to a muddy river. All traces of the trail suddenly disappeared. Wendall stood on the inclining bank watching Raven Sky hunt for sign. The current in the deeper waters appeared swift, but the two men would have no trouble crossing.

Wendall waited as Raven Sky returned to the bank to where he stood. He could not read the Indian's implacable expression.

Finally Raven Sky spoke. 'We will cross the river. Perhaps we will pick up their trail on the other side. The water has risen, and I cannot tell how far they followed the river.'

Wendall stared at the reeds along the

riverbank and at the jagged rocks and mingled stone and clay all around them. He had to choke down the frustration he felt. Any man in this right mind would have turned back long ago. But if there was still a chance that they could find Kathleen, he could not give up.

Raven Sky urged his horse forward.

★ ★ ★

Kate thought she could go no farther as they rode through a small grove of trees and passed out into sunlight that was less generous with its warmth as it had been only a week before. Still the plains stretched in front of them, swelling and receding in low hills. She began to wonder if Billy meant to press her forward until she died on the trail.

He had kept her out of sight whenever they approached settlements where he or Hutch bought supplies. She surmised they also tried to find out whether the U.S. marshals were after them.

They rode up a crumbling incline where the moss-covered skull of an unlucky longhorn lay in a deep gully. The horses picked their way through brambles and grapevines. Billy stopped at the crest of the hill. As Kathleen's horse caught up, she drew

415

in her breath and blinked unbelievingly, thinking that what she saw was a mirage. On the horizon stood a collection of buildings. She had difficulty focusing on it, for the sunlight seemed to dance in front of her. But the longer she stared, the more certain she became that she was looking at a town, a large one at that.

'Amarillo,' Billy said.

'Amarillo,' she breathed. This was no small settlement but a major crossroads. A real town with a railroad. Could it be that he now trusted her enough to take her there? She dared not try to guess what was on his mind, but kept silent, hoping her hammering heart would not give away the surge of hope that lifted her tired spirits.

As they walked their horses forward, the town slowly began to take shape. They joined the main road, and as they came nearer, Kathleen could see how the streets were laid out. At one end of the town there were neat houses, each with its own yard. Where the railroad passed out of town in the other direction, shacks tilted toward the dust, looking as if a gust of wind would knock them over and crush the dark men who squatted there. From the stockyards, cattle bawled, waiting for the freight trains.

Daring to hope that she might actually be

able to appeal to the law here, she felt her stomach churning. How she would love to get Billy and Hutch arrested, but she would have to find someone to help her.

Suddenly Billy let out a shout and spurred his horse along the path that led into town. 'Party tonight,' he yelled, whooping it up as if already drunk. Kathleen followed more slowly, letting her horse pick his way down the rocky path. Hutch brought up the rear. Billy led them down the main street and pulled up in front of one of the town's many saloons.

'Boy, do I have a thirst,' he said. He turned to Hutch. 'Take her to the hotel and book two rooms. Put her in one of 'em and make sure she can't get out. Stay there till I come. I'll just wet my whistle, then come on along.' He looked at Kate. 'And don't try anything. You're still expendable.'

Hutch grumbled something and then led the way down the street, where they dismounted and he tied the horses to the hitching post. He approached Kate, his hand on his gun.

'Don't forget, little lady, you're still a prisoner, even if Billy there's taken a liking to you. Don't try anything foolish.' He extracted a knife from its sheath and ran a finger across the blade, just so Kate would get the message.

She held her tongue as they walked into the hotel. Slightly worn overstuffed armchairs sat on one side of the lobby, under a brass chandelier that looked like it could use a bit of polish. Still, the plank floor was clean, and the brown velvet hangings over a door to the left gave the lobby an air of faded elegance.

Hutch pulled her across the lobby to the desk. It seemed odd to be thrust so suddenly from sleeping on the ground and wearing threadbare clothes to such a civilized environment. It took her some time to gather her thoughts. Perhaps she ought to make a scene now, while she had only one enemy. Surely she would be able to get away from her captors in a place like this without causing any bloodshed. But Hutch's hold on her wrist made her hesitate.

'Two rooms,' Hutch demanded of the clerk. The small man behind the counter nodded and got two keys. Then he pointed to the ledger.

'Sign in, please.'

Hutch made his mark, then handed the pen to Kathleen. Turning away from the clerk and leaning his elbows behind him on the desk, Hutch spoke to Kathleen in a low voice while toying with his knife handle. 'Don't sign yer real name. I can read, so don't try to trick me.'

This confused her. If he could read, why

418

hadn't he signed his name? Perhaps he had made a mark to throw the clerk off. He wouldn't want a signature for a lawman to examine. She dipped the pen into the ink and poised it over the ledger.

In a bold, clear hand she wrote a name: 'Molly Ladurie.'

Hutch squeezed her arm so hard it hurt and guided her up the stairs to their rooms. He opened her door, pushed her in, and followed, locking the door behind him. He checked the windows that looked out over the street. There were no balconies, and the drop was too far for her to make without hurting herself. He looked in the wardrobe and under the bed.

'You stay here,' he said.

'Wait just a minute, Hutch.'

'What is it?'

'Billy said I could have a bath.'

Hutch grunted. 'I guess I'll have to send for one, then.'

He lumbered off. Kathleen didn't want him watching through the keyhole, but she would take that chance. She figured that Billy would stay in the saloon longer than he anticipated and get raging drunk. She had learned by now that his weakness was alcohol, not women. She just hoped her luck would hold.

The bed had a few broken springs, but anything would have been welcome after sleeping on the ground and in occasional haystacks for more than two weeks. She had lost count of the miles, but her bones could attest to every step she had taken. She could have fallen asleep right then, but had things to do. She had to have a plan.

Two maids brought in a large wooden tub, but Hutch watched them and didn't allow Kate to speak to them. After they'd gone, she climbed into the warm soapy water, keeping her back to the door. She closed her eyes and luxuriated, feeling wonderful for the first time in weeks. For a time she was able to forget everything, letting the water slosh over her limbs. She never knew water could have such a soothing effect.

Finally she got out and toweled herself dry. She wrapped herself in the large, fluffy towel, then looked around the room for something to garb herself in. Her dress wasn't worth cleaning. She would have to throw it away.

She had a choice: the curtains or the bedclothes. The curtains were too thin, she decided. Since her underthings were as soiled as her dress, she would wrap a sheet around herself, then use the bedspread as an outer garment until something could be done about clothing. She was clever with folds and knots and could make a respectable-looking garment even without the benefit of her sewing needle.

When she was finished, she examined herself in the gilt-framed mirror. 'You look almost respectable, Miss Calhoun,' she told her reflection staring at her brown skin and her hair, which was still damp from the bath. If worse came to worst, she could escape in this getup, although she wondered how many people would take the word of a woman dressed in cast-off bed linens.

Next she had to decide how to get rid of Hutch. She bent and looked through the keyhole. He was guarding the door, and she knew he had a gun. She had to work quickly, before Billy came back.

She tried the door, but it didn't budge. Hutch had the only key on the other side. She would have to persuade him to let her out.

'Hutch,' she called. She heard him shift his weight on the other side of the door.

'What?'

'I'm thirsty, Hutch. How 'bout getting a girl a drink?' She hoped her voice carried enough bravado.

'You gotta wait till Billy comes back. He tol' me not to budge.'

'But what about you, Hutch? You haven't had a drink all day. You could get us both a little something, just enough to wet our parched lips. Sure would taste good.'

'No, ma'am. I gotta stay sober while I'm on the job. Soon as he comes back, I get my turn. Then he'll be busy with you, so he won't need me.'

'Hutch, how long do you think he'll be gone? I'm getting awful bored cooped up in here. We could share a little drink now.' She prayed that she didn't sound too inviting. She didn't want him to take her up on her invitation until he had gone out for some liquor.

She listened. What she said must have had some impact. He seemed to be trying to make up his mind. She bent to the keyhole once more.

'Hutch, what if he's gone for a long time? You and I gonna sit here and wait? Don't seem fair. Let's start the party now. He can join in when he comes back. He'll be ahead of us as it is.'

'He'd shoot me for that.'

'Then we'll just have a party and never tell him.' She was growing desperate and wondered if any of this was sinking into the big man's thick skull.

'Well,' he drawled, 'maybe one drink. I'll just have one little drink with you. Then I'll come right back out here and you won't tell him?'

'That's right, Hutch, 'cause I'm so thirsty.'

'If you squeal, I'll tell him it was your idea, and then he'll kill you,' he said. Then Hutch was silent, thinking.

'How long does he usually stay in the saloon after such a long ride?' she asked.

That seemed to decide it. Hutch must have calculated that they would be stuck at the hotel for the rest of the day and all of the night, if Billy ran true to form. Not wanting to wait that long for a drink, he moved his big body.

'I'll be right back,' he said. 'You make any noise and you'll feel my knife in your ribs.'

'I'll be quiet, Hutch. Just hurry.' She heard him lumber across the hall and down the stairs. Her heart beating against her chest, she looked around for a weapon. The only thing available was an empty porcelain vase on a dresser near the window. A blow from the vase might not even bruise Hutch, but she would have to try it. The thought of spending the night with Billy reinforced her decision. She would rather be dead than raped by that outlaw. She didn't care what she had to do.

She picked up the vase and climbed up on a chair near the door, trying to stop her legs from trembling. If Billy got here first, she would use the vase on him, but she felt even less certain of being able to surprise him. His reflexes were bound to be faster than Hutch's.

She stood poised on the chair listening for footsteps. Finally a heavy tread sounded on the carpet outside. Hutch mumbled as he struggled with the key. From his cursing, Kathleen figured he had taken a few swigs of whiskey on the way. She raised the vase, clutching it in her shaking hands and the door opened. As Hutch stepped into the room, she brought the vase down on his head with all her strength, stunning him. Before he fell, she kicked him in the jaw. He grunted and fell backward.

Before he hit the floor, Kathleen raced out of the room and down the stairs. If she could just get out of the hotel!

She got as far as the sidewalk in front of the hotel and stood there. Sunlight momentarily blinding her she caught her breath. The exhilaration of escaping the clutches of the two outlaws sent her hopes soaring.

A greasy-looking man who'd been leaning beside the door slid toward her.

'Hey there, missy,' he said, blocking her path. 'Where ya goin'?'

'What business is it of yours?' she asked. She needed to ask someone for help, but she didn't think this man looked like the type to be trusted.

'You're Billy Durke's woman, ain't ya?'

She shrank back against the brick building, but he moved in front of her.

'I got instructions not to let you go nowhere. How'd you get past that big brute upstairs, anyway?' he asked, coming closer.

'He went to get a drink,' she said belligerently.

'We'll see about that,' he said, jerking her arm.

'Let go of me,' she said, but she felt cold steel against her side. His hot breath sizzled in her ear as he pushed her back across the lobby.

'I'd be mighty happy to push this knife between your ribs,' he hissed. 'Now, just walk nice and easy up those stairs until we find out what happened to yer friend.'

Fear paralyzed her. She looked for someone who might help her, but the few men in the lobby weren't paying any attention. Her skin was clammy, and beads of sweat broke out on her forehead as she imagined what Billy would say if he came back now.

All of a sudden her foot caught in the loose folds of her garment. With a little cry, she went down, causing her captor to stumble. A woman coming down the stairs screamed as Kate lunged toward her. The knife flashed, then paused in the air as a hand reached out and grabbed it. Billy stood over her, clutching the knife.

'Get up,' he growled, yanking Kathleen to her feet. Then he turned to the other people in the lobby who had turned to stare. 'Sorry folks,' he muttered. He turned to his hired guard. 'Get lost,' he told him, handing the dark man his knife.

Billy jerked her up the stairs and kicked open the door to her room. He wrestled her inside and slammed the door behind him. Only then did she notice a large box he was carrying. He threw it on the bed.

'What'd you do to Hutch?'

Her teeth chattered as she said, 'Nothing. He went to get a drink. I found a key in the dresser, so I decided to look for you. I — I was thirsty too, that's all.' She fought to maintain her control as Billy eyed her.

'Don't know as how I believe you. I oughta kill you, but I went and spent good money on this, and now you're gonna wear it. Put it on. You're gonna deliver on all those promises tonight. Then, I dunno. If I get tired of you, I still might kill you.'

His eyes were bleary, and Kathleen began to hope that his fondness for whiskey might be her salvation once again.

Billy sat on the bed and took another swig from the bottle he carried in his hip pocket. Then he slapped the box. 'Open it.'

She reached for the box. Inside was a red satin gown with sequins on its low-cut bodice. The skirt swished as she held the dress up. There were also stockings and a garter belt, and a pair of slippers.

The dress would make her feel — and look — like a hussy, she knew, but pride made her thrust her chin out. No matter what anyone thought about her, she still had enough self-respect left to fight for it, even as tears welled up in her eyes.

'I'm gonna get cleaned up,' Billy said when his bottle was empty. 'Then you're gonna bring me luck at the faro tables.'

Kate swallowed hard as he left. It was no use trying to escape again until they were out in the open. He must have men posted all around the hotel.

She ought to be thankful she was still alive. She wondered what had become of Hutch. Evidently he'd feared reprisals from Billy and fled. One less robber to worry about, she thought with a grimace. If Billy was as gullible as he sometimes seemed, she might still have a chance.

* * *

A tall Indian on a red stallion and a saddle-weary cowboy on a black mare rode down Main Street in Amarillo. Both men were fatigued. Raven Sky was no longer sure he had read the signs correctly. Along the banks of the river there had been no prints, and on the road to town there had been too many. It was impossible for him to be sure that Kathleen had been brought to Amarillo. The last person who had seen her had been twenty miles the other side of the river. Now he was only following his instincts.

To have come all this way for nothing was hard for Wendall to bear. Still, he could not blame Raven Sky. The man had done his best. They had spoken less as they rode, more discouraged with every step. There was a chance that someone here in Amarillo might have seen her.

Raven Sky had persuaded him to search this town, since some of the signs had led here and because he figured that Kathleen's captors would want to get drunk and spend the money they had stolen. So they had come to Amarillo.

Raven Sky could not give up. If he had to hunt to the ends of the earth for Kathleen, he would, for he acknowledged the hold she had over his heart. They were bound together by words and deeds, almost as if from another lifetime.

People turned to watch the two men pass. Raven Sky's impassive face belied the murderous rage that lay underneath, waiting until he found the men who had Kathleen. He didn't let Kathleen's brother know his innermost thoughts. Even Wendall might not approve of what he intended to do to the men who had taken her.

25

Billy looked almost respectable in a clean suit of clothes, with his two weeks' growth of beard shaved off. He also looked very different from the description of him that was probably circulated after he had held up the train, Kathleen thought wryly.

She stood before him in the red sequined dress while he nodded approvingly and walked around her.

'You'll do,' he said.

She stiffened under his glance. Her only hope was that she could get him so drunk in the saloon that he would leave her alone. Maybe then she could solicit someone's help and get out of this place. She could send a wire to the ranch to let Wendall know where she was.

Billy walked behind her and reached around her from behind. Cupping her breasts with his hands, he gave a deep, guttural laugh that made icy shivers crawl down Kathleen's spine. She remembered threatening to stab Jesse Smith when he had tried the same thing. She welcomed no man's touch, except that of Raven Sky.

Thinking of Raven Sky made her shiver. How she longed to see him, instead of being chained to this mongrel of a man.

'Ouch,' she said as Billy squeezed her arm. A wave of self-pity overcame her. Raven Sky would probably laugh at her for getting herself into this scrape.

Then to her horror, Billy turned her around and planted a slobbery kiss on her mouth, making her nearly retch. All he wanted was a kiss, however, for he let her go. He walked to the door and opened it.

'After you, madam,' he said with false gallantry. As she hurried into the hall, he reached for her arm again. 'Not so fast,' he snarled, closing the door behind them. He walked her down the hall, keeping an iron grip on her elbow.

'Just want you to know I've got my derringer, in case you decide to play dirty this evening. I'd hate to put a hole in you before I'm through with you, but don't think I won't if you try to double-cross me. I was beginnin' to trust you, but since this afternoon's little show, I ain't so sure anymore.'

Kathleen gave a saucy toss of her head. 'I don't know what you mean. I'm not going to double-cross you. Not if you're planning to share some of that money with me.'

He eyed her suspiciously, but she cocked

her head at him defiantly. He laughed and said, 'Come on, then.'

As they walked down the red-carpeted staircase to the lobby, several people turned to stare at them. He was nothing to look at, but the woman on his arm was striking, with the hair the color of sand piled high on her head and the red dress complementing her fair complexion. Her swanlike neck and shoulders gleamed above the sequined dress. The gown belied her look of innocence, and so did the hard features of the man she was with.

She tried to catch the attention of people as they passed, but everyone looked away, not wanting to meet the eyes of a harlot. With one glance, the citizens they met passed judgment on her knowing that a man would not allow his wife to dress in such a manner.

Billy steered her across the lobby toward the dining room. They passed through the velvet hangings at the door and took their seats at a round table to one side of the room near the wood paneled walls.

Kathleen ordered steak and Billy ordered the biggest, hottest Mexican dish on the menu, with champagne to quench his thirst. It sickened Kathleen that outlaws like him stole other people's money just so they could come to a place like this and spend it all.

'Well, now, pretty lady, what'll we talk about?' He leaned back in his chair, patting the derringer in his pocket.

Her mouth jerked involuntarily as she remembered she would have to keep up her act and watch for an opportunity to make her move.

The champagne arrived. She didn't want any, knowing who was paying for it, but she choked back a refusal. She raised her glass when he indicated he wanted to make a toast.

'To success,' he said.

Her eyes narrowed in spite of her resolve to flatter him.

'Ah,' he said after taking a sip. 'Do I have a tigress on my hands tonight?' He laughed then turned up the glass, swallowing its contents. 'I like a feisty woman.'

She sipped from hers then put it down. 'Tell me,' she said, beginning to feel bolder, 'what do you do when you're not robbing trains?'

He curled his lip in an ironic smile. She wondered again if the wisest move might not be to stand up and scream. That could start a shootout, though. Innocent people might get hurt. That derringer in his pocket made her nervous.

'Well, I guess I plan other robberies when I'm not livin' a peaceful life,' he answered, mirth still apparent in his eyes.

'Why do you rob at all?'

'Now, you wouldn't be thinkin' of reformin' me, would you, little lady?'

'I doubt there's any chance of that,' she said.

The food arrived, and Kate stared hungrily at the thick cut of steak before her, her mouth watering. Having lived on short rations and ill-cooked gruel for the last two weeks made her appreciate the steak, and she plowed into it.

'Just like I like it — makes my eyes burn,' said Billy after swallowing a big forkful of enchiladas with hot green chilies. He shoveled the food down, stopping between mouthfuls to slug down more champagne. Kate found his table manners, like everything else about him, abhorrent.

She refrained from drinking any more champagne, wanting to remain clear-headed. Eating vegetables and hot bread and butter with her steak, she looked casually around the dining room. Nobody seemed to be paying any attention to them.

'How long do you plan to stay here?' she asked.

His mouth full, he answered, 'Long as the money runs, an' I feel like it. Why? You don't have any plans, do you?' He laughed again.

Kathleen's skin crawled. She wondered

what his plans for her were. To use her and then murder her so she couldn't talk? Or did he really believe he could turn her into an outlaw and travel with her, always out of reach of the law? In any case, she wasn't going to wait long to find out. She knew how to shoot, and if she could get hold of that derringer, he would be a dead man.

She finished her dinner, and he ordered dessert. But when it came, she pushed hers away. Remembering where the money was coming from to pay for this lush meal, she had eaten enough to give her strength, but no more.

'Not hungry?' Billy asked.

'Guess my eyes were bigger than my stomach,' she said.

Billy wolfed down his dessert, then belched and pushed his empty plate to the side. He took the last swig of champagne from the bottle and waved for the check.

'Now for the real fun,' he said.

Kate gave a start, then realized with relief he was talking about gambling. Billy scraped his chair back and got to his feet. She rose, trying to avoid his touch, but he grasped her elbow and guided her between the tables to the double doors that led to the saloon.

A gleaming mahogany bar stretched the length of the room, and a huge mirror hung on the wall behind. At one end of the bar there were whiskey advertisements featuring drawings of nude women. Elsewhere, images of noble womanhood and thoughts of home were prominently displayed to turn the men tearful and make them drink more.

Several men surrounded a noisy roulette wheel, and there was an equally large crowd at the faro tables, where the stakes were high. Billy decided to try his luck at roulette first. He nudged Kathleen, and she moved forward.

'A chair for the lady,' he called out, and someone handed her a chair. Billy pressed her shoulder, making her sit down.

If she was supposed to be his good-luck charm, she hoped it turned sour. She glanced around and noted the other women in the room. They were dressed even more gaudily then she was, and they flirted outrageously with the men. There didn't seem to be any respectable women in the place at all.

Someone brought her a drink, which she pretended to sip whenever Billy looked at her.

After winning a little and losing more, Billy moved to the faro tables, dragging Kathleen along. She sat behind him on a bar stool with a comfortable backrest. From her perch she could see the swinging door and watch people pass in and out. Whom could she speak to who might help her? Whom could she trust in a place like this?

Suddenly, Kathleen stiffened with surprise. At first she thought she must be dreaming. She blinked, stifling a little choking sound, and looked again, but they were still there — two men who had walked up to the bar. One was her brother, or at least looked like him from where she sat. The other was a tall, dark Indian dressed in jeans, a blue hunting shirt, and a green neckerchief.

At first she was too stunned to move. Her heart pounded in her chest, her skin prickled from head to foot. Then she started to get up, but she felt a hand on her knee.

Without looking at her, Billy muttered, 'Where you goin'?'

She instantly stopped moving toward the bar. Assuming it was really them, that she wasn't dreaming, she didn't want to endanger Wendall and Raven Sky.

'I just wanted a refill,' she said.

Aware that Billy wouldn't know her brother and Raven Sky, she wanted to catch their attention without alerting her captor. It was all she could do to keep from shouting and running to them. Her mind still could not grasp the fact that Wendall and Raven Sky were here together. She tried to breathe evenly as a thousand questions crowded her mind.

'You sit right there,' Billy told her. Then he turned and yelled, 'Bartender a drink for the lady.' His shout attracted Raven Sky's attention, and he turned around.

He started forward, but she shook her head imperceptibly and glanced at Billy. Her head began to spin. Salvation suddenly seemed so close, and yet so dangerous.

Raven Sky would have cast safety aside and attacked the man across the room, but Wendall, who had turned said, in a low voice, 'They don't know us. She might get hurt.'

Perceiving the wisdom of this, Raven Sky stood where he was, his face frozen into harsh lines. He wanted to slit the man's throat, but he didn't want to endanger Kathleen.

Wendall faced the bar. 'Turn around,' he said, 'and act normal,' and Raven Sky slowly turned back to the bar. 'We'll get Kate out of here,' Wendall added. 'Then we'll bring the bandit in.'

'The law will not get him if I get to him first,' said Raven Sky. His voice was low, filled with murderous vengeance. The cords in his neck stood out as he stared straight ahead into the mirror. Wendall looked down at his whiskey. He didn't want any killing if he could avoid it. He merely wanted to turn the outlaw over to the authorities. His desire for revenge was tempered with respect for the law.

'I'll stay here, then,' said Raven Sky. 'You go get the sheriff.'

Kate had her head down, trying not to look at them, but she looked up and caught Wendall's glance as he moved toward the door and went on outside into the darkness.

Raven Sky turned and leaned on the bar. She could see that he seethed with anger and was surprised that he was able to stand still. But she understood that both men feared she would be hurt in a fracas. She would have to get out of the way.

As she looked cautiously at Raven Sky, his eyes seared into her body. She could see in his look the anger and passion that raged within him. Ignoring his whiskey, he stared at her. Then he seemed to realize that he must not draw attention to himself. He deliberately turned back to the bar and held out his glass. Time stood still as Kate wondered how the two men had come together. How did Raven Sky even know of her plight? Had he been the one tracking her all this time?

She looked away. She couldn't risk staring at him, for fear Billy or his cronies would notice. She would have to try a ploy. She leaned toward Billy, who was flushed with winning at faro.

'What is it?' he asked gruffly.

'I have to go to the . . . you know, outside,' she said.

'You what? Oh. Hey, Lou,' he yelled to one of the ladies of the establishment. 'Come over here.'

A red-haired woman in a low-cut blue dress trimmed with black lace climbed down from the lap of a man on the other side of the table and swished over to Billy, chucking him under the chin. 'What do you want, honey?' she said.

'Show her the way,' Billy said, motioning to Kate. The men at the table guffawed, and Kate turned crimson.

'Right this way, honey.' The rouged woman crooked a finger at Kathleen, who slid off the stool and followed the woman, not daring to look at Raven Sky.

Kathleen was three paces away from the faro table when Wendall returned followed by a man with a badge. A big fellow with broad shoulders and a tall black felt hat, he was a good six inches taller than Wendall. Kathleen hastened her steps toward the back door as the men approached the faro game. Billy didn't look up when they stopped in front of the table, but the din of conversation in the room died.

'I hear you're wanted in Arkansas,' said the sheriff.

Slowly Billy raised his eyes, sliding his hat back on his head. 'I don't know what you're talkin' about, Sheriff. I never heard of Arkansas, and I'm just here having a friendly game. You got no cause to bother me, seein' as how I'm spendin' my money in your town.'

When the sheriff reached for his gun, the other partrons in the saloon abandoned their chairs and backed away. Billy cocked his derringer under the table and aimed upward. Kate shrieked as Raven Sky leaped the distance and flew across the table, grabbing Billy by the neck as the gun went off. The sheriff had sidestepped, and Raven Sky knocked the gun out of the bandit's grasp with a downward slash of his hand and rolled with him onto the floor.

Raven Sky never let go of Billy's neck, choking him, and the men playing faro with Billy took sides randomly. Two men grabbed Raven Sky from behind and pulled him up. Wendall worked his way through the crowd to Raven Sky, but was waylaid by a punch to his jaw.

There was an eruption of gunfire, and the sheriff grabbed Billy by the scruff of the neck. Then he yelled to Wendall, 'If I were you, I'd beat it out of here,' and clamped handcuffs on Billy. 'We'll keep this one under lock and key till your marshal sends for him. Meanwhile maybe he'll decide to tell us more about that train robbery.'

With two upward thrusts, Raven Sky sent his attackers reeling to the floor. Then he looked around for Kate. Seeing her crouched between the bar and the red velvet curtains that led to private rooms behind, he ran to her.

He grabbed her wrist and pulled her toward the door and out to the street. Wendall came crashing through the doors as Raven Sky lifted Kate onto his horse, then swung up behind her. Wendall untied his horse's reins from the hitching post and mounted up.

'Let's go,' he yelled.

Kathleen sank back into Raven Sky's arms. They wheeled the horses and thundered out of town as the fight spilled out onto the street behind them.

They rode out of town into the darkness, and Kathleen's heart beat as loudly as the flying hooves on the hardpacked road beneath them. Finally they slowed, the beasts heaving from the run. Kathleen fought for breath.

'There wasn't anyone with him,' she said,

panting, as they pulled up under the overhanging boughs of a sturdy oak. Raven Sky dismounted and reached for her, and she slid into his strong arms. He held her against him, his own heart thundering as he caressed her hair. Finally she raised her head and looked into his black eyes. He stared wordlessly at her as they held each other, afraid to let go.

'Hey, I helped, too,' said Wendall, coming around his horse. Kathleen laughed and turned to him, and he crushed her in a bear hug, swinging her around.

'I know, and you don't know how grateful I am,' she said, still shaking. 'I never thought I'd see either of you, or anyone from home, again. I still can't believe it.' She looked at Raven Sky, who watched her as tears spilled from her eyes. She tried to decipher his expression.

'How did it all happen?' she asked softly.

Raven Sky shook his head almost imperceptibly and came to her again.

She looked at Raven Sky with wonder. 'You tracked me here?'

'Most of the way,' he said, the glimmer of a smile coming into his eyes at last.

Chills ran up her spine as she clung to him, his soft breath feathering her hair and his heart pounding against her.

'How did you know what had happened to me?'

Raven Sky answered, 'I have ways of knowing what I need to know.'

She raised her hands to his shoulders hesitantly. He gazed at her, his eyes smoldering with passion and exultation at having gained his prize at last. He brought his face close to hers and she closed her eyes as his lips met hers. His hold on her tightened.

Clearing his throat, Wendall said, 'I hate to interrupt the party, but we have to get out of here. We didn't wait to see if that piece of slime back there was confined to jail. I say we'd better hit the road.'

Raven Sky released Kathleen reluctantly, but her heart leaped up at his look. He looked back in the direction of town.

'Forget him, Raven Sky,' said Wendall. 'It's not worth it.'

'That depends,' said the Indian. He gripped Kathleen's arm and turned her to face him. 'Did he touch you?' he asked. 'If he did, the man will be meat for vultures.'

Amusement touched Kathleen's face, but then her expression was softened by compassion. 'He didn't touch me, thank God,' she said, grinning. 'I was smarter than he was.'

Raven Sky frowned and looked down at her as if to assure himself that what she said was the truth. Then relief came into his eyes as he gazed at her radiant face.

They mounted. This time Kate rode behind Raven Sky, thrilling at the feel of her arms around his lithe body. They rode through the night, guided by a bright moon, and arrived at the junction before daybreak. They located a small hotel and roused the clerk, who found them rooms.

'We might as well get some sleep,' said Wendall as they climbed the stairs. Stopping in front of the room that Kate would sleep in, he said, 'Rest well, Sis.' He gave her a quick hug, then grinned down at her.

'I will, brother,' she said, returning his smile. 'And thank you.'

Raven Sky stood somberly against the peeling wallpaper. Tired as he was, Wendall couldn't resist teasing the Indian. 'I do declare, Raven Sky,' he said. 'You sure don't smile much.'

Raven Sky tossed his hair over his shoulder as Wendall turned to the room the men would share and went inside. Still, his lips lifted slightly in a smile.

Kate turned to her own door, but Raven Sky touched her shoulders. As he turned her to face him, she couldn't help the eagerness that came into her look. He studied her soft shoulders, and she glanced down, realizing she still had on red satin dress.

She blushed as his eyes strayed down the bodice to the soft curves of her breasts. He kissed her, pressing himself against her as she leaned on the door. She could feel his hardness, and her own body cried out in the same need. She thought of the bed inside. It would be so easy. But thoughts of her brother stopped her. He would not permit any impropriety, and it was clear that Raven Sky would not betray Wendall's trust.

But Raven Sky did not hesitate to make his wants known. He gently caressed her skin, letting his fingers wander to her nipples. A tingling began in the center of her and climbed upward in a dizzying sensation. She had almost forgotten what it was to experience desire. But it was an expression of love, a love that had grown in her heart since the first day she saw him. Even when she had feared him, she knew somehow that she belonged to him. And now she knew it had been only her memories she had feared.

As if hearing her thoughts, Raven Sky ended the kiss and whispered, 'My heart lives for you, my white dove.'

He held her a few inches away, piercing her gaze with his eyes. 'I must know if you love me,' he said, his eyes demanding and pleading at the same time.

'Of course I love you. I have always loved you. I just didn't know how to love you before.'

He held her close to him again, and she laid her head on his shoulder. 'Then we will be married,' he said.

'Yes.' She couldn't stop the tears of relief and love that flowed from her eyes.

★ ★ ★

The citizens of Tulsa sat in the makeshift church awaiting the ceremony. Those who couldn't squeeze in stood outside, and some of the cowboys sat astride their horses, watching the ceremony through the windows.

The Reverend Mr. Haworth stood behind his lectern. To his left was Raven Sky, handsome in a dark suit and snowy white shirt with a stiff collar, contrasting with his deep bronze skin.

As Mrs. Haworth pumped the organ pedals, Kathleen entered on Wendall's arm, and all eyes turned to her. Molly had made her a dress of white gauze with lacy leg-of-mutton sleeves and a neckline that plunged to reveal her delicate shoulders and a hint of her breasts. The full bodice tightened over her flat stomach, and the generous folds of the skirt floated to the floor.

Kate's nerves were taut as she walked toward Raven Sky, but when she met his gaze she knew their hearts were bound forever. Hardly aware of the words they spoke, they communicated as spirits, forming agreements that outdistanced time and space.

'You may kiss the bride,' said Mr. Haworth, and Raven Sky enfolded her in his arms, kissing her tenderly, a promise of the lovemaking that was to come.

Outside, friends came to wish them well. Molly, rustling in her blue taffeta dress, was the first to hug her.

'Oh, Kate, I know you'll be happy.'

'Yes, at last,' said Kathleen, looking at her blushing sister-in-law, new happiness radiating from her since she had become a mother. 'If I'm as happy as you and Wendall are, I'll be satisfied.'

Others, even Jesse Smith, came forward. Evidently having decided to be polite, he bowed from the waist. 'My congratulations, Kathleen.'

She smiled warmly at him. 'Thank you, Jesse. I hope you mean that. I've always counted on you as a friend, even if it didn't always seem that way.'

He gave a half shrug, but she could see the hope that sprang into his eye. 'In that case, you may consider me at your service.'

She had to smother her amusement at his formality, for she knew he was behaving stiffly to cover up his true feelings, and she was touched.

'There are too few of us out here to hold grudges, Jesse,' she said. 'I apologize if I've ever hurt your feelings.'

'I accept your apology.' He nodded, cleared his throat, and bowed again. As he walked away, Kathleen allowed herself a sentimental smile.

With much difficulty, Raven Sky got his bride away from the crowd and into the wagon. The crowd cheered, and she waved at them as Raven Sky clucked to the team, and the wagon pulled off.

The new home that the community had built for them was a large two-story frame house in town, with bedrooms on the second floor. Friends and relatives from both sides had furnished the house, so that nothing was wanted. Raven Sky helped her down from the wagon in front of the newly erected picket fence, lifted her up, kicked open the gate, and carried her into the new house. Bittersweet tears came to her eyes as she remembered how he had once carried her off to a cave.

'What is this?' he said. 'Tears on your wedding day?'

She smiled, running her hands lovingly up

to his broad shoulders. 'Tears of happiness.'

That night Kathleen stood proudly in front of her husband as he slowly undressed her. Now there was no hurry, for at last there would be no recriminations. They could indulge their love and take their time with it.

He unfastened her dress, and she stepped out of it. Then he removed her undergarments. Sensations flooded over her as he gazed at her breasts in the moonlight that spilled through the window. Then he lifted her up and placed her on the soft feather bed, then removed his own clothing.

'You're beautiful,' he said as he slid in beside her.

Kathleen had no words for the emotion she felt as she gazed at him. She had seen him like this before, but now he was all hers to touch and love. She tentatively reached for him, and he guided her hand in her explorations.

He kissed her arms, her neck, the sloping mounds of her breasts, his hands rubbing gentle circles on her stomach until he worked his way downward, preparing her to receive him. He held her close to him so that she could feel every inch of his skin on hers. It was even more delicious than she thought possible.

Every inch of her throbbed for him as her

body matched his rhythm. They moved closer, lost in the joy and feeling of love. Finally he burst forth in her, pulsing life into her body. She met his fierce cries with her own, her fingers gripping his shoulders to steady herself as she floated upward.

As they lay in each other's arms, Kathleen gazed out at the moon, knowing she had finally found happiness. Thoughts floated in and out of her mind as she rested her head on Raven Sky's strong shoulder. She contemplated what their lives would be like, and the lives of their children, as this territory was fast absorbed by the nation.

Would the Indians hold on to their land? Would Tulsa grow into a metropolis as some people said it would? And what of the outlaws who roamed the hills? Kathleen had no answers to these questions. As her eyelids grew heavy, thoughts of the future blurred. She nestled against Raven Sky's back and joined her husband in sleep.

We do hope that you have enjoyed reading this large print book.

Did you know that all of our titles are available for purchase?

We publish a wide range of high quality large print books including:
**Romances, Mysteries, Classics
General Fiction
Non Fiction and Westerns**

Special interest titles available in large print are:
**The Little Oxford Dictionary
Music Book
Song Book
Hymn Book
Service Book**

Also available from us courtesy of Oxford University Press:
**Young Readers' Dictionary
(large print edition)
Young Readers' Thesaurus
(large print edition)**

For further information or a free brochure, please contact us at:
**Ulverscroft Large Print Books Ltd.,
The Green, Bradgate Road, Anstey,
Leicester, LE7 7FU, England.
Tel:** (00 44) 0116 236 4325
Fax: (00 44) 0116 234 0205

Other titles published by
The House of Ulverscroft:

THE WILL

Patricia Werner

When Leigh Castle returns to the mansion she grew up in, it is not a happy occasion. Her mother has died, leaving an estate entangled by a questionable will. It is more than reason enough to rekindle the old rivalries among Leigh and her three sisters, Hania, Anastasia and Claudia. When Anastasia is discovered dead at the bottom of an abandoned mine, chilling fear takes hold of the sisters, compounded by suspicious events. But Leigh's return has also afforded her the chance to meet Braden Lancaster, the engaging young lawyer hired to handle the estate. Despite the circumstances, the attraction they feel is immediate . . .

THE DECENT THING

C. W. Reed

David Herbert lives a privileged life in Edwardian society but is dominated by his sisters, Gertrude and Clara. At public school he suffers bullying and at home his only friend is Nelly Tovey, a young maid . . . Living on a pittance in London after being disowned by his family, he becomes seriously ill and is nursed by the devoted Nelly. Although certain of their love, Nelly is aware of the gulf between them. David must find the courage to defy convention and breach the barriers to their happiness.

LOVING HIM

Kate O'Riordan

Connie and Matt Wilson, once childhood sweethearts, have worked hard to achieve their dreams — their lovely London home, their three beloved sons and a stable marriage. When they go to Rome for a romantic weekend, they enjoy exploring, eating, drinking and making love. But a random encounter sets off a chain of events that turns Connie's existence from predictable, but blissful, domesticity to dangerous obsession, when Matt announces that he is not coming back with her and she returns to London — and their three boys — alone.

WINDS OF HONOUR

Ashleigh Bingham

The Honourable Phoebe Pemberton is beautiful and wealthy, but is the daughter of the late, disgraceful Lord Pemberton and Harriet Buckley . . . Phoebe escapes her mother's plans to teach her the family business of wringing profits from the mills. She dreams of running away, and, when she learns of her mother's schemes for Phoebe's marriage as part of a business transaction, she calls on her friend Toby Grantham for help . . . But Harriet's vengeful fury is aroused, leaving Phoebe tangled in a dark and desperate venture.

FLYING COLOURS

Heather Graves

With a broken romance behind her and a promising future ahead Corey O'Brien intends to concentrate on her chosen career. She certainly doesn't expect to come to the attention of someone like Mario Antonello, a racehorse owner and heir to a fashion house . . . Their first meeting isn't friendly so she is surprised by the interest he shows in her later. It all seems too much and it will take a while for Corey to find out the truth. Then she discovers a shocking secret and feels she must turn her back on him forever.

THE LADY SOLDIER

Jennifer Lindsay

Spain, 1812. Jem Riseley is the perfect soldier in Wellington's army: brave and daring — but also a gentle-born lady! Her deceit is tested when she meets the handsome Captain Tony Dorrell, who knew her as Jemima. When the pair are trapped behind French lines, Jem has to battle the enemy as well as her desire for Tony . . . From the fighting in Spain to London's drawing-rooms, Jem will preserve her secret. However, the reappearance of an old adversary causes Jem to confront her past in order to save her own, and England's, future.